Excelsior House

By: Lance Lund

For them.

Sarah Hillsbrook did not want to live anymore. Or so she thought. She was sick of being fucked up on drugs: crystal, speedballs, pills, ludes, weed, and any other shit she decided to put up into her system. So she pulled the trigger on her life. Pumped all the scratch she had left in her bedroom stash up into her arm at one time. In her father's guest bathroom. She was sure he wouldn't miss her. Already caused his political career so much damage to begin with. She could see the headlines now, though she knew she would never read them. 'Assemblyman's twisted daughter meets a tragic end.' How cute it would be. They would both be better off without her. So she buried the syringe deep into her skin, injecting the last of its contents into the collapsed vein, and rolled her eyes back, finally enjoying the warmth of the water in the tub where she lay. Only a few minutes more of this, she mused. Then everything would be nothing....

She could only remember flashes of what came next: the bright light of the paramedic's magna flooding deep into her eye, her iris' failing to shut, then the straps tightening around her arms and legs, locking her body into the gurney, then the sounds of her mother's crying over the rolling of the stretcher into the Emergency Room (how had Dad discovered her so fast? he was supposed to be at that fundraiser until eleven!), then the doctors forcing of that long plastic tube deep into her stomach, the transfusion, fuck the pain of that pumping as her arms and legs slowly came back to life, then the wave of hurt flooding her body, the numbness of over-saturation, and finally, a return to physical sobriety unremembered for years. Then darkness.

Sarah awoke to her parents bickering beside the bed where she was cuffed. She saw the shackles but did not move. The hell if I'm going to give them the dignity of chewing me out here. Like this.

It's all your fault. If you hadn't been so busy-
If I hadn't found her, she'd be dead.
She may be yet.
I don't like this any more than you do.
She's just acting out because you left us.
It was you who walked out on me as I remember.
You've been tuned out of our lives for years.
And so on.

Sarah tried in vain to return to the permanent slumber she so desperately sought with her failed suicide attempt. At any rate, this is all temporary. They'll never make me go back home like this, she thought. Not after this. Still, the bickering persisted.

You've failed me as a husband, now you've failed your daughter as a father.

Fine. But it's both of us who've failed her now. Look at her.

I want full custody. If you can't take care of her then I will.

You walked, remember? You're never going to get it.

But our daughter just killed herself in your home!

Don't be so dramatic. Doctor says she's still got a 50/50 shot.

Sarah didn't even blink. 50/50? What the fuck do they pay those doctors for? If only she had it so good.

If she survives, I'll never let you have her again.

Well you can rest easy there, Lorraine. Because with her little stunt she's violated her probation and they're probably going to make her a ward of the state. This is going to look so bad for me, you don't even realize.

Yeah, well it's always been about you anyway, hasn't it? You should have thought of that before you destroyed our family sleeping with that floozy.

That floozy is twice the woman you ever were-

You're such a bastard.

Sarah heard her mother sobbing as she briskly left the room. Mom was such a baby sometimes. I mean, sure, dad was an asshole, everyone whose ever met him knows that, but couldn't she ever find a way to maintain? She'd always been so weak like that. That's why she left home. But now I'm screwed. They must have given me new blood, because all that shit I pumped into me was supposed to do the trick. The pills I swallowed were only supposed to put me out just long enough to let the killer take hold. I was never supposed to survive, let alone become a ward of the state. What the fuck is that gonna mean? Probably a stint in juvie, then what? A foster home? Or worse. As much of a prick as dad is, he's always let me do whatever the hell I wanted, no questions asked. Maybe I can make the case for giving him a second chance with me. That'll be better than whatever else they'll have planned.

My PO will understand. He's cool, can't play no bullshit off 'a him. As long as I show some inner-life-crisis-moment-of-clarity remorse, he'll understand. But fuck if I'm going into foster care. Because that shit ain't for me. That's for really fucked up kids with completely screwed lives and nowhere else to turn. But I'm too clever for that. 'Cause I know better than anyone how to take care of myself. Always have. My PO knows it too. Even the judge thinks so. Just get me in front of her again. She won't know what hit her, like when she agreed to let me live with my dad. I'll be back up in no time, back to the same shit. No shit. But I won't make the same mistake again. Next time I'll get the job done right. Guaranteed.

SAN FRANCISCO FAMILY COURT DOCKET CASE NUMBER 220145: MS. SARAH HILLSBROOK

Ms. Blancecourt, are you ready to make your recommendation?

Yes. Thank you, Your Honor.

You may proceed.

As Ms. Hillsbrook's Social Worker, it is in my best professional judgment, in accordance with the psychological evaluation conducted by our staff, to conclude that Sarah will reattempt suicide if not immediately placed in a residential treatment program serving the Severely Emotionally Disturbed. Because of her extensive history of leaving home, her family history of neglect and her parents demonstrated inability to provide adequate supervision to meet her unique medical and psychological needs, it is the opinion of the Department of Child Protective Services to recommend that Sarah remain in custody as a ward of the State of California until reunification with her father is determined possible. Reunification will be subject to the terms of her parents' divorce settlement, and contingent upon their successful completion of family counseling, as well as Sarah's adherence to the provisions imposed by her treatment program. Success will be determined in consultation with Sarah's therapist, probation officer, and CPS when the court reconvenes to decide on said possibility for reunification.

The court hears and agrees with the sum of these recommendations, Ms. Blancecourt. Thank you.

Thank you, Your Honor.

Sarah, is there anything you would like to say on your behalf?

You bet your ass I would-

No, Your Honor.

Sarah was scared. Her PO Marlon Willburton had no pull over CPS after this last episode. And they were out to get her. Besides, Marlon didn't trust her anymore. Said I was a junkie, and won't do nuthin' for myself until I get free from the need to cop my next fix. Which is true. Detox was a bitch, and I still think about how I'm gonna get my next high. But all this court shit is going real bad. I gotta find a way outta this. But none 'a them are havin' it.

Fine, thank you Sarah. And thank you to each member of Sarah's treatment team for your presentations. In consideration of the sum testimonies presented to the court today, it is my judgment to adhere to the Department's recommendations in the interest of best serving Sarah's unique supervision needs.

Sarah's PO nodded as Mom sobbed at the thought of her daughter undergoing treatment outside of her parents' care. Dad could only roll his eyes at the ruling.

It is the judgment of this court that Sarah be admitted immediately to Excelsior Children and Family House where she will undergo substance abuse and psychological counseling under the supervision of the onsite residential treatment team there until her next hearing in 90 days. At that time her treatment status will be reviewed and options for reunification with her mother and father will be assessed.

Sarah sighed loudly, exasperated at the verdict.

The judge peered down at her with a combination of compassion and mild disdain.

Sarah, you are obviously a very bright, talented young lady with much potential to achieve success in this treatment program. At the same time, you have demonstrated a keen ability to manipulate not just those in your immediate family and case managers, but this court as well-

Why do judges take so friggin' long to say what they've got to say?

...Drug treatment in residential placement is not a punishment, it is a chance for you to get yourself clean so you can make the most of your life and to realize your full potential. It is my opinion that you have loving parents who only want to see you get well. I therefore believe you have a strong chance at success for reunification and strongly hope and encourage you to make the most of this opportunity. Because ultimately what happens with you will be up to you and will depend on your performance in this program. So will you do that, make that commitment to succeed, not just for them but most importantly, for yourself?

Fuck you! You don't know the first thing about me or them!

Yes, Your Honor. I will. I mean, I do.

The judge smiled for the first time in the proceedings.

Great, will the Clerk then please note that this court will reconvene in 90 days to review treatment performance and to assess options for reunification? This hearing is adjourned.

And with that, Sarah was on her way.

***

Lucinda Gutierrez punched away furiously at the keyboard in front of her. This was her first practice test at the Centro De Empleo (Employment Opportunity Training Center) on Mission Street. After several hours of classes, reviews of office etiquette, lessons on how to dress, and watching the safety in the workplace video, Lucinda was ready for the typing exam. Anyone looking to work in an office had to be able to consistently type between 60 and 70 words per minute. Many of the women in the room had brought their children. Despite the muffled cries of young babies in the daycare office and friendly chatter of the likeminded women around her waiting their turn on the computers, Lucy was determined to succeed. If she could type fast enough, the workplace training staff would know she had potential and immediately move her into the Microsoft Word and Excel course. If not, she would be confined to practicing her typing speed. Lucy had worked with these computer programs before in high school, and know that if she was ever going to land a job anywhere, as an office assistant downtown or with a dentist or travel agency on the block, she was going to have to know her way around that software eventually. But no mind to that right now. The task at hand was typing, and Lucy knew she had to succeed here and now. But she'd never learned to type fast. In school, she would always look at the keys, and chicken peck with two fingers. What was the correct hand position again? Did the pinky go over the F or the G key? Which index finger is supposed to hit H, or B or Y? At any rate, none of this mattered at the moment. What did matter was that her infant son needed her to land a job with a temp agency as a typist, where then she would maybe get a foot in the door of a business where she could make a good impression, learn Microsoft Word and Excel on her own, and finally be hired on full-time, if everything worked out to plan. That was the strategy she and her Independent Living Skills Tutor, Darien McDowell at John McConnell High School, had come up with to get her out of her financial rut. Lucy had just turned eighteen as a ward of the State of California and was now out on her own after recently emancipating from a transitional home for teenage mothers.

Joe Rodgers and the staff at her old group home had been wonderful, offering her a place to stay while she emancipated, even though the facilities there were not adequately staffed to support the needs of young mothers with children. Lucy had grown up at Excelsior House, and only moved into transitional living once she'd had Tre, but Joe never forgot about her and always let her know there was a place for her in her old home if she ever needed it. He was the closest thing to a father she'd ever known. Most directors of group homes would never have said those things to her that he did. But Joe cared. And he always put his money where his mouth was.

But her mind quickly returned to the keys. She typed something about Accounts Payable Annual Summary Reports…no, not numbers! They were really testing her now. She wasn't proficient on the number keypad, so would really have to hustle. Hopefully she wouldn't make too many mistakes that would offset the accuracy component of her score. Because Tre needed her now more than ever. And when she emancipated, she would need a high enough paying job to move them into a place of their own. At least until she could patch things up with his father, Keyshawn.

Keyshawn, also known as Special K., was a drug dealer, but he had feelings for her and for his boy, she knew he did. He told her as much. Key had been in jail on a short stint for beating up some fool who lost his dope. But he always provided for their son through thick and thin, even though being a slinger meant that he never knew when or where he'd be there in person. Lucy always knew he could drop off in a quick minute if a business deal went sour, or some fool out to cop his smoke or settle a score decided it was time to do him in. In her heart, Lucy loved Keyshawn, and she knew he loved her, but there were no shortage 'a fools who he had beef with, and Keyshawn was a tough motherfucker from the street, so as far as Lucy was concerned, nobody who be steppin' to him come out straight 'less they readz to pay the consequences. You come at my man, you best bring your game correct, or it wuz all 'n out war until one 'a y'all's dead. 'Cause Keyshawn be crazy, he'd flex on a fool full force, pull out all da stops no doubt. Lucy liked the fact that Keyshawn was strong like that, along with the fact that he kept hisself off the smoke. But on those rare occasions when he did get high, when she came home and was either too loud or otherwise inattentive of his needs, he had to put the hurt on her to remind her of her proper place in the household. That's just the way it had to be with him. So Lucy overlooked the demon side of Key as much as she could. Just the smoke taking hold, she reasoned, it wasn't who her man really was, for sure, 'cause in his tender moments he was always quick to show how much he really loved her, bringin' flowers around, buyin' her that beautiful platinum plated rose pendant she liked from that jeweler shop down on Mission Street. There was real history between them. But with Keyshawn in and out of prison so much, Lucy knew she had only herself to depend on. And so when the baby came, she was all her only son had. So Lucy understood better than anyone else how she really had to make her life work now. For both of them.

Lucy quickly finished typing the document from Morgenson's Accounts Payable and waited patiently for the test results to print. Keyshawn would most likely beat his most recent flap, because that trick bitch who he'd sent to the hospital three times over for smokin' what he should a been slingin' decided with Keyshawn locked up and no more direct line on another fix so quick and easy, best let a bad rap beat a bad rap, bygones be bygones. And Keyshawn would surely hire him again once he got out, because for all his faults, Key was loyal like that. He may 'a disappeared from time to time, but he always came back and hooked up his peoples. Even them dopefiends workin' his corridors in exchange for their daily smoke, always robbin' him of shit, Keyshawn didn't really care. 'Cause when he caught your ass skimmin' you got your beatdown fair and square, tit for tat motherfucker, then you picked your ass back up and went back to work distributing his product. That's just the way Keyshawn ran his game. Tight as a motherfucker.

***

Julio Hernandez strolled up Carolina Street across from Garfield Square playground. His homies was waitin' on him. But he had other plans. Something was going down. Usually the park was all kinds of full with kids and parents after school. But not today. Even the dopefiends were scarce, so something must be up. Of course, his old friend Hector was still out representin' on the block with Edgar and Tootz.

Julio walked up to Hector and put his hands out, giving him the requisite handshake. A two fist knuckle tap followed by the up and down.

Ordeley.

Whassup rogue?

You're late ese-

Naw blut, I'm right on time. My time.

Shit. You got the goods?

Right here, blut.

Shit, you betta.

Julio tossed Hector a bag of the weed he copped earlier that day. Edgar pulled out his Zig Zags while Tootz smelled the stash and laughed.

Homie straight bringin' da purple hair buds up in here.

Damn...

What's up wit' all dis whiteboy Humboldt shit?

They do chicken right, yo.

The boys laughed.

Yeah, mang, shit's off the hook. Take you for a ride, homie.

For realz.

Hector engaged his old friend.

So you readz to get yo' scrap on tonight, Julio?

Who you swoopin'?

Rodrigo Suarez.

You mean that Sureño frontin' up on 16th?

Bitchass think he own the block now.

Gon' flop his ass fo' realz. Show him whassup.

Dude knows he claimin' neutral territory.

Fool straight don't give a fuck...

Shit blut, that bitchass beat down Little Eduardo this afternoon over some dumb shit, no doubt blut.

He crossin' hoodlines, yo.

Damn, blut, yeah. But that fool know Shorty ain't flossin' north of 22nd.

Man, dude got off the bus to buy hisself a taco. Ain't throwin' up his numbers or nuthin'.

Dude straight popped him in the face rat-tat! Just fo' walkin' by.

Shit is fucked up, blut.

Hella.

So we's goin' at all those scraps hard up on Shotwell, straight up. Some fools gettin' capped tonight, know what I'm sayin'?

Hector held out his hands out in the shape of a gat. Bap bap!

We smoke all 'dose fools, blut.

Word up.

So whus up Julio, you rollin' wit' us tonight?

Julio hesitated at his friend's not-so-subtle invitation.

Naw, blut, I be takin' my moms to mass tonight.

Aw, fuck that! We need you, homie, Hector implored. Shit's gonna get tight.

You know I ain't about to violate my probation sweatin' some Sureño scraps-

Hector grew pissed. Aw hell naw, blut, Julio growin' a pussy on us.

What, you too good for your homies now?

You know it ain't like that, I'm just kickin' it right, mang.

Check out Julio, Tootz mocked. Hangin' all high and mighty wit' his moms, taking her to church and shit. Yo, they let you walk in that place?

Dude, just 'cause you punked out on us don't mean you'z out da life. You got enemies like all 'a us, blut. And when they'z comin' at 'chu, the only motherfuckers got yo' back are your homies from back in the day, you feel me?

Hector and Edgar clasped hands. Thas' right. For realz.

Julio understood the life he'd worked so desperately to leave. Hector was right. To his old homies, and 'specially to them scraps lookin' to put a slug in him for his past misdeeds, Julio could never be completely out. Never mind how desperately he wanted to change.

Mang, you's crazy bringin' it to some flip ass scrap ain't none a yo' concern-

What it do, blut? Hector hissed, throwing up his arms in disgust. Maricón lost his cojones! He spit beside Julio and turned away from him.

Yo Hector, step off, blut. This ain't your fight, yo.

Man, take your flip-ass bitch self out here fo' I knock you to the curb! Hector waved him off.

Julio, taking his cue, backed up and stepped from the corner.

Go on then, fuck you then, pussy-ass bitch...

Julio gave his other two patnas, Edgar and Tootz, a wave as he turned the corner down the block, away from Hector and the trappings of his old life at the park.

***

Sylvia Sanchez came home early. Her mami was lying fast asleep on the living room couch. She passed out most days after working a double shift at the 99 Cents store on Mission and 23rd. Her papi was a day laborer who found work maybe twice a week, standing out on the corners of Cesar Chavez with those other *jornaleros* waiting for any Jefe needing landscape work on the cheap to come rolling through. Must 'a been one of those days, 'cause Papi was nowhere to be seen. None of them had green cards. Sylvia had made El Viaje de Mexico with her madre when she was 8 years old. They came to meet her papi who she only remembered seeing once in her childhood, when her abuela died and he made the return journey back to Jalisco to bury his madre. That world, her old village, the campos where she played with her primos y hermanas every day after school seemed a lifetime away. But when they arrived in San Francisco, Papi took her under his wing as his own. She loved her papi, who always brushed her hair and made her *muñecas* and told every guest at her Quinceañera that she would make the worlds' most beautiful bride someday. Papi had no money but had thrown her the biggest party she had ever seen. All her relatives and juanitas from the neighborhood came to celebrate her ascension to womanhood. But things changed after the Quinceañera. Papi started looking at her different, talking to her like a woman, annoyed that she didn't do more for la familia. So Sylvia took it upon herself to change Papi's mind about her. She worked at the bridal gown store on Mission and made tamales with mama on weekends to sell to people at Dolores Park in order to make ends meet. But Papi was still unsatisfied with her. She wanted nothing more than to please him until the night her Uncle Juve came home from the Coco Club muy burracho and lookin' for a good time and raped her. She never told Mama, didn't much see the point. Mama would've never kicked her own brother out of their house, that wasn't the family way. *Los ancianos* set the rules, and the women lived with them. She knew that Mama knew, but Mama never pressed it and never said nothin' to Papi, so neither did Sylvia. Until Papi beat her up the night when she came home and told him she was pregnant with Juve's child. Then the shit really hit the board. Papi insisted she had to keep it, but Sylvia knew this would scar her family with God and their church community, so she copped outta class one afternoon on her own and got an abortion at Planned Parenthood Women's Community Clinic on Valencia Street, not needing parental consent at 15 in California, in and out, no questions asked. She was pretty torn up about the whole thing when she came home that night and confided everything she'd done to Papi. She wanted more than anything for him to know everything, she wanted him to love her again like he done when she was still his Niña Princesa back in the day, before she came of age. She prayed real hard to God for Papi to still love her despite what she'd done. But Papi blew up instead and beat the living shit outta her when he found out, something he'd never done ever before and never since. His daughter was dead to him, and after that he just stopped talking to Sylvia. The bruises would heal, but his dead silence with her from then on out was what hurt the most.

He wouldn't say two words to her after that night, he just stared through her like the ghost of Guadalupe whenever she walked into the room. So she went to school the next day with the splotches Papi put on her, and a call got put in by one 'a her oversuspecting teachers. That damn Hispanic CPS worker Clara Rodriguez knew right away what she was looking at when she met Sylvia, and then again after the nosy vecinos called the po-po when Sylvia threw her abuela's vase and knocked Juve straight out after a verbal scuffle turned physical. She never admitted to no abuse from Papi or Juve, but Clara knew someone in that house was fucking her, so she pulled her out right quick, makin' a case to that Family Court Judge Donna Rogers downtown with the threat of a pap smear and a hunch. Papi and Mama never wanted to press charges, they didn't want no police up in *los cosas familiares* and that was cool, 'cause Mama had nowhere else to go if Papi caught a case as an accessory to child abuse and found hisself in jail or deported. So Sylvia took the rap and moved into Excelsior House to avoid a trial. She was not yet considered a "ward of the state." She was just in temporarily relocation status pending reunification because her parents were deemed "unfit" to provide a safe living arrangement for her. Even though she had visitation rights and all 'a that, and could come around on weekends or after school or pretty much whenever she felt like. Papi knew better than to lay a hand on her again now with the court watching, and Juve was out of the house to avoid arrest, so that felt pretty good to Sylvia. Mama hadn't changed her room at all, all her stuff was left just like before they pulled her.

Sylvia had big plans. She didn't need to be livin' here no more no how; she planned to move to New York to make it big as a hip-hop dancer, just as soon as she graduated from Mission High at the end of the school year. So she was just biding her time. But it was her mama that Sylvia worried about most. Mama started drinking heavily when it came out that Juve had raped her and Papi wanted nothing to do with Mami after that. She knew Mama blamed her for all that had happened, but that didn't matter no how. Sylvia was a tough bitch who could scrap with the best 'a them fools, take a beatdown and always handle her own. But because this was her Mama, she wanted her and Papa to have what they did before Sylvia got into all this trouble. 'Cause Mama was never gonna leave him, that much Sylvia knew for sure. And Sylvia wasn't gonna be around forever. So she had to find a way to help Mama get herself right so Papi would want to be her man again.

Sylvia crossed the room and smelled the stench of alcohol on her mama's breath. She wasn't going to wake up tonight. With a touch of grace, Sylvia kissed her gently on the forehead, covered her madre with a spare blanket from the closet, carried her empty bottle to the trash bin underneath the kitchen sink, and left the house before Papi had a chance to know she'd even been there.

***

Joe Rodgers shifted in his chair. As the Executive Director of Excelsior House, he had a lot on his mind. Placement for his new intake, Sarah Hillsbrook, would be tough, though somewhat routine around here. Another client requiring constant monitored supervision as did each of the other children of Excelsior House. They were all special needs kids, diagnosed as Severely Emotionally Disturbed (SED) boys and girls, the victims of tumultuous childhoods and random instances of fate that would have sent any normal adult flying over the edge, let alone an impressionable and unformed personality of a young child. And Joe knew all of his charges well: Tyrone, with his abusive prison guard father and lesbian mother who left him with his dad to pursue a new life after 'coming out', had his share of issues, but at least he'd had a home. Rydell's grandmother gave him up to the system when he was five; being the energetic personality he was, he never stood a chance in a reasonable home, and at forty placements before coming to Excelsior House, he held the record for time spent among all the kids. The sexual abuse he suffered in his 2nd placement pretty much guaranteed he was never going to be a normal child. But Joe took him in like he did the others, because as far as juvenile placement facilities in California went, Excelsior House was his last stop before permanent institutionalization in youth camp or jail.

Joe was a leader in his field, and had had unmatched success with several disturbed kids during his six years working the group home circuit. Joe was also a product of the system himself. He, too, had been a victim of childhood violence and was pulled from his family and made a ward of the state at 8 years old, bouncing between group homes like Excelsior House for the rest of his childhood as he came up yet another product of the system. He never saw his parents again after his father killed his mother and went upstate to jail for thirty years. Let the motherfucker rot in there as far as he was concerned, but Joe himself was never going to go that route. By some miracle of fate he beat the odds, worked the state funded programs and avoided becoming one of every 4 kids who aged out of foster care who spent time in prison within seven years. Back then, they didn't have programs like Excelsior House to help youth transition to the working world, instead throwing them out of public assistance on their 18th birthday, when most were still in high school. But Joe was one who made it out alive himself, so he knew the example he had to set. For the way you got out and became a man in this world, starting with nothing and making up for lost time, he dedicated his life to helping disadvantaged youth like himself beat the odds and find a way out for themselves the way he had done. Hell, as a black man alone, by just having a job he'd already exceeded the fortunes of 34% of young African-American males his age in the US, and by never ending up in jail or on probation, he was ahead of 30% of them. This concerned Joe, because he knew these kids and understood that with the decks already stacked against them, it took a superman to make it out in one piece with the tools needed to survive in this world. And he never would have done it without someone else to look up to, someone to depend on. Joe had that, a black male role model like himself in his life, someone who looked and acted and talked like him, but who had made it, and who was willing to help Joe do the same.

Without his Boys and Girls Club counselor Ron Thompson, Joe would've been lost to the wolves with no one to check him the way he needed as a young thug in training, and he surely would have ended up either in jail or dead without Ron's intervention on numerous occasions. Ron looked out for him the way no one else could, no matter how hard staff in his numerous group homes tried to care for him or to help, they just never knew how to relate to Joe in the same ways Ron did. So Joe understood well the need for role models in the lives of children who came up as he did, for someone permanent who was committed to checking them constantly, staying on top of their issues and keepin' their heads straight so they didn't make the reckless mistakes they'd otherwise be destined for as young adults with limited judgment, fucked-up emotional instincts and no other choice but to manage life on their own. Joe knew his place in their world, and it was right here at Excelsior House. But now, shit was getting especially tight, and he didn't know how he was going to hold it all together.

What it came down to, as it always did in the non-profit world, was money. Joe didn't yet know how he was going to pay rent for the rest of this year. He had staff to compensate, pipes that needed fixing, salaries for his onsite therapists Rita and Jamey to cover (those angels worked for reduced pay because they were loyal and believed in him and the mission they shared here at Excelsior House, but he had to get them up to full competitive compensation, because they deserved it), and with two of his kids soon to age out and enter into transitional living, he had to come up with the funds to match their Section 8 government assistance in order to keep them afloat until their jobs became permanent and their government papers got processed. Three months tops, but still that was three months of scrill Joe didn't have handy to float on his own. Then there were the essentials for the kids; cash for movie tickets, sports equipment (the boys still needed a decent rim over the garage), clothes (especially for his girls, there was no way Rhona and Sylvia were going to school as tenth graders sporting threads from Giant Value or Target, they had to front at least Marshalls or Ross to stay in the game), then came gifts for birthdays and holidays, school club fees, and memberships to the Excelsior Boys and Girls Club. And Marcus might be headed to basketball camp this year: he was a truly gifted baller and Joe understood that it was something he was born to do; he needed this to keep his life in one piece, but nonetheless it was an extra expense that as his legal guardian Joe needed to kick in for. All combined, this would have been manageable had his funding from the state not been cut in half for next fiscal year. This meant Joe was going to have to beg his donors for even more than what they'd already so generously offered, which was no light task, but something Joe knew he could probably pull through if need be.

What made Excelsior House different was that it was the first program of its kind in the State of California to treat SED children in a fully integrated, community-based residential treatment facility. Excelsior House, in effect, was an experimental pilot program designed by the Strategic Task Force committee assembled by the California Department of Youth and Families, Child Protection and Family Support Branch, endorsed by the Governor of California, and launched by the Mayor of San Francisco, the San Francisco Board of Supervisors, and Director of the San Francisco Department of Youth and Their Families. Their collective intent was to find a way to incorporate these children directly into a group home campus situated in a residential neighborhood and comprised of two living units interspersed among the private residences of "regular" citizens in order to promote integration into community-based living. This approach was intended to ease the transitional process for SED children re-entering society. Instead of keeping their clients cordoned off in hospitals, hidden within quiet city neighborhoods, or spread across the countryside as was typically done, the Strategic Task Force Committee believed that the livelihoods of these children with special needs would be best served where their unique psychological dysfunctions could be addressed in a pseudo-public medical setting as they readjusted to society after placement. Joe believed in this idea and endorsed their approach wholeheartedly, but he knew from a practical standpoint that it would be challenging, at best, to keep any group of unruly young thugs and emotionally damaged adolescents in a neighborhood setting, let alone the members of his unique population of special needs kids, as had been proposed for Excelsior House. Nonetheless, Joe had applied for the position and had been hired immediately based upon his background, inspirational life story, and tireless ability to cultivate donors as director of another group home he'd managed for two years prior to his arrival at Excelsior House.

But none of that seemed to help him now, with Excelsior House already over-budget for this year. Joe's most compassionate and avid donors - a few prominent families of San Francisco's philanthropic community - could always be trusted to come through for him if he begged them, as it always seemed he had to the more successful his program grew. But with the new budget allocations proposed by the deficit-strapped state legislature, any and all alternative experimental social programs branded with that scarlet letter known as "temporary status" were on the chopping block for defunding or removal altogether, and Joe knew any hopes he had for recouping his usual 40% of Excelsior House's $247,000 annual operating budget from Sacramento was a pipe dream. He'd have to press his donors right quick and hard to make up the difference. He didn't trust those empty suits in the capital any farther than he could toss 'em to continue supporting any programs they'd already vowed to cut, and so he could no longer be sure how to keep his kids afloat if they pulled the rug out from under his bottom line, even with the increased generosity of the sizable donor pool in his rolodex. All he knew was he'd have to work every angle he could in the coming year: attending grant writing workshops, submitting proposals through local NPOs such as United Way of the Bay Area, networking at foundation fundraisers, working the phones on cold calls, and talking up his program to every last reference he could squeeze from his contacts, if Excelsior House was going to remain open come the first day of the new fiscal year, July 1.

Surprisingly, he wasn't overly concerned about any of this. Joe knew his business well, and through a combination of applying for new grants, working the phones, and developing at least one new partnership with an upstanding member of the local business community, he might have a shot. Besides, that deadline was at least a year away. Joe had total confidence that he'd come through for his kids in the end, as he'd always done. That's just the way Joe worked. Still, he knew there were more pressing challenges to focus on which made him less sure of himself. In addition to Marcus needing help with his basketball scholarship to attend the Boys and Girls Club's Summer Training Camp in Atlanta, Joe had not only the intake of a suicidal girl to wrestle with this afternoon, the daughter of a State Assemblyman nonetheless. The gears in

Joe's mind churned furiously as he thought through all the potential ways he could work this. Local attention to the care Excelsior House provided the community, maybe a local exposé in the Chronicle, possibly even enough appeal to tug the purse strings of a sympathetic Bay Area public to keep the Excelsior House program miraculously continuing on. But no, ultimately that idea had no legs, because Joe was always wary of media attention; in fact it went against every fiber of his instincts to allow the press into the lives of his children. They had already endured so many hardships and they were his to protect. So guard them he did, never letting a single reporter or story exploit their situation for public spectacle or prurient interest. Fame and notoriety were never going to be the golden geese Joe was looking for, but as a fantasy he entertained it often within his few quiet moments, dreaming up ways to conjure new funding sources for the house. Within the safe confines of his imagination this scenario always played well. Still, Joe never lost sight of the fact that within the political circles that ran San Francisco, any program that successfully and anonymously treated a State Assemblyman's drug-addicted, suicidal daughter would be impossible to cut, even without a direct link to the kids themselves. Investigative reporters Matier and Ross could surely skewer his board of directors and the mayor very publicly in their biweekly column in the Chronicle if they caught wind of such double standards being applied by the city in providing foster care services for San Francisco's most underprivileged and needy. Joe imagined the headline now: "Are San Francisco Youth Undeserving of the Same Programs Offered to Children of Our City's Political Elite?" So with the intake of an Assemblyman's daughter came not only burdens, but options as well, including protection for all. As long as they succeeded with her.

More immediately, however, Joe worried about his other girls. Rhona was still acting out sexually with some of the boys from Cottage 2 across the street. Part of the success of Excelsior House was due to Joe's insistence that the integrated program be coed in order to promote therapeutic interaction with peers of both sexes. Under his plan, which made Excelsior House as controversial and cutting-edge as it was, male and female clients were separated only by living arrangement, with two houses situated directly across the street from one another in San

Francisco's Excelsior District. The clients (as staff referred to kids) were allowed to eat together, attend public school, and engage in private and group therapy sessions to promote equity in their peer relationships while allowing onsite therapists and staff to model positive interactions between members of the opposite gender within their communal group setting. In addition to Rhona's behavior, which Rita was already having some limited success with, Sylvia was still all over the place, recently arrested for vandalism twice while in Joe's custody. He had to admit, Sylvia was an amazing street mural artist and spray paint was her game. Before she came to Excelsior House, she made it her habit to tag every wall in her sight, and it took just about all the patience and favors Joe could muster from his personal relationships with the local police to keep her out of the juvenile justice system permanently by bringing her back to the house in place of a trip back to the halls. This must have happened at least six times since Sylvia came here, and although Joe never gave up on her, the patience of his friends in law enforcement was running understandably thin on this. But Joe held credibility with a number of people throughout the community, having come up in the city himself, and so he knew a lot of bangers, cops, civic leaders and neighbors alike, and many of them admired the progress he'd made with the kids in his charge, for their neighborhood and their city. So for the most part, they backed him whenever he needed to bend a few rules another Exec Direct could never swing to keep his program alive. And his commitment to his wards had already paid off in small ways. Sylvia had, for the most part, stopped tagging up her old neighborhood and was getting healthier within the Excelsior program. Instead of acting out, she now channeled her need for expression through art therapy and hip hop dance. She and Rydell, Joe's biggest head case by far, were even entering themselves in poetry slam classes together at the Mission Community Center. Imagine that, Sylvia spittin' her wisdom to youth, telling them how to behave. My God…And Rydell, he even had himself thinking he could rap! Of course that fool had no flow to speak of whatsoever. But these activities kept them both outta trouble, as did Rydell's twice daily dose of Dexedrine and Sylvia's steady regimen of Ritalin. But still, Joe always had to keep one eye out for Sylvia especially, 'cause with that girl's mouth, and coming off 'a her parents abuse, not to mention the fact that they lived here in town, anything was still possible.

Interestingly, it was Joe's biggest Excelsior House success story for whom he was most worried now. Joe had held a special place in his heart for his best girl, Lucy Gutierrez from the moment they first met. Lucy was the classic tragic case. Parents killed in an automobile accident when she was just a baby. Raised in the system all her life. Sexually abused numerous times, first by an uncle and then by an older brother in a foster family with whom she had lived in "stable" placement for over four years. Lucy had always been responsible, always held her own, but needed support the way any developing young woman does. She now found that support in her thug of a boyfriend, Keyshawn - Special K as he was called on the street - whom she'd dated on-again-off-again for several years. Joe knew his kind: he'd grown up with the type. In fact, Joe had been just like the dude until Ron Thompson, his mentor at the Boys and Girls Club, had turned him around. But as for Keyshawn, it didn't matter no way no how who did or didn't take care of him when he was coming up, because that dude was a thug for life. No excuses, no disenfranchisement, no second chances, he was pure hood and all mean simply 'cause he wanted to be. But unlike Joe, who'd always had a place inside him that wanted to change, with Keyshawn there wasn't nowhere like that to be found, best as Joe could tell. And if nothing else, Joe could read people. Ain't no one ever gonna reach that boy, just a matter 'a time before he kills someone, he truly believed. Joe was a Christian and so he valued the power of forgiveness and redemption above all else, but he also came up knowin' that even with help, some dudes just didn't wanna be reached. And Keyshawn was that kind of banger, pure and simple. But Lucy loved him nonetheless, 'cause he was just about the only thing rock-solid in her life. Though she knew he was a menace to society tried and true, slingin' drugs to young'uns and thuggin' on any fool with a need to step to him, that still didn't matter enough to Lucy. For some fucked-up reason that Joe had no mind to comprehend, Lucy's trusting heart always held a special place for Keyshawn. Maybe she wanted to save him, maybe she needed to believe there was some good left in him, or maybe she just wanted someone to fill that void in her life. But whatever the reason, Lucy was loyal as hell to that boy, and so she became his woman.

It hadn't always been that way for her. After Lucy's court case freed her from her abusive foster family several years back, Joe took her in to live at Excelsior House. He could see the fire in this girl's eyes right from the get-go; she desperately needed a strong parental figure who could show her a way to live in this world right, someone from whom to learn how to trust in people again, who could teach her how to depend on others in a healthy way. And for whatever reason, Lucy seemed ready to take that chance with Joe. So he did what any good mentor would do: he became the dependable role model Lucy needed, and she loved him for it. But Joe also had his own secret feelings of longing for her, even though he knew he could never act upon them if he was going to be the man Lucy needed him to be. Still, you can be goddamn sure he had those thoughts. They were several years apart in age; Lucy was 17 when she arrived at Excelsior House, while Joe had just turned 26 - he was the youngest Executive Director to ever run a group home anywhere in California. But in order to keep his true feelings hidden from Lucy, to be the man she needed, he put up an emotional wall she could never cross, as much as she tried. And try she did, may times. But she could never fully reach this part of him. So even though he could never give her what she really wanted from him, Joe gave her what he believed she needed most: he ended up being Lucy's father figure, the first she'd ever really known in her life, and Joe reveled in his role, 'cause this girl deserved to have someone care for her in the way only Joe could.

But since Joe could never be Lucy's man, it never crossed Lucy's mind in a serious way to shake herself of Keyshawn. With all that girl had been through, she'd still believed she needed a man in her world to make her happy. And for better or worse, from the day Joe met her, that man was Keyshawn. Key, as stubborn a motherfucker as he was, had stuck with her through all her drama, from the rapes to the court cases to her placement at Excelsior House. Of course, out of everything Keyshawn hated about Lucy's new life most, he despised Joe's presence, 'cause he sensed where Joe's true heart lay for his girl. So Keyshawn called Joe out on this straight up when they first met, and they almost came to blows right then and there in the street, which would've landed Joe immediately in the penitentiary for assault, causing him to lose his gig and his kids. But after momentarily contemplating the ins and outs of putting that fool in the ground, Joe's cooler head prevailed and he gave homeboy a choice: either get hisself whupped in front of his woman or never come around Excelsior House again. Surprising everyone, Keyshawn backed down, either 'cause he knew on account 'a how Joe came up it'd be only one them left standin' if they threw down, or because he understood what Joe meant to Lucy's life now and in the twisted workings of his mind he actually respected Joe for that. For Joe's part, regardless of how he dealt with Keyshawn, he knew he could never get Lucy to drop that gangbanger without pushing her out of his life altogether, so he begrudgingly accepted her continuing to see Key, so long as that motherfucker kept himself nonexistent around Excelsior House.

Thus, Joe's pact with the devil was signed and sealed by his unrequited love for Lucy. She stayed without incident under his roof for several months until she got herself pregnant with Key's child. That alone should have disqualified her from remaining at Excelsior House, but come hell or high water, Joe wasn't about to give up on his girl. He leaned on several of his donors to pay for additional maternity resources that allowed Lucy to remain in Joe's care instead of being transferred to a transitional living home for pregnant mothers. Of course Joe loved Lucy and didn't want to see her go, but it was only because Lucy herself wanted to stay that it worked. Joe's only condition was that Keyshawn kept his bitch ass away from them. For their part, again for inexplicable reasons, Lucy and Key both complied with this arrangement, so Joe did everything within his power to make sure Lucy had everything she needed to raise her little boy, Tre, right during his first year of life.

Until her eighteenth birthday: like any one of his clients, Lucy aged out of the foster system and was no longer a ward of the state. According to California law, due mainly to lack of funding for such programs, Lucy was left to her own financial devices and emancipated after a short period of transitional living in another group home. This was pure suicide for tons of foster kids living within the system, to be abandoned by every support structure they'd ever known just because they came of age or finished high school, and it wouldn't have been any different for Lucy unless she kept herself enrolled in school, but with the demands put on her by raising Tre alone and dealing with Keyshawn's incarceration just after the birth of their son - he caught a case upstate to Folsom, sentenced to 30 years as a repeat offender for damn near beatin' the life outta some slinger who was skimming off a his stash (Good riddance to the both of them, Joe not-so-secretly thought to himself, Three Strikes and You're Out Motherfucker) - Lucy dropped out of high school in the middle of her Senior year because she just couldn't take the pressure of havin' her baby's father out the mix for the remainder of Tre's childhood.

For all his faults, Joe did recognize that one good thing that thug had done while he was still in the game was float Lucy enough money to get her own place and to raise their son under a roof 'a they own. As psychopathic as that motherfucker was, and as unhealthy as Lucy's attachment to him may be, he cared for that little boy. And for her too, so it seemed. But with Key outta the picture for good and Lucy without the means to provide for herself, it was Joe who came through. He arranged to have her emancipate while providing her a special scholarship to help her make rent and pay the electric bill until she finished her GED and could go to work to support herself and the baby. Joe also kicked in outta pocket to provide her the difference for food, diapers, and clothes when the food stamps Lucy received through government assistance came up short. But with Keyshawn off 'a Lucy's radar now permanent, Joe was only too happy to fill the role as her provider once again. He never told her he was paying for her himself. That much was gonna stay his secret – his gift for his own baby girl, now with a baby of her own.

But sure enough, as fate would have it, several months later Keyshawn got his sentence commuted for what Joe believed to be a fuckass manipulation of jurisprudence by his defense attorney, who claimed improper search and seizure by the police during Keyshawn's arrest. Why cops can't drop a motherfucker in his own home and have a look around the bedroom while they're cuffin' the fool was beyond Joe, but nonetheless upon prudent review of the details surrounding the arrest, the judge declared a mistrial and Key was back on the street, livin' back with Lucy now in the house he'd paid for before gettin' sent to the pen. And even though Joe kept coverin' Lucy's bills to keep her livin' right, as far as that motherfucker Key was concerned, now his baby, their son, and the rest 'a her shit was rightfully his, even though that thug hadn't fronted her one dime in over a year. Key was right back to his old ways, rebuilding his crew and slingin' in the most desperate neighborhoods of San Francisco to finance his gangsta life and his baby mom's crib. Key didn't give a fuck that he was on his last strike, somehow the dude was too delusional to comprehend it. But sure as hell, once he started back up Lucy stopped taking Joe's money, talkin' some stupid mess like 'Now Key out, he gon' provide for me and Tre. He already payin' my rent, bringin' home diapers and the like.' Joe wanted to right about smack Lucy for the first time in his life when he heard her spittin' that mess, and it took all the strength he could muster just to hold himself back, 'cause she was an adult making her own decisions now, and there was nothing he could do but sit and wait it out for that thug to fuck up again like he would for shore. But this time might be Lucy and Tre's last chance to get out, 'cause Joe knew Key's kind, and he was sure it was only a matter of time 'fore that fool got back to his old ways, puttin' the beat down on Lucy whenever he got too high or pissed off 'bout some street bullshit, though Joe couldn't prove it none. And Lucy was never about talk no shit 'bout her baby daddy in front 'a Joe 'cause she knew it only made her look a failure in his eyes. Naw, Lucy was hell-bent on avoidin' any kind of drama with Joe all costs, 'cause nothin' was more important to her than makin' Joe proud 'a her by raisin' her little man right and takin' her lumps the way a real woman does, and providin' fo' her own any way she could. Joe was left with no choice but to wait for that punk motherfucker Key to explode, and when he did, he just betta hope neither Lucy nor Tre was caught up in the fallout. 'Cause if that dude so much as thought about doin' damage to his people again, it was Joe who was gonna be the next nigga to find hisself catchin' a case upstate, murder for life. And they would never find the body. That much was for damn sure.

***

Julio shifted in his chair. He snorted, rubbed his face, scanned the other expressions of those tattered frames sitting around him. Some looked like ghosts, memories of their original selves lost now in physical decay; others were stringers, hangers-on to a semblance of their regained selves by only a thread. And then there were those addicts in full recovery mode, sober each day-by-day, all keeping themselves alive by finding a way to those chairs every chance they could, when it felt like they couldn't hold on to a life of sobriety any longer, they all filed around him now, and they were watching Julio intently, eagerly supportive, yet all with an increased desperation for his gathering of words the longer he sat among them silent. Julio had been attending Narcotics Anonymous for several months. He'd done the twelve steps. He'd slipped and found his way back. He still had trouble getting from 11 to 12. But he believed in the process. Divine power, it must exist, Julio reasoned, because it allowed him to find his way back. From pullin' half the shit Julio did in his past, from clockin' knocks, runnin' sleeping missions, beatin' down fools and cappin' scraps who dissed his crew, he should be dead for half 'a those things by now, though nobody could never prove nuthin', not even them fools who witnessed his deeds direct, legit. So he believed in the divine spirit. Pure and simple. Because he had to. This is how Julio saw the world. The only way it could work, the only justification for all the horrible shit he'd seen done and been a part of. The reason for all of it to go down the way it did, for all those motherfuckers either laid up or dead while he was still out walking was for him to overcome his evil and find love in Jesus Christ. By any other account Julio knew he should be dead, either rottin' in the ground with the rest of them decayed corpses or burnin' in hell for all the shit he pulled in a previous life. But with the Love of Christ filling his heart now, with his surrender to the divine love of HIS guidance and HIS spirit, everything was so simple now, there was a reason for his second chance, there had to be. With so many people out there weak and fragile, slave to their addictions, lost along the path of darkness, there was always a choice of surrender to the higher power, the love of our creator. Only then could each of us have a second chance. This is what NA had taught him.

The rest he already knew himself. God was not to blame for all the evil in the world, we were all just a part of some shit that's much too big to comprehend, of that Julio was for damn sure. But if we just accept the Lord into our hearts and embrace our place within his divine creation as His children, regardless of what we've done, the love of Cristo, our savior, will deliver us from evil, and that shit is guaranteed. As long as we remain humble enough to accept our own shortcomings and embrace His acceptance and His love, to kick drugs, to stop killing one another, to make the most of our lives filled with the strength of his divinity and his grace, in the spirit of his master plan, anything is possible. And for that, anyone who escapes, anyone who comes clean is a rarity to be admired, an example to be followed.

Julio believed that he was that example now. Because he was living proof. He'd been clean for going on six months, so it was Julio who was leading group this week. Julio understood that world and he was going to share his experience with everyone who would listen, because it had changed him; because his survival might help another vato survive his own situation. Because as long as Julio could make it, he had something to stand for, something to live by, and he wasn't afraid. But like always, just like every other night like tonight, rain or shine, in the depths of a Rodgers or when calmness swept over him, however arbitrarily those feelings came and went, triggered by shit he still couldn't explain, he was now just looking for the right words. They would come, he thought, they always did when he needed them. Again he clasped his hands in front of his mouth to disguise his frustration. They always did. Still nothing. Finally a stir in the crowd. Those basket case motherfuckers would have to wait. But not for long. Almost as if roused to the challenge by the mild grunts suppressed by the other members wading through the burdening thickness of their own uncompromising silence, waiting for him to speak, the lion roared and the beast was unleashed, flying out its cage. With visceral confidence Julio started the meeting in his usual stream-of-consciousness free flow.

What up y'all?
Whaz up man.
Yo I'm Julio.
His fellow addicts loved him.
I'm thinking all kinds 'a crazy thoughts tonight…
That's cool man.
Stay strong brother.
You got this.

Y'all know how I been straight for going on like six months and shit.

Yeah!

Applause.

And you know how I's always frontin' on y'all to stay strong.

You go brother.

Tell it true.

Well I'm tellin' you sumpin' real now. This shit don't get easier the longer you go, hell no. It just gets clearer why you stay doin' what you doin'.

Ayite. We feel you.

It's like, man, some days, you know, that Rodgers be kickin' and shit ain't goin' right at all, and you's like damn, I don't know if I can handle this one more motherfuckin' day, know what I'm sayin'?'

But I'm tellin' you fools, it don't make no sense, and it don't mean much when that Rodgers be kickin' how long you been sober, you just want to get yo'self straight and nuthin' no motherfucker says gonna change none a that.

Julio paused. He had to gather his words.

Man, I almost used last night. I came this close, you know?

Julio pinched his fore finger and thumb nearly together, leaving only a small gap in between.

Yeah, hell yeah, Julio, we know-

And I been sober like six months and shit. I been comin' home from work every night thinkin' 'bout that shit, after gettin' all grease monkey changing tires and shit, and sumpthin' triggers sumpthin' up in here, man, I don't even know where it comin' from but that shit creeps up on a motherfucker sumpthin' real. And all I wants to do is get high.

Keep going, man. Stay solid brother!

Tonight I wanted to shoot my shit up more than anything.

We hear you. We know.

But you know, I held my game tight, was fightin' through some motherfuckin' cold sweats and shit. It was like detox all over 'gain in my room I even went for a run out in the rain and shit. Ha!

Everyone laughed.

But you know man, somehow, some way, that shit just disappeared 'bout as soon as it come on. I dunno what happened, and I don't know what I woulda done if it'd lasted more than a couple 'a minutes, yo, but what am I thinkin'? Mang, it didn't mean nothing. When I left my crib to score how's I's gonna get all messed up and break my probation and shit, end up in jail, yo. But when I was 'bout to do myself right, all I couldn't stop thinking 'bout was y'all...

The room erupted.

And I thought, mang, damn, there ain't no way y'all motherfuckers gonna let me creep back up 'round here tellin' y'all how I relapsed and shit. Naw, man, fuck that. I wasn't havin' none 'a it y'all; didn't matter how bad I had t' get high. Facin' y'all motherfuckers was my worst nightmare, so I copped my ass right back 'round opposite side da street and kept my shit goin' for like three hours straight, standin' out in da rain all soaked front 'tha house, no shit. But man, I tell ya, when the Rodgers came back bangin' hard, I had the power to fight it off, yo, you feel me? And so here I am today, tellin' y'all what I wanted to say. Yo mang, I'm Julio. I'm a drug addict. And I been sober now six motherfuckin' months!

With that, his group couldn't restrain their whistles and cheers. Julio laughed and high fived a few of his fellow addicts. He was all too happy to be able to bring it to them in this way tonight.

***

Lucy eyed her favorite dress at Mi Encanta's on Mission Street. The one in pink with the white frills. She had played the scene in her mind a hundred times since she first saw the dress hovering over her in that storefront window. Lucy hadn't had a Quinceañera, because her foster family at the time never saw fit to give her one. But it had always been Lucy's dream to have all her homegirls around her, praising her beauty, all center-of-attention and the like, a celebration of her transition from little girl to full-fledged woman, adulthood-style and all. In her mind, champagne was poppin' and all them wannabe thugs from her 'hood was out checkin' for her and her girls, but it was her man K that stood by her side that night. He was the only thing she'd lived for until Tre came along. As unceremonious as that had been, with her falling into labor at the liquor store and an ambulance ride to San Francisco General, where Tre was comin' in breeched after something like 15 hours labor, damn he was a fighter from the get-go. They C-sectioned him out and there he was, God's gift of glory smiling back up at her, and she knew right then and there what her new purpose in life was. While K was busy out workin' his hustle on the block, he couldn't be around to hold her hand come time for delivery or none 'a that. It was Joe who did all that, but she didn't pay it no mind, because Key came when he could, and he was the only one besides Joe who showed up. But none of that mattered anyhow no more, cuz now there was her and there was Tre, a heavenly angel in whose eyes nothing tarnished or evil or dirty ever existed. Seeing him come into this world this way, he was pure as anything she'd ever seen, and she intended to keep it that way, by raising him right: free 'a all that drama and misery and pain that came along wit' da upbringings 'a just about everybody she'd ever known, like the baggage she brought to her own circumstances. But now with Tre, it wuz' gon' be different from the get-go. Lucy never wanted him to know the struggles she'd endured as a child; he was never gonna have to keep from killing himself the way she'd done, after that maricón foster uncle of hers diddled her for three months when she was seven and her foster mom left her alone with him time and time again to babysit. Or how her stepbrother started fucking her when she was eleven and Lucy couldn't say shit about that 'cause she wanted nothing more than to be adopted by his sweet grandmother; then for all those years after when she dealt with her sexual abuse issues in residential treatment at Excelsior House and how Joe and Rita taught her to stop acting out and how to become a normal woman with a normal life who could bring up her new baby right, God's blessing to her in this world now for sortin' herself out, as she believed. She saw Tre's life as her mission now, her quest to rise up and give him all the things she never had, and she was determined to teach him what she'd learned on her own so he wouldn't come up broken the same way every other fool she knew done. K was no different from the rest in that way, but Tre would be a happy boy if she had anything to do with it. And she did. Because she kept true to the man who brought him to her, who cared for both 'a them when she got herself pregnant. Key was willin' to stick wit' her and be his baby's father and that shit meant more to Lucy than nobody's business, given how so many mommies out there tryin' to make it on they own, wit' all these playas fatherin' kids and no intention 'a providin' for them, no way, hell naw. Her life was gon' to be different from all that so Tre's could be, too. They was gon' break that cycle, and Keyshawn was the man to help her do it. So any other problems 'a his she was quick to turn a blind eye to, cuz in his heart she knew he was good. Good to her and most important, good to his boy. He just had to keep his punk ass outta jail long enough to raise his son into a young man. But he was workin' that out.

Lucy came home to find Keyshawn on the Sony Playstation. The sweet smell of marijuana smoke permeated the house. Key must 'a been up with Tre all day. He always played his games to unwind after a busy day wit' their son. He nodded in acknowledgement as she walked through the front room of their flat, waving the smoke outta her face.

Hey boo.

No response.

Where Tre be at?

Sleepin'.

Lucy wafted through the thick cloud in the room. Man, you gon' wipe your boy's brain out 'fore he even have a chance to use it.

Keyshawn let out a snicker of mild disgust. Boy gots to be able to get his smoke on 'f he wanna be a man someday.

Lucy face took pause at Key, who hadn't yet looked up from his game on the TV screen. What, like his daddy?

Straight.

Lucy smiled, though Keyshawn, facing the TV screen, wouldn't have known it.

She walked into the kitchen and started unloading the groceries she had purchased with food stamps from Cala Foods on South Van Ness. With Keyshawn back in her life she was makin' rent again, and payin' all her bills on time.

On government assistance as a single mom with a dependent, she was able to afford the basics: diapers, powder, wipes, baby food, eggs, bread, bologna, fresh fruit, and cheese

slices to keep her strength up, and Kool-Aid with Flaming Hot
Cheetos and Shortbread Chocolate Chip cookies plus some
microwaveable popcorn for Key's snacks. He could buy all his
beer his damn self, 'cause she had neither the time nor the money
for any 'a that. But by keeping the shelves stocked with foods her
transitional home counselor called 'dietary essentials' for the baby,
along with some junk food, it kept K and his friends off 'a her
stash when they comin' around. She also bought herself and Tre
some milk and fresh vegetables for salads, because she was told
she needed these for fiber, and she was still breastfeeding.
According to the doctor, Tre still needed her milk for at least the
first year to keep his immune system up. And that meant gettin'
her full value of daily nutrients each and every day, from greens
and tomatoes and rice with a multivitamin kicked in for good
measure. The doctor stressed the value of a balanced diet from the
very start as crucial to her baby's bodily development in those
early formative years, and since she wanted Tre to have every
chance in life she never did, she was becomin' Miss Nutritionist to
do her and her baby right. There was no way she'd be havin' Tre
scroungin' the corners of the house for his bread crumbs the way
she done in a few of her placements, hells naw, and he was never
gon' have to shoplift off 'a grocery store carts neither to keep
himself eatin'.

Lucy had never been much of a cook, but she was learning.
Seemed easy enough to add water to mashed potato mix and steam
vegetables for ten minutes on the stove or bake a piece 'a chicken
marinated in some quick-mix sauce. Before her maternity classes,
she'd only cooked on the Foreman Grill Joe had bought for the
kids at Excelsior House. Man, none 'a those fools never knew how
to heat up nuthin' but a bunch 'a burger patties and French fries
broiled in the oven up in there, but some 'a the staff wasn't so bad
at makin' a little go a long way, doin' plenty more with what they
got. Carly made some mean enchiladas more than a few times, and
Maurice whipped up his gumbo like nobody's business that done
kicked your stomach's ass up and out each and every time! Those
meals was tight! About the only gripe Lucy ever had 'bout her time
in Excelsior House was nobody never taught her to cook nuthin'
'till she had Tre and her health worker showed her some recipes.
But it was all good, 'cause with her training now in full effect Lucy

was learning fast. And with Tre still on baby food, she had plenty 'a time to get it right for him. But she had to keep herself correct as well, 'cause there was no way she was gon' die 'a no heart attacks supersizin' on no fast food just 'cause she wuz workin' two jobs. Naw, 'cause this shit was about buildin' some new habits, to pass on to her boy. And with cookin' healthy, Lucy was comin' in quick to more than a few 'a those.

Lucy put the groceries away in a hurry before they spoiled. She couldn't wait to see her boy sound asleep and give him a big old kiss on his forehead. Even though she'd only been away for a couple 'a hours, with Tre only six months old, that shit felt like an eternity. And damn, Lord only knew how the fuck she was gon' make it through the next few days even if she DID get that part time job she applied to at the hospital to keep them government assistance checks rollin' in. And wit' two hours a day lookin' every-which-way for employment, if she was gon' keep floatin' above water she'd have to get used to bein' away from her boy more and more, at least 'till Keyshawn got his hustle straight to pull in some legitimate dough.

Out of nowhere, Keyshawn wrapped his arms around Lucy and gave her a hug from behind, kissing her gently on the cheek.

Hey boo...

Your boy missed you.

She smiled coyly. Who dat?

Both 'a dem.

He nuzzled her neck more forcefully. It felt so good to have him want her the way he was comin' for her now.

I need t' check on Tre.

He good. Stayed awake half the day waitin' fo' you to come back. All missing his moms, thinkin' if he just kept his eyes open, you'd get here quicker.

Key always knew how to make Lucy smile. She turned around to face him.

Our son already actin' just like his father.

Keyshawn laughed. Yeah, you know that's real.

He gave Lucy another gentle kiss on the lips. She loved Key's tender side.

Baby?

Yeah boo...

I think I'm gonna land that job with the hospital. I tried real hard on the entry test today you know, and I think I be makin' it happen, she proclaimed proudly.

Girl, you know I'm 'a float you any and every way, come hell or high water…

Lucy appreciated his gesture, but was a bit despondent at his taking the wind out of her sails. She wanted nothing more than his approval, his acknowledgement or encouragement, anything. But she knew Key was trying, and that had to be enough, at least for now.

I know. But if I get it, I'm 'a be gone at least eight hours a day. So we needs to figure on findin' someone to watch Tre.

Key stopped kissing her and cradled Lucy's cheeks firmly with both of his caressing palms. Hell, I'm a be here.

Lucy hesitated at this thought a quick minute, because deep down she knew Key planned to keep on runnin' his original hustle, and if he wus homebound, chances were his business'd make it back 'round the way sometime. And she didn't want none 'a them smokers near her boy ever, 'specially when she wasn't there.

Key, you know what I'm sayin'. With you's busy doin' what you do, we'll be needin' professional care 'a some kind.

What, you think I ain't qualified? He seemed to utter these words almost half sarcastically. 'Cause I'm his daddy, and any motherfuckas you ask tell you I take care 'a my own, know what I'm sayin'?

Lucy laughed off his posturing. Key was always playing the tough guy, which in a weird way still made him seem strong in her eyes.

Yo what 'bout his grandma? She got this.

But baby, she all the way out in Richmond. I'm thinkin' serious now, you feel me?

Yeah I feel you girl, for real. Come on now.

Key groped her hard in his temporary moment of sobriety. She was sure he must have understood what she was spittin' was the God-honest practical truth 'a da matter. 'Cause if he wus out thuggin', he ain't got no time to care fo' their baby. 'Specially when there was work to be done.

Yeah, well you know. Child care ain't no thang neither, 'cause now I'm back out da pen, I'm 'a be pullin' in grips real quick, you feel me?

Yeah, I know, Lucy pondered out loud. But for how long?

Keyshawn flashed her a serious look before locking his hands forcefully on both her shoulders, to force eye contact. But seeing the uncertainty in her eyes, his violent side drew back down to a simmer, as he held his woman gently, but commandingly.

I done told you I ain't never going back in dere.

His voice was simultaneously assuring and uncompromising in its tone.

'Cause come hell or high water, if it between me and some smoker, you can believe that fool ain't seein' the light 'a day, know what I'm sayin'? 'Cause my son and my girl be my world now, and whatever else, what it do. Ain't no bullshit gettin' in my way no 'mo', hell naw!

Lucy smiled and dropped her stoic stare, backing down from the sheer force of his grasp, while at the same time enamored with his intense commitment to their family. Yeah baby…I feel you.

So we's all good den.

She held back tears, though not of pure joy.

Yeah baby. We all good.

Key returned to kiss her on the lips gently once again.

Ayite then. 'Cause my baby be one 'a da smartest women on this here planet, yo, you know what I'm sayin', and I can tell these things. Real soon dem fools in that office job gon' be beggin' for you to bust on in through they doors and show 'em how it do, you feel me boo?

Yeah.

Yeah?

Raising her chin now with his index finger, he brought her stare back up to meet his own.

Yeah, she reiterated again to assure him, tapping him on the chest playfully, trying to make the most of his awkward tenderness. You know you's so sweet when you wants to be…

Ain't no thang when you mean every word.

She nodded again, this time relieved. At least he didn't hit her. He promised never to do that again. And for now, he was keeping all of his promises.

Ayite den, let's go say g'night to our son.

***

Oh shit here come the new girl!

The girls of Excelsior House saw Sarah Hillsbrook walking up the steps with Agnes Washington, Intake Coordinator for their living unit.

Ah, hell naw, Sylvia grimaced at the sight of her. Homegirl be pale as fuck.

She look like Casper the Unfriendly Ghost and shit.

Shit, she best keep her hands to her damn self fo' we have a exorcism up in this.

Damn Syl, you's wrong, Brenda admonished.

Rhona laughed. But that wuz hella funny 'dough.

None of them knew what to expect from the sight of her, but they tried to size her up just as they did every new client who arrived at Excelsior.

Yo Sylvia, you know whitegirl be bunkin' wit' 'chu, Rhona taunted.

Sylvia started right in. Hell naw, I'm 'a tell you right now I ain't sleepin' wit' dat snow bunny up in my room.

Rhona smiled. Carly gon' rearrange us 'cause you's the youngest and she promised me my own room when the new girl come.

It'll be fine, Lucy consoled them both. Just give peace a chance.

Uh-uh, Sylvia squeaked noxiously, I ain't givin' that bitch shit.

I'm sure she'll be fine.

Easy for you to say, Loosey Wit' Cho' Poosy. You already got a place to call yo' own wit' your drug dealer baby daddy, shit.

Yeah, well I already done my time with y'all.

Shit, and I was the best roommate you ever had, Sylvia threw right back at her. You know that the truth. Better than that dude you shackin' wit' now. He shady.

Lucy ignored Sylvia's mouth. Just get to know homegirl and I'm sho' y'all be fine.

Did you even see that bitch? She obviously whack. Probably snores and speaks crazy devil shit in her sleep. But it don't matter none, 'cause she ain't bunkin' wit' me. Hell naw, I'm 'a tell Carly and Joe that straight up right now.

Shh, hold up, here they come, yo.

Agnes opened the door and the girls immediately silenced themselves.

Hey, Agnes.

Hey, ladies.

Agnes gave a smile, implying a question she already knew the answer to. Y'all's quiet today.

She turned to Sarah, who, mortified at the very thought of living here, blushed nervously. Here she was, just another girl figuring out for the first time how to walk through the door to a new home to meet her housemates. Agnes had watched the same combination of emotions - fear, anticipation, hopefulness and contempt - flash across the faces of hundreds of girls, as they negotiated their first steps through the threshold into Girl's Cottage 1.

You can come on in now.

Sarah fidgeted with her bag and walked through the stoop, looking up to see the seemingly hardened girls in the front room staring at her with a mixture of childlike sympathy and curiosity. They, too, remembered walking through that door on that first day at Excelsior House. This might not be so bad after all, Sarah reasoned.

Ladies, this is our new client, Sarah Hillsbrook.

Sarah waved. None of the girls changed their expressions.

This here is Sylvia, Rhona, Lucy, and Lucy's son Tre.

Sarah feigned a polite smile. Hi.

Just get me the hell outta here was all she could think to herself. But she decided to make small talk to try and break the tension filling the room.

You're baby's cute. How old is he?

Lucy smiled at the compliment and gently rocked Tre in her arms to keep him asleep.

He goin' on six months.

Cool, Sarah replied. She knew she had to make friends fast and with this moment, she seemed off to a good start.

None of the girls asked Agnes what each of them was dying to know. An uncomfortable silence fell over the group. Agnes maintained the introductions demanded of her by the intake process seamlessly, having shepherded each of the other girls into the house either months or years before.

Y'all got anything planned today?

Immediately, Sylvia responded. Naw, we just kickin' it round here.

Agnes smiled. That's good, 'cause maybe y'all can show Sarah 'round the neighborhood when we finished with orientation.

The girls all nodded but cringed at the thought. Yeah. That's cool. Shoure. We could do that.

Sarah smiled, but likewise cringed at the thought. All she could hope for now was to get into her private room so she could close the door, put a blanket over her face and forget this place...

But before any of them could maintain their own fantasy of what was to come, Agnes dropped the news all of the girls were waiting for: new room arrangements.

So Rhona, since you and Brenda are the youngest, Joe decided you gonna share the single room.

What! Sylvia sounded off in horror at the news.

Syl, you gonna stay where you is and Sarah gonna bunk up wit'chu.

Immediately, Sylvia protested. Damn, Agnes, if I'm the oldest then I should get the single room like Lucy did!

Agnes, having expected Sylvia's reaction, calmly tried talking her down.

Girl, now listen here a quick minute. First of all, with Sarah here, you aren't the oldest client in the cottage anymore.

Lucy and Rhona couldn't help but smile as Sylvia gave Agnes a look of dread at the thought that this new girl had usurped her status as eldest in the female unit, thereby negating her unspoken but customary claim to single room privileges.

And second, since we ain't got space left with four a y'all, Joe felt it best since you been here the longest that you help Sarah with her transition.

Sylvia immediately looked at Sarah, No offense none, then quickly turned back to Agnes, But hell naw! You know this is whack, Agnes.

Agnes agreed, but still couldn't offer Sylvia the real reason she needed to shack them up together, not in front of the other girls.

I hear what 'chu sayin' Syl, but you know if you got room change issues you gotta take it up wit' Joe.

Sylvia blew her off with a wave of the hand. Naw man, this is some fucked-up shit here and y'all knows it.

Lucy scolded Sylvia for her vulgar outburst toward staff. Girl, be cool now and run your program right. You know she ain't got no say in the matter.

Seems like all y'all got say but me, Sylvia steamed, but restrained herself from any further outburst that would get her in trouble at the cottage. Last thing she needed now was to come off 'a her weekend sporting a Verbal just in time for her weekly behavioral review.

You know I'm a talk to Rita come Monday.

Well, you need to do what you gotta do, Agnes agreed.

Oh, I will.

Agnes smiled at the resolution. OK, ladies. Well Sarah, let's show you your new room.

Sarah nodded to acknowledge the girls. It was nice meeting you all.

Cool, the girls responded tersely.

Yeah.

Whatever.

Sylvia turned to Lucy and Rhona as Sarah and Agnes left the hallway. She rolled her eyes petulantly. This is some bullshit runnin' up in here, she whispered, And I'm 'a sleep on dat couch 'till Monday, y'all watch.

She ain't trippin' on you none. Who knows, maybe y'all'll end up friends.

Hell naw, Sylvia scoffed. Homegirl be hella maddoggin' me with them devil eyes. I already hate that bitch.

***

Clara Rodriguez hated Sunnydale. Every time she came to these projects on the far side of Visitacion Valley, she saw things that make her stomach churn. As a Child Protective Services Worker for the County of San Francisco going on twelve years now, she had witnessed her share of misery in the untold number of interventions she'd made in that time. Children eating cat food to survive; the soggy carpets and leaky pipes in dozens of public housing units across her territory, causing chronic cases of asthma in kids living there; or mothers turning tricks in another room while their husbands, boyfriends, uncles or fathers collected their cut; gunshots; kids dealing drugs and babies left in dirty diapers on a mattress soaked in vomit - Clara was no stranger to the worst of their world. However, on this particular day, she had no taste for her job. There was no sign of abuse beyond neglect in the house she was about to visit. Beyond the groups of the pushers and their clients, through the vacant stares of those housing project dwellers who surrounded her during every intervention and made her clasp her keychain with the mace sprayshot held tightly in her pocket. Many of them - the ballers, knockers and tweakers; the daddies and their tricks; the gangstas with their patnas; and withered elderly alike - condemned by an indifferent society to waste away in this place, yelled profanities in her general direction as she passed, but none could do anything to keep her from her grave task. It was always the same voiced grievances: 'How you comin' in here takin' babies away from they mama? You one 'a them!' These comments always stung the most. Clara was a mother herself and knew enough to understand the gravity of her business whenever she approached a family who was otherwise off the radar to society, and why these project dwellers, regardless of who they were, universally hated her for entering their world; like a cherry picker, she was a stealer of their youth, for many a last source of joy, inspiration and hope; plucking the most preciously vulnerable of their community away from them, those young souls the world had to believe might blossom out of what they'd surely become if only given the chance.

But Clara had no illusions. Condemning children to a life under CPS (Child Protective Services) was a fate she would never wish upon anyone's children, certainly not her own. Through her numerous interventions, Clara could only guarantee these kids the possibility of escaping a certainly-short life behind the barrel of a gun; if they never got to come home, the kids she "saved" by the age of 6 would end up in an average of 23 foster homes by their 18th birthday, before they aged out and moved on into the world with no further assistance allotted to them. Forty percent would be unemployed on their 21st birthday, over half would be arrested at least once for petty theft or drug crimes, and forty percent of African-American boys would be serving drug sentences in jail. No, what Clara offered was not safety, but a clear path to institutionalization for many of these same kids she saved from almost certain death. If the numbers proved correct - and Clara did not believe they were, given the lack of adequate reporting across county agencies - two-thirds of those children would go on to be physically abused, one-third sexually assaulted, and about half the girls molested at some point by a member of the foster family. So Clara knew that the path she set these kids upon in extracting them from their birth families was not a way out of misery - no, surely it was not that - it was only a stopgap from the immediate neglect or abuse or threat of death these young children would surely continue to face if they remained in their current homes. So what Clara really offered was only a chance. At hope. For the possibility of something more. As far as Clara could tell, hope itself would never be enough. But it was a start.

How you doing, girl? Clara's supervisor, Loretta Harris, asked as her colleague stared
distraughtly at the placement file open on the desk before her. Clara sat with her chin buried in the palms of her hands, her elbows dug firmly into her cluttered desktop at the Child Protective Services offices of San Francisco General Hospital.

I've been better.

Sunnydale got you down again?

You know the drill. Pulled two more from Number 12 this morning. Was like a public hanging up there.

Yeah well at least you're not a man. Then they come after you. Ask Harold.

She shits you not.

Harold Vargas, the only male CPS worker servicing the Outer Mission, Visitacion Valley, and Excelsior districts with

Clara and Loretta, walked up and smiled, nodding in full agreement.

Just last week in Potrero I had three dealers run up on me with a gun to my head telling me to back off before I got capped, how I wasn't about to take their favorite trick's baby away cuz she was a good mother and that little boy was the only thing she was livin' for. Man, when I realized my job was bad for business, that's when I got really scared. But you do what you got to. Went back up there that same afternoon with three black and white units and we pulled the kid without incident. Sure as shit made me feel good until he AWOL'ed the next day from his placement 'cross town and found his way back. So I did it the same again that day. Much as those cats hate on me, that doesn't happen every time. You just can't let the bastards get you down.

I dunno, Clara mused. I just can't keep pretending we're really helping these kids. At least in the Mission, the Hispanic families see me coming and they know I'm givin' them a fair shake. Even the fathers back off. But in Sunnydale, hell I'm always La Diabla, spreading misery wherever I go.

Clara came up in the Mission; it was her home and so everyone knew her there. But even that made working the area a mixed bag. On one hand, as a Hispanic American, she had the community's trust; as a neighbor, she knew the players and they knew her. But that only went so far when you had to pull your neighbor's daughter for suspicion of domestic violence with a possible arrest for a father or uncle if endangerment charges turned up signs of abuse. You became a savior and a traitor in one fell swoop.

You think you ain't making a difference, girl? How about Turner…How's he doing?

You mean Marcus, our model citizen? He isn't talking to me right now. But he's fine. Even working on a basketball scholarship.

See? And remember how you felt pulling him and his brother? You just about wanted to kill yourself.

Clara chuckled strongly enough for her coworkers to see. Yeah. That was a tough one.

But look at him now. You know you're making a difference, woman.

Clara agreed with her colleague. Although she never told him directly, Marcus did give her hope. He'd always been a good kid, tried so hard and given so much for his family, caring for his drug-addicted mother and raising his little brother on his own for so long. Truth was, pulling Marcus away from them was the hardest task Clara had faced in her fourteen years with CPS. He was such a kind soul, a strong, good kid who'd already been through so much and had so much generosity to give to the world if just given the chance at a real childhood himself. So even if he never forgave Clara for breaking up his family, Clara said a silent prayer for Marcus each night before falling asleep. Because if anyone deserved to make it, it was him.

But Clara never dared let Marcus know how much he meant to her life. Because that could never be fair. It was too much responsibility to put upon any one kid, let alone one with Marcus's past. No, this was his time to worry only about himself, to work on his own life, to build his own future. Though she never acknowledged it, he'd always have a champion in his CPS worker.

***

Rory Binder woke with a rustle. His therapist, Jamey Sherwood, napped in the car seat beside him. They had left San Francisco at two-thirty this morning to make the three-hour drive south to Chowchilla Women's State Prison in California's Central Valley. Rory looked around at the other cars just like theirs, parked along the roadside near the prison entrance; he could imagine the other broken families like his sitting inside of them, the kids with their grandmothers or aunts or social workers, all waiting out the dead of night just like him to see their mommas too. Visiting days were run strictly by the prison's management and guard staff; if they hadn't driven down the previous night, they might have missed visitor roll call at 8 AM sharp. Because too many other families all wanted to get in (which only happened twice per month) and since the prison could only accommodate so many people on a given morning, if you were late, you missed your slot, whether if you had an appointment or not, no ifs ands or buts about it, no matter how far you came or how early you'd dragged your butt out of bed to get there, you were shit outta luck. So most people just did like Rory and Jamey, they came up from wherever - L.A., Chico, Sacramento, Fresno, Oakland - and camped out in their cars, waiting for their chance to visit with their kin. From the looks of it, no one was going to miss roll call today. Rory could barely see through the foggy windshields of the other vehicles parked along the main entrance road. There must be a hundred people in front of us, he thought out loud, but Jamey assured him as he awoke that they would get in today.

You sleep OK, bub?

Damn, got me a couple a winks at least.

Excited?

Rory looked down at the floor. Yeah.

Nervous?

Naw, Rory brushed off the question. Maybe a little.

Jamey smiled. Rory was one of his favorite clients. It made him happy to know he was the reason Rory saw his mother at all. The last time they came up here six months ago, Rory went ballistic for three weeks after the visit. Jamey had to up his Ritalin dose twice to get him to therapeutic levels manageable for the Excelsior House residential staff. But what short-term behavioral tumult might result in Rory's life now as a result of this visit didn't matter much to Jamey, even though as his therapist he would inevitably be one of the principals managing the fallout. They had done a lot of work together in Rory's biweekly therapy sessions leading up to this weekend visit. And against perhaps the better judgment of his colleagues, including Joe and Agnes and the rest of the Excelsior House line staff who had to deal with Rory running his program every day, it was up to Jamey to make the executive decision to bring him here, come what may. Because what was most important for Rory's well-being right now was for him to see his mom again.

The prison guard at the entrance checked over them with a mild impatience.

Please empty your pockets, put your hands up, then turn around.

The guard noticed Rory's muscular arms through his sleeveless white muscle t-shirt. After passing both hands across the child's sides and down the insets of his denim jean shorts below, the guard then spun his index finger in a circle, motioning for Rory to turn.

You work out?

Sometimes.

That's good. Helps keep the mind clean. And strong.

Rory put up with the mild humiliation of the guard's frisking until he pointed to the woman behind the plexiglas wall. She buzzed the door and Rory and Jamey stepped inside.

Make your momma proud.

Rory nodded. Yes, sir.

Rory's mother saw him coming from across the visitors' room floor. As they hugged, she wanted more than anything to swell with tears. But in typical fashion, the best she could muster was to maintain her gruff front. This isn't too bad, she thought. Once every six months with her son. At least she had a son. And at least he came to see her. At least they had each other.

How you doing Rorybear?

Good, momma.

Yeah, I bet you been. How's school?

Fine. I done good on my report card. Three C's. In PE, Social Studies and Art.

That's great bumpkin. You keepin' out 'a trouble?

Once in a while.

She laughed at her son's honesty. He was so much like her growing up that it hurt now to look upon him. Still, holding back her tears, she mustered enough of her own courage to turn to Jamey.

He behaving hisself OK?

Jamey was required by law to be present during their interaction. Rory's assessment team had agreed that monitored visits were the only option currently appropriate for Rory under his treatment plan, given his troubled relationship with his mother in the past.

He's doing very well.

See momma, told you I was good. And if Jamey says it's true, you know it must be.

The three shared a quick laugh, but Jamey quietly disengaged himself. There would be plenty of opportunity over the coming weeks for replaying the visit and sharing his input with

Rory in therapy. But for now, right now, this was Rory's time. Their time.

Oh, how I miss you, bumpkin. His mother pinched his chin softly.

You talk to Uncle Jarrett lately? Rory smiled.

Says he's gonna come up and see you soon, his momma confirmed. You know your uncle loves you just like I do.

Rory looked down, unsure but wanting desperately to believe his mother about his uncle.

Listen bear. We've been talking a lot about having you go live with him and your sister, at least until I get out of here. Because he's your family.

Rory seemed to draw himself down after hearing her words. His mother noticed his discomfort.

Something nice to look forward to, bear.

How long you got left, momma?

Dolores wanted to cry every time Rory asked her this question, because she could never give him a straight answer, however much she wanted to. She didn't really know the answer herself.

They say maybe a year with good behavior.

Rory always felt a swelling of hope, anger, despair, and distrust, regardless of how momma answered this question, each time he asked. Because as much as he wanted her out so they could live together again, every time his dream seemed to come closer to becoming true, it didn't.

First it was the drugs she stole to pay off her boyfriend the Meth Chef. Then it was the drugs she done in jail, violating her chance at probation. Then it was Rory's own acting out, the Ritalin, the medication he needed to stay well, and all the other decisions made by Jamey, his assessment teams, and the parole hearing board members to keep them apart because of child endangerment, because she could not be trusted to keep herself away from Crystal, because the fiery explosion which torched her boyfriend's lab in their garage had almost killed her and her children; with his uncle having to take care of his baby sister now and with Rory's own chemical imbalance and dependency problems, he was too much for his momma to handle alone. Even if she did get out and could keep herself together enough to avoid coppin' another fix.

All of this thinking made Rory want to lash out in tears. But he had to stay strong for his momma now; last thing she needed to see in jail was her own grown son cry.

That's good, momma. Then we'll be together.

The visitors' hall floor guard cut the group visit short as always. Before all of the families in the auditorium sitting on the rows of benches with their incarcerated kin across the pale white tables had a chance to make their amends, give their countless hugs and make up for lost time, which could never be regained or forgotten with each subsequent visit, the one yell of the floor guard mercilessly returned them to the uncompromising realities of parental incarceration that these momentary fantasy visits of togetherness allowed them to temporarily escape, but always on such short and final notice.

TIME!

***

Brenda McIntyre fixed her makeup in the Quick and Go gas station bathroom. She was primped and primed, ready for her debut. All her other homegirls woulda thought she was nuts, but now she had nowhere else to turn. Kicked out of her grandmother's house and AWOL from her most recent group home placement, Brenda had no skills, no job, and no otha' way a payin' fo' herself. So she was 'bout to hook up what some 'a the other girls she met in placement done when they needed a fix. She was gon' prostitute herself. But she knew dem streets of East Oakland ain't kind to no bitch. They be crawlin' wit' tricks her age and younga. At the hard age of fourteen, Brenda felt sorry for dem girls who was 11, 12, already trickin' and hoin' theyselves just 'cause they got wrecked up or pimped out by they eldas somethin' awful like. Those girls had no options, and neitha did Brenda. At least she'd hooked up wit' a few dudes befo'. Or somethin' like dat. She'd sucked a couple 'a dicks, had a few fools up her shirt and down dem draws, the shit ain't complicated far as she'd been through it. Dudes all the same, they just wanna bust they nut, don't matter how you be gettin' da job done. Easy enough how it do. So she grabbed her purse and moved out into the street.

Brenda never wanted to be a ho. Most a dem Billys 'dose girls be trickin' for'z nasty, and all dem bitches she knew in da game wuz all the same, though some'd been nice to her. Told her what she needed to avoid dem daddies and to keep herself standin' tall, come what may. 'Cause Brenda wasn't 'bout to have no punk motherfucker takin' all 'a her money she puttin' in work fo'. Hell naw, cuz she wuz out to survive, no two ways 'bout it, and fuck gettin' her ass bitchslapped or kicked in the stomach like her girlfriends by some trick daddy tryin' to get up in her stride. Mang, fuck that shit. Brenda wuz go'n be careful, for realz.

'You look dem pimps in the eyes and then they's yo' daddy.' These wuz the rules 'ccording to her girlfriend Rhona, who'd been workin' the 20's for, like, months. So Brenda was careful not to cop a stare to no shady dudes end up bein' a daddy in disguise. But Brenda knew she was a good judge 'a character. It was easy to tell who wuz funny and who wuz busted, comin' up how she done. Though DFS moved her out of the city when her PO caught wind 'a her turnin' tricks to pay f' her clothes and smokes, Brenda wus always just a BART ride 'way from her favorite spot in da Murder Dubs. But out here fools be cappin' each otha over some whack ass shit. So da cops be keepin' they distance, leavin' some flip ass niggas who be tryin' run' da block to fight over some dumb ass little-boy mess, they all be up in whose checkin' fo' who's trick, who in dis set or dat, some skandless-type activities no doubt. But Brenda was too smart to get caught up in none 'a that. She was just out gettin' hers, and the only fools Brenda be scopin' out wuz dem pimps she had to go dodgin'. 'Cause dem dudes was a special kind 'a ugly, slappin' you around, takin' all yo' money, all just 'cause you his. Some a these fools came off real nice-like in da beginnin', buyin' they tricks jewelry and shit. Then once they got 'em, they turn a girl out for realz, makin' 'em fuck for they hustle, no two ways 'bout it.

Brenda could never understand how a bitch could run wit' some dude just to be makin' him dey money. But most daddies neva give a trick no choice, they just come step to you when you's least 'xpectin' it, then dey drag you inta some alley o' shove yo' ass in a trunk put the hurt on you bad 'till dey 'bout wreck a bitch.

Mmm hmm, couple 'a near death 'speriences and then you his, no ifs ands or buts about it. So a girl had's to be careful out here. And dere wuz some desperate-ass hos out workin' dey hustle. But Brenda also understood the game well enough to know that if you's ever slippin' in yo' head, den dat's when anything goes. So you had's to run yo' game tight as a motherfucker, never lettin' no creep step to you. Most 'a them tricks thinkin' dudes they be fuckin' wit' wus straight enough 'till they let they minds go. Then they go bustin' on some lonely old dudes from the Westside who got jobs and families and shit, and if you go quick on 'em it ain't no thing. Those Billys wuz usually too scared to pull any type 'a wicked shit on a trick no how. So they just made theyselves easy targets for sleepin' missions or workin' da easy hustle. Shoot, Rhona even be runnin' her own stick-up game on some 'a dem dudes, waitin' for 'em to pull out they willies fo' beatin' 'em silly wit' her curling iron. Damn that bitch was crazy! But Brenda knew it best to run her game on the up and up. 'Cause when word be gettin' out, what goes around comes 'round, Brenda concluded to herself. But for the most part, the Johns she wuz funkin' wit' wus the easy score. So long as she kept her head straight and rubbers on dey Jimmys, Brenda knew she was cool.

***

Rydell Prince and Sylvia Sanchez walked down Mission street after their spoken-word tryouts at Café DuNord.

Mang, I straight turned dem fools out tonight. Ain't no one spit flow tight as mine! 'Cause I'm the best they is. For realz.

If you call that stupid shit flow, den you truly is dumb.

Oh yeah? Then how come I qualified for finals while you's walkin' yo' broke ass home wit' cho' tail between yo' legs?

Rydell tried to wave his hand between Sylvia's thighs as she slapped him off.

Bitch you best git! They just picked you 'cause they felt sorry for your nappy ass, passin' yo' shame game off like you wuz.

Aw hell naw, them fools wuz feelin' me. Folks straight bankin' the knowledge I'm droppin', Know what I'm sayin'?

Uh, no. 'Cause no one understands a damn thing you say…

Rydell waved his hand at her in disgust. Pshh. Forget 'chu then! 'Cause we all know my game's unstoppable. Shit's for real. Holla back.

Chump, you's delusional! I hate to break it down to you, but listen up: YOU CAN'T RAP, OK? Damn, my buck tooth gramamma float betta rhymes than yo' stuttery ass.

Rydell pouted.

Aw, there you go now, gettin' all sensitive 'gain. Shit, I'm just tellin' you like it is so you don't go makin' a damn fool 'a yo'self thinkin' you all master 'a the universe.

I see how it is, you just one 'a dem skandless-type bitches be hatin' on a brotha cuz he got his game tight.

Shit, I'm just tryin' to save yo' ass some 'barrasment next time you go act a fool.

Oh OK, so then when I'm on stage holdin' up my Grammy statue for the all world to see, who gon' be the fool then? You!

She just shook her head.

You best fix that lisp first, whack toothed ass motherfucker.

Whud 'chu say? He tickled her hard and fast under her arms.

Damn mang, cease and desist!

Bitch betta recognize.

Shit.

Proper.

Rydell and Sylvia continued down the street past a vendor cooking carne, bacon and onions on a rollcart.

Yo, I'm hungry.

Then buy yo' ass a diarrhea dog.

You got fifty cents?

Not for you, shit. That's why we'z walkin'.

A group of scantily clad older girls walked by on their way to a club down the way.

Rydell cat called, AY MAMI!

He turned to Sylvia. Damn, you see that booty? I'd tear her up sumpthin' real.

Nephew, you couldn't work that pussy 'f it fell on yo' dick!

Rydell stuck his tongue out at her.

Aw hell naw, 'cause I been practicin'. He spelled the first 4 letters of the alphabet with his tongue as if he was licking the inside of a vagina.

You's nasty.

As another group 'a girls passed, Rydell started faking a limp.

Fool, what's wrong wit' 'chu?

I'm gettin' my thug on. He yelled out to the older girl, who smiled back this time. Yo, I took two slugs for 'Pac!

Rydell smiled back. Check it yo, she be checkin' me out. Girl, you way too fine with all that behind!

Sylvia couldn't help herself but chuckle. You's stupid.

Yeah well I'm gettin' all the bitches.

You need to stop smoking that dank 'cause it be wreckin' yo' head.

Aw let's get some Popeye's.

OK.

As they approached the next corner they saw the lights off in the restaurant.

Whassup? It ain't even eleven o'clock yet.

They be closing hella early!

All 'cause them wannabe Mission gangstas shootin' demselves up over a three-piece.

Rydell and Sylvia crossed the street. Rydell entered the corner liquor store and left with pork rinds and grape juice.

That fool tried to cheat me out my eleven cents change! Cheap ass.

He gobbled down the rinds and washed them down with the juice. Sylvia watched him devour the grub with mild disgust.

Fool, you representin' just about every stereotype tonight, you know that?

Shoot I don't care, shit tastes hella good. Wait-

Just then, Rydell spotted a White Cutlass Ciera with its lights off creeping up Mission Street slowly towards two Hispanic boys standing just past the corner in front of Popeye's.

Yo, hold up now-

Sylvia looked over to the boys. They wore long white shirts and black pants, but sported red laces on their shoes. She and Rydell both immediately switched into hyper-alert mode.

Those scraps out dey territory.

What they doin' this far down Mission Street?

Lookin' for friction, no doubt.

Well looks like they found some.

From across the street, they saw Hector hang his body out the side passenger window of the Cutlass as it rolled to where the scraps stood. With Edgar behind the wheel and Tootz in the backseat, the Sureño boys on the corner finally caught wind of the Norteño hit squad upon them and threw up rival gang signs to call out their attackers. But Tootz was unfazed. He yelled out to the shorter Scrap.

Yo, Rodrigo Suarez!

Thirteen bitch! What it do!

Rodrigo immediately reached for his clip under his long white t-shirt.

This is from Nacho! 24th Set motherfuker!

But Rodrigo was not quick enough. Before he could pull his clip out from under his belt, Hector rotated his body to reveal the barrel of a shotgun squarely in his hand. He fixed on his target and fired.

Rydell immediately grabbed the back of Sylvia's head with his hand and pulled her down onto the pavement across the street.

Giddown!

He instinctively pressed his other hand under her cheek to protect her face from the fall while spooning her body to cover her from the path of any stray bullets that were about to fly.

Hector pumped two slugs directly into Rodrigo, who fell lifeless to the ground below. The second Sureño, who was not strapped, immediately sprinted for his life up Mission Street away from where his dead homie lay.

Roll up on that sucker! Rydell and Sylvia heard Hector yell out to Edgar.

Edgar tore the Cutlass up Mission Street to catch up to the fleeing Sureño, who was two solid blocks away from crossing into his own territory. Hector unceremoniously took aim at the young kid hustlin' to the next corner. Sensing his enemies upon him, the kid stopped running, knowing he was beat. He turned to Hector and threw up his hands.

Rydell pulled up his head briefly to watch the action unfolding down the street.

Yo' mang, fuck the 24th Crips!

Hector didn't blink. He unloaded two shells into the kid whose guts splattered across the metal storefront shield behind him. What was left of the Scrap fell the concrete below, dead as dirt.

Rydell threw his head back down. Damn!

Hector pulled himself back into the Cutlass as Edgar swung an immediate U-turn, speeding back down the remainder of the block and screeching left through the 22nd Street intersection near where Rydell and Sylvia lay. They smelled the filthy burnt rubber of the tires as the Cutlass swooped through the stretch of 22nd toward Potrero Avenue and to the freedom offered by the 101 freeway entrance beyond.

Sylvia and Rydell heard the roar of police-car sirens and of the ambulance from General Hospital approaching, passing the Cutlass whose occupants created the carnage now laid bare at their destination.

You cool?

Yeah mang.

Yo' then let's get the fuck outta here 'fore we witnesses.

Word.

The two friends stood up from the sidewalk and jetted down the opposite direction of Mission Street together as fast as they both could run.

***

Marcus Turner drove the ball hard and fast down the gym court of the San Francisco Excelsior Boys and Girls Club where Donna, his fiercest competition of 5 foot 2 inches, made it her mission to steer his onslaught away from the hoop. This girl was vicious, and she kept Marcus's game in check. Marcus normally would have no mind to pay attention if she came at him any other way, but if he was gonna make regional placements in Atlanta, he had to spar with the best of 'em.

Man, why you's cupcakin' when you should be gettin' it? Donna taunted, stalling his advance at the free-throw line.

Wha' 'chu know 'bout me, huh? He chided back.

Enough that you can't ball for shit!

Admittedly, his come back on this girl talkin' head right to his face wasn't very biting, but it bought him enough time to pull a reverse fake and throttle past her. Once in the paint, Marcus scored easily with a solid rim shot, skippin' the backboard assist all together.

From courtside, Ron Thompson, Marcus' coach and head of the Excelsior Boys and Girls Club, clapped. Nice rally, Marcus!

Donna shook her head. Ayite then, I see how we doin' it.

Marcus moved to the opposite side of the court for a quick winner take out. He passed it to Donna, who checked him one-on-one style, quickly shotgunning the ball back to him before he regrouped, charging the net.

This time, Donna was on him like white on rice.

What 'chu know 'bout me Cuz?

Bitch, you all talk and no game.

Donna caught him easily off guard, knocking the ball from his distracted dribble while he ranted. She ran it expeditiously down court for an easy two points, settling the tab for his last shot with a layup.

Who the bitch now? Donna mocked. She threw her hands up and made a victory lap around the court before returning the ball to Marcus, waving her index finger at him in a not-so-mild rebuke of his previous efforts.

Eat 'chu live, now bow down!

Their coach, along with several other boys on the court, Cleon, Little Stevie, and Bunky, all couldn't believe the mess she was spittin' to Marcus. 'Cause as good as he was, her shit was on tonight, and ain't nobody up and down this court got past a girl rallying on them without a little shame rubbed off on his game. So the other boys were all too eager to jump on his case. Though Marcus was a straight shooter and hood certified, when it came to basketball, everyone around him had a combination of mad love and jealousy for this wunderkind on his way up from the Altegard Projects about to go pro and bring glory into all 'a their lives. But Marcus could also become a crybaby bitch quick when things weren't flipping his way on the court. And of course, any fools to catch him slippin' were quick to remind everyone of his sensitivities, whenever they smelled an opening. Especially Donna.

Man, once you start losin' you one foulin' ass motherfucker! Donna ribbed.

Marcus blew her off with a wave of his hand.

She swooped you fair and square Cuz'.

The boys continued to ridicule him.

Dude she got 'chu!

Gettin' played like a bitch!

That's skandlous!

Donna hollered out to encourage the other boy's scorn. Whassup now! Bow down peasant!

Marcus waved her off as the other boys cracked themselves into stitches on the bleachers.

Man, y'all's flip, he whined.

Donna lifted both of her arms into the air to elevate their taunts while her fans scuffed him.

Bow down peasant!

Aw hell naw-

Bow down!

Later off court, Marcus and Donna shared a burger and fries away from the gym at McDonalds on Ocean Boulevard, where they could be true to each other without fronting for the others.

Man you best get my change back, damn.

Hold on.

'Cause I ain't eatin' no frozen ass Whopper.

They sat down at a booth and scarfed down their meal. Donna swallowed several bites before reviewing their practice with her teammate.

Wha' 'chu doin' I be doin' like all day!

Marcus shrugged, It ain't no thang.

You made' some good shots dough, I'll give you that.

He smiled. Oh you will, huh?

But try and run you game up 'gainst Tommy Clayton come All City, dude gon' knock yo' ass back to the free-throw line.

That boy ain't all that. Shit, I wus hittin' 30's on his bitch ass my Freshman year. And besides, they don't play no JV up at

Lowell. Just Freshmen and Varsity. They got no experience.
Marcus took a bite of his cheeseburger. Buncha' weak ass players
up there.

Yeah, well when you goin' toe to toe 'gainst them chinos
from Mission, they some cheatin' ass motherfuckers.

Marcus looked annoyed. Then I take' 'em at they own
game.

Not dribblin' wit' yo' left like you been doin'.

OK, so I wuz slippin' towards the end, I ain't makin' it no
habit.

Donna laughed at Marcus' calm confidence, but quickly
grew serious toward her friend.

Fool, you hold that arm back 'gain and I'm a slap you
myself.

She lightly tapped his left elbow, which he retracted with a
not so mild wince.

Damn girl, you know it ain't healed yet!

What you needs to do is stop knockin' around wit' them
ghetto chumps in yo' pickup games and let that shit heal. 'Cause
you got bigga fish to fry. Scholarships to think' 'bout. Gettin' yo'
ass up outta dis place for realz, shit.

Man, I do what I do. None a' them's got the skills to pay
my bills.

Yeah, well if you ain't got yo' game worked out come All
City, them youngins gonna bring it to you direct, know what I'm
sayin'?

Marcus agreed nonchalantly. True 'nough. Some a' them
ayite.

Shoot, Clayton already hit 20 a night 'gainst Portola and
Washington.

Marcus clicked his tongue with disapproval. Pssh! He can
mix it up wit' any janky-ass teams he wants, but I'm 'a bring it to
'em right and tight all night when we go. You watch.

Learn how to cut through the perimeter and maybe I give
you that.

Oh, you will huh? Marcus playfully cracked. Shit, I hope
so.

What you really need is a consistent free throw,
motherfucker.

Marcus took particular offense to her insinuation. Because ultimately Donna was right. He was a great driver and a pretty good passer, and could dominate any position due to his natural ability, fact was fact. Ron had mentored him on the mechanics of group ball as well as anyone in his division could, so Marcus made for a pretty functional Center and Point Guard if need be, in addition to running his one-man stinger show.

But free throws were always Marcus' clearest weakness. He never had much practice with them when he was up and coming, 'cause none 'a his patnas never called no fouls on dudes when they wus ballin' in the street, and no one never did much passin' neither. But shootin' the ball when you's pressed was easy enough to habituate. It was makin' yo' shots consistently without the juice of some knock up in yo' grill that wus a challenge. 'Cause wit' that free shot, it wus just you and the ball. All the pressure and none of the glory. But Marcus needed to keep it movin' to stay sharp and stay correct. Just like with livin', 'cause that's how you beat the struggle. So no two ways about it, no one from the pickup games of his upbringin' was callin' no fouls 'less shit crossed the line, and then if it did, that shit got handled fo' good. Some fool got his ass knocked off his two toes and that wus that. So Marcus played his best game just drivin' the ball down court. And the sad truth of it wus, he never developed much practice with his free shot as a result.

But playing off Donna challenged his game right. Damn, who dis?

Donna shrugged. Just callin' it like I see it.

Mang, dem bitches ain't runnin' they skirt games up and down my court. I take 'em anytime, anyway. You watch. I'm a be takin' out da garbage come All City.

Blood, you don't put in some work on yo' free throw and they got us by twenty.

Girlfriend puleez, I'm a' take that bet just to see you cry.

Uh huh. Donna mocked. Only thing cryin' is yo' raggedy ass next time I bitchslap it up and down the court 'gain front 'a all 'a yo' boys.

Shit, was all Marcus could muster as he took the last bite of his burger.

***

Johnhay DeGuzman climbed the overpass rail with care just after midnight. It was a weekday, so the passing cars were surely apt to miss his presence on the freeway sign. One slight misstep however, one slip of the foot and he'd be pancaked across 280 below. That is, if the cars didn't smash him up across the shoulder lane first. But he was on a mission to advertise. The big race was coming this weekend and everyone had to know he was back in the game. What better way to stage his reintroduction? John had climbed plenty of fences in his day, so this obstacle was of little challenge to him. But now he had to focus. Nothing short of glory awaited. He had everything he needed: ropes, three spray cans, touch up rags and enough pure gumption to make his name known again. Given how well-traveled this corridor was, all 'a them weekend warriors, commuter bridge-hoppers, and local yokels would surely take heed of the fastest street racer this side of Fresno if he pulled this off. So he focused his mind, throwing the ropes over the top of the sign's base board, and pulled himself up with this makeshift harness. From his hip bag he drew several spray cans and immediately went to work. Within four minutes, his moniker was sprayed golden across the sign and he was back in his 2002 Toyota Celica GT whizzing onto the freeway to view the glistening paint drying in its solid metallic verse. None of the previous lettering remained. All that was in view now, in big block shiny print letters for all the world to see was just one word, his street-racer moniker on display after three long years of retirement: PANOY-1.

***

Lisa Gatwyn gathered her books and her purse from the trunk of her car in the parking lot of Thurgood Marshall High School. It was the first day of her internship as Assistant Guidance Counselor and she was ready to perform. Having recently landed the opportunity of a lifetime through her master's degree program in Counseling at San Francisco State University. Her thesis adviser had linked her up with a fellow colleague and previous mentor at Stanford University, Dr. Larry Metcalf (who had just received a sizable grant through the American Union of Psychologists in conjunction with the National Institute of Health) to conduct groundbreaking research into the effects of Post Traumatic Stress Disorder on the academic performance of urban children living in high risk environments where exposure to neighborhood violence was commonplace. To her knowledge, the idea of linking PTSD with academic performance in high school was revolutionary, certainly the first study of its kind in the country, and Dr. Metcalf had granted Lisa extreme latitude as his point person on campus in San Francisco. Lisa was assigned to design her own program over the course of twelve weeks to treat a test group of four individuals identified by school administrators and Dr. Metcalf's team who were failing to thrive academically as a probable consequence of first-hand exposure to severe incidents of domestic and/or community violence within their neighborhoods in the past three years. Each individual was carefully screened and handpicked for the study by Lisa, Principal Joanne Wilkins, and Dr. Metcalf. Though the test subjects were given an initial psychological evaluation by Dr. Metcalf to confirm a PTSD diagnosis, to control for demographic and environmental factors, all subjects in her test population were African-American children originating from the San Francisco Bayview District and Sunnydale housing projects of Visitacion Valley. The high per-capita murder rates per square mile for a densely populated urban area compared directly to those of other neighborhoods nationwide of similar demographics and size to be the focus of subsequent phases of Dr. Metcalf's study. But for now, to control for the subjects in his initial experimental group, all members resided in San Francisco's Excelsior House group home, where their responses to the PTSD treatment regiment could be easily monitored in the subjects' living environments away from the test site. For the San Francisco cohort, administration of the program on-site at the high school was entirely Lisa's responsibility. This being the first day of her big shot, she was understandably nervous. It certainly must have shown. This is all you, girl, she quickly muttered to her reflection in the car window as she closed the door, briskly flicking at her bangs with her fingers to compose herself. With as much ease as she could muster (she'd popped 2 Beta Blockers on the way to school that morning to quell her fear of public speaking), Lisa took one last deep breath, briskly adjusted her blouse, and entered the building confidently, ready to change the world.

***

Johnhay Deguzman let himself into Cottage 2 the following Saturday morning, carrying a bag of McDonald's as the boys inside all stared at him. Johnhay squinted as light filled the darkened front room. As was typical for every weekend morning at his former residential placement, the house was pitch black inside.

What up Carly?

Hey John.

Rydell immediately chafed at his appearance. Dude, what you doing here, you don't live here no more.

Johnhay completely ignored Rydell, two years his junior, and sat himself down on the couch next to Duane.

Man, you fools need to wake up and drag your lazy butts outside. It's nice out. Ain't even no fog rolling through.

The boys were all wrapped in their blankets on the couch this lazy weekend morning.

Whatup playa? Johnhay slapped Eric's open hand. Rory, Duane, Tyrone and Rydell all gathered around him.

Where's Little Man Kendrick?

He still on restriction in his room.

He just got out da halls.

Gotta work his way back up to group privileges.

Johnhay laughed. Little tyke be crazy. Yeah, I remember those days. He laughed mockingly, overchewing his tasty McGriddle in front of the other boys.

Rydell whined. Damn John, how come you never bring any Mac Donald's for the resta us?

'Cause you all some broke ass little boys.

John, language!

Sorry Carly-

Dude, take yo' ass back to Daly City where you belong-

Rydell! Language.

-Wit' the resta them Filipinos. Y'all be taking over that town and sh-

Carly eyed Rydell hard.

Shooooot.

Eric changed the conversation.

So what's up John, you racing again this weekend?

Naw, I don't do that no more.

When did you emancipate?

Three months ago.

Damn. You scared?

Hell naw. I ain't trippin' off it none. 'Cause I already have a job. And Joe said he gonna help find me a new place to live.

Joe ain't gon' do nothin' for your punk ass. Tyrone countered. He broke just like y'all.

Yeah mang, and he gots to hook us up first, Marcus insisted. Dude promised me some basketball shoes.

Y'all know Joe be handlin' his business when the time comes. I lived up in here long enough to figure that out.

Yeah, well he ain't even fixed our hoop yet.

And we still don't got our new stitches for winter. It be cold as hell outside and all I got is some t-shirts, Tyrone whined.

All of this bickering was annoying Johnhay. Damn youngsters, y'all some complainin' ass bitches up in here. None 'a y'all's cripple. Marcus, why don't you go get up on the roof and fix that hoop your damn self? And T, get yo' butt to the dollar store and buy yo'self a sweater already, damn. That's what I done when I wuz comin' up. But, naw, y'all some lazy sacs.

Carly walked in with a tray of half dozen small plastic Dixie cups filled with pills for each of the boys. She poured water into a second one for each of them to wash the contents down.

Alright guys, time for morning meds.

Damn Carly, you know we're supposed to eat first!

Then have some cereal.

I don't want none…

Well you know the rules, Rydell. If you refuse your pills again, I've gotta report you, and If I do Rita said she's gonna have to send you back to the hospital.

She won't do nothin' and you know it.

Tyrone disagreed. Mang, I hate that place. That mean lady Charlotte be crazy.

And she's Rita's boss now…

Shoot, she all whacked in the head.

They all whack up in there.

But naw, blut, I heard she turned two 'a her staff into lesbians, no joke.

Rory was now interested. No way!

Tyrone nodded to his friend. Jerome said he be seein' 'em kiss when he wus up there two months ago.

Man, I ain't never going back.

You know you want to get booty busted by Zeke.

Rydell! Language.

Staff caught that dude in the closet with Miguel suckin' each other off.

Marcus and Duane could no longer contain themselves. DAMN!

Tyrone! Be appropriate!

That's why they ain't livin' here no mo'. Them dudes just ain't right in the head.

No doubt mang, Zeke crazy as all hell-

Tyrone! Language!

Sorry Carly.

Marcus chuckled. No you ain't fool.

But that dude is crazy as hell, Carly!

Fine, express yourself. But be appropriate!

Ayite, I know.

But Miguel, he cool sometimes.

Not when he suckin' on dudes' willies, he ain't.

Well he ain't coming back here, that much is for damn sure, Duane proclaimed confidently.

Carly felt the need to correct them. Don't be too sure about anything. Haven't you guys learned that by now?

Johnhay was already over the boys shallow talk. Why don't y'all show your staff some respect and clean up your language? Act like some grown-ass men for a change. I'm getting hella bored listening to your little boy chatter...

Then leave, Rydell reiterated his earlier wish.

Yeah, forget you John, Tyrone dismissed.

Nobody asked you PIN-OYE.

Why don't y'all just behave? Johnhay enjoyed practicing his disciplinarian skills on the rest of them. And take your meds like the good little mentally disturbed children you are?

Shiiiii-

Carly once again stared daggers at Tyrone.

-oooooot.

Rory immediately swallowed his pills down. Marcus and Eric followed, then Tyrone, and finally, Rydell.

But Johnhay was not satisfied with their apparent display of obedience. Yo Carly, you better double check Rydell's mouth.

You cheeking your meds? Carly asked him plainly.

Rydell flipped off Johnhay as he bitterly gulped them down, sticking out his tongue to show Carly the empty inside of his mouth. He briskly handed her back the empty plastic cup.

Carly finished her rounds with each of the other boys opening their mouths to visually verify they had ingested their allotted doses for the morning.

OK, now you guys can get dressed and go outside once you clean up your empty cereal boxes...

But none of the boys moved. They were all much more interested in sitting around and comparing the severity of each others' medications.

Johnhay began with Rory. What' 'chu takin' these days Roryman?

Ritalin. 500 megs.

Damn. That's harsh.

It ain't no thang, Rory dismissed easily.

Tyrone disagreed. Yeah, not 'till you come off it. Then you be hella goin' AWOL an' shit!

All right, Tyrone, you're losing your language points this morning!

Mang Carly, I don't care, shoot. Tyrone boasted before redirecting to finish his conversation with Rory. But you gots to admit, you do get hella squirrelly without yo' pills.

Rory laughed, mildly embarrassed. Yeah.

Marcus offered new details of his own regimen. They just took me off 'a Prozac.

Great, so what, now you gon' start sheddin' yo' tears again? Rydell always took pleasure in mocking Marcus.

I ain't no crybaby.

Dude, you get hella sensitive over some dumb-ass stuff, Rydell insisted.

Tyrone nodded in agreement. It's true.

Marcus ignored both of them and addressed Johnhay instead. Anyway, now I'm on Zoloft. But that ain't even a real antidepressant.

Rydell balked. Blut, they all is fool. That's why we all takin' 'em. 'Cause you's just as whacked as the rest of us.

Marcus scoffed. Shoot, if they want me to chill, then gimmie some weed…

The boys all cracked up at the thought, while Tyrone high-fived Marcus for his bright idea. Hell yeah. I hear dat.

Rita said she gonna reduce my Dexedrine dose by half if I'm good this week and don't end up kickin' nobody, Tyrone bragged.

Meanwhile, Duane stood proud. Shoot, I ain't even need no meds.

Yeah, but that's 'cause you's already brain dead from all that crack you momma smoked when she had 'ju.

Rydell snickered at Tyrone's dis. Because all the boys knew that it cut deep.

Shoot, Duane responded despondently. But he had no other words to come back with.

So what about you Prince? Johnhay prodded Rydell. But by now, the glossy look of vacancy in the eyes had already overtaken him. There would be no more smart-assed comments from Rydell this morning. In fact, there wouldn't be much of anything from him until about noon. All he could do now was curl his body into a ball and maintain a hollow stare at the television, where Carly left repeats of 7th Heaven episodes running on loop to entertain what was left of him.

Damn, that shit kicks in with the quickness don't it? Johnhay inquired from Carly. She didn't bother to chide her visitor from transitional living for language. He on Dex too?

Only thing that keeps him from acting out all morning, Carly informed him.

Damn dude, I know he's an asshole and all, but shit. That ain't right.

None of the boys knew if Rydell could even hear them at this point, even though he was sitting right beside them. Like a vegetable, all he could do was stare catatonically into the TV screen and glare at the Carter family living out their fantasy television life together. Maybe in Rydell's consciousness somewhere, if there was still enough of him in charge to comprehend what his eyes and sensory apparatus appeared to absorb, hopefully he was wishing for a family of his very own someday, and a place like that on the show to call home. But no one in the room around him could really tell one way or the other.

Naw dude, it'll wear off soon enough, and then he'll be right back to his asshole self 'gain, Rory surmised for John.

Johnhay looked to Carly sympathetically. Damn, at least y'all get the morning off.

Carly nodded with a deep undercurrent of ambivalence towards her clients' medical regimen, an opinion betrayed by her own solemn stare. But quickly enough, she recovered and called out to the boys. All right, everyone who can walk…outside!

***

Sylvia Sanchez walked into her bedroom at Excelsior House to find Sarah Hillsbrook unpacking her things into Sylvia's clothes drawers.

Sylvia pointed down. Naw girl, those shelves are yours. Mine are the ones up top.

Sarah looked up, clearly unsettled. Because Sylvia's were all empty.

Oh. OK.

Sylvia walked to her bed and sat down, eyeballing Sarah menacingly as she redistributed the linens below, organizing her socks, underwear, jeans, sweaters, and shirts into neatly folded groups.

You got any tops with no sleeves?

Sarah didn't want to answer her, but she had to.

Don't need any...

Sylvia noticed that all of Sarah's shirts had the same practical function, to fully cover her arms.

You best be careful wit' cho' stuff, 'cause there go some thievin'-ass bitches up in here, Sylvia offered, seemingly polite.

Sarah looked back up expecting to dog her out, but realized Sylvia was actually trying to be helpful.

Can't lock nuthin' up here, so you best be careful what 'chu be wearing in front a these hoes.

Sarah wondered if this was why Sylvia's drawers were empty.

Thanks.

It ain't no thang.

Sarah moved to the closet to hang up her jacket. Sylvia couldn't help but fixate on her new roommate's pale skin.

How come you so white?

Sarah instinctively counterpunched. How come you so Mexican?

Aw hell naw…

Normally Sylvia would flip this chick. But she let the new girl off with a pass. Because after 6 group homes, Sylvia knew how much of a bitch intake could be. With everybody checkin' you right off the mark, nerves always be a bit edgy at first. Besides, there'd be plenty a other opportunities for fuckin' up this whitegirl if it came to that.

Sarah turned back to hang her only jacket in the shared closet. Couldn't this girl just leave her alone?

Naw, I'm serious 'dough. How come your skin so pasty?

Don't you know how to mind your own business, or did they not teach you that here?

Damn whitegirl, I's just askin'. Shit. You don't need to be gettin' all sensitive.

Sarah paused, sensing an opportunity to connect with her new bunk mate.

It's vitiligo. My skin cells don't make pigment. So it looks white.

Sylvia's expression moved from defensive to surprised.

Then how come you got so many freckles? Her question was innocently curious now.

It doesn't happen everywhere, just on most places.

Does it hurt?

No, only when I get sunburned. I can't be outside for too long.

Damn, Sylvia snorted. Ain't that a bitch…

Sarah laughed. No shit.

Another silence fell between them, but it was less awkward now.

So what 'chu do to be in here?

I tried to kill myself.

For realz? Sylvia turned her head skeptically. You's lyin'.

No, Sarah replied simply.

Then how'd you do it?

I OD'd…First on heroin. Then I made these for good measure. Sarah held up the scars lining her wrists.

Damn, you serious?

Sarah nodded solemnly.

Then why you ain't up in no mental hospital?

Isn't that what this is?

Naw, mang, nobody in here tryin' to whack themselves 'less you Tyrone or one a them horny little boys 'cross the street. But you crazy girl, they need to lock you up at General or sumpin', not in my room. 'Cause I ain't havin' no bitch cut herself up where I'm sleepin', hell no.

Sarah could see where this was ultimately going. Relax, I'm not gonna do nuthin' to you.

Damn straight you ain't! Sylvia cracked. Cause then I'd have to kill you myself, straight up. But damn…

Sarah looked firmly to Sylvia to reassure her, though she was pleased with the idea that Sylvia might fear her enough now to leave her alone.

Relax, I'm not staying. I'm out first chance.

Sylvia seemed surprised by this information. Where you gonna go?

I know people.

I tell you straight up, you go AWOL or break your probation up in here, it ain't straight to the halls, that's fo' sho'. First they send yo' ass to the hospital. For realz. But damn, maybe in yo' case that 'a be a good thing.

They ain't gonna catch me.

Oh yes they will, they always do.

I sprang from my last placement three times and nobody saw me before I came back on my own terms.

Shit, then maybe you do know what you's doin'.

Always have, always will.

Sylvia was pleasantly surprised by Sarah's moxie. Well you best think twice 'fore you try sumpin' stupid, 'cause as far as placements go, it's ayite here.

Yeah? Sarah offered.

Shoure, staff be buggin' sometimes, and Agnes can be a real bitch, but mostly her and Joe cool as fuck long as they ain't up in yo' business tryin' to get you to do some whack stuff like pullin' good grades or sumpthin'. Damn therapists think they all that, but you's lucky if you get Rita, 'cause she cool. Just don't go gettin' up in no fights or cussin' out staff 'cause then they fuck you up real quick, put yo' ass on restriction and you can't go nowhere, watch TV or do no kind a dirt. And Joe be knowin' all the cops in da city too, so if you's sprung they bring you back up in here 'stead of a trip to the halls. Pshh, after a couple a times, it ain't worth da hassle. So run yo' program right, and even dough the food sucks, ain't nobody gon' mess with you in here, know what I'm sayin'?

Sarah took all of this in and, after a minute to process, smiled. Yeah, I think I got it.

Ayite then. So for us, the rules are simple, yo. You stay on your side da room, I stay on mine. And don't get freaky wit' none a my shit or I'll go to work on yo' ass for realz. Sylvia waved her hands as if conjuring up a spell. 'Cause all 'a dis demonic satanic shit you frontin' don't even phase me fo' like a quick minute, you feel me?

Fair enough, Sarah nodded frankly.

Sylvia checked her up and down again and shook her head. Damn, you's one crazy-ass bitch, ain't 'chu?

Sarah curled a smile. After a pause, Sylvia jumped off her bed.

Yo, I'm 'a get with my homegirls at the park. You wanna come?

Cool, Sarah replied.

So together, they left the house.

***

Sylvia and Sarah walked the five blocks to Excelsior Playground to meet up with Rhona and Brenda, who sat on the benches behind the basketball court watching Marcus, Tyrone, Duane, Kendrick and Rydell trade hoop shots in an impromptu pickup game. Josh Crenshaw, Excelsior House Line Staff for Boys Cottage 2, supervised.

What up, ladies…

Hey Josh.

Sylvia led her and Sarah over to Rhona and Brenda.

Y'all know homegirl.

Hey.

Whassup.

She gon' kick it with us.

Wha' 'chu doin'?

Watching Turner ball over these fools.

Sylvia pointed him out to Sarah. That's Marcus there.

He good?

Hell yeah, shit, dude be makin' All City this year 'less he fuck up his game. But he cry like a coochie-ass bitch when you smack 'im down. All dem little boys easy to break. 'Specially Tyrone.

The girls agreed with Sylvia as she pointed each of the boys out. Yeah, but the one with the funky hair, oohh he talk a lot 'a shit but he ain't worth no worry. He cool once you put 'im in his place.

Bunch a whiny-ass kids if you ask me, Rhona concluded.

Brenda offered an exception, Duane pretty nice 'dough.

Aw there you go 'gain, Rhona made her blush.

Yeah.

Brenda be checkin' for little Duane, Sylvia explained to the newbie.

He the short one?

'Bout as short as Chita. Rhona compared.

But he cute!

How you go gettin' sprung on Duane B?

I dunno. He just crazy I guess.

Boy messed up in the head is what it is.

His momma smoked so much crack that fool came out brain dead.

For realz?

But he sweet.

I guess.

Way to pick 'em Bern, Sylvia mocked.

But Rhona found Brenda's affections endearing. So you gonna ask him to the dance or what?

Girl, he only in eighth grade!

So what? Brenda in the 9th.

Sylvia backed down, waving her hand back and forth in the air. All I'm sayin' is, B, you can do way better for your goddess self than that damn scrub.

Sarah felt the need to contribute to the conversation. So you gonna ask him out?

The girls all looked to her.

I dunno, Brenda replied shyly.

Rhona rose to the occasion. Here, I'm 'a get they attention right now. Yo Duane! A! A! A! Whew! Whew!

Brenda blushed again. Stop!

Rhona prodded her. Naw girl, you got this. Check it!

The boys all turned to ogle the hollering girls.

You Duane, come kick it with my homegirl! Rhona shouted out, cupping her hands to her mouth.

Brenda slapped her arms under her jean jacket, embarrassed.

Oh shit, now it's on!

To Sarah's surprise, Sylvia and Rhona seemed to take full pleasure in embarrassing her. You done did it now!

Tyrone and Duane strutted across the playground and through the door of the court's chain link fence while Rydell and Marcus continued their one-on-one game. Kendrick shot baskets by himself at the far hoop across the yard.

Hey T-

Hey Rhona.

What it do Duane?

Duane replied shyly. Whassup…

Man, Brenda be crushin' hard on you, dawg.

No she ain't.

I'm tellin' you, you should go fo' her tonight if you want.

Shoot.

Tyrone motioned to Sarah. Who dis?

She the new girl.

Sarah. She offered her hand. Tyrone just looked her over.

She's cool, Sylvia assured them.

Right on, Tyrone offered, nodding his head in her direction. Welcome to Excelsior.

Thanks, Sarah returned curtly.

I can see you already met the rest 'a these skeezas den.

Rhona took particular offense to his insult. Who you callin' skeezas fool?

Y'all, Tyrone admitted, nonchalantly.

Yeah you wish. 'Cause you ain't never gettin' up in none 'a this, Rhona grabbed her own butt and squeezed it to rile up the boys, because everyone knew Tyrone crushed hard for her. Oh yeah, but I forgot, you ain't tappin' no ass, so who made you authority on the matta?

Damn! Sylvia and Brenda cracked.

Tyrone fronted. You know I'm 'a keep you next chance I get.

Shoot, in your dreams. Rhona shot him back down.

You be seein' plenty 'a me...

Go get yo' stanky ass outta here. You smell funky! Sylvia waved an imaginary cloud away from her face.

Tyrone stepped to her, attempting to hug her. She put up her hands fast in revulsion, afraid to touch the perspiration soaking through his shirt.

Naw, Tyrone balked. 'Cause here go some real man's sweat right here.

Hell naw, 'cause I ain't checkin' for no scrub!

Good. 'Cause I ain't gettin' wit' no fat ass ho'.

Boy, you best step yo' Kobe Bryant wannabe ass back fo' you get bitchslapped.

He checked her up and down with revulsion. Shit, last time I tapped that thick ass boo-tay, I had to splash some water on it and poke around for the wet spots.

Only Duane chuckled. Aw man, that's cold.

You best shut yo' mouth Duane, Sylvia hissed. Skinny-ass bitch.

Shoot, Duane rebutted.

Y'all a bunch 'a skandless haters up in here, Tyrone countered. 'Cause you can't handle no love from a real man.

Real man? Where he at? Sylvia dramatically looked between the boys for any sign of one.

Tyrone flipped her off. Sylvia slid her hands down her arms from opposite elbows to palms and flicked her fingertips open towards Tyrone, as if spraying him with her sweat. Back at 'chu, fool.

Meanwhile, Rhona took the opportunity to change the subject. So Duane, when are you gon' holla at my girl already?

Now Duane was on the hot seat.

Mang...

There's a dance at Leadership next week. And Brenda ain't got no date yet.

Shoot.

Rhona pressed him. Ask her out, fool.

The girls and Tyrone stopped in their tracks. Their awkward exchange suddenly became interesting.

Mang, I ain't no dancer, shoot. Duane looked shyly to the ground. But then he came back with, So you checkin' to go Brenda?

Brenda blushed. It ain't no thang, really.

Sylvia rolled her eyes as Rhona prodded Tyrone to intervene. You best talk some sense into your boy here.

Tyrone took the cue. Dude, ask her out already, damn! You wanna sit around the house all Friday night? Shoot. Maybe you'll even get your dick wet, who knows!

Rhona turned livid. Why you always gotta bring it there?

Shoot, 'cause that's how it is.

Blushing, Duane looked back down. I dunno...

Sylvia tisked. You already said that fool!

Everyone knew this was Duane's moment. Because even though he was shy as hell, he did like Brenda a lot.

So what time the dance be at? He inquired sheepishly.

Next week, Bern offered. Eight o'clock.

Then shoot, if you's lookin' to go, I be around...

Nephew pleaze, Rhona huffed. That's 'bout the most sidestepped way 'a makin' yo' play a bitch ever heard!

Yo, Sylvia interjected. I think that's the best you're gonna get.

So I see you next week then? Duane finally asked, hollowly.

Ayite then, Brenda blushed.

Damn Duane, you let this coochie rope you in easy as that? Tyrone needled his friend.

T, shut your mouth! Rhona and Sylvia retorted together.

Oh hell naw, mang, my boy ain't goin' out like that. Tyrone grabbed Duane by the shoulders. Lemmie spit some wisdom 'tween yo' ears.

Nice goin' Duane, Rhona rewarded with encouragement as they left. You might be a little mack yet!

Duane flashed a smile back to Brenda as Tyrone ushered him away from the crew.

Once the boys returned to their game on the court, Sylvia chided her friend. Well you want him, now you got 'em.

Yeah, Brenda replied, seemingly happy with herself.

You done good fo' yo'self today girl, Rhona agreed.

***

Later that afternoon, Tyrone, Eric, Rydell, Duane and Kendrick sat on the front porch of Excelsior House's Boys Cottage 2 watching Rhona, Brenda, Sarah, and Sylvia "walk the circle" in pairs around the cul-du-sac, down the street from where both residences were located. Tyrone filled the rest of the boys in on Duane's most recent achievement.

Yo dude, Duane be askin' Brenda to the dance.

No shit? Rydell ruffled Duane's head. Little crackhead be little mackhead now. You's big pimpin' baby!

Gots to be, shoot, Duane laughed in agreement.

You gonna make her pay, or you goin' all baller status?

Hell naw, dawg, she payin', shoot, Duane laughed.

The boys all cracked up.

Man, this fool ain't got no skrilla, Tyrone interjected.

Not unless he got his little brother to front him. Yo Kendrick, how that job at Mickey D's workin' out?

Kendrick waved him off. Shoot, I'm makin' more than all y'all broke asses combined, so don't even try to bag.

Rydell laughed. That's it, mang, tell 'em how you's stackin' paper. Little Kendrick be havin' more game than all y'all skandless niggas combined.

'Cause you got to get paid 'fore you get laid.

Hell yeah.

Sylvia chimed in from across the way as she passed the boys' cottage with Brenda and Sarah. You still tryin' to rap, D? Step off wit' them fake-ass wannabe rhymes.

Rydell tossed Sylvia the obligatory finger. But the other boys didn't reply, still not sure what was up with the new girl yet.

Yo' mang, check out whitegirl, one of them muttered under his breath.

There go one pale-ass bitch.

She be lookin' like a ghost and shit.

Long as she fuck like one, ain't no thang, Duane cracked.

Yo' mang, what's that even mean? Rydell chimed in.

Don't listen to him, Rory interjected in Duane's defense.

This irked Rydell. What, you want some now too BILLY?

Rory blew him off.

Rydell turned back to Tyrone. Your roommate stupid.

Whassup snowflake! Rydell hollered out once she passed. What you hangin' wit' them skeezies fo'? Come kick it wit' us! We show you some love!

The girls retreated back into their house, Sylvia with her palms out sayin' 'talk to this.'

Eric's eyes opened wide as Sarah disappeared from view. She's hot.

Mang you gotta get cho head checked, 'cause that bitch is busted.

It ain't no thing. I'd love to get up in that-

Rydell scoffed. Listen to Eric thinkin' he some kind 'a playa now.

Yo mang, just 'cause she white don't mean she gon' fuck you.

Oh I'm sorry, 'cause I thought that's how it worked around here, Eric sarcastically shot back.

What 'chu think, she gon' give her pussy up to you fo' playin' your guitar?

You'd be surprised how that shit works. Bitches droppin' they draws when they see you got some skills to pay the bills. Eric smirked as he high-fived Tyrone.

Yeah, well, the only skills you got is sucking Tyrone's dick balls deep! Rydell sneered.

How you know so much 'Dell? Eric mocked back.

'Cause he be fightin' you off just like yo' sister did.

You best watch yourself or I'm 'a come bootybust you in yo' bed tonight.

You do and I'm 'a fuck you up right quick, perpwalk. Rydell was now all kinds of agitated. 'Cause I wus walkin' down the hall last night to take a piss and I seen this fool all bent over his bed trying to suck hisself off.

The other boys revolted. Ugh!

Bitch, stop dreamin' about me. At least it's a wet hole.

Yo fuck all that...

The girls sauntered scantily past them again. This time however, the boys noticed a tattoo imprinted on the small of Sarah's back. It was a pentagram.

Aw, hold up now-

Man, damn.

Tyrone suddenly showed some interest. Snowflake don't look too bad from behind.

I bet homegirl just frontin' wit' all that devil shit.

I still wouldn't stick that with Tyrone's dick.

That's cool, Rydell concluded, 'cause we all know Eric be lovin' dem crazy bitches. Mang, she the girl 'a yo' dreams dawg.

Naw that's still you 'Dell.

Shit, that be your sister.

Maybe she can carve some devil horns in you dick.

I bet you'd like that.

Naw blood, 'cause then his sister wouldn't wanna fuck him no mo'.

She probably like one 'a dem vampires bitches from Twilight, Tyrone asserted. Shit, I bet she'd suck the blood right out you, dawg. Wrap her nasty-ass fangs 'round yo' jimmy and homeboy be turnin' into a bat and shit.

Eric laughed out loud. You're talkin' stupid now.

Yeah, just wait.

Sarah couldn't hear their conversation, but threw a flirty glance towards the boys anyway to get their attention. Let them know she was down for whatever. But clearly to all, her glare was directed solely towards Eric.

Whoa, hold up now!

MMNMMN.

Oh damn.

Y'all's gon' be a bunch 'a fools when I hit that.

Pshh.

Mang...

Yeah right.

Eric fixed his own gaze back on Sarah as she returned to the girls cottage across the street, satisfied with the reception her message received. Eric entertained fantasies of hooking up with her. But the other boys couldn't let up on their jealousy trippin' until Rhona and Brenda walked past to distract them.

Of course, all attention shifted immediately back to the girls. Tyrone started right in on Rhona to impress Rydell.

Damn Rhona, who let you loose wit' all that caboose?

Rydell snickered. Yo Brenda, yo' booty look like it done swallowed the Goodyear Blimp and shit.

Little boy, don't you go talkin', Rhona sniped, 'cause you ain't never gettin' no love offa this. She grabbed her friend Brenda's butt and badonkadonked it hard for the boys in the grip of her two hands.

Damn, she clownin' for realz!

Hell yeah.

Yo Duane! Rhona called out as the girls swooped by. Why you let these scraps bag on your girl like dat?

The boys were obviously perturbed that Duane now held the girl's flirtatious attentions. Duane sheepishly obeyed Rhona's prodding.

Mang T, why you gotta talk shit?

Thad a' boy D! Rhona waved her finger at them. Way to defend yo' woman! He da only real man outta y'all.

Tyrone shook his head in mild disgust. Shut up Duane, I'm tryin' to help you out.

Shoot, I don't need your help...

Dawg, that bitch'll tear you up spit 'chu out and not think twice 'bout it. You know she a prossitute?

Yeah, I know, Duane admitted.

It's 'prostitute', dumbass, Rydell corrected Tyrone harshly. Go read a dictionary or sumpthin'.

Rhona shook her booty provocatively at the boys once more. From the porch of Girls' Cottage 1, Agnes called them out. Alright ladies, bring it inside!

The girls promptly headed back to their residence.

Meanwhile, from across the street on the porch of Cottage 2, the boys hollered out. MMMNNN!

Man, damn!

You really gon' tap that Duane?

Shoot, hell naw.

Brenda's booty so big, Duane be fallin' in that shit pokin' his head around, yellin' help, y'all! Throw a nigga a rope! Rydell flailed his arms around violently for dramatic effect. Both Tyrone and Rory cracked up.

I bet that coochie so loose when fools eat her out, they be hearin' the ocean and shit.

Rhona could tell they were spittin' no good from all the way across the street. So she checked them with a threat. Boy, you keep talkin' yo' shit and I'm 'a come over there and knock you out!

Duane, you best get lost fo' sho.'

Don't you go listenin' to dem little boys, Duane! Rhona shouted back before being dragged lightly into the house by Agnes. Brenda looked to Duane from the front window of Cottage 2 and smiled. We holla at you later!

Tyrone couldn't help himself, after not receiving any real attention from Rhona. Tha's right, get that big ass outta here. You blockin' my sun!

Rhona turned around through the door once more, charging the front porch to face off on Rydell and Tyrone both. Tyrone, you don't need no sun! You's so dark, you be disappearin' at night. Fools steppin' to you be like, damn mang, smile I can't see ya'!

Aw she's crackin' on you dude.

Fuck naw...

Rhona continued to yell from across the street. And 'Dell, don't you be talkin', cause yo' skin so ashy, nigga look like Frosty Freeze with a fudgesickle stuck up his booty!

Ohhhh!

Hell naw!

The boys were beside themselves as Rhona just worked them up and down something real. Brenda watched from the front window of the house as Agnes finally pulled Rhona inside. But before she could, Rhona launched one final taunt. She triumphantly turned with her hand raised in the air and slapped her own ass to hit it home before disappearing beyond the threshold of the door. All the boys winced.

Mang…

Girl be killin' it wit' that booty!

Fo' sho'.

***

The Excelsior House boys sat around on the couches of the front room of Cottage 2 as on any typical night, passing time and waiting for dinner to be served. Julio was busy cooking one of his signature Mexican dishes in the kitchen, while Eric worked in solitude at the round dining table, sketching a dragon from one of his fantasy graphic novels. Kevin McClaskey, the new line staff, ready to begin his evening overnight shift, was greeted at the front door by Carly, about to make her way across the street to finish her evening supervising Girls Cottage 1.

As Kevin settled in to supervise the boys, Duane intimately recounted a story from his childhood to Marcus, Kendrick, Rydell, Tyrone, and Rory, who all sat captivated, drinking in all the sordid details. Duane's animated gestures always found their way out of his otherwise awkward frame whenever he spoke of life in the Oakdale Projects in San Francisco's Hunters Point.

Mang, I tell you, shit was off the hook yo, know what I'm sayin'?

Rydell and Tyrone enjoyed every twist and turn of Duane's narrative. As tough as Rydell acted toward the other boys, he'd never known any life other than in placement. Tyrone, on the other hand, grew up in living with his father in Richmond. His father worked as a security guard at Folsom Prison and commuted back and forth every several days between shifts to be with his son. So Tyrone was left on his own most days. Still, he knew to stay out the way of the local thugs doin' they dirt round the way, 'cause his dad would have fucked him up real quick if he ever caught him wrapped up in that mix. But he understood their game well enough to know the score Duane now described. Marcus too. He himself came up in Western Addition, so none of this was exotic to his weathered ears. Rory, however, lived in a trailer park before coming to Excelsior House, while Eric remained on the move with his hippy dope-dealing parents for most of his young life, so neither of them had ever experienced any of the ghetto life Duane so vividly recalled.

This made rare shared moments such as these so special to each of them. With Duane the expressionist, Tyrone and Marcus providing insights or clarifications, everyone in the group shared in the mystery of peering into the window of someone else's life when revealed to them in such an honest and uncompromising way.

But I'm tellin' y'all, shit was hot. Niggas comin' 'round strapped, jackin' fools over some bullshit. We wuz sittin' on da step once when this one fool run up on Tiny...

Aw hell naw, Kendrick cracked a devious smile.

You rememba', huh Kendrick? He quickly filled the room with his gargling, high pitch cackle.

Yup, Kendrick recalled gravely.

Tiny be hella big, know what I'm sayin', like 400 pounds and shit, and he ain't about t' take no mess from no hood rat, hell naw, dude fuck you up over a Dovesack straight up, know what I'm sayin'? So this young dumb-ass kid Neeka, one day he grindin' near where Tiny's crew be doin' they dirt and they ain't feelin' this nigga one bit 'cause he movin' in on they business, so Neeka walk right up wit' his clip and the dude straight slugged Tiny in the face and Tiny be hittin' the ground, boom! Fool straight dropped the dude, and Tiny be hella thick so he fell hard, and now Neeka thinkin' he all Machiavelli now, know what I'm sayin'? Walkin' round da hood wavin' his clip lookin' fo' fools to step to him so he c' take out the rest 'a Tiny's crew, and we all be like hell naw, we ain't with that dude, but all kinds 'a fools be duckin' and runnin' while Neeka shootin' shit up, straight out da gate...

But now Tiny's homies from Palou caught wind 'a this dude's thuggin', so they all come flexin' on Neeka hard wit' da quickness, and all'va sudden twelve 'a dem Oakdale Boyz swooped on homeboy straight up, know what I'm sayin', and they's all takin' turns kickin' that fool, and we wuz hella spooked watchin' out da window 'cause Tiny be pullin' the dude up on the curb to smash Neeka's head in, teeth be flyin' 'round the pavement and shit. Then Tiny pulled out his clip and he capped that nigga in da face straight up, rat tat tat! Shoot, I ain't never seen so much blood come out 'a one dude my 'tire life. Then he grabbed whas left 'a Neeka and pulled a grip out his pocket, that dude had a Dovesack, know what I'm sayin', and from there on out Tiny owned da block like it ain't no thang, shoot, cus them peoples wus hood certified, and then nobody be sayin' nuthin' when Tiny come 'round.

Damn, Rory sighed.

Hell yeah, Tyrone agreed.

Duane finished. But Tiny be hella cool. Shoot, I carried bags fo' him 'round da way plenty 'a times. One time, I brought a grip 'a his cash to this dude, cus the cops and Knockout Posse wus all hella lookin' to get at him, so they sent me instead...And shoot, I walked into the house, and dem fools wuz strapped to da nines sittin' round da table wit' they glocks and they AK's, and one 'a dem grabs this bag and he be pullin' out a Dovesack!

The boys laughed as Duane cracked himself up midsentence.

Shoot, so I dropped Tiny's grip on him quick, then I grabbed that Dovesack and walked right out like it wuddn't no thang 'cause all them fools knew Tiny'd fuck them up 'f they tried steppin' to his boy, know what I'm sayin'?

Damn Duane, represent!

Straight clockin' da dough.

Shoot, I know...

Kendrick chimed it. You wuddn't all that, shoot. They wus just some weak as fools up on Palou.

Wus you ever strapped on your runs, Duane? Rydell asked, genuinely interested.

Hells naw. I wusn't down with none 'a dat, cuz den dem up and comers be checkin' for you fo' sho'.

But I thought Tiny had yo' back.

Yeah, but that dude couldn't be everywhere all da time. And 'f fools thinkin' you's out on yo' own frontin' all gangsta like, then they come at 'chu hard.

Damn Duane, you wus doin' yo' thang...

Naw mang, 'cause the game's changed yo. You ain't shit 'less you runnin' yo' own hustle, know what I'm sayin'?

It was here that Marcus felt compelled to chime in. Shoot, in the Addition, they smoke yo' ass just for walkin' down the street 'less you runnin' wit' somebody's crew. They take you out like you's a snitch, cus dem dude's got no love for fools who ain't affiliated, damn straight.

Shit, Western Addition got nuthin' on Bayview.

Oh, OK D, whatever, Marcus quickly admonished Rydell's feeble attempt at dropping some street cred.

My homeboy got shot up there just 'cause he had hisself a fine-ass girlfriend, for realz, Marcus explained. Niggas be grabbin' yo' bitch however the they want, straight don't give a fuck if she wit' someone, for realz.

Rydell checked Marcus. Shoot, then if y'all so bad up there, den how come yo' crybaby ass didn't get capped already? Cause you's such a bitch when you ball, I'd 'a done it myself by now just to shut you up.

Still, it was all too easy for Marcus to flip the script on Rydell, You ain't know nuthin' 'bout how I come up.

Know enough to know you's a whiney-ass bitch.

Rydell! Knock it off, Kevin finally interrupted them.

Rydell hated this new line staff. First, Kevin was white. Second and more importantly, he was a buster. Third, he only seemed to hear whenever Rydell talked out of turn. And fourth, he was inexperienced, which made him an easy target for Rydell's aggression.

Dude, don't even talk to me. You know nobody like you.

That doesn't matter, Kevin replied evenly. You still gotta run your program like everyone else.

Rydell reveled in his chance to escalate the tension. Why you gotta call me out when everybody else swearing? Shoot, I didn't even say no bad words, so you best get your ears waxed and stop swoopin' in conversations that ain't yo's.

Annoyed, Kevin tried not to increase Rydell's displeasure, only to match his intensity.

Nobody should be swearing, but you're antagonizing another client. So stop being rude.

Rydell knew he had Kevin bargaining now, right where he wanted him. Because Kevin needed the boys to respect his authority in order to do his job. But what Kevin didn't yet understand was that Rydell would never give him that satisfaction on his terms alone, not ever. Because here, locked in this space, Kevin was far too easy to manipulate. So inexperienced!

So Rydell checked him. You's a hypocrite, Kevin, 'cause you ain't even supposed to let no one use foul language, but you only callin' me out and I ain't even done nuthin'.

Kevin maintained his composure, though he knew he was losing this battle.

You need to be a good citizen.

Oh, OK. Whatever, dude. Don't talk to me. Rydell stated plainly.

Kevin's blood began to simmer, because he'd already given this kid several chances earlier this week to respect him, to no avail. And he needed to build some credibility quick with the boys, especially tonight when he was the sole staff supervising the cottage. So tonight, Kevin insisted this was the evening Rydell would learn to respect him. Bad move.

Rydell, you have to respect your peers and listen to your staff or else-

Or else what! Rydell quickly jumped from the couch, yelling at him.

Kevin was briefly taken aback but remained calm. He could always contain the boy if the situation called for it.

Or you won't earn your citizenship points for the evening.

Shit, you think I'm worried about that? He waved Kevin off dismissively.

Kevin's hold on the situation was clearly slipping. Rydell, no swearing. Or I'm going to have to give you a Verbal.

Fuck you then! Do what you do best, hater! Rydell reacted out of sheer frustration, flipping Kevin the finger which made the other boys laugh while he sat back down defiantly. But he knew he'd already overstepped his game showing more emotion than he wanted. Get outta my face bitch…

Kevin's blood was at a boil now. Against his own better instincts, he walked directly over to the couch and leaned his body down, towering over Rydell to intimidate him.

Alright, you've just earned yourself a Verbal Abuse. Go to your room.

Fuck you.

Go to your room! Kevin pointed his arm toward the hallway.

I said FUCK YOU! Rydell screamed. He was about to kick Kevin in the pelvis.

The boys sat silent, wondering where this pissing match was going. Everyone knew one of them had to back down, but neither one was about to, so shit was real tense now. Kendrick began rocking himself back and forth in autonomic reaction to the charged energy while Eric mumbled nonsensically behind him, his Tourette's Syndrome settling in. Tyrone felt increasingly disjointed while Marcus, Duane, and Rory remained perfectly still. All were quiet, awaiting the meltdown about to be unleashed.

Julio walked out of the kitchen, knowing full well it was up to him alone to diffuse the impending standoff.

He pointed his own finger down the hall. Damn 'Dell, go run your program already. When staff tells you to get in your room, go. Stop being such a little boy about shit, damn!

Rydell had been institutionalized since he was an infant and so he instinctively knew better than to take on a line staff with a model client like Julio backin' him. Rydell was sure to have better luck agitating the other boys into action against Kevin later, over the coming weeks and out of Julio's born-again watchful eye. The boys were already growing restless, and Tyrone always had his back in a crisis. Kevin was clearly afraid tonight; it would only be a matter of time before he had to perform his first containment. Better to have it be on Rydell's terms then.

Get your Mole-makin' butt back in the kitchen Julio, this don't concern you.

But Julio's tone was even more uncompromising that Kevin's.

Dude, get in yo' room 'fore you cause yourself some real problems.

Oh and what you gonna do probate boy? You lay a hand on me and you go right back into the can.

Rydell chided him, but his voice betrayed a deeper respect for Julio. Julio meanwhile didn't flinch.

Dawg, you know Rita ain't keepin' you around with any more major incidents against staff. Best go to your box and beat it out there. This ain't no fight worth havin', D.

Whose fightin'? We's just talkin'.

Yeah, Julio sighed.

It was clear to everyone in the room that Rydell had made the decision to back down the minute Julio entered the fray. He used Julio's words only as a pretext to save face with the group. And Julio, well schooled in the ways of intimidation and crushdown, clearly understood enough to not press the matter any further.

So without incident, Rydell stood up and whisked past Kevin toward his room.

Punk-ass staff can't do nuthin' wit'out help from clients anyhow, he hissed under his breath, turning to face Kevin mid-hallway. Nobody likes you dude, and ain't nobody ever gonna. You don't got anybody's respect now.

Go to your room 'Dell, Kevin phrasedsaid in a vain attempt to reassert his authority and recoup any dignity he might still hold with the other boys.

But Rydell would have none of that. He calmly flipped him the bird again and trailed off down the hall. Crisis averted. For now.

***

The staff of Excelsior House Cottages 1 and 2 conducted their Monday morning meeting to review their clients' compliance with their treatment plans over the past month and to prepare for the week ahead. Their supervisor, Joe Rodgers, hastily walked into the room to greet his employees. Under his arm, he carried a basketball hoop.

What up y'all.

Hey Joe, Deirdre Monaghan, one of Excelsior House's weekly rotating line staff, beamed.

Hey doll, Joe walked over and planted a kiss on her forehead.

Joe, you're gonna mess up my hair before my big report tonight at school. She fixed her bangs, tousled by Joe's affections.

That's alright, then they'll know you's spoken for.

You finally bought the hoop! Carly proclaimed, excited.

The boys are gonna go crazy. I'm 'a have to hide it 'till they all get home. Joe turned to Maurice Wilkins, his longest serving line staff. You around this afternoon Moe?

Naw Joe, you got me workin' all evenings this week.

Then I guess I'm 'a have to put it up myself.

I'm sure Marcus and 'Dell will help you, Agnes claimed. Those boys been talkin' 'bout that hoop you been promising for weeks.

Yeah, well now they can keep they bitchin' to a minimum.

You know they'll find something else to fixate on 'fore too long.

Ain't that the truth.

The staff laughed in agreement.

Ayite, so where's Rita?

She's still on the phone with CPS, Jamey, her therapist colleague reported.

Then we'll wait. Joe looked over to his probie line staff. Man Kevin, you look shot.

I'm still getting used to these overnights.

Didn't I tell you to get some sleep already, Maurice playfully advised.

Agnes hit Maurice in the arm. Don't you go teaching our new staff your bad habits! He laughed playfully as she turned back to face the group.

I don't want anyone going AWOL on my watch, Kevin reiterated to Joe.

And ain't no one knockin' you for doin' your job correctly, Joe agreed.

Those boys ain't going nowhere, Maurice insisted. Those evening meds be knockin' their lights out 'fore they even hit the pillow.

Everyone laughed. Because he spoke the truth.

Maybe when *you're* workin', Carly challenged.

Maurice smiled. Medication is a beautiful thing in this place.

Kevin laughed with him, as Maurice returned with at earnest tone. But seriously dawg, I'm just trying to help you out, because you got to admit, those are some bloodshot eyes you're sportin'.

Maurice jovially put his hands over his own as if the dark red in Kevin's exhausted gaze was blinding him. Kevin chuckled with half of the others at Maurice's dramatization.

They really had me goin' for a ride last night, Kevin sighed.

Maurice patted him on the back. It ain't no thing dawg, you still just growin' yo' house legs.

Rita Wilson, Excelsior House's lead onsite therapist, quickly entered the room and sat down to join the discussion.

Hey Rita.

Sorry everyone, she offered, I just got off the phone with Tyrone's social worker. DFS is finally gonna permit him to see his mom.

That's great news.

Nice work, Rita.

When is that gonna happen? Joe inquired.

Soon as I can coordinate with her PO.

You wanna do an onsite visit?

It depends on whether or not Tyrone wants her coming to the cottage. It has to be monitored, and if he doesn't want the other boys to see her, we'll probably go out to her home in Richmond.

Well keep us posted, 'cause we all know how he gets whenever he has phone contact with her, Agnes shook her head. OOHH, she recanted, remembering his past blowouts. He's like a bulldozer on demolition duty up in here.

I don't expect him to have any more episodes, Rita conceded. He's been making great strides in therapy, and changing up his meds has seemed to calm things down for him a bit.

That's true, he's been much mellower lately, Carly agreed.

Deirdre added, As long as nobody else is making fun of his mom.

The boys *have* been better with that too, Rita gathered from the notable absence of recent conflict around this point.

True.

Yeah, they haven't brought her up at all lately.

We've discussed it extensively in group.

That's a good thing.

Rita changed the subject in order to assess her other clients' more recent conditions. So how was the rest of their weekend?

Carly quickly inserted herself into the discussion. Speaking of new meds, Rydell sat on the couch for several hours again on Saturday and Sunday morning. He was like a zombie until 3 o'clock.

That must have been heaven for you, Kevin chimed in.

That boy sure ain't got no in between, Agnes added.

So do you think upping his Dexedrine dose is helping him overall to manage his behavior better? Rita inquired.

Maybe if you wanna drug the life right outta him, then yeah, Deirdre mocked. It was no secret that Deirdre was heavily against medicating children to squash their emotional expressions of trauma, an opinion reinforced by what she had learned so far in graduate school.

I think it's just delaying the inevitable, Kevin chimed in, in defense of Deirdre's position. He was intolerable last night. I think we would have come to blows if Julio hadn't chilled him out.

So that knucklehead is still giving you grief? Joe asked.

He can't stand me. Said as much several times last night.

You doing fine, dude, Maurice offered. 'Dell's like that with everyone in the beginning.

What set him off this time? Rita inquired from Kevin.

I gave him a verbal restriction. He knew it would drop him down to level one for the rest of the week, so he wasn't happy about that.

The boys are looking forward to the Warriors game on Wednesday, Agnes observed plainly. If he's on restriction, then he can't go.

Rita appeared very disappointed by the news. I was hoping he would done better with his new dose. He's behaved so much better in session, I was really hoping he could have this.

Maybe he could, if he stopped being an asshole, Kevin suggested, obviously still pissed from the previous evening.

Maybe we can work something out, Joe pondered out loud. Let him go to the game, but run the restriction an extra day.

Maurice openly disagreed. I think its best that he pay the consequences straight out. He knew what he was riskin' when he called out Kevin last night.

I agree, Agnes nodded. Fair is fair. Kevin ain't gonna build no credibility with the rest of the boys if we ain't in line on this.

Deirdre also fell in favor of Rydell not going to the game. He isn't going to get that he can't keep behaving this way if we let him go. And we have to think about the fact that he's emancipating next year. He needs to be prepared for dealing with real people on terms that aren't always his.

Rita backed down. OK, then. Fair is fair.

It was clear that Rita's favorite client had exasperated the patience of many members in the group, for various reasons. But Rita remained his tireless advocate. In part because she was the only parental figure he'd ever grown to trust in his seven years in placement with them, the longest of any of their clients. So Rita considered it her obligation as his therapist to continue offering a tint of sympathy (and to push for clemency from time to time) for Rydell with the group.

I think maybe his behavior came from crashing off his old meds, Rita speculated out loud. Maybe if I spread the increase in dose across the entire day instead of loading him up in the morning, we can stabilize this little guy's behavior.

I think he's gonna continue to be a jerk either way Rita, 'cause that's what he really is, Deirdre evenly surmised.

Still, Agnes and Kevin betrayed some sympathy for Rydell as well.

It's probably worth a try. Might keep evening staff from bearing the brunt of his aggressions, Kevin asserted.

You do what you do Rita, 'cause we all trust you, Agnes offered.

Carly agreed. Yep.

As did Joe. That sounds about right.

Rita recoded a note in her composition pad. All right, I'll make the adjustment.

Listening to all of this back and forth, Jamey Sherwood was obliged to ask about his own clients. So how were the rest of the boys?

Carly reported her observations from the weekend. Tyrone and Marcus chilled out together all weekend. Kendrick kept mostly to his room, but he played ball with the other guys in the afternoons. Rory was mellow too.

Jamey sighed, remembering their trip from earlier in the week. That's good. I think seeing his mom really made a difference.

There any hope of her getting out yet? Deirdre asked him.

We're not sure. Her parole hearing is scheduled for next month. Could go either way.

Deirdre nodded solemnly.

Oh, Carly blurted, and by the way, apparently Duane's got himself a new girlfriend.

Joe and Maurice immediately cracked up. Because they both knew he'd been crushing on Brenda for something like months before Carly even finished her sentence.

Agnes laughed along with them. That Rhona won't stop at nuthin' to hook them up, mmn mmn.

Joe snickered. That girl be up in everybody's business lately!

Carly reaffirmed his assessment. Apparently there's a dance coming up at Thurgood Marshall and Rhona got Duane to holla at Brenda to be his date.

The entire group bellowed with laughter.

Maurice shook his head. Man, that boy got no spine when it come to the pretty ones.

Joe was still smiling. So if now she's checkin' for Duane, we gonna be havin' ourselves some more AWOL's again. Kevin, you best bring your bottle of Visine to your next overnight, 'cause you gonna be up late talkin' with the police before too long.

Maurice couldn't contain himself from cracking up. Yeah dawg, you ain't gettin' no sleep now!

Joe laughed hard again, then grew serious. But seriously, I'm still a little concerned 'bout their blossoming friendship. 'Cause we all know it's just a matter of time 'fore Rhona takes Brenda on one 'a her nocturnal field trips 'cross the bridge. Far as we know, Rhona don't have any connections with no Frisco pimps yet, so if they go, they gotta spring before midnight, 'cause the BART trains don't run after 12:30.

The mood in the room turned to one of sober reflection.

They could always take a cab across the bridge.

Then y'all need to be checkin' the beds early and frequent these next couple a weeks.

All the staff agreed.

And be sure to stagger your rounds, that should throw 'em off.

Or at least discourage 'em.

Yeah, right.

Deirdre frowned. Brenda doesn't seem like the type to get herself mixed up in Rhona's nightlife.

Who knows? Joe wondered aloud. Brenda might even invite Duane out on a little nocturnal adventure 'a their own so they can get to know each other better. And y'all know if Rhona be there, Tyrone and 'Dell will be comin' too.

Agnes agreed. Oh yeah, and she checkin' hard for Tyrone now. She ain't admitted nuthin' to the girls, but that boy sure got enough sense to know it.

Oh great, the staff collectively moaned.

Then we need to keep an eye out for them too, Joe inquired.

Agnes gave him a sardonic stare. As if that's anything new.

Rhona knows she goin' right back to the halls if Oakland PD pick her up again, Joe reasoned. And I ain't got no pull with the officers out there. She's headed straight for youth camp if she catches another case for solicitation.

Rita chimed in to bolster his case. We've talked about this in session on more than a few occasions.

But y'all know sometimes that girl just ain't got no sense, Agnes bluntly pointed out. So all y'all gotta keep an eye out. Cool?

Joe's staff all agreed. Yeah.

Alright.

We got your back, Joe.

Good. Anything else?

Oh yeah, Jamey interjected. I'm working on getting Nate and Brandon's parents up here for a visit but nothing's finalized yet because DFS insists that the parents' urine tests come up negative for least a month before any contact with the boys is permitted. And so far the longest either one of them has lasted is two weeks. So I'll keep you guys posted if anything changes.

Do the boys know yet?

Yeah. But if their parents fail the tests again, be sure to watch for any triggers that will set our guys off, especially Brandon.

OK, will do.

Joe decided this was the best time to drop his new news on the group. Ayite y'all, well, we all know we have ourselves a new client. Some 'a y'all have already seen her, she just had her intake yesterday. Her name is Sarah Hillsbrook, and she's suicidal, manic depressive with diagnosed ADHD. You'll see the cuts on her body when you meet her up close.

Uugh, Deirdre gagged.

Even Maurice, the veteran of the group, sighed. Damn...

And it only gets better, Joe continued.

The staff appeared nervous.

Who diagnosed her? Deirdre demanded. And if she's manic, why is she here?

Isn't she dangerous? Carly wondered out loud.

Joe stiffened to project a sense of calm. She's outta General on probation under Charlotte's direct responsibility. Charlotte has assured me she poses no immediate threat to staff, peers, or herself.

Oh, what a big relief that is, Deirdre replied sarcastically.

Joe paused, then continued. But she told me staff needs to be careful with her during the transition.

Uh, yeah-

Apparently she has successfully detoxed, but her manic episodes might return and 'cause her to relapse if she refuses her meds-

Is she still on Methadone? Deirdre interrupted.

Buprenorphine, Rita clarified for Deirdre, but reported to the entire group. We also have her on Clonodine to stabilize her mood swings.

That sure doesn't sound like 'no immediate threat', Deirdre snarked.

Her suicidal ideation is apparently limited, but because her heroin use was a chemical trigger in her previous attempt,

Charlotte thinks if she attempts an AWOL and gets ahold of any drugs and relapses, she might try to kill herself again. So we have to be very careful to monitor her these next few weeks until her adjustment to the treatment program is clear. Charlotte will reassess her continued admission to our program based upon her performance then.

Joe, in all honesty, it really don't sound like this girl should be here.

Agnes furrowed her brow. I agree, this is not the right place for her.

So then why is General dropping her off here? We're a transitional residence for SED youth, not a mental outpatient facility.

They've got the space, especially if she's suicidal.

And it's not safe for anybody, clients or staff.

All right y'all, I hear what you're sayin'. Joe patted his hands on the table to calm the group. The real reason she's here, and I ain't got no better way to sugarcoat this, is because her father's a State Assemblyman.

No shit?

Mitch Hillsbrook, 12th District, San Francisco.

Aw, man...

Then we don't have any choice here, is that it?

This is about some political bullshit then, Deirdre winced at him, infuriated.

Well what if we don't feel safe treating her?

Joe tried calming them all down. Listen y'all, her father knows we're the best in the business. That's the God-honest truth 'a why she here with us now. And y'all are right. I don't like this anymore than you do, but I was told under no uncertain terms that if her situation gets outta control, they gonna pull her at first incident.

Yeah, that's all well and good unless she does some real damage the first time she flips out, Deirdre insisted.

Then we deal with it like we always do. Look, I wouldn't put none 'a y'all though this if I had a choice. But we've got no cash left in hand by the end of this month 'less the state decides to reach up in its golden coffers 'n cut us our check. And her father made it pretty clear through his channels that he wanted us to treat his girl. So our funding is pretty much tied to taking her on.

What, so now he and his crazy daughter get to decide how we provide safety for the rest of our clients? Deirdre raged. This is bullshit, Joe, and you know it!

Joe was clearly distraught with the understanding that his decision to take Sarah on was potentially compromising the safety of both the clients and his staff. Believe me, y'all, come first incident and I'm 'a pull the plug on her, even if it means my job. Now we've got Charlotte's assurances that we're all safe with her here, so if something don't run as smooth as we like, we just send her right back to General.

You know that don't mean nuthin' if Assemblyman Hillsbrook is pressuring them, too.

Hold up now, Joe paused. We all on the task, and that means a lot to me. So all I'm askin' is that we all try and make it work with her here, see where it goes. I have full confidence we can give this girl the same shot we give the rest of our clients.

By this point, everyone seemed about as exasperated with Joe's explanations as he did with his own.

But Joe finished his request. And hey, then if it don't work, it don't work. Give it a try is all I'm askin'.

Agnes was the first to come around. Well if it is as you sayin' Joe, then we gonna try for you.

Maurice followed her with, Yeah man, it ain't no thing.

With Maurice's agreement, Agnes redoubled her backing of Joe on this. We'll just keep on doin' like we always done.

Deirdre however remained unsure. The two therapists sat quietly. Finally, Deirdre relented. So when are the boys gonna meet her?

Tonight, Joe replied.

Well, we'll see what happens then, won't we? Deirdre smirked.

Joe could only look to his crew with a small glimmer of the greater anxiety withheld beneath his face.

Then we'll see...

***

Officers Michael Moreno and Tommy O'Shea drove their unmarked Ford Sierra down Capp Street, wearily looking for information. Last night two kids had been shot dead right in the heart of their beat. And early word out of shift change was that the 16th Street Sureños had it in for the three Norteños, most likely from the 24th Street set, responsible for the deaths of their two homies for simply walking out of their territory. No good deed went unpunished between those bangers, so Moreno and O'Shea didn't need to speak of what was now running through each of their minds. If they didn't cop a quick lead to the identity of the suspects, pressing their snitches or shaking down some newbie with a miracle tip, come this evening or next, there'd surely be more dead teenagers on a one-way trip to General. As members of the SFPD Gang Task Force with fifteen years of experience between them - O'Shea, the old man of the unit, had walked his beat in the Bayview for 11 years before getting shot on a routine assault call, only to be transferred to the Mission, while Moreno spent four years after the academy working the Chinatown Gang Unit before moving to Mission Station - each knew the players in this neighborhood especially well. The priests, the shopkeepers, community leaders and activists, legals and illegals, and especially the kids: who ran with which crews; who was taking orders from whom, who was aiming to make a name for themselves in their sets or within their crew; who was on the hustle or on his way to some hard time; whose brother/father/uncle/cousin was under house arrest, incarcerated, or out on parole; and who was automatically subject to pat downs as a result of being listed under a newly implemented (and controversial) gang injunction by the D.A.'s office. Moreno and O'Shea knew the ins and outs of which sets controlled which blocks and corners, their illicit drug operations (mostly meth and heroin cooked up in labs run by Nuestra Familia and Mara Salvatrucha gangs in the Central Valley and sent to their surrogate sets in California's major cities for distribution), whose crew was moving through whose turf, who was buying and selling, and, most importantly, which crew at this moment had beef with another crew.

What made Moreno and O'Shea especially desperate today, however, was the knowledge that whatever they did to run their usual shakedown game, cultivate their contacts, learn the nicknames, keep tabs on who was in and out of which set, dot all their I's and cross every T, none of it made a difference if they couldn't finger last night's perpetrators before nightfall, when the cycle of violent retaliation was sure to come full circle. Under normal circumstances it was never easy. Call it mothererfucking hood code, a community living in fear of retribution, no one was willing to risk becoming a witness for the prosecution under subpoena, even to save their own skins. Not the oldest grandmother, the most loving parent or sibling, or most sympathetic of neighbors, because once word got around that YOU were the snitch, no one in your family was safe. The reasons for that were all too clear. Fewer officers assigned to evening shifts created a permissive environment for violent crimes to continue with impunity in areas where rates were highest and ignored. Reduced funds for witness protection/relocation programs hindered law enforcement efforts to guarantee the safety of residents who did come forward. And for the rest who lived in the neighborhood, their families and friends, their jobs, their lives were all here. They didn't want to leave. And they shouldn't have to. So what was left to prevent the most vulnerable of this heavily undocumented, economically and politically marginalized immigrant community from falling victim to gang life?

Motherfucking Code of Silence. That was the game changer. The grand bargain for those living at the margins of a society indifferent to crimes committed in the 'hood. And it just about always went down like that. When it was time for people to step up or step aside, either to report the details of a violent crime or point the cops in the right direction of those who perpetrated them, no one saw nothing and no one did nothing. Fuck you very much, have a nice day. And so it went, with a legal system unable to provide safety for those going out on a limb to see justice done, as long as residents tolerated the occasional stray bullet through their windows at night or looking the other way heading to work, school, the market or church, if everyone just kept their mouths shut, then everyone and everything kept on keepin' on. As a result, the two warring factions of Norteños and Sureños effectively held the Greater Mission neighborhood in a stranglehold, slowly killing one other along with the entire community they held hostage under this unending cycle of tit-for-tat violence and retribution.

Thus, it was no surprise to Moreno and O'Shea that ID'ing the perpetrators of last night's crime before the next kid got shot would be anything short of a miracle, as it was on most days. Even in private, with so many residents of the mindset that 'snitches be gettin' stitches', no one had come forward with reliable details. Hell, these bangers could even roll into the middle of a house party packed forty deep with a mix of innocent bystanders and gang affiliated alike and wet t-shirt a dude right in front of all to see, but once it came time to speak to the police, nobody knew shit, even if it was their own siblings or cousins or brothers or sisters cut down for Chrissakes. And keeping the cops out of the loop was acceptable to all, because everyone knew hood justice would eventually play itself out on whoever had it coming. Problem was, once shit got escalated, nobody knew how or when it would stop.

Payback might be a bitch, but in reality, the young up and comers lookin' to make a name for themselves by dropping thugs in rival sets were just victims creating more victims. Alive or dead, each of these kids was still somebody's brother, somebody's son, and in many cases, some kid's father. Moreno and O'Shea always kept mindful of that fact above all else. That any loss of life in the community was a loss to all, be it a gangbanger, a bystander, neighbor, or police. And with no end to the violence in sight, a culture of fear, resentment, helplessness and finally, hopelessness gripped everyone in a crippling fatalism that became the greatest barrier to stopping it. So breaking the cycle of escalation and reprisal, just long enough for people to grieve their losses and heal was the crucial job of Moreno and O'Shea as they saw it on this day. This was what was at stake for the community they served, against the odds that consistently favored the reality of otherwise, if they didn't end up with at least one arrest by tonight. Pure and simple, fact was fact…

During their mid-afternoon run down Capp, Moreno spotted an old familiar face from the neighborhood walking south toward the corner of 24th street. He and O'Shea acknowledged this sighting with a mutual smile, deciding it was time to catch up with the young man they now knew to be a "former" Norteño. As

Officer O'Shea rolled up to stop the car, Moreno popped his head out the passenger window and called out to him.

Yo Julio!

What up Moreno.

Get over here.

Aw, man.

Let's go. 3479.

You ain't got no evidence of public nuisance from me just standin' here, yo.

The officers stepped out from the car as Moreno cited the city's civil gang injunction code, allowing him to frisk select members of the city's 24th Street Mission Norteños upon sight. So Moreno approached Julio as O'Shea scanned the sidewalk up and down the block. He spotted Edgar and Tootz, two of Julio's known Norteño homies also identified in the injunction, sitting on a front porch about halfway down the block from where the officers were standing. The Norteños watched the shakedown and dogged the officers with their stares. Any information the officers could use to question these boys later would hopefully begin with Julio.

You remember, do not associate within the Safety Zone?

Man those fools are halfway up the street. Julio voluntarily spread his legs and raised his arms up over his head. Damn, you call this probable cause? He busted on them more out of adherence to ritual than from any real personal discomfort incurred.

Staying clean? Moreno asked his suspect with mild concern.

Blut, you know I gots to.

Yeah, you do.

Moreno finished the search and Julio put his arms back down, but maintained a confrontational posture to keep up his front for the onlookers streetside.

So what do I owe the pleasure? Julio offered sarcastically.

We haven't seen you in awhile man, thought you might be starting to miss us. Moreno replied with mock concern.

Aww, Julio laughed. Mang, never.

Moreno and O'Shea chuckled back.

So how's rehab treating you? You still attending your meetings? O'Shea inquired.

Damn, O'Shea, you know I got myself right after you busted me. Shit homie, that was 'bout the best thing that ever happened to me, know what I'm sayin'?

Glad to hear you think so, O'Shea returned sincerely.

So I'm grateful mang, you know. You's lookin' at one reformed Twelve Step motherfucker, you feel me?

Moreno cut right to the business at hand. So you know anything about those Sureños got themselves lit up on Mission last night?

Naw, I ain't got nuthin' to do you for that. Julio threw up both hands, holding his palms out to convey sincerity.

How 'bout your homies? They know anything? Moreno flashed a look back down the street toward Edgar and Tootz, who immediately took their cue to walk in the opposite direction before Julio gave these officers any more reason to come creepin'. 'Cause your crew's been droppin' way too many bodies recently.

O'Shea pushed his eyes to the side, indicating to Julio that he wanted information on Edgar and Tootz without calling their names out directly.

Julio responded with all sincerity. I don't know nothing 'bout that. They ain't my homies no more.

What, you gave up on your set now? O'Shea cracked.

Mang, I'm clear now. All lucid like. And wit' them injunctions y'all be implementin', my probation don't allow me no contact with those dudes. I ain't lookin' to get locked up again.

That's good thinking, Moreno agreed.

'Cause we're gonna bring a serious crackdown on y'all if the bodies don't stop dropping, you hear me? No more drugs. No parties. No infractions of any kind.

Well y'all gonna have to talk to them 'bout all that, 'cause like I says, I'm out da life now.

Oh really? O'Shea mocked. That part of your Twelve Step?

C'mon man, we all know that ain't how it is, Moreno chided him, thinking Julio was full of shit.

Naw Moreno, I'm serious blut, Julio maintained. I been using my probation as an excuse to stay out da 'hood. Since I got locked up I ain't got nothing to do with none 'a that, 'cause y'all know trouble be havin' a way 'a finding me up in here. He looked around to see if Tootz and Edgar were still watching. Of course they were.

You know if we find you're blowing smoke up our asses and still on the hustle, it ain't gonna be pretty next time we see you.

Naw mang, I'm tellin' you, I ain't blowin' smoke up nobody's nowhere. I'm done. Out. For realz.

The officers finally believed him.

So whachu' doing up here then?

I just came to see my babymoms. You know she livin' up here with our niña.

Julio pointed up the street to a decrepit beige house where a young Latina girl stood on the front porch, holding a small child, watching the interrogation intently.

Moreno nodded to O'Shea to confirm Julio's alibi.

So how is Leticia?

See fo' yourself. He pointed her out down the block. Julio nodded. She straight. 'Dogh she hella pissed off I ain't comin' 'round lately, shit you can go ask her yo'self.

The officers looked back down the street and confirmed his story with the daggers she stared in their direction, most likely for Julio bringing police attention back on himself.

The officers laughed. Yo I bet.

But I tell you mang, since I's been sober I been doin' right by my family.

That's good, Moreno replied. And your niña? We heard she was up in General recently for a respiratory infection.

Aw yeah, Julio confirmed, but she cool now. Doctor said she got bronchitis, most likely from the mold up on walls in the apartment, 'cause it be hella damp and shit in there. But I'm on that. Gonna buy me some paint. Can you believe it, O'Shea, I'm one home improvement motherfucker now.

O'Shea laughed. Man, you come a long way, holmes.

Julio smiled. Hell yeah, no doubt.

Moreno interjected. So you make sure the landlord checks the pipes, then. If your baby moms is a legal tenant, she's got rights. If there's a leak, they gotta fix it. It's the law.

Julio shook his head. Mang, that's what I'm sayin', but I don't know 'bout havin' to deal with no landlords now with all them tenants, you feel me? Julio nodded to Moreno, referring to Leticia's abuela, whom the officers knew was living with her as an illegal immigrant.

Moreno agreed. Well, those walls ain't gon' paint themselves. Can't hurt to ask, huh?

Fo' sho' Moreno, I hear you.

So you're sure you ain't still slingin'? Moreno pressed him seriously again, returning the conversation back to business. 'Cause if you is, you know we gonna find out.

Yeah, I know. But naw, mang, like I said, I quit all that. Straight up.

Ever suspicious of Julio, Moreno looked over once again to Tootz and Edgar, who broke their gaze after briefly mad-dogging the officer.

'Cause you got your people to worry about now, know what I'm saying? Moreno finally counseled.

Yeah mang, fo' sho'.

And your little niña, she's gon' need her father around a long time, especially with the world being the way it is and all now, know what I'm sayin'?

Yo, holmes, I feel you. Believe me I do…

So you gonna keep doing good now, OK?

Yeah, mang.

Ayite then.

Solid.

Julio and Moreno tapped fists.

So, see you around, O'Shea, Julio laughed him off.

Hopefully not too soon, O'Shea returned dryly.

Aw mang, that's just wrong, Julio brushed himself off as the officers returned to their car and continued on their beat. After the officers left, Julio caught the business end of his woman's disapproving eye one more time. Instead of trying to turn her out and explain himself to his old crew, Julio walked instead to the end of the corner and hopped on the next MUNI bus back to Excelsior House.

***

Duane, Julio, Eric, Rydell, Tyrone and Marcus sat around the front room table in Cottage 2 of Excelsior House, discussing the most important information of the day.

Damn, you see our boy Kobe hit three off the shot clock?

Fool went for thirty six today my patna!

Marcus and Tyrone slapped hands in mutual admiration for their idol. Rydell scornfully watched their camaraderie build.

Damn, I told you dude's game is tight.

Like mine, Marcus declared.

Rydell hissed. Shit fool, you ain't never ball like Kobe.

Oh, we see about that.

Yeah we see. Rydell turned his admonition to Tyrone. And why you gotta always go copyin' what Marcus do, wit' that comb stuck in yo' hair and yo' pant leg all jacked up on one side? Yo' ass can't even dribble, fool.

Tyrone pouted while the others laughed. Because it was true. Although both of the boys idolized Kobe, only Marcus had any game on the court.

Just then, Duane and his less-scrawny younger brother Kendrick entered the room.

Whassup y'all?

What up crackhead? Rydell mocked.

What up criminal? Tyrone added.

Handslaps all around from the boys.

Kendrick smiled mildly. Nothin'.

The boys couldn't wait to hear about his recent trip to the halls.

So how you like it in there? Tyrone inquired.

Ain't no different from this place, shoot, Kendrick replied.

You get booty busted? Rydell wondered out loud, half seriously.

Kendrick shrugged him off. Mang, those dudes ain't nothin' compared to Tiny's crew.

Duane nervously laughed at the memory of the man who ran all the major sets in their old neighborhood.

So what did you go in for? Eric asked innocently. He wasn't even aware that Kendrick had been gone.

The rest of the Excelsior House boys were fascinated for more details. Of them, only Kendrick and Julio had ever been locked up.

Duane scorned his younger brother not for his bad behavior, but for gettin' hisself caught. Mang this fool be pullin' some kid's shoes right off his feet outside 'a class just 'cause he wanted 'em'. He could barely contain laughing at his brother's audacity before even finishing his sentence.

Mang, that's just stupid, Tyrone chided.

But Rydell couldn't get enough. Kendrick, you's too much!

Kendrick dismissed Rydell's admiration with a half smirk because he knew this behavior was beneath him. Meanwhile, Tyrone tried to snap Kendrick out of his funk by rubbing his scalp.

Well you're back out now boyee...

Man damn! Step off, 'cause y'all don't know when to quit, shit! All the boys hated having their hair scuffled. Especially Kendrick.

Carly, supervising the boys' cottage this afternoon, scolded him for swearing. Kendrick! Language!

Man I don't care! Shi-

She waited for him to complete his cuss but he didn't, so she let it slide.

Bunch 'a haters up in here.

No doubt.

Oh damn, check it 'chall!

The boys all looked out the front window to find Rhona shaking her butt at them from behind the main window of the girls' cottage directly across the street.

Man, that chick is whack!

But damn, she got dat booty goin' on.

MMM MMN.

I'm 'a get her pregnant. You watch.

Bitch, you wish.

Hell yeah, I do!

A few of the boys laughed. But most kept their eyes locked on Rhona's strip tease across the way.

Damn, that bitch got skills!

Tyrone!

Sorry Carly! I mean, damn, that trick got skills, Tyrone revised.

Carly was already on the phone with Agnes across the street. You better check Rhona before the neighbors freak out…Yeah, you should see the riot she's causin' up here...They're going to be washing their OWN sheets tomorrow. Carly hung up the phone and drew the front shades to the boys' cottage. All right, show's over.

Mang Carly, why you gotta kill my erection?

Only Tyrone laughed. Yeah Carly, why you gotta hate?

I see you got yo' PhD in full effect, Rydell unpleasantly observed.

What's that 'Dell? Carly asked naively.

Your player hater degree, Marcus informed her bluntly.

Carly just shook her head with a disapproving smile.

But you know you always had one 'a those, shit, Rydell finished.

Rydell, inappropriate language. Your losing your citizenship points for the evening.

Hell, I already done that.

Duane quickly changed the subject. Mang, I don't know about none 'a y'all, but I'm goin' outside. He nonchalantly gestured toward the door to catch the rest of Rhona's display.

Hell yeah, Rydell bolted for the exit along with Tyrone and Duane while Kendrick, Eric and Julio hung back.

No! Carly insisted. It's time for dinner chores. Get to 'em!

Mang! A brotha can't have no fun up in here.

If you wuz cool, Carly, you'd understand, Duane pouted.

Eric and Julio shared a laugh over the frustrated boys' tantrums while Kendrick retreated to the bathroom to attend to his pre-dinner hygiene.

After chores, the guys sat down to dinner. They took turns shoveling out their evening meal from the aluminum pan sitting at the center of the table.

Mang, lasagna again? This stuff tastes like prison food.

I tell you, we's institutionalized up in here.

It's good practice for when you get older, Josh Crenshaw bellowed, playfully deriding of the boys. Evening, gentlemen!

Aw, man, Carly, what's he doin' here? Rydell complained immediately.

Maurice called in sick. So Josh is your staff tonight.

What up Josh? Julio greeted him with a raised fist. Josh tapped it firmly.

What up, dawg.

Hey Josh!

Eric.

Mang, shoot, Tyrone pouted.

What, you ain't happy to see me, T? 'Cause right now I ain't feeling the love.

Tyrone only shook his head in disappointment. I ain't hatin' on you Josh, but Maurice was supposed to bring Transformers over tonight.

Well, I guess you're gonna have to watch it some other time.

Why don't you go crawl back under your rock, baldy? Rydell challenged without looking up from the food he'd slopped onto his own plate.

Hey Rydell, why don't you worry about your own hair. 'Cause right now it looks like your bunk buddy Tyrone pissed on yo' head again.

The boys laughed hard at this, because Tyrone was notorious for wetting himself in his sleep. Two birds checked with one stone.

Man Josh, why you gotta go bringin' stuff up? Tyrone moped.

Rydell passed his hand across his own gelled mini-afro in a display of self-admiration,
while the other boys snickered. Josh, don't even try to bag. 'Cause you ain't all that.

Meanwhile, Josh rubbed his own glossy dome. What you see goin' on here is Paul Mitchell skin toner, but I guess you wouldn't know nothing pimpstyle like that.

Bald-ass bitch.

I'm your worst nightmare tonight, Dell, so shut the hell up and eat your food!

Eric guffawed. At least Josh never hands out restrictions for bad language like some haters I know.

Tyrone agreed. That's 'cause he's got the worst mouth of all.

Duane offered his two cents. Almost the worst.

Tyrone shot Carly another dagger stare as Carly briefed Josh on each of the boys' behavior that afternoon. With Kendrick just returning from the halls, he was back on Level One. And because Tyrone received a verbal earlier, he also had to go without TV privileges for the night.

Josh was all business. Got it, Carly. Thanks.

Great, then I'll see you later.

Yeah doll, g'night.

Most of the boys chimed in. See you Carly!

Goodnight, she returned back as she left the house.

Finally, Josh was alone with them. He instantly put in a video for all of them to watch, including Tyrone, overlooking his earned restriction altogether.

So T, So why you gotta go puttin' yo' grief on Carly? Josh huffed at the boy.

Mang, she stupid is all, Tyrone whined. She all strict and stuff.

But not Josh, Duane immediately jumped over to him, obviously trying to curry favor with the utterly caustic line staff. 'Cause he's my dawg.

That's right little man, Josh rubbed Duane's head in approval. Unless of course you piss me off. He pushed his knuckles deeper into the boys scalp to noogie him and left a red mark.

Duane grimaced, waving Josh off with his hand. Man, why you gotta mess up my fade?

You call that a fade, pubic head? Josh cracked. That's funny.

Damn, that fool just called you pubic head! Tyrone snickered.

At least I got me some hair, shoot. Duane defended weakly, patting his 'do back into place. And the ladies be lovin' to run they fingers through my stuff.

Eric and Julio cracked up at the very notion of this. Listen to Mac Duane up in here!

Finally, Tyrone had to throw some salt into his game. Shit Duane, you know your crackbaby ass ain't getting no bitches-

Shoot.

Josh interrupted them all. First you boys go grow some fur on your balls, then you come back and talk to me when you got some real women checkin' for you.

Shoot, I'm the only one up here representin' manstyle, Rydell proclaimed, grabbing his crotch as he fondled the prepubescent beginnings of his goatee. The rest 'a y'all nutsacks be as shiny as Josh's head and shit.

Duane and Eric quickly dropped the subject. But Julio chimed in, surprising all of them. Hey Dell, how come you know so much 'bout other dudes ballsacks? You checkin' D's nuts? Julio riffed on him hard. You turnin' gay on us and shit?

Rydell didn't miss a beat. Naw blut, I don't even need to be lookin' at 'chu, cause everyone knows you hairy-ass Mexicans all lookin' like monkeys since you fell out 'cho momma's pussies and shit.

Tyrone pulled out the front of his sweats to check out his own situation down below. Mang, I'm straight!

Nobody care 'bout 'cho business T.

Shut up, chump!

Whatever, fool. You still cry like a bitch.

Julio interjected. Yeah keep frontin' D, 'Cause we all know you never had no woman go down on you, for realz. He tapped Tyrone beside him to recruit him for a laugh. Shit, homegirl comin' up for air spittin' yo' baby hairs out her grill, be like, damn! Where yo' dick at nigga?

Oh, hell naw, Tyrone busted up on cue. Julio just clowned your ass!

Shit, Rydell slurred, pouting.

Emboldened by the gang's belittlement of his nemesis, Eric had to jump in. I think we're still years away from that.

Yeah, and what do you know Eric? Rydell deflected. Just 'cause you ain't get to fuck yo' sister no more don't mean you gotta hate. Shit, I heard you whackin' it last night, don't even try to lie. Rydell made a juicy lip sound with his mouth.

Tyrone and Rory both cringed at the thought. Uuugghh!

That's right, Dell continued his onslaught. Dude be walkin' 'round da cottage with some chalky ass hands this mornin'.

Eric immediately tried rubbing Rydell's cheek with his right hand to deflect his criticism.

Mang, get yo' spermy palms out my face!

Uughh!

Eric threatened him squarely. You best watch yo' back or I'll leave another present in your pillow like I did last night.

Shit perpwalk, Rydell balked. I catch you anywhere near my room and I'm a cut yo' jimmy off myself, I swear to God. But Rydell appeared disgusted enough by the thought of Eric unloading into his pillow to back off. Josh, you hear that? 'Cause I'm 'a need yo' testimony when I sue this fool fo' sexual 'rassment!

You ain't suing no one D! Josh commanded. Quit your whining and shut your trap! You spew it, then you take it.

Rydell waved his hater staff off. Naw blut, 'cause Eric here be crazy, yo.

Crybaby.

Naw, that be Marcus.

Eric smiled as Rydell clicked his lips at him.

Tyrone changed the subject. Well I don't know 'bout y'all, but I'm jockin' all the bitches.

Collectively, Josh and the other boys dismissed him. Yeah, OK…

Yo' momma maybe.

Naw blut, 'cause she only like pussy.

Y'all's flip, 'cause my game is tight. Tyrone flicked his hair quickly with the pitchfork comb lodged in his tiny Arsenio to sharpen the edge of the sides.

So then why you frontin', T? Josh challenged him. 'Cause if you wus so busy hittin' it, you wouldn't gotta talk so much.

Shoot, I'm 'a tap Rhona tonight just to show y'all whussup, Tyrone boasted.

Marcus was unimpressed. Naw mang, fuck all that. Cause that chick's nasty.

Rydell dismissed him outright. That skeeza ain't gonna mess wit' no fool who can't grow no hair on his nuts.

Julio counseled Tyrone. I'm tellin' you T, trim yo' shit. It'll make yo' dick look bigga.

How you know so much, Don Julio? Rydell chided.

Been laid more times than you can count, ese.

Eric kept after Rydell. Yeah, maybe that would mean something if he could count…

Rydell turned to Eric and dismissed him with a puff of his chest. Nobody talkin' to you Chester.

The molester! One of the boys hollered out.

Eric had no rebuttal. So Rydell, smelling defeat, redirected his vitriol back to Julio. Shit, just 'cause you wetbacks all be gettin' wit' yo' cholitas 'fore they out da cradle, and they all be havin' yo' babies when they like twelve and shit…

Don't be talkin' 'bout my babymoms blut.

Rydell showed his proper respect for Julio. Naw blut, 'cause I ain't even gotta bag. Everyone know dem little-ass Mexican girls be horny as hell, yo.

Hells yeah, Tyrone agreed. Look at Sylvia. She got pregnant hella young. And with her cousin, no shit!

Shiyte, all them bitches be marryin' they cousins.

True dat.

And she still wants to get stuck.

I'd hit that, Duane admitted.

Shit, you'd hit anything, Tyrone jibed. That's why you all up in Brenda's stank.

Rydell agreed. Mang, I wouldn't fuck that skeezer with Rory's dick.

Man, screw you, Rory deflected.

Naw, seriously blut, 'cause I hear she a prostitute now.

No way…

Yeah.

Then maybe you got a shot after all Duane.

Mang, fuck all y'all.

Naw blood, I think it's cool you crushin' on B, Julio encouraged him.

Yeah mang, I mean, sure that bitch is big, but you know 'f she hoin' then she got skills to pay da bills, Tyrone and Marcus high fived, cracking each other up.

You really checkin' for her Duane? Rory asked.

Duane hung his head down. Naw mang.

'Cause I bet she could suck the chrome off a trailer hitch.

A few of the boys snickered at this remark.

Check out Rory, all bustin' out his redneck expressions!

Yo Rory, Tyrone cracked, You betta take yo' ass back to the trailer park with that.

Rory blushed.

And wash them stanky ass feet while you at it, Rydell sneered, waving his hand in front of his face. Shoot, 'cause no fool be hookin' up bitches 'round here 'till you clean out yo' funk. Get some deodorant fool, damn. Rydell held his nose, shooting Rory a putrid grimace.

At this point, Tyrone felt it necessary to intervene in his friend's defense. Why you gotta bring up the dude's medical condition?

That ain't no condition, he just nasty, Rydell intoned. Rory, get some hygiene dawg, for realz.

Marcus brought the discussion back full circle. Yeah, well Duane ain't never gonna hook it up with Brenda anyhow, 'cause she a lesbian.

That don't mean nothin', shit. Tyrone dismissed outright. Them neezy ass bitches need some dick too when all they been eatin' is rug.

Who made you the expert on lesbians, T? Marcus tossed out, unwittingly opening Pandora's Box.

His momma's one, or did you forget? Rydell reminded them all. Tyrone immediately grew quiet.

Rory didn't hesitate to call Rydell out for this. Dude, that's messed up.

I don't give a fuck, Rydell hissed back, completing his disrespect on this kid. Go wash yo' feet already, damn.

Dude, don't go bringin' up blood's mom, fool, Marcus insisted.

Don't get all sensitive, son, Rydell dismissed to Tyrone, who sat across from him, pouting silently. We just choppin' it up, yo.

Julio interjected angrily. Yeah, well, we ain't in group now, D, so shut the fuck up!

With Julio pissed, Rydell knew he'd overstepped his bounds. So he quietly backed off. Shoot...

Seeing no chance at a positive outcome from any more of this, Josh immediately cut off the conversation. Alright maggots, clean it up! I want this place spotless or you ain't watching wrestling tonight.

The boys finished their evening chores quickly in order not to miss WWE Monday Night RAW. Kendrick continued wiping down the table and counters long after the others moved into the front room.

C'mon Kendrick, you gon' miss the beginning, Rydell called out to him. That kitchen ain't gonna clean itself while you gone, shit. For some reason, 'Dell always showed mad respect for Kendrick as well.

Ayite.

Hurry up-

In a minute, shoot! Kendrick diligently scrubbed the last surface of the countertop with his sponge.

Back on the couch, the boys tuned in with a focus unseen in any other aspects of their lives. Jon Cena, Alberto Del Rio, Zach Ryder, The Miz, R-Truth, CM Punk and The Rock dominated their attentions for most of the evening. As the battles came and went, a few of the boys reenacted the wrestlers' best moves, reciting their full commentary word for word.

I'm gonna lay a smackdown on your candy ass! Rydell declared as he pounced on Tyrone, mimicking his idol Dwayne Johnson. Can you smell what The Rock is cooking?! Tyrone returned with a quickly administered pile driver driving Rory into the couch.

Brown Regal, damn it's illegal! Marcus and Rory rallied together, rushing Tyrone and Rydell as a tag team.

The boys replayed each scenario from TV to near perfection, but of course their routines grew predictably out of hand and devolved into a rapid free-for-all once it was time for one of the groups to lose.

Meanwhile, Eric sat across from them at his favorite table, writing down his personal thoughts in a journal while Josh and Julio chatted casually in the kitchen. Kendrick kept to himself on the couch, transfixed by the TV matches, and huffing in mild disgust anytime one of his peers inadvertently knocked into him.

Man, damn! Kendrick whisked away either Tyrone or Rory, the usual suspects bumping him.

Josh laughed aloud at Kendrick's annoyance with them. You chumpstains settle down before I come over there and take out the garbage!

Rory and Marcus quickly ceased and desisted. But Tyrone still couldn't break from the full-nelson Rydell had him locked in.

I said knock it off! Josh roared.

Rydell immediately let go of Tyrone, whose blue face now showed color returning.

C'mon Josh, I thought you was goin' to be cool tonight.

Did Rita forget to change up your meds again? Josh asked with all apparent seriousness.

Rydell waved him off without a second thought. Dude, you just a PHD like the rest of 'em.

Josh bellowed in his deep, brooding laugh at Rydell's frustration with him. Because nothing made Josh more happy in life than to put 'Dell in his place.

Tyrone however, felt compelled for some reason to pout again. He rubbed his head for dramatic effect. You see that Josh? I think I'm bleedin'. Now you need to write a incident report.

Stop being such a wuss, T.

Naw mang, it really hurts...

Lemmie see it.

Tyrone walked over to a seemingly sympathetic Josh for inspection. Josh moved his hand across Tyrone's scalp, clearly determining it was only a rug burn. Once he found the sore spot, he rubbed it hard with his hand balled together, making Tyrone wince out loud.

OWWW! Damn!

You'll live, Josh dismissed with no sympathy.

Tyrone huffed as he pulled away. Mang, staff ain't got respect for no one up in here...

But then he caught a glimpse of what Rydell and Marcus were already staring at outside the front window - Lucy Gutierrez walking down the stairs of the girls cottage across the street. She turned down the block to catch the bus on Mission Street.

Damn, check homegirl out!

Lucy be hella smokin' tonight.

Man she always smokin'.

Mmn mmn.

I would tear that up.

You ain't gettin' nothin' off a her blood, 'cause she's mine, Rydell insisted.

Keep dreamin' fool.

Y'all watch, she'll be on my tip soon enough.

Yeah whatever.

Girl be fine 'dough.

And DARK as a motherfucker…

Naw blut, Rydell corrected. She half and half.

Where you think she goin'?

Back home wit' that dope slinger boyfriend 'a hers.

That same dude who stepped to Joe that one time?

That's what Sylvia said.

I thought that fool been in jail…

Naw, he just out.

How you know so much allva sudden? Rydell beamed at Marcus pointedly. I ain't heard 'bout that.

Shoot, that's cus you ain't never hear nuthin' 'bout nuthin'. Marcus chided him.

What she doin' twisted up wit' that dude anyway? Tyrone lamented. Damn, that girl's too fine to get sprung on some thug.

Julio scoffed. Yeah, but he's her niño's papi, holmes. So he got hisself up in her heart permanent now, know what I'm sayin'? Regardless 'a how they front, bitches be in it fo' realz when it comes to they baby's daddy. Believe dat, for sho'.

Guess it takes one to know one, huh Julio? Rydell mocked him pointedly.

Shit, my old lady couldn't survive a quick minute wit'out me 'round to go knockin' heads wit'. And we ain't even togetha.

Then you best make yo' move quick 'Dell, Marcus surmised.

Shit, you need to hit that and quit it, straight up!

You ain't got no chance a gettin' with Luce while Key all up in her world, Tyrone reasoned. Come on, now.

I got more goin' on in spades than that dopeslingin' boyfriend 'a hers yo', you feel me? She been my girl foreva, and that's always how it gon' be.

Julio knew exactly where Rydell's particular crazy was coming from with this girl and it disturbed him. Yeah, so then what D? When Keyshawn come at you for swoopin' his woman, what then?

Shit, then I take 'im out, Rydell declared evenly.

Ah, hell naw! Tyrone blurted.

Marcus balked. Nigga please! That dude'll waste you easy he stroke hisself.

He ain't got nuthin' on me, Rydell scoffed.

Fool, Keyshawn been runnin' Eddy Rock for like three months...that's Western Addition dawg. And them OG's ain't forfeit they corners to no hood rat suckas. Dude put in work to get his, you feel me? So you best get yo' head on straight before you get GOT. Mmm hmm, that's what I'm sayin'. For realz.

Shit, I still take 'im, Rydell declared as plain as day.

Den you's gon' be one mo' dead nigga on da block, Marcus concluded.

It's cool D, Duane mocked, 'Cause 'I'm a wear your picture on my t-shirt, dawg.

Tyrone joined in the fun, pretending to cry in his hands. 'Dell, we'll never forget chu!

Marcus added coarsely. Mang, 'fore you know it, they gon' be pilin' up Hennessy bottles on da curb and lightin' Jesus candles for yo' ass.

Duane mocked the gesture. Dell be gettin' hisself a ghetto shrine!

Mang, fuck y'all, Rydell rejected their ridicule. Just watch what happens.

Julio better understood the true extent of Rydell's obsession with Lucy, so he shook his head and assumed a more serious tone. Don't go gettin' yo' ass smoked over some little-boy jealousy shit blut, you feel me? 'Cause Keyshawn a grown-ass man, and so his woman be off-limits. Shit, even if you did go afta her, then you's just stupid, and I ain't cryin' at cho funeral, you know what I'm sayin'?

Oh, OK, Julio, Rydell dismissed outright their concern. We see about that.

Marcus and Julio could only raise their hands in the air, dumbfounded by his uncompromising naiveté.

Shit...

***

Julio sat on the floor playing with his daughter Cecilia on his lap, singing an old Mexican nursery rhyme to her while his ex-novia Leticia folded clothes on the bed across the room. Between stacking each linen in its properly sorted pile, Leti took the opportunity to stare daggers in his direction whenever she managed to make eye-contact. Julio, for his part, tried to enjoy his visit with his niña while averting every angry glance she threw his way.

You gonna tell me what's on your mind or keep givin' me the evil eye?

You know why I'm mad.

Shoot, I ain't no mind reader, girl.

What wuz up with you and Moreno yesterday?

We wuz just choppin' it up is all.

Don't play me Juli, 'cause we both know what kind 'a scandalous activities you into wit' Edgar and Tootz.

Julio was irritated with her tone. Then why you askin' 'f you know so much already?

That shit with Rodrigo Suarez Saturday night, Leti blurted out abruptly. Somebody capped that scrap right in front 'a his crew' and words out you was in the mix.

Julio blew off her badgering. Girl, you musta got yo' signals crossed 'cause I got nothin' to do wit' any 'a that.

You promised you'd stop bangin' Juli, you told me when our baby came you was gonna be the father you never had!

And I been doin' that, shit, he replied evenly.

Ahh! She waved her hand at him as a dismissal.

Damn girl, man can't catch no kinda break with you! What?

Ain't kickin' the Rodgers and jumpin' out my crew mean nuthin' to you? He pulled up his shirt to reveal the remnants of stab wounds across his lower stomach, exit scars from leaving his set. What other kind 'a proof you need?

He stared at her hard to punctuate his frustration with her lack of confidence in him. But by now Leti had heard enough of his lies and she wasn't impressed.

Oh yeah Juli, thas it, always talkin' big shit 'bout how you all rehabilitated, then you go do what chu want anyhow. You know all kinds 'a people up and down da block been talkin'…

What they say? Julio commanded her to respond.

But she wouldn't answer him. Julio took one look at her and saw beneath the anger in her stare lay a genuine fear for him. Fear for Cecilia, for herself, and for the life she still wanted for all of them together, buried deep within her broken heart. This rift between them had grown much more serious than he'd initially realized.

Wha'd you hear?

Oh hell na, don't go actin' like you don't know nuthin' 'bout nuthin'.

Leti, I'm serious. What are them bitches spittin'?

She paused to read his own nervous stare, which seemed genuine enough. So she continued.

Some trick-ass skeezas from 16th up in the lunch yard yesterday talkin' 'bout how one 'a they cousin's be bringin' in da Maras from Bakersfield to come hunt down dem bustas who took out Rigo, sayin' Eme comin' at the 24th Street Norteños hard for all they people they dropped, talkin' 'bout wiping out Slum Francisco Ene for good. And none 'a them fools been showin' up to school rest of this week.

They goin' to war all over some flip-ass scraps?

You know that dude you went funkin' wit' wus the little brother of Antonio Suarez.

You mean that Eme who runnin' Chino? Oh shit. Julio was clearly swept aside with the distress over this news.

Don't you go actin' all surprised and what not, 'cause you knew who you wus swoopin' on when y'all pulled the trigger!

What? You think our beef wit' 16th street bitchpunks started over some dead scrap? Julio tried recovering his cool. Shit's been started.

Screw you Juli fo' all yo' thuggin'! For gettin' me and your daughter in the middle of all this. For what you promised to change! Forget you!

Girl, I told you I didn't do nuthin' to that dude! 'Cause I'm all about you and Cecilia now. Keepin' on the straight and narrow for y'all.

Damn you Juli, you can't fool me! Remember what you promised! For our baby! Now her father gonna be one mo' dead busta too. Leti started to cry.

Naw girl, it ain't like you think. Just 'cause shit around us outta control don't mean we can't pull through dis together, you and me. C'mere. He held Cecilia tight with one arm and moved across the room to comfort her distraught mother. But Leti pushed his hands away.

I ain't your baby no mo'.

Leti, I'm steppin' it up for realz now, you feel me?

Pssh. And what you gon' do for us when you's dead?

I told you I'm out the life. Done. We can go away. Leave Frisco behind us tonight. Fo' good. Just me and you-

And go where Juli? Leti seethed. Huh? You still on probation. Where you gonna take us? Pack up Celia and mi Tia in a suitcase? Wherever we be, you know them scraps'll hunt you down just like y'all did to Rodrigo and his boy.

Then I call a truce.

Pshh, Leti just shook her head in disgust, tearing up. Cecilia watched her mom weeping and cried herself into a lather. Julio tried calming her by lightly bouncing their daughter in his arms, but Leti would have none of it. Because she knew him all too well, and understood that any hopes of extricating him from the life he still clung to were delusional.

That's it then, huh, that's all you got? She snapped at him, taking their daughter from him into her own arms.

Girl I'm fightin' for you, fightin' f' us now, you hear me?! You just got to put some trust in me a while. We got our baby, and we got each other to look after, no matter what. And that shit means somethin'-

Leti's rage turned conspicuously to a serene, cold calm. Because at some level, she always knew even in the first moment she fell in love with this gangbanger that he was a thug for life, and that in a moment all this would end between them one way or another. Someway, somehow. That's just the way it was always meant to go down. His way.

No it don't. Not no mo'.

What chu mean babygirl-?

You need to go Juli, just go.

Finally resigned to their fate, she pointed to the door.

Naw, hell naw wait a minute-

Kiss your daughter goodbye Juli and leave this house. Leave us before you dead on the block wit' tha rest of em'. You owe yo' daughter that much.

You know I'm out da life, I swear-

Just go. 'Cause you ain't never gonna change. You can't.

Julio resigned for the moment to kissing his daughter. He then moved to give Leti a peck on the forehead; she dismissed him simply with her palm covering her forehead, mouthing the word, Don't. She raised her arm into the air, gently pressing his face away.

You know I'm 'a be back when all this shit cool down.

She turned to her daughter and looked her over solemnly, condemning herself inside for making this man her father. Knowing that because of her falling in love with him so many years ago, Cecilia would now never have the papi she'd always hoped he'd become.

I check you later...

No response. Only silence.

Ayite then, I see how it is.

But deep down, for the first time in their relationship, Julio didn't.

***

Lucy rode the bus home with her shopping bags filled with groceries. It was anniversary night. Can you believe it, she mused to herself, five years with this man? He may have his problems, but who don't. Lucy was amazed that anyone could love someone like her for so long. So she was going to surprise Keyshawn with his favorite dinner. Steak with collard greens. Her baby loved empanadas too, so of course those would be on the side.

Tre had cried nonstop earlier. He was fighting off some kind a stomach flu going into yesterday, and threw up all over his daddy, but Key bein' the good father he wus didn't even flinch. He just wiped the lip of his baby boy, proud as a poppa could be, and said, 'Wouldja look at that? My dawg, kickin' it however he feels like, ain't takin' shit from nobody. He a soldja, like his daddy.' That's the kind 'a good people Key was. Always looking out for his son. Even when Tre started crawlin', Key couldn't help but take two steps outside 'a hisself. 'My boy gonna grow up real strong,' Key bragged, grinning like she'd never seen him before, 'He already more man than half the suckas you meet.'

And now Key was even spittin' 'bout how he wus gon' put them up somewhere in a real house, maybe up in the country, as long as his boy could still grow up hard, 'cause he ain't never raisin' no sucka. But not too hard 'course, 'cause he wanted his boy to have everything he never done. Like all 'a them famous rappers who was pullin' in grips 'a scrilla and spendin' it all on they kids, Key was plannin' for the future. A betta life wit' his son and his baby's momma. Lucy loved it more than anything when Key talked like that.

Baby, I'm back, Lucy yelled as she pulled the groceries in through the front door to their house. She found Key and his boys sitting in the living room getting high and playing the street racer video game as she dragged the groceries into the hallway beside them. Immediately, she caught the eyes of several 'a Key's homeboys sittin' on the couch. Tony, Rolfie, and Bizmark. When she appeared, Rolfie waved his hands frantically in front of his face to disperse the cloud of smoke lingering around them. He then stood up, apparently to help her with the bags. But Key's quiet, commanding voice instructed him otherwise. Don't even trip, she cool.

Awkwardly, Rolfie sat back down.
Hey baby, Lucy smiled at them.
The boys hollered back.
Whassup Luc!
Whas happenin' mamacita?
Key, engrossed in the game, didn't bother to turn his head.
You bring our snacks?

Right here, baby. Lucy beamed, proudly pulling out Flaming Hot Cheetos, Pringles, and beef jerky wraps for Key and each of his boys.

Keyshawn crashed in the game, yelling to Antonio. Aw man, mufukin' cheatin'-ass bitch!

Nigga, I whupped you fair an' square, Tony retorted.

Just 'cause you's up in my crib playin' this shit all day don't make yo' no winna.

Some niggas be out workin' for theirs, for realz.

Shut up and eat yo' food dawg! You too, Biz.

Keyshawn's oldest homeboy, Tony, was the only fool you'd *ever* hear checkin' Key like that without gettin' some serious hurt put to him.

Yeah, well I'm 'a whip your ass next time, believe dat! Key laughed off as he got up from his couch and walked over to Lucy, who was busy in the kitchen putting the groceries away.

MMMN, he looked her up and down like he wanted to sex her up right then and there. Ain't you just 'bout the prettiest thing this no-good soldja ever laid his eyes upon.

Lucy blushed as the other boys offered they two cents.

Yeah Luce, you the real deal!

You's the finest ghetto princess 'round da world.

In the universe!

Whattup babygirl, Keyshawn smiled, planting a tender kiss on her cheek right in front of his boys, making her his all over again. You hear what they sayin'? Cause it's all true.

Aw Key, Lucy almost came to tears. You always so sweet to me.

That's 'cause I appreciate you, baby. And everything we got goin' up in here. And its' all good...

Happy anniversary baby.

Lucy looked deep into his eyes, and although he was high, she was sure she could feel his true affections permeating through that glossy stare.

He wrapped his arms around her and moved in for a slow, romantic kiss. His strong, assured embrace drove the butterflies in her stomach wild.

But other business called from the other room. Yo, you gonna suck her tongue out her mouth all night or bring yo' rematch, bitch?

Key laughed as his boys finished their razzing of him. Then he spoke to her again with his tender talk. I gotta go handle this.

She smiled and nodded right back to him. Yeah, you do that.

Be right back...

You betta.

You know that's real.

Good.

She blinked and pushed her face forward to his, stealing one last kiss.

How's Tre?

He sleepin'. Just waitin' fo' his momma to come home.

Keyshawn returned to the couch and grabbed the controller from Bizmark. Ayite bitch, interruptin' me wit' lady makes y'all some dead motherfuckers.

As the boys resumed their game, Lucy retreated into the bedroom to find her baby sound asleep in his crib. She turned Tre from his side and slid him onto his back. He puffed but did not wake. Lucy had been reading a lot recently about Sudden Infant Death Syndrome a.k.a. crib death and so she wasn't leavin' nothing to chance for Tre to suffocate hisself sleepin' face down. She would have to talk to Key about that later.

***

Skreetch dusted his leather jacket off briskly as he shuffled his emaciated frame down Haight Street. He was in no mood for anything but attending directly to the pressing task at hand.

Spare some change?

He needed at least a few more coins to cop his next fix. It was a cold day. Raining. And his Rodgers was kickin' bad this morning.

Give a dollar, make me grow taller-

His go-to shtick of waving a plastic chicken at passersby always brought a laugh from plenty of unsuspecting tourists and young suburban kids looking for a thrill in the Haight Ashbury.

Cock a doodle doo...

Was that the sound a rooster makes?

Any change'll do...

Next came a pair of pretty teenagers. He focused on the brunette. Because by the look of her hot-assed friend, she was probably the one getting less attention.

Hey cutie, was your father an astronaut? Because he put the stars in your eyes.

The girl smiled at this burly mohawked skaterpunk using a rubber chicken to make romantic advances on her. All these Barbies were the same. Trendy, extreme, usually rollin' up to his hood for some excitement, looking to get a piercing or tattoo, but naïve as all hell 'bout the real score. Their inexperience was written all over their faces. Give 'em at least three days on the street with Skreetch, and he'd break 'em. Like he'd done with the last few he took a liking to. Thought they was hard because they'd left home, they wanted a taste of real livin' on they own. So he handled 'em right, delivered just what he wus givin' right on a silver platter. First he'd butter 'em up, telling them they was just about the prettiest little things he'd ever seen, then they'd get all sweet on him long enough to start hurtin' from the chill of being outside a few days. Then he'd pump some of his shit right into their arms for that much needed relief, before dragging them down to the park near Amoeba Records, where above the tunnel bridge with a cupped hand to the mouth that bitch became his to do with whatever he wanted. Soon she was workin' her pretty little suburban snatch up and down the panhandle with all the proceeds finding their way right back into his arms, with all his needs gettin' met. It was all too easy back then playing those lipstick wannabes, but there was no time for that now. Because Screetch's veins were screaming now. Screaming to get fed.

Fuck this.

Spare some change motherfucker!

That old man passing by with the look of shock would 'a never been a taker no how. Screech threw his fist through the air towards the man's general direction as if to flail and assail the old timer into submission. But he had to chill out. No Rodgers ever got squashed soliciting these assholes. Not unless you was ready to rob the prick outright. But Skreetch couldn't resort to such measures this morning. With any more assaults on his record, ending up in lockup was a guarantee of swallowing detox the hard way, cold turkey. No way, fuck all that. Screetch had kicked his habit once before in jail and fuck if it didn't near kill him. So naw, he had to keep his profile low this time around if the knocks were out and about hunting him off the block.

And his Rodgers was still kickin'.

He started scratching himself violently. He needed the pain now as a distraction from the hunger choking out his veins.

Just then, an elderly woman walked up. She looked like one of those churchgoing types.

Fucking needle exchange Jesus freaks seeking their salvation! He could smack her up and down the street for being so stupid! Believing in a God that didn't exist to any of his kind. But maybe she could reach him, that one desperate soul willing to throw down his sins, absolve himself of his misdeeds, seek penance in forgiveness, and embrace her almighty fucking Lord with wide open arms simply 'cause she fucking asked him to. Bunch 'a hypocrites! But maybe it would take his mind off his pangs to let her make the first move. Fuck it. No time.

Spare some change for a hamburger?

Yes actually, I can, she replied. Here's five dollars.

Bingo!

Thank you ma'am. He laid on his fake southern drawl to make him sound all the more sincere. God bless.

Fuck you very much. Time to get fixed up.

Skreetch ran like hell to his dealer in Buena Vista Park.

Paid that motherfucker 15 solid. Then a bag to the hand. Maybe enough to last a few hours.

You pinch this?

Fuck it, no time left to bicker about volume.

He found his favorite tree. Pounded the hash into a puddle of spit in his rusted spoon.

Goddamn the shaking of his hollow arms...

Fired up the Bic. Boiled the hash. Shaking so hard now he couldn't even hold down a vein to tap.

Fuck it, pump it right in, hope for the best.

The needle hit its target. Oblivion. Now the eyes rolling back. Everything blurry, everything right...If only for a few hours…All except for the tiny carving at the base of the trunk…In his favorite tree…Sarah and Skreetch it read…True Loverz Forever…

His last Barbie-

How he really did love that skank-

As much as he'd ever loved anyone…She would pay for leaving him…If he could ever find her…

Where the fuck'd she-

Out cold.

***

Sylvia Sanchez found her way to Almas Apasionadas Youth Artist Studio on Monday afternoon. For several days straight she'd made the trip down from Excelsior House to her old hood on 24th Street to put work in on a mural commissioned by her mentor, Rosaria Hilgada, to focus community awareness back on the plight of struggling neighborhoods in crisis, plagued by youth violence sprouting up across the city. Rosaria was recruiting all her big guns for this partnership, involving several street sprayers from the block and around San Francisco to promote a unified message of peace and tolerance. Sylvia and her homeboy Manny Alvarez planned to throw down as their set piece a rendering of an unnamed Central American country occupied by its state military, complete with peasants linking arms in solidarity, planes and tanks attacking the citizens, requisite bodies of the disappeared all piled up together with the dumping of subsidized crops to bankrupt the local farmers and destroy the local economy taken over by foreign investors. Sylvia's concept incorporated the struggle of the local Mission youth with the countless number of refugees who fled the civil wars of their home countries across Latin America throughout the 70's and 80's to start families in the US. Whether of Mexican, Nicaraguan, Guatemalan or El Salvadoran descent, the legacy of most people living in her neighborhood, 24th Street had them all.

Rosaria liked Sylvia's idea so much she asked an Ashkenazi Jew and a Palestinian artist from across town to cross tag a Peace Not Apartheid wall in solidarity with the plight of their Arab and Jew brothers and sisters locked in their struggle for equality in Israel and Palestine. Rosaria was famous for bridging cultural divides and whatnot, and she typified La Raza both in how she carried herself as a "non-violent subversive" of her community and in the history she made over the years lining the corridors of the Mission with her numerous murals and collaborations. From Potrero to Valencia, 14th Street to Precita Park, each reflected a piece of our history, depicting our unity in struggle, our connectedness as a people, teaching us who we were and where we needed to go, regardless of what set you ran with or which piece of the block you claimed your own. Rosaria's art brought us together and made us one, though many a fool had little conception of this, still stuck on chasin' they monay and they bitches and they status, all to gain some respect from they patnas 'till they wound up dead with they face on some suckas t-shirt at they funeral. But she also taught the youth of the 'hood how to express themselves creatively, through spray murals as she'd done through the years. Rosaria was the best, and she wasn't afraid to speak her own mind and have it speak for itself through her teachings to others. And Manny and Sylvia were her best and most dedicated students.

So when word came out that the wall on the corner of 24th and Harrison Streets was to be repainted, Rosaria put them up for that commission. Sylvia had learned all she knew from Rosaria, pretty much how to build a street piece from the bottom up, how to mix her paints just right and create the illusion of depth in her features, and most important, how to give it all a social-historical purpose. Her mama and papa taught her what it meant to be El Salvadoran, cause she was first generation growin' up in America. But it was Rosaria who taught her how to find her own voice. And so Sylvia wanted to be just like Rosaria in her own life and future telling it like it was, throwin' down her own brand of knowledge and wisdom on the masses, and if those deaf and dumb motherfuckers refused to listen, she was gonna holler loud enough and def enough that they had no choice but to hear.

***

Marcus Turner took the 25 MUNI bus to the Altegard Public Housing Complex in Western Addition. His moms and brother needed checkin' up on. It was three years ago to the day that Clara Rodriguez from CPS came into their home and took him and his little brother Boyce away from their momma. While Momma got herself cleaned up at SF General, Grandma got Boyce. But Clara insisted Marcus be placed in a group home because their grandma wasn't equipped to cope with his emotional fits of rage, or 'teenage exuberance' as Clara put it. Truth was, Clara believed Marcus was a member of the Eddy Rock crew which ran the Addition back in the day. It was true that Marcus was cool with them dudes, but he never had no chance a gettin' wrapped up in none 'a they scandalous-type activities, because even though Momma was lost in her binges most nights, she never allowed Marcus the time alone to hang with those cats. The only contact he had with most of them bangers was playing ball either at Kimball Playground or Jefferson Square Park after school or on weekends. But he always had to be home on Momma's strict orders. Cause she'd whup the living mess outta him regardless how high she wus if she found out he'd stayed out past the streetlights coming on. But Marcus had to get hisself home most nights anyway, 'cause by about 4, momma was too stretched out to do nuthin' 'bout Boyce. So it was up to Marcus to make sure his little brother had dinner to eat, got his homework done and put himself to bed. Then Marcus would throw a blanket over momma when she passed out on the couch before he got himself some sleep. And when momma woke the next morning, she'd forget all that went down the night befo', packing their lunches and see 'em off to school just like any other day, befo' makin' her 20 hour a week job with the city in her bright Orange throwover, cleanin' sidewalks and dumpin' out them neighborhood trashcans to keep them paychecks for Section 8 comin' in. Momma took care of her business every morning when she was lucid, but then it was up to Marcus to watch out for Boyce in the evenings. That was their deal. Cus they wus a team. Until that bitch Clara came in and broke everything up. Of course Momma couldn't kick her Rodgers 15 years in the making right away, so her urine tested positive for crack cocaine and opiates one too many times for Clara's satisfaction, and Clara threw Marcus and Boyce into placement until Momma got herself serious treatment. In the hospital, the methadone worked mom's addiction up somethin' real, so she stayed clean eight months for realz, and eventually got Boyce back from Grandma, whose steady-onset Alzheimer's gave her no business caring for a ten year old no how.

But with Marcus, his arrangement for returning home was different, 'cause with CPS considerin' momma's habit of leanin' on him for household duties to be child abuse, he had to remain in placement to keep his momma from fallin' back into drugs, should he come home and watch over Boyce so well as he done befo'. Therefore, Marcus's current home visits with momma and Boyce had to go under the radar of CPS. Fuck the courts, fuck visitation "rights", fuck monitored sessions with the therapist and fuck that hater caseworker Clara! Because Marcus was gonna see his family however he wanted, no ifs ands or buts about it, on his own terms, as he'd always done. CPS couldn't stop him or give no grief to momma 'long as he made his way all stealth-like, he was just keepin' sure they stayed a normal family, far as he saw it.

So Marcus exited the MUNI bus and walked trenchantly down Eddy Street towards his momma's unit. He carried a bag of groceries bought with his allowance money from Joe. He was sure Boyce and Momma would be short on eggs, seeing that it was already the 23rd, and that Momma's welfare check usually didn't stretch past the 15th, even on a good month.

Yo Turner!

What up D?

Whuz poppin'?

What, you ain't got no love fo' yo' boyz no more?

Now you some big ass basketball star…

Nigga be on the hustle and shit.

Damn straight in and out, you know how it do.

Who you's swoopin'?

I'm just checkin' on my moms and B. He stayin' outta trouble?

Mang, I ain't seen nuthin' foul outta that boy.

Yo he ayite. Sportin' hisself a black eye dough.

Whut, one 'a y'all roughin' on him?

Naw mang, but some dudes at Leadership been checkin' him fo' his lunch money.

What dudes?

Yo, I ain't tryin' to hear no names mang.

I'm 'a have to handle all that, Marcus nodded.

You hear about Jute?

You mean that bitch from Knockout Posse who can't dribble?

Yeah, he the one.

Damn nigga ain't got 'nough sense to keep from crossin' Key on his own.

Fool be runnin' up on 'em wit' his clip, and motherfuckin' Keyshawn didn't even flinch, you feel me? Put two up in his chest rat-tat straight up, dude was dead fo' he even hit the flo'.

When dat happen?

Shit, last week. That nigga Key come right out da pen, droppin' fools left and right.

RIP motherfuckerz what I say...

D poured his beer into the gutter.

But naw blut, I'm serious, that shit ain't right. K ruthless, you feel me. Shit, he claimin' the whole block, takin' out both our crews.

Y'all handlin' yoselves straight I hope.

Shit, dude got the rest 'a dem bitch-ass punks from Knockout runnin' scared. Neighbors be snitchin' us out to the police sayin' we'z gangbangin' when we ain't even done shit. And dem pigs even be puttin' up cameras and shit. But we took 'em down for realz, you feel me?

'Cause Eddy Rock don't give a fuck, y' feel me?

Dude be cuttin' into our business, know what I'm sayin'?

Motherfuckers slingin' everywhere and wastin' anybody try to take they cut.

Mang fuck that!

Nigga think he all Donald Trump out here and shit.

Yo D, be careful. I hear Key got muscle.

Who said dat?

Deantre.

Aw mang fuck all that. And fuck Deantre too. That flip-ass bitch don't know shit. I'm a go bitch slap his ass right now just for spreadin' shit!

Yeah and I'm 'a put a cap in that nigga Key's skull next chance I get. His old friend put his hand shaped as a gat into Marcus's temple. Den shoot him straight in the dick so his crew all know he went out like a bitch!

Damn, you's cold...

Well y'all betta get it done of there ain't no more 'a y'all.

Naw mang, fuck all that! 'Cause Eddy Rock been ownin' the block since we wuz kids, you feel me?

Damn straight. You feel me?

For realz.

Yo mang, you want in when we go knock the dude out?

Naw mang, I ain't even supposed to be here.

Then you best get to yo' moms fo' we kick your ass for not comin' wit' us.

We gamin' on Sunday. You in?

I'll try to make it 'round, y'all.

Cool Cuz, you do that, 'cause I been workin' out my dunk.

I catch y'all later.

Fists tapped. Straight.

Marcus walked up the steps to the second floor and knocked on the front door to the third unit down the hall. He entered to find his momma passed out on the couch. He put the groceries down, covered her with a blanket, and walked into Boyce's room. Sure enough his brother was sitting there, sporting a shiner on his left temple.

Yo B?

Hey Marcus.

Yo little man, come give yo' bro a hug.

Boyce stood up from where he sat with his truck toy and hugged Marcus.

I missed you mang. How you doin'?

Good.

How's momma?

She sleepin'.

Mang, let me see you, Marcus moved down on one knee to get at eye level with his brother, holding the young boy's face gently in his hands. Who did this to you?

Some fools at the bus stop.

What fools?

Dequan & Barry.

You mean from Knockout Posse?

Yeah.

They take yo' money too?

Boyce didn't answer. So Marcus grew impatient. Yo mang, did they rob you?

Yeah.

And so whad'ju do back?

Boyce hesitated.

How'd you retaliate? His brother insisted that he answer.

I hit Dequan twice in the nutsack, the young boy revealed.

Marcus smiled. Did you drop 'em?

He too big, Boyce replied, somewhat defeated. But he wus hurt a bit.

Then what?

Barry came up and held me down...

And then Dequan went to work, Marcus finished his brothers sentence for him. Boyce nodded, embarrassed.

But you didn't let 'em run you.

Boyce looked up. Naw, I threw down just like you show'd me.

There you go, Marcus smiled, proudly rubbing his brother on the head. My man. They may 'a took your money, but you makin' 'em think twice 'fore they check you again. For realz.

Those dudes don't know when to quit.

You let me handle them suckas, you feel me?

Yeah, OK. Boyce could only look down to the floor.

'Cause you know I will, yeah?

Yeah, Boyce replied, more forcefully.

Good. You finished all 'a yo' homework yet?

I still got math.

Then you best get on that. I'm 'a fix us some dinner.

Alright.

Marcus?

Yeah B?

What 'chu gonna do to those guys?

Never you mind now, lemmie take care 'a all that. You just get ready to eat.

What we havin'?

Egg sandwiches.

We all outta food.

Not no mo' y'ain't.

Marcus?

Yeah B?

When you comin' back to live with us?

This time Marcus hesitated. Because he really did not have a good answer for that.

When CPS let me.

When is that?

Soon I hope.

Me too…

Boyce walked to his blue backpack and pulled out his homework.

Marcus?

Yeah B?

Momma misses you.

I know. Marcus was solemn. I miss y'all too.

Boyce considered this for a moment, then looked back down to his homework and began writing.

Marcus walked into the kitchen to fix his brother an egg sandwich. Out of his bag came the bread, then the eggs, bologna, butter stick, Velveeta cheese slices, ketchup, mustard, milk, Flaming Hot Cheetos bags, apple cider packets and Capri Suns he'd bought to pack with Boyce's lunches. As much as Momma was tempted to scrounge money for her drugs, she never sold the food Marcus brought. She was a good momma, despite her faults.

He searched the cupboards and found a clean plastic bowl which he rinsed in the sink along with a tiny fork. After breaking several egg shells on the edge of the linoleum counter and swirling the yolks together into a scramble, Marcus tried the stove. No gas. He'd be sure to remind Momma to press Clara to have the San Francisco County Housing Authority have it turned back on. Next he tried the microwave. Stupid piece of shit, nothing worked in this fucking house! No matter, Marcus thought, Joe could front him 40 bucks to pick one up at Costco next time Agnes and Deirdre went shopping for the other boys. As a last resort, he opened the door tenuously to the top cupboard to find…YES! The hotplate he'd stashed deep behind the other bowls, hidden away from the sticky fingers of Momma or one of her boyfriends. No one ever cooked around here besides Marcus.

Marcus wiped the dusty face of the hotplate and poured the egg batter onto it. Several minutes later he toasted a pair of buttered bread slices and added the scramble between the two pieces, warming up some cheese layered throughout the middle for his brother. A fresh pitcher of Kool Aid already sat in the fridge, so Marcus poured a glass for Boyce. He made a second sandwich for Momma. Then after rinsing the hotplate off in the sink and re-stashing it safely away, Marcus called Boyce into the kitchen for dinner.

How's the sandwich, B? Marcus inquired as his brother wolfed it down.

Good.

Let me see your homework.

OK.

Boyce dutifully pulled the assignment sheets out of his binder. Because Marcus always liked checking it was done while they ate together.

You got an A on yo' spelling test last week. Nice job, yo!

He rubbed his brother's head just as Boyce tried to finish his Kool Aid. It splashed all over his face.

You made me spill.

Aw that ain't nuthin'. Dem red lips match yo' black eye, Marcus teased, posting the homework on the refrigerator with a Golden State Warriors magnet.

He returned to the table to watch his little brother eat as he shuffled through the rest of the papers. So you finished all your work tonight?

You gonna check it?

Marcus looked it over. Times tables huh?

Yeah. Ms. Ramos has us practicing them. Says they the most important things you can learn in math.

Shoot, Marcus replied shyly, I wish I knew mine. Now you's finally passin' me up, shorty.

Marcus smiled as he watched Boyce finish the last of his dinner. My man.

You gonna stay over tonight Marcus? Boyce asked with a wish in his voice. Marcus' proud smile faded.

Naw little man, I gots to get. If I'm back too late and Clara finds out I wus here, shoot, CPS ain't never gon' let me come live at home again.

Boyce looked defeated.

But it's all good B, Marcus rubbed his brother's head again. 'Cause I be back later this week, you hear?

Boyce nodded his head. Yeah.

Good.

And don't you go worryin' 'bout them suckas at school. Just keep yo' head high and do like you been doin', you hear me? We don't need you in no mo' scuffles, gettin' suspended over some bullshit, bringin' any mo' 'ttention to our situation, you feel me?

Boyce nodded.

Ayite then, Marcus smiled again. My man.

Marcus stood up and walked over to his Momma who was still passed out on the couch. He moved his face gently toward hers. She had that all too familiar, sweetened stench of smoked cocaine on her breath.

Marcus leaned down and gently kissed her on the forehead.

Out of nowhere, his momma awoke in a panicked, violent rage.

Get in your room and lock the door! Marcus quickly directed his brother. Boyce, all too familiar himself with this routine, quickly retreated from his brother's orders. Marcus could hear his bedroom door shut and the lock twitch into place.

Don't come back out until she asleep! Marcus yelled.

Without warning, his mother lunged in full panic attack mode, slapping her hands forcefully into Marcus's toned body.

You sonofabitch youmothafuckin' son of a bitch get out GET OUT GET OUT!

Momma it's just me, momma, it's Marcus-

Her arms continued flailing at him. Instinctively, he grabbed her wrists to suppress the onslaught directed his way.

You motherfuckin' sonofabit-

He could never control her whenever she awoke like this in a full-fledged manic attack induced by the drugs flooding her brain.

Momma stop it stop it just stop!

Her strength was insurmountable, fueled by whatever shit was in her system. Maybe PCP, maybe pure crack or crystal or some mix cooked up with Drano or Clorox, Marcus didn't have time to know. He just had to get out of there fast. So he pushed his momma to the floor and ran for the front door.

You no good sonofabitch I hate you I hate you get out get out leave me and my children alone get out GET OUT!

Marcus did just that. He slammed the front door while his mother banged her fists into the hardwood now separating them. If all went down normal-like, she would settle down soon, fall back asleep within a few minutes, and wake up tomorrow mornin' not remembering a thing about how she got them cuts on her hands and who wrapped her up in those bandages. Boyce knew what to do. He would stop the bleeding once she fell back asleep. So there was no sense to be had callin' anyone for help. Soon she'd calm back down on her own with no one else the wiser. But if the police ever got notified, Boyce'd be right back in placement and then who knew if they'd ever see each other again. So naw, fuck all that. For now, Marcus had no choice but to let Momma calm herself back to sleep on her own. She wouldn't remember Boyce was even in the house. And Boyce knew not to come out 'till he heard her snorin'. As long as the neighbors kept to they own business, all would be fine, all forgiven. But either way it wasn't safe for Marcus to stick around. He had to get back to Excelsior House before Agnes discovered he'd blown off basketball practice at the Boys and Girls Club in the first place. And it was already getting dark.

But Marcus had one more quick task. On the way to the MUNI stop, he made his way over to Kimball Playground. He knew Dequan and Barry was slingin' round tha' way wit' the rest of Knockout Posse, unless Keyshawn already cleared them out too. Sho' 'nough, there they wus sittin' wit' the rest of they crew.

Pumped with adrenaline from the scuffle with his mother, Marcus approached the benches overlooking the yard.

Yo' if it ain't crybaby Turner!

You mang what rock you crawl out from unda?

He headed toward them with such an aggressive swagger that several of the boys stood up.

Yo this ain't your block Eddy Rock!

Marcus retorted as he came upon them fast. Y'all know I don't run' with none 'a them!

That ain't what I heard.

Then you best clean out 'chour ears fool-

Who you think you checkin' f-?

Whassup nigga! Marcus called out Dequan, pushing him to the ground.

Aw hell naw.

You go punkin' my little brother think I'm 'a let that slide?! Marcus seethed. Get yo' ass up!

Dequan stood up with his arms extended, holding the bottom of his shirt up to reveal the exposed chrome clip of a .38 gleaning from his belt.

Oh yeah, thas right, whassup now crybaby, you ready for some a dis? Little bitch.

Before anyone could flinch, Marcus lunged for Dequan and pummeled him back to the ground.

Oh damn…

Aw hell naw!

The crowd surrounded Marcus scuffling down on Dequan but he was unfazed. He balled his hands into fists and landed punch after punch, bloodying Dequan's face. He couldn't control himself at this point. Because if he stopped the onslaught, the cracking bones in his hand would excruciate, not to mention Dequan would reach for his clip and all of this would be over. So he kept pounding away. The only way this motherfucker would leave Boyce alone wuss with the right payback, if Marcus dropped him fair and square in front of all his crew to see.

Damn, Turner be fuckin' D UP!

After several moments, the Knockout Posse set pulled Marcus off their patna, with two of them holding Marcus by the arms.

Dequan reached to his belt, flexing for his clip but the others stopped him.

Yo hold up D! Jay, the leader of KOP demanded, focusing his attention back on Marcus. What' 'chore beef nigga!

You best stop robbin' my bro! Marcus insisted to Dequan.

Jay turned to Dequan, who was bloody. You fuckin' with Boyce, D? The leader of his crew retorted. He in 5th grade, fool!

Mang I don't give a fuck, a bloodied nosed Dequan mocked defiantly.

Upon this revelation, Dequan's set quickly turned on him.

Mang that's some fucked up shit right there!

Naw hell naw...Dequan cooled as the others grabbed the clip from him. Jay signaled to them to let go of Marcus.

It's all good Cus. He had it comin'.

Dequan held his nose, flicking blood to the ground, Mang fuck you, and fuck that! Your little brother, he a dead motherfucker now!

Another member of the Knockout set chimed in, hitting homeboy across the arm. Mang shut the fuck up!

Marcus knew his former neighborhood boys well enough to gauge D's threats to be idle.

You's one weak-ass nigga pickin' on a ten year old, you know dat?

Shit.

What now, you robbin' bitches fo' they lunch money?

That's fucked up blut-

Pussy ass bitch-

Because the Knockout boys wouldn't have none of their own disrespectin' no shortys from the block without payin' Dequan further attention, Marcus walked away from the group, satisfied.

Jay called out to him as he left the park. Yo Turn, we ballin' on Sunday 'f y' want to come out!

Maybe, he replied to the crew. Gots to see what it do.

You best hope I don't see you later bitch! Dequan yelled out.

Mang shut the fuck up. You ain't doin' shit. Jay lambasted him with a slap to the chest.

Dude fucked you up blut...

Marcus caught his bus back down the block. His hand was bloodied. Hopefully not broken. Or sprained. If so, his chances for making All City and impressing those college scouts would now be in jeopardy. Fuck his hands hurt. But he did what he had to, so fuck if he had a choice. It is what it is, Marcus thought to himself, assured. At least he'd make it back to Excelsior House by the time basketball practice was scheduled to end.

***

Joe Rodgers installed the basketball hoop he purchased for the boys of Excelsior House over the garage of Cottage 2 after school. The residents all helped him to varying degrees with the setup; all except for Eric, who sat drawing sketches in his notebook on the driveway step.

Rory, man damn! Stop bouncing that ball, shoot, a frustrated Kendrick chided him.

Rory ignored him. He couldn't contain his excitement. Kendrick turned back to watch Tyrone holding the ladder for Joe.

Yo 'Dell, make yo'self useful by handing me that screwdriver.

Rydell dutifully did, but could not let Joe's directive tone slide without retort.

Mang, it's about time you be puttin' up our hoop, shoot. How long he been talkin' 'bout this?

Months, Tyrone offered.

Damn staff ain't got no love up in here.

Quit your whining D, Joe miffed, 'fore I come down there and really give you something to complain about.

Mang, you ain't gonna do shit.

Y'all lucky you gettin' anything, Joe screwed the bolts in. Little disturbed children. Only reason I'm doin' this is so you stop scarin' all them normal kids at the park.

Mang I'm sick 'a walkin' over there anyhow.

Shoot.

I think that does it, Joe proclaimed as he tightened in the last screw.

Rydell grew excited. You Rory gimmie the ball, I'm 'a take the first shot.

But Tyrone dogged Dell out to Joe. Hell no, he don't get to play 'cause he on restriction.

That don't mean nuthin'. 'Cus this is a special occasion.

Joe shook his head. You know the rules D. You can't go messin' with staff 'n be expectin' special privileges.

Come on Joe, Kevin hatin' on me for some bullshit. You know how we do it.

Yeah and that's why you sittin' yo' butt out while my boys try out they new hoop.

Mang that's fucked up Joe. You's the king 'a playa haters!

Sit yo' punk ass down, Joe forcefully commanded him.

Rydell waved his arm at him in disgust but did what he was told. Because he had mad respect for Joe. He knew Joe and Rita's dedication to his betterment were the only reasons he hadn't been shipped outta Excelsior House long ago.

Meanwhile Rory, holding the ball, took the first shot. It bounced off the rim with a firm twang.

Aw hell naw, Duane and Tyrone yelled out together as they competed for the ball in the rebound.

Y'all's a bunch a fools, Rydell pouted.

What up Duane, whut up now? Tyrone noogied Duane to distract his shot.

Mang Tyrone you's dirty. Joe! It was clear Tyrone was imposing his larger figure over Duane to outmuscle the ball from him.

Joe! Duane called out. Tyrone playin' dirty!

Boy, you best stop yo' whinin' and handle your own damn business!

Aw, you gonna let T punk you like that? Joe now instigated. Yeah I see how it is.

You's a punk T, Duane dismissed as Tyrone stripped the ball from him and shot again, this time swooshing the net of the basket.

So? You see me give a fuck?

Watch yo' language boy.

Aw my bad Joe, Tyrone dismissed as he slapped Duane across the head for snitchin' him out.

Duane looked once again over to Joe. You see that?

Joe returned his glare with feigned disdain.

Yo, come here boy!

Unfazed, Duane walked over to him.

Once within reaching distance, Joe snatched Duane by the shoulders and forced him into a headlock.

Whassup now? Whassup? You need help or somethin'?

Duane couldn't stop laughing as Joe playfully dragged him around the driveway.

Come on now, fight back or somethin', shoot, you makin' this too easy!

Duane feebly swung his scrawny arms around trying to escape Joe's grip as Kendrick and Tyrone laughed at them. Rory took the chance to run the ball down court and shoot a flawless layup off the backboard.

Aw hell naw Joe...Help! Duane continued yelling out from Joe's death grip.

You done yet? Joe taunted his prey.

OK! OK! OK-

Joe paused for a moment, if only to establish complete dominance over his ward, then released him.

Thas what I thought youngin'.

Mang I'm 'a take you next time.

What?! Joe fired off another grab for Duane's skinny frame.

But this time, Duane was ready. He ran down the street cracking up as Joe chased him. But Duane could not escape because of laughing too hard.

Aw naw!

Joe overtook him three houses down and wrestled the boy maybe one quarter his size to the ground.

Kendrick continued watching with amusement as Rory and Tyrone traded hoop shots. Rydell still moped on the stoop.

Mang y'all's whack...

Soon enough, Maurice walked up the driveway, arriving for his evening shift. He called out to Joe, who was still busy overtaking a subdued Duane.

That kid givin' you mess Joe?

Nothin' he ain't already sorry fo'!

Duane winced on the pavement. Maurice! Help!

Boy I told you to be quiet, Joe demanded, jabbing the hell out of him.

AWWWWWW NAWWWWW!

Maurice started laughing. Let me know dawg, 'cause I can put my gear down.

Duane knew he was screwed. Mang Maurice that's jacked up!

Maurice walked toward the hoop to check the installation. Rydell immediately jumped up, excited to see his favorite male staff.

You Maurice, my dawg. He put his hand out to slap Maurice's. Maurice obliged him.

Sup Dell'. So why you ain't ballin'?

Mang, Joe and Carly be playa' hatin' over dat mess wit' Kevin last night.

You dawg, you gots to be cool with the new staff.

That dude don't like me...

Well who do? Maurice responded.

Mang screw you.

Yo, you best run your program or they're gonna run you outta here, feel me?

Yo it ain't nuthin, I'm just breakin' in new staff is all.

Be cool yo.

You know how I do.

Ayite den, Maurice hit fists with Dell.

Yo, so you bring the new Rainbow Six?

Yeah, got it right here. He pulled the new video game from his bag.

Wifey still letting you buy that junk? Joe interjected.

She ain't callin' the shots on ALL 'a my purchases.

Yo Maurice, you know thas' whussup! Rydell put his hand out sarcastically to slap Maurice's again. But on this occasion Maurice refused to oblige him.

Yo that's my woman you dissin' now...

Shoot, my bad, Rydell redacted honestly.

Maurice gave him a fake dirty look. Rydell stepped from the cottage door to let him pass.

Tyrone, Rory and Kendrick finally spotted Maurice, realizing he would be working the evening shift in Cottage 2.

Whattup y'all?

Yo Maurice! Tyrone hollered, Watch this!

He tried to pull a fake reversal on Rory for an alley oop but missed the rim entirely as the ball bounced off the backboard.

Yo Joe this hoop ain't up to regulation! Tyrone tried dismissing his poor shot as Rory copped the rebound. Maurice instructed Tyrone to take the shot a second time but he missed the target again. Rory caught the ball and took the same shot against Tyrone's fresh attempt to block him. This time, the ball seamlessly passed through the hoop.

Yeah like that's gonna help yo' sorry game T, Maurice blurted to Tyrone.

Whattup Maurice!

Roryman, show this little boy how it's done.

Rory shot the ball again for three points at the edge of the driveway upon Maurice's prompting. This time, he missed too.

Mang y'all need some work! Maurice shook his head in disappointment.

Tyrone redirected his embarrassment. Yo Maurice, drag you fat ass out here and I show you how it's done.

Maurice could only laugh. Naw, I think I'm 'a go set up my new Xbox 360 instead while y'all learn to ball.

You bring Rainbow Six? Kendrick shouted excitedly.

Yeah and you'll be the first to play it when you make it back to Level Three.

Shoot, you know that's only a matter of time, Kendrick dismissed his own brief stint in the halls as merely a fluke. I'm 'a take you later.

Now that's what I'm talking about. Maurice smiled before entering the house. Rydell followed him with a shameless ploy for his mentor's validation.

Yo' Maurice check out my new rhyme…

Maurice shot him a sarcastic frown.

Mang, why you gotta do me like that? Rydell put out his arms again, genuinely hurt. You ain't even heard it yet.

Maurice maintained his disapproving look. After a quick minute, Rydell shrugged him off as Rory, Tyrone, and Kendrick finished their three way game, just in time for Joe to finally release Duane from his grip down the street.

***

Later that evening, Marcus Turner arrived back to find the boys in the front room of Cottage 2 engrossed in their game on the

Xbox. Eric continued along with sketching his scrapbook drawings at the kitchen table.

What up cuz, Maurice threw his hands up as he tagged Marcus passing by on his way to the kitchen.

Holla, Marcus dropped five into Maurice's palm with his good hand.

How was practice, dawg?

Straight mang, he replied, continuing on down the hallway to check the damage of his wounds in private.

Whattup, Eric offered to his roommate without looking up from his tracings.

Yo.

The boys on the couch continued with their game.

You'z cheatin' Maurice!

He always do.

Y'all can't step to none 'a dis.

Mang when you gonna let me play?

When you'z off restriction, fool.

That means never.

Maurice cracked up. Damn dawg, they'z all on you tonight.

Mang, fuck y'all, Rydell pouted.

Maurice paused the game with his controller. Yo D, why you gotta get all sensitive?

Shit, Rydell pouted, but had no other comeback.

A few moments later a knock sounded at the door. The boys were all too lazy to answer it. Another knock.

Maurice! It was Carly's voice.

Yo Kendrick, will you handle that?

OK. Kendrick opened the door to find Carly with the new girl, Sarah Hillsbrook. They entered the cottage congenially.

Hey guys.

All the boys sounded off. Whassup Carly!

Yeah I see how it is, Rydell scowled. Now y'all be throwin' a hater convention up in here.

Maurice, you got the new Rainbow Six already? Carly exuded excitement.

He could only laugh. The missus picked it up for my birthday.

You're gonna have to let me borrow it.

Naw Carly, you best step off 'till we'z done, Tyrone insisted.

Ain't no haters get to play, Rydell interjected in a feeble attempt to check her.

Carly just shook her head and pointed to her companion. Everyone, this is Sarah. Sarah, everybody.

Yo. Whassup.

You guys even gonna pause your game? Carly suggested, annoyed by the boys' indifference to the new client.

It's cool, Sarah shrugged them off.

Yo, we already met, Tyrone offered plainly.

So much for male chivalry. You guys have some extra sugar?

Take whatever y'all need, Maurice offered.

Damn Carly, why y'always go raidin' our stash every time y'all be runnin' outta stuff? Rydell pouted. I best have enough fo' my cereal tomorrow.

Too much sugar'll rot your teeth, Carly retorted with ease.

Mang I don't care, shoot. Who y'all should be worryin' 'bout is Rhona. 'Cause that bitch's smile ain't nuthin' polite.

Damn! Tyrone and Duane both cracked up.

Carly yelled from the kitchen. Language 'Dell! I'm gonna tell her what you said.

Go ahead, shoot. Rhona know betta than to believe any 'a y'all haters anyhow.

Maurice finally scolded Rydell for disrespecting staff. Yo shut yo' ass up, boy, 'fore I start talkin' 'bout you're stank-ass yellow teeth front 'a everybody.

Rydell dismissed him plainly. Naw blut, cause you'z the one with the hot breath, fool. He waved his hand over his face. Everyone be knowin' when you's comin' round befo' you even walk thru the door.

Maurice paused the game as if to start some mess. Mang, I'm just playin' wit' you dawg, shoot. But you always gotta take it there, D.

Why you gotta go gettin' so sensitive Maurice? Rydell smiled. Damn, ain't no haters able to take a joke no mo…

Yo chill out D, Tyrone shot back, we want to finish our game.

Duane followed Tyrone's lead. Yeah D, shoot.

With the group firmly against him, Rydell silenced himself. The boys returned to their Xbox 360 match.

Meanwhile, Sarah looked over to see Eric drawing some elaborate body structures in his notebook. She walked over to him. He raised his head from the page and smiled to this girl he'd had his eye on for several days now, appearing interested in learning what he was all about.

Hey, Eric greeted nonchalantly.

Hey, she returned wryly. She looked over his drawings. Full anatomical tracings of the insides of human bodies. Skeletons, muscle systems, and nervous tissue all separated from each other and arranged in orderly parallel rows on the page.

Those are tight.

Thanks.

You into the body?

I'm mostly interested in its limits.

She scanned his page again. Saw a yellow light passing up the frame from the crotch of one of the tracings to fill the upper crest of the skeleton's chest cavity.

What's that?

Most people think it's an orgasm. But it's really a Kundalini.

Sarah looked puzzled at this dude who had so much going on in his art. A what?

Kundalini. It's an energetic charge which shoots up the body from the spine into the crown chakra when a person reaches enlightenment. It's described to look like a coiled snake slithering up through the body to numb the other chakras to the pain of the world.

Sarah was intrigued. So it's better than an orgasm.

Eric laughed as he continued to fill in his sketches. Much.

She paused to take him in. You some kind a spiritualist?

Naw, I'm more of a Satanist. But I'm really into Gieger. He's the artist who does all of Tool's artwork on their albums.

I like Geiger.

You know Geiger?

I'm into Sepultura.

They're pretty dope. But it takes a special person to get Tool. Ever listen to them?

No.

I'll rip you a CD.

That'd be cool.

Right on.

Sarah was beginning to like this guy. Have any others?

Yeah. Wanna see?

Sure.

He turned the pages as she scanned his book. What she found inside was much darker than the visions laid out in his more recent renderings. Here, a variety of decapitated heads wearing various expressions of pain were being pumped with a dark green fluid by several rusty dialysis machines.

What's that all about? She asked, simultaneously disgusted and fascinated.

Oh, these are just my plans for some experiments I'd like to carry out someday.

For what?

To prove a human head does not need its body to live.

And how you plan to do that?

Eric grew excited by her interest in his macabre vision.

Easy, when you first chop a head off its body, it has about one minute of blood left in it. That's why when the French used to decapitate their enemies, they picked up the head to show it to its body, so the person had to stare at themselves as the last image they saw before they went unconscious. But if you hooked a head up to a machine to pump blood into it before the brain dies, you could probably keep it alive for as long as you like.

Why the fuck would anyone want to do that?

I think it would be the ultimate form of torture. Keep the person's brain alert and awake to think about whatever it is they have done, but they are completely out of control to stop you or to kill themselves, 'cause they no longer have a body to manipulate. Like a vegetative state, but they're always aware, always watching you, and always powerless to stop you doing what you want to them, or forcing them to see.

Sarah was instantly nauseated by the thought of one day becoming a head plugged into one of Eric's blood machines, never being able to take her own life if the pain and suffering he chose to inflict upon her became too much to bear.

I think that's horrible, honestly, she admitted to him. Demented, really. But genius at the same time.

Thanks. Eric seemed to accept her criticism warmly. It's still in the planning phases mostly. But I'd never advocate doing this to good people. Only criminals. The scum of society that can't be saved.

What, you mean people like us?

Eric laughed. Yeah, I guess so.

It was then that he noticed her wrists. So I see you're no stranger to darkness either, he offered, pointing to her lower arms with a flick of his eyes.

I've had my moments, she returned dryly.

That why you here?

Supposedly I'm on suicide watch, though this place seems pretty lax.

But you had to come over here with Carly.

Partly. I really just wanted to see what you all were about.

So what do you think? He raised his arms to encompass the room. Welcome to paradise.

She laughed at his intended absurdity. Yeah. Well, you don't have it too bad.

At least I ain't livin' with a bunch 'a crazy chicks.

No doubt.

Just stay cool and you'll be all good, Eric offered plainly.

Yeah, well I don't plan on stayin' long.

He smiled. You and me both.

Yeah? Sarah perked at the thought. Where you off to?

My mom and dad live in Venice Beach, they sell weed to the locals down there. I'm goin' to live with them once I get off probation. They said anytime I'm ready, I can come down and they'll make a place for me.

That's cool, Sarah nodded. Sounds like you've got a plan at least.

An awkward pause.

What about you? Eric inquired, though seemingly only to bridge the chasm of silence between them.

I'll probably go live with my old boyfriend in the Haight.

Eric's heart fell, crestfallen at the very mention of another man in her life. Well if you jet, that's the first place they'll look.

That's why once I find him we're outti. Gone. Gonna take a Greyhound up the coast to Oregon and live on the beach together.

That sounds cool I guess. He returned. What's his name?

Sarah instantly became defensive. Why you gotta know so much all of a sudden? Gonna NARC me out to staff once I bounce?

Naw, just trying to make conversation is all. But he was surprised at how quickly Sarah read his true intentions. It made Eric believe this was the girl for him all the more.

Finally, Sarah finished her thought. Skreetch.

Eric nodded. Cool. A pause. You in love with the dude? Absolutely.

Then I hope everything works out.

He would have seemed indifferent to her if not for the furious shaking of his facial muscles taking hold of his inner rage.

Sarah was unsure what to make of their conversation now. But thankfully, Carly all too soon interrupted them. Eric, snap out of it!

After several seconds he did. As if it never happened.

Well we've got to head back.

Just wait until I can get that mix to you, he replied coolly to Sarah as she and Carly walked out the front door of Cottage 2. Sarah smiled to herself at the thought, though Eric could not see her do so as she left.

***

Back at Girls Cottage 1, barely two minutes after lights out, Rhona burst through Sylvia and Sarah's door and flipped on their light switch.

Yo bitch! She pulled Sarah's blanket immediately off of her feet. You best give me my shit fo' I cut you!

What the fuck? Sarah moaned, still half asleep. Sylvia rolled over in bed to see a wrecked up Rhona hovering over her new roommate.

I ain't playin' wit' you bitch! Rhona pushed Sarah hard back into her bed as she tried rising up to confront her accuser. Get up. 'Cause I'm 'a fuck you up right quick!

Again, Sarah tried to rise. Rhona moved to slap her, but Sarah shielded herself with her arms, eyes still half shut. I didn't take your stuff!

Rhona swiped at her instead with her nails, backing Sarah into the wall behind her. Rhona pointed at her ferociously. You's a lyin' 'ho! Ain't nobody come in my bathroom stealin' from me!

What 'chu lose now Rhona? Sylvia grumbled from her bed. Shit.

My crimping iron, and I know this cunt's got it.

Rhona turned to Sarah's dresser, opened the first drawer, and threw Sarah's clothes onto the floor one by one.

What the hell? Sarah moved toward her to stop her, but Rhona whisked the air in front of her with another pass of her nails. Sarah backed up again to avoid getting sliced.

Bitch, don't even think 'bout steppin' to me. I make you bleed, give you AIDS, you feel me? I straight don't give a fuck.

Sarah resigned herself to staying on the bed as Rhona continued dumping her clothes all over the ground.

You best stay out my business! Sylvia hollered from her bed, covering her head with her blanket indifferently. Bitches always be losing sumpin' up in here…

First rule da cottage bitch, don't go touchin' shit ain't yo's!

Rhona you's whack, Sylvia dismissed her cottage mate briskly. Homegirl just got here!

When Rhona finished emptying the dresser and found nothing, she quickly turned to Sylvia's area and began rifling through her closet.

Girl, you best get out my threads! Sylvia hollered from her bed. Ain't nobody know where yo' stanky prossitute fingers been.

Fuck you Sylvia, if I even find my shit up in yo' mess I'm a fuck you up nuthin' nice, you can believe that, fo' sho'.

Yo girl, check Brenda's stuff fo' you come up in here runnin' yo' commotion. She always be stashing things she can't remember where.

Naw, 'cause Brenda ain't seen it.

Eventually, Rhona turned the whole room apart. Nothing was found.

Mang, I told you we ain't got your curler, damn! You happy now? Sylvia hissed, pissed as hell but too groggy to do shit about it.

Rhona, clearly frustrated, tried to leave. But Sarah was having none of it. She stood in front of the door to block Rhona's exit. Yo, why don't you try cleanin' up the mess you made fo' you go, she demanded.

This made Rhona explode, waving her palms and moving her neck side to side. Oh hell naw whitegirl, you don't tell me t' do shit! You got that? 'Cause I'll wreck your world up real quick!

She threatened another advance on Sarah, but this time Sarah'd had enough of her. You wanna fight, 'ho, then let's go right now-

Sarah drew her fists and advanced toward Rhona herself, who continued flailing her palms and curling her fingers.

Just as Rhona was about to lunge, cottage supervisor Agnes appeared at the door.

Rhona! Back up now. You know where you headin' f' you start any mo' trouble.

Rhona could not stop madogging Sarah, but retreated with Agnes's stoic command.

Agnes surveyed the mess on the floor and sighed. What 'chu outta your room for girl?

This bitch stole my crimping iron!

Agnes could only shake her head. You have any proof 'a that?

Shit, I wuz just usin' it this morning fo' whitegirl moved in, and now it's gone...

So you're sure it had to be her, Agnes chided. You re-check yo' bathroom drawers?

Naw, 'cause I left it on the countertop dis mornin'!

Sylvia and Sarah both rolled their eyes.

Rhona remained recalcitrant. What 'chu lookin' at spooky? OOH, I'm a slap you silly right quick!

Rhona! Agnes yelled. Did you find it in her things?

Naw Agnes, but that's just 'cause she good hidin' it, shoot. Rhona eyefucked Sarah hard. I know you have it bitch.

But after several minutes, with no contraband to be found, Rhona slowly admitted defeat with a dispatch of her hostile posture and a slumping of her head into her shoulders.

Listen up ladies, Agnes lectured when all was settled. You know you got to respect each other's property. This happens all the time with y'all. So whatever you do, you gon' have to find some way to work it out.

This bitch know what she done...

Rhona, watch your language.

Sorry Agnes, but she is one.

Agnes scowled at Rhona, who clearly knew she was in the wrong. Agnes then turned to the other girls in the room.

Do y'all have the crimping iron?

No Agnes, Sylvia replied immediately.

Nuh uh, Sarah shook her head.

Well then, y'all can't go around accusing people 'bout thieving fo' no good reason. Rhona, you owe your housemates an apology.

Rhona shook her head defiantly. Then finally, Sorry Sylvia...

It's cool crackhead, Sylvia mocked.

But Rhona gave another evil stare toward Sarah.

Pshh, she hissed. Hell if I'm ever 'pologize to you.

Agnes interjected. Rhona, you know exactly what you got to do to run your program right and be a good citizen.

Naw Agnes, 'cause she only up here one day and already she be causin' trouble. Rhona turned back to Sarah. You remember what I said. If I ain't got my stuff tomorrow, some bitch 'bout to find her shit disappearin' like a motherfucker. I ain't gonna name no names, but y'all feel me...

Sarah was perplexed but had no response.

Agnes waved Rhona out of the room. Come on then. Go back to sleep. 'Cause y'all gonna have plenty to talk out in group tomorrow.

Rhona walked out without another word.

Y'all OK with cleanin' up in here?

Yeah Agnes, we cool, Sylvia replied.

Agnes scanned Sarah up and down with an obvious mixture of sympathy and suspicion.

You good girl?

Yeah, Sarah responded. That was all Agnes seemed to want to hear, for now.

Alright then, goodnight ladies.

Night Agnes.

And fuck y'all very much! Rhona yelled from down the hall. Agnes rolled her eyes and left the girls' room to deal with her.

Sarah and Sylvia picked up their clothes off the floor and packed them back into the dresser. Finally, Sarah worked up the nerve to ask her roommate.

What's eatin' her?

Mang, that bitch be crazy as a motherfuck is all, Sylvia surmised. Sometimes for God knows why. Maybe they switching her meds up or sumpthin'. Who knows? Maybe she bleedin'. Fuck if I care…

Everyone knows y'all 'a couple a rug munchers up in there!

Can she hear us? Sarah asked with a whisper.

Naw, she just talkin' head is all.

As they folded their clothes back into place, Sarah locked eyes with Sylvia.

Hey. Thanks for having my back tonight.

It ain't no thing, Sylvia shrugged it off. But don't get used to it homegirl. 'Cause it's anything goes wit' these crazy bitches, you feel me?

Yeah, Sarah nodded.

Good. Then wanna know a secret?

Sure.

Just as she finished packing up, Sylvia pulled out Rhona's curling iron from under her bed and brazenly placed it in her top dresser drawer.

Sarah was shocked. You?

You ain't no snitch? Sylvia grew darkly cross. 'Cause ain't nobody round here got love fo' no snitch bitch.

No.

Cool, Sylvia nodded intently before packing herself into bed. Then I guess we's even.

***

So how you doing honey?

I'm straight.

School going OK?

Fine.

Do you like your new teacher?

Ms. Gatwyn cool I guess.

Rita pressed him to open up. Are you enjoying the new program?

You mean in the stupid class?

Do you really believe that? Rita treaded lightly.

Brenda, Rhona, and Rydell all up in there. They da dumb kids. Everybody knows that.

So you think you were picked because you're stupid too? Is that it?

Shoot. That's what y'all think.

Well I don't think you're stupid Tyrone. Not at all. I actually know you to be quite bright.

Then why am I goin'?

Because it's designed to treat students who've experienced a lot of stress at home.Silence.

We can move you out of there if you don't want to continue the program.

He paused.

Do you want to leave?

Man, I don't know...

Rita understood this to mean no. For now. You wanna talk about what's bothering you?

Ain't nuthin buggin' me, Tyrone insisted. But he still wouldn't meet Rita's eyes. So she gave him some comfort with a courtesy pause.

How was your phone call with your mom this weekend?

He nodded, pursing his lips as if agreeing with some communication left unspoken between them. Still, he said nothing aloud.

She seemed really happy to talk to you.

More nothing.

As far as I'm concerned, I think it's good that the two of you are speaking again.

Tyrone twitched. How come staff always gotta be listening in on our conversations all the time?

He was clearly animated now in his frustration with her intervention. I mean shit, ain't no kids never get no privacy up in here.

We've discussed this, honey. On weekends when I'm not here, staff has to supervise the call, because we don't know how stable she is yet.

She cool now, he defended.

But if she gets abusive with you again, staff has to intervene. That's the only reason your conversation is monitored. It's to protect you.

Yeah but it be annoying as fuck sometimes, 'scuse me for cussing.

Rita nodded. I understand.

More silence.

Are you OK? Rita scanned him for any noticeable signs of vulnerability, any point of entry to crack through that rough veneer of his defensive exterior.

Yeah, Tyrone flatly admitted. But I don't need no protecting from that queer bitch 'cause I'm 'a handle her just like I always done.

Rita was mildly taken aback by this effrontery toward his mother.

So her sexual orientation is still embarrassing to you? She said this not to infer, but rather to inquire.

Naw mang, I just can't stand havin' staff all listenin' in all the time when she talkin' 'bout her girlfriends.

I see, Rita nodded, affirming him. But you know staff understands whatever they hear is confidential-

Then tell that to Kevin, shoot, 'cause he always be makin' faces whenever she say stuff, and I'm like oooh, but I can't say nuthin', 'cause then the other kids c'tell whassup.

Do you think Kevin's reactions are intentional?

Tyrone pondered this for a moment. Naw, he don't mean nuthin' by it. And better him than Josh. Shoot. I just can't be havin' them up in my business all the time.

Well if you have to blame someone for that, dear, blame me. Because I made that decision for having them monitor your calls. They're just doing their job.

He paused, not yet ready to make her responsible for his current predicament.

But I will talk to Kevin, OK?

He nodded. Ayite.

And Josh too if you like.

Hell naw! I'd never hear the end of it from that fool.

Rita found herself pleased with Tyrone's ability to set this personal boundary with her. He'd come so far. She paused a moment to let him process their exchange. Then she offered, out loud, I think it's healthy that you're feeling safe enough in your relationship with your mom to share these concerns.

We wuz just talkin' like we always done, Tyrone dismissed.

Did she bring up your father again?

Tyrone shook his head again. Naw. But I guess you already knew that too. He shifted uncomfortably at the thought of Kevin briefing Rita on his weekend call.

Your mom understands that's he's still off limits right now. So I'm glad she's following the rules.

Mang, y'all and yo' rules...

Would you like to talk about him today?

Naw, Tyrone was certain. If she don't get to talk to me about him, then you don't neither.

I can arrange to have the three of us discuss him together, if that's what you would like.

Naw, I'm cool. Tyrone dismissed flatly. He obviously did not want to continue this line of conversation. And for today, they were almost out of time.

Honey, did your mom mention wanting to come visit again?

Tyrone's demeanor shifted with the question. He looked silently to the floor.

Honey?

She said she could come up this month.

Rita risked a short smile. A hint of progress. Maybe today-

Does that feel OK to you? She asked intently.

Tyrone was obviously conflicted.

Because I think you are ready for monitored visits.

He still would not look her directly in the eye. Do they still got to be here at the cottage?

Yes, Rita confirmed. In the beginning.

Tyrone's body language suggested a complete physical withdrawal from her response as he cringed his shoulders tightly in his chair. Then naw, I don't want her to come.

Rita also cringed inside. Because rules were rules.

Maybe we could meet at my office downtown? She left a short moment for his consideration.

But his withdrawal from the conversation now seemed complete. Tyrone did not change his disposition with her offer.

But then, seemingly out of nowhere, his mood shifted. Well If she makes the drive down, maybe we see, he posited, punctuated by a few more awkward twitches. But she gotta be da one to ask, he insisted.

Rita smiled once again. Finally. Progress.

***

Tyrone, Rydell, Rhona, and Brenda unloaded from the Excelsior House Astrovan the next morning at Thurgood Marshall High School, each carrying a brown bag. Joe hollered out to them from the drivers seat.

Y'all be good. Don't go sellin' off yo' lunches now.

Shit, ain't no hoodrats gon' eat no Excelsior food, Rhona mocked.

Even dem niggas from da projects be eatin' betta den us, Rydell agreed.

Joe playfully lunged for him. Boy, get to class 'fore I whip your ass 'front 'a all these civilized folk.

Rydell closed the van door before Joe could grab his arm. Mang get 'cho janky-ass van outta here fo' you embarrass yo'self. Oh I forgot. Too late!

Joe drove off to leave the four of them in front of the school, and together they walked to class. The other kids moving through the hallways ignored them.

Some weak-ass scrubs up in here, Rhona observed.

Shit, dees fools smart enough not to tap yo' stanky ass.

Fuck you Dell, Rhona swung at him with her open palm. But he leapt forward in front of the group just in time to dodge her.

Bitch you best keep runnin' fo' I slap you silly.

Bouyahhh!

The other students now noticed them, but none responded. As group-home kids, nobody wanted to have anything to do with them. A few of the girls flashed Rhona and Brenda dirty looks as they walked past.

Rhona immediately acted out in retaliation against their judgmental stares. Who you rollin' yo' eyes at bitch? Rhona hollered out.

The girls laughed out loud at her. One in particular, Taniqua, went so far as to mock Rhona's frenetic hair style.

What 'chu do, roll right out yo' trash can dis mornin' forget to comb yo' hair? No weave havin' mothafucker.

Fuck you bitch, I'm 'a check you right now!

Tyrone held Rhona's arm back firmly.

Yo Bern!

Brenda grabbed Rhona's other arm to pull her away.

Yo fuck these haters mang, Tyrone reasoned.

Yeah Rhona, these skeezas ain't worth no 602.

Rhona agreed, but still turned to holler at them as her friends led her down the hall. That's right 'hoe, now you don't say shit! I see uh huh...

Taniqua yelled back to her. Bitch we standin' right here, what it do? She pushed her hands against her chest to call for a tussle. Who da bitch now! Oh OK! That's right, get on wit' cho' group home up to class den...Go on. Y'all ain't shit.

Whoohh I'm a fuck that hoe up next time I see her, Rhona swooned.

The four made it to class without further incident.

Damn girl chill out, you hella hot, Tyrone insisted to Rhona as the four of them settled into their desks.

What 'chu got so much rage fo' today, shoot? Rydell asked, genuinely concerned.

Brenda outed the true source of her friend's aggravation. She on her period again.

Rhona rolled her eyes at Brenda. Now why you gotta go bringin' these flip-ass niggas up into my bus'ness like that?

Rydell popped off. Shit, yo' foul mouth already done that.

Frustrated, Rhona took her desk with the others.

Hi everyone.

Whattup Ms. G.

Hey.

Yo Ms. Gatwyn? Tyrone raised his hand perfunctorily.

Yes Tyrone.

Tell me we ain't in here 'cause we the stupid class.

Rhona rolled her eyes. My god, not again.

Brenda laughed. But Rydell was pissed at the comment. Naw 'cause then I shouldn't be in here with y'all.

Ms. G, let me apologize on behalf 'a these two fools right now, Rhona implored.

Is this a serious question Tyrone? Lisa focused upon him.

Naw, he just tryin' to rattle you, Rydell admitted.

He bein' a little punk is all. So don't listen to nuthin' that little boy be sayin' today, or any day for dat matta', Rhona agreed.

No, I'd like to be serious now, Ms. Gatwyn insisted. Tyrone, why do you think this class is for stupid people?

Tyrone smiled, unwittingly taking the bait. 'Cause you have us drawing stuff all day. I mean, it ain't like I'm complainin' an all that, but why you ain't makin' us do any REAL work?

Boy, quit runnin' yo' mouth and let the teacher teach!

Lisa nodded to Rhona to acknowledge her defense, but continued to press him on his own line of reasoning. OK Tyrone, I can see how you think that. I guess I didn't explain my approach to your lessons clearly. This is called cognitive therapy. We mix your academic work with art therapy in order to activate your brain's creative centers. This makes you more receptive to opening up and processing your emotions in our controlled setting without letting your defenses get in the way the way they might if you felt pressured to explain them to someone with words. By integrating your creative work with standard rote learning, we're trying to access any unsettled or residual feelings that might unconsciously be holding you back from focusing, or concentrating in a traditional academic setting.

Rydell immediately raised his hand.

Rydell, asking permission to speak is unusually out of turn for you.

Ms. G, I can tell you right now what's makin' it hard for ME to concentrate.

And what is that Rydell? Lisa asked incredulously, just waiting for his sarcastic response.

He turned to Rhona. That shirt. I mean damn Rhona, I knows you's a 'hoe, but mmmn girl, you's sportin' some big-ass titties today.

Rydell! Lisa shot him one of her rare scowls.

It's cause she on her period, Brenda chimed in again.

Brenda! Rhona finally lost it with her friend. My God!

Naw, 'cause you only get swollen titties like that when you's pregnant, Rydell insisted, turning to Brenda. She ain't on no rag. You get knocked up by one 'a yo' tricks Rhona? Rydell finished his train of thought aloud.

Rhona just shook her head to Ms. Gatwyn with complete embarrassment that she had any affiliation with Rydell whatsoever. Like he ever be getting' any 'a this.

Look Ms. Gatwyn, Rydell pointed to his classmate. She been goin' AWOL like every night, I'm serious, you can see them circles she sportin' right under her eyes.

Rhona stared daggers at Rydell, utterly insulted. What 'chu insinuatin' boy? You don't know shit. But uh-uh, you's done fo' now.

Alright enough, Lisa finally demanded, clearly annoyed by their childish behavior. Rydell, you need to be appropriate. And Tyrone, I want to get back to your question, if everyone thinks we can actually have a civilized conversation about this.

The Excelsior House kids all quieted up, not used to seeing their teacher's firm side this early in the morning.

You all may be SED, but you aren't stupid, and neither am I.

The kids couldn't say anything back to that.

Now you all know each other really well, and from what Joe's told me, you are more than a little bit comfortable getting up in each other's mess.

Lisa paused for a moment to refocus her comments. Now that can be a good thing for your therapy, with all of you quite

familiar with each other's traumas, but this drama you keep
bringing to class needs to quit, 'cause it isn't helping you in here,
and it certainly isn't helping me help you.

Rydell fronted again. So what if we don't want to help you?

Then you don't have to participate.

Fine.

So now what?

I don't know, you's the teacher.

You wanna give it a shot or not?

Rydell considered this. I'll get back to you, he posited
sarcastically.

Well you can always get back to Ms. Ellinwood's class.
Lisa couched the idea as a suggestion, knowing full well it would
be taken as a threat.

Oh hell no! Rydell shook his head. Ms. Gatwyn, you can't
send me back there, please! It's hell! He quickly turned into a
manipulated puppy. That lady's hella mean, I mean for realz.
Meaner even than you!

Brenda agreed. It's true. She make him clean everything in
the classroom every time he acts up even a little bit.

And them hamsters she be keepin' as pets is nasty, Rhona
offered.

She already stanky enough to begin with, Tyrone finished.

The students all laughed in agreement at this.

Then, what I'm hearing is that you want to stay here? Lisa
firmly concluded.

Hell yeah! Rydell finally relented.

Good. Because your classmates have done a lot of good
work here this past week, and your presence, as remarkable as this
might seem, has actually provided some stability for them to open
up.

See malfunctions, I'm helpin' y'all even despite myself.
Ms. G. just said so. Rydell was mildly proud of himself at the
thought of this.

I wouldn't go that far yet Rydell, Lisa interjected.

The students all laughed, sensing the cynicsm in Lisa's
honest observation.

Mang, why you gotta do me like that? Rydell sounded
genuinely embarrassed.

I can't be any worse than Ms. Ellinwood, she responded.

True dat, true dat.

Then you're staying?

Mang. Well then can I perform one of my raps during art therapy?

Rhona and Brenda rolled their eyes together. Ms. G, no, please send us out instead! 'Cause his whack-ass rhymes is torture!

Fuck y'all then, Rydell retreated, pouting at his desk.

Of course you can share them with us Rydell, Lisa assured with much resistance from the others.

Shoot.

As long as you're not going to be disruptive until then.

Ayite then, Rydell agreed with a newfound sense of purpose. You watch Ms. G, I'm 'a write a fly one just for you.

I can't wait, she smirked, giving him a wry smile.

No you can't, Rydell agreed, and started writing energetically into his notebook.

Oh yes you can, Rhona contradicted Ms. Gatwyn, in her defense.

OK then, Lisa smiled as she nodded to the rest of the obliging students to pull their Social Studies homework from their bags and formally begin with class.

***

Outside Cottage 2, the boys of Excelsior House played a game of basketball. The brothers Nate and Brandon, having just returned from a brief but unsuccessful trial reunification with their parents, were easily frustrated by their teammates' insufferable need to maintain possession of the ball at all times.

Yo Tyrone, pass already, shoot!

Mang I'm 'a take a shot off you Brandon.

Dude you never even hit the basket.

Quit your whining B, line staff Josh Crenshaw yelled from courtside. You're beginning to sound like Marcus.

Mang, yo it be kind 'a bright out here. Brandon held his hand over his eyes, mocking Josh's bald head. But he did not dare check Josh directly. Rydell, however, had no problem doing that for him.

Yeah Josh, turn your head away, I'm seein' sunspots off 'a yo' forehead.

What game you playin' D? From the looks 'a things, you spend too much time jerking off to make a damn shot.

You would be watching that wouldn't 'chu? Rydell threw right back to him.

Ugh, Nate intoned from the sidelines.

So are we ever gonna see some real ballin' outta you doggy dicks today? Josh huffed.

Yeah, if Tyrone ever takes a damn shot!

Mang, that dude ain't never givin' it up, Brandon complained.

Kendrick, Nate, and Rory made up the opposing team. While Nate and Brandon were gone, Kendrick and Rory had developed a good passing game. They easily traded shots, occasionally dropping off to Nate, whose standing free throw shot was good even if he couldn't dribble to save his life. Brandon, his smarter and more physically dominant younger twin, easily entered the key and laid it up after stealing the ball from his brother. Rory returned the gesture with his trademark hook, but missed.

Damn Rory, put your arms down, shoot, even the bugs be dyin' out here, Rydell mocked his body odor to impress Brandon.

Naw blood, they just be smellin' his feet, Nate returned.

Y'all hillbillies are hella stanky, Brandon dissed as he pulled his t-shirt over his mouth and nose.

Everyone laughed. But Rory couldn't very well defend himself as the only whiteboy in the group.

Meanwhile, Eric drew a picture of Sarah in his sketchbook as he sat on the wooden fence in the front yard, while Duane chimed in to the game from the sidelines. So when y'all gonna let me get in?

Soon as you grow about five inches you little runt, Josh ruffled Duane's shirt playfully.

Man dawg, why you gotta bag Josh?

'Cause you can't do shit about it, his staff replied plainly.

Yeah Josh keep him quiet, Nate called out.

You're next if you don't step it up son. Let's go!

The boys sprung back into action on the court. Brandon went in for another layup but Rory, clearly the most skilled of the players, easily stole it off, passing immediately to Tyrone, who shot from where he stood; the ball bounced off the rim, close enough for Rydell to lazily attempt a recovery, but Rory was all over the rebound before anyone else could react, jumping in front of Rydell to score off a single bounce.

Rydell gave Rory a small push mid-air, hard enough to cause him to land on his back. But it was Tyrone who put his hand out to pull him back up.

My bad dawg, Rydell offered.

It's cool, Rory dismissed.

But Brandon was pissed. He brought back up Rory's hygiene to downplay the kid's clear superiority on the court.

Man Rory, why you stink so bad?

This time, Tyrone defended his roommate. Why you gotta bag when you can' even make a shot?

Look whose talkin' T, Brandon hissed. I don't see you makin' nuthin', shoot.

Rydell, still feeling somewhat bad he ran Rory into the ground, didn't immediately jump into the mix.

But Brandon wouldn't let it go. 'Cause I can't be playin' with yo' stank cloud up in my face all the time.

This escalation prompted Josh to yell out from the sidelines. You need a time out B?

Naw I'm cool Josh. But underneath, Brandon clearly seethed.

Then stop acting like a queer bitch and play the damn game, Josh riled him on.

Brandon was not about to let it go. Bullied by Josh, he redirected his anger back to Tyrone.

Naw mang, I think you got me confused wit' these booty busters over here. He pointed out Rory and Tyrone.

Rydell and Nate cracked up. Uugh. Damn...

Rory tried to retort. How 'bout checkin' yo' mirror? He knew instantly that his comeback fell flat.

Brandon just looked to him as if he was a worthless piece of trash. Man, I hear y'all up in your room, suckin' off each other's dicks every night, that shit be carryin' all da way down the hall, case you're wonderin'.

For some reason, Tyrone got all sensitive over this. You ain't heard shit when you was gone...

This provoked Brandon, whose home visit plans were rudely interrupted, to funnel his rage at Tyrone. Dell, you best keep watch ova' dis fool right here, 'cause you might be next. 'Fore you know it he'll be crawlin' up in yo' bed tryin' to stick his willy in yo' booty while you's sleepin'.

I put a cap in his ass straight up! Rydell insisted.

Ugh, y'all's grimy, Brandon continued mocking Tyrone and Rory as he dribbled the ball.

Tyrone harped back. Why you gotta talk shit, just 'cause you ain't wanted by yo' folks?

This set Brandon off into his hyper-offensive mode while Nate clearly coped by withdrawing into moping, hunching his frame to let the more dominant Brandon defend them both, as he'd always done. Mang, all's I'm doin' is puttin' two and two together, Brandon dropped the ball to tick off reasons with his fingers. Rory be hella stinky, you always comin' to his defense like he your bitch, and you's a momma's boy son of a faggot...

Tyrone blew into a livid rage. He stepped toward Brandon to knock him out.

What 'chu gonna do? Brandon held his arms up outstretched.

Josh finally realized that his allowing the boys to crack on one another unrestrained had led far enough. T! Take a walk!

With Josh's bellowing roar challenging his stride, instead of hitting Brandon, Tyrone lunged into the house, kicking the front door hard into the back wall against its hinges, causing a loud reverberating shockwave to sound out across the garage door of Cottage 2 and ripple into the neighbor's yards across the circle.

From inside the house, Joe yelled from his office. Tyrone, what the hell!

More banging and kicking of objects inside the house could be heard by all the boys outside, before Tyrone trotted back out of the house with Joe following him.

Boy, you best check yo'self right now!

Naw fuck all that Joe, fuck you and fuck this place! He kicked at the short wooden fence surrounding the yard as he passed and stood firm out in the middle of the street.

Tyrone I ain't playin' with you, bring it down a notch, Joe commanded.

Tyrone was so steamed he couldn't even break himself into tears. The boys on the driveway basketball court watched the scene unfold on the circle as Joe motioned to Josh to follow him out into the street. By now, Agnes, Carly, Rhona, Brenda, Sylvia, and Sarah cleared out of Girls Cottage 1 to catch a view of the drama. Agnes and Carly tried shooing the girls from the porch back into the house, but once the nature of the situation became clear, they quickly realized any further efforts to do so were futile. With the audible yells emanating from the street, several neighbors eyes peered from behind the curtains lining the front windows of the surrounding houses.

You need any help Joe? Agnes called out from across the street.

Naw we got this, he replied calmly.

You ain't got shit! Tyrone barked.

T, check yourself now.

Mang fuck all that! Tyrone yelled out now. I ain't got nuthin' to do wit' none a y'all no mo'!

Josh and Joe strategically surrounded him.

You know you can't go walkin' off like this T, Joe reasoned.

I ain't on restriction! Josh, you best step off, Tyrone warned.

Be cool T, you just gotta settle down.

Tyrone started kicking the manhole in the center of the street.

Naw mang, fuck this! I ain't calmin' down 'till those motherfuckers stop talkin' they shit!

Sensing a break in Tyrone's rage, Joe gave Josh the signal. Together they lunged for him. Joe instantly took Tyrone's arms behind him and locked him into a full nelson, dragging him down onto the street forcefully with his own body weight. Josh quickly subdued Tyrone's legs before he could kick at Joe after using them to brace his fall.

A few of the boys were aghast at the fierce efficiency of the containment they had just witnessed.

Man, Joe dropped that fool quick!

He lucky Joe didn't box him-

Excelsior House protocol dictated that Tyrone be contained so he couldn't hurt himself or anyone else. So Joe and Josh opted to restrain him on the street outside rather than drag him back into the cottage.

They calmly sat there and waited for him to regain his own composure, until his breathing slowed and he realized he was still safe, though completely immobilized. Then they held him there for several more minutes until he was fully subdued and relaxed.

You OK big man? Josh finally offered.

Yeah Josh, I'm cool now.

Boy you getting stronger by the day, Joe hollered out playfully.

Tyrone started to laugh. You ain't had to do that in awhile huh Joe, he offered as an olive branch.

Son, you gonna put me in the cripple house you go off like that again.

You just be glad you didn't kick me, Josh interjected.

I may be stupid, but I ain't crazy, the subdued boy responded gravely.

Alright now, up you go, then back in the house, Joe directed. We straight?

Yeah mang.

The two men let him up. Tyrone picked out several pebbles embedded in his arms as he walked peacefully back into his room. None of the boys dared confront him on his way in, and he casually avoided their stares.

Alright ladies, show's over. Agnes and Carly shepherded the female spectators of Cottage 1 back inside. Agnes directed a concerned look of 'That could have been worse' to Joe. Joe agreed with a nod.

Alright you doggy dicks, in the house now! Josh now commanded to the boys on the driveway. Dinner chores are getting done early tonight.

Mang, the boys protested lamely, but they all did immediately what they were told.

***

Kevin arrived at 7 PM to work the overnight shift at Cottage 2. Duane, Nate, Eric, Rydell and Rory sat around on the couches watching Rydell and Kendrick play Tom Clancy's Rainbow Six on Xbox.

Hey y'all, Kevin greeted the boys.

Whassup Kevin, Duane and Rory responded.

Welcome back Nate. Kevin was happy to see him.

Nate tossed a nod his way but nothing more.

Oh no, not you again tonight, Rydell blurted.

Nice to see you too 'Dell.

Mang why you always gotta be workin'?

Cause I'm on the schedule, that's why, Kevin dismissed simply.

Man Josh, when Maurice coming back?

Don't you worry about it, Josh commanded.

Bunch 'a haters up in here… He returned to concentrating on his game with Kendrick.

What's up Josh? He and Kevin exchanged handshakes at the kitchen counter.

Kevin nodded toward the couch where Rydell sat. What's got into him?

He's just a little asshole, Josh described loudly so everyone could hear them. Ain't that right Dell?!

Rydell nonchalantly flipped off Josh with his free hand without losing his focus on the TV.

Josh laughed with a deep, bellowing roar, relishing the success of his provocation.

Mang, it be kinda bright in here again, Rydell feigned having to squint at the TV. Go put yo' hat back on, Josh, shoot.

Man, damn! Kendrick sighed, clearly annoyed by Rydell's chatter during their game. He compensated by flicking at his controller with increasing intensity.

Chill out Kendrick, we'z on the same team-

Man, fools always gotta be talkin' while they playin'!

It was clear Kendrick needed absolute quiet to concentrate. Kevin and Josh resumed their conversation at a lower volume.

Where's everyone at? Kevin inquired.

Marcus and Julio have late curfew tonight. Brandon and Tyrone are on room restriction.

The entire night?

Yup.

What up Kevin, Tyrone interrupted them with a yell from his room down the hall.

Yo T! Kevin shot back.

Uugh! Kendrick hollered from the couch, pounding the controller against the cushion.

Nate laughed at Kevin's response. Aw, he be sounding hella white when he yell Yo! The boys cracked up hard over this. Kevin let it slide.

Kevin tuned back in to his debriefing with Josh. Those aren't the two I'd expect to be on shutdown. Didn't Brandon just get back?

Yeah, and already the little bastard provoked T into kickin' out the front door and knockin' the kitchen table over.

Kevin shook his head. He was doing so well too.

Duane chimed in, getting off the couch to seize his opportunity to suck up to staff, Mang Kevin, you shoulda seen it, Josh and Joe straight dropped that fool!

Nate and Rory cracked up. But Kendrick choked, Damn y'all some loud-ass kids!

Josh immediately scolded Duane. Nobody asked your opinion! He playfully faked a lunge toward him. Am I gonna have to go to work on those naps again?

Duane retreated to the couch laughing. Aw hell naw Josh!

From their rooms, Tyrone and Brandon chucked at something shared between them.

Shut up in there, y'all are on shutdown! Josh yelled in their general direction.

Brandon immediately hissed under his breath, Bald-ass bitch...

What was that?! Josh yelled again.

This time, no response.

So Tyrone needed containing?

Yeah, but he was real good about it. Calmed right down when we grabbed him.

That's 'cause he knew y'all woulda tore him up Josh, Rydell inserted his opinion from the couch, You know you woulda.

Yeah, you're right about that one D, Josh bragged. Though you'll never hear me say it. His bellowing laugh filled the room again.

Mang, y'all love any opportunity you get to beat on us kids, Rydell retorted.

Kendrick was now beyond frustration. Mang will you EVER stop runnin' yo' mouth while we'z playin', shit!

I don't think he can, Rory observed honestly.

OK little Kendrick, don't go gettin' in no tizzy, we still gots to take level six.

Then do it and shut up already...

Anything else I should know? Kevin returned to his conversation with Josh.

Naw, that's about it. Good luck with our little disturbed children tonight. Josh packed up to leave.

Finally, Rydell seemed pleased about something. One hater staff down, one to go...

See you girls in the morning, Josh threw out to them as he left.

Later Josh.

See you baldy.

Soon after, Kevin walked down the hall to check on Brandon and Tyrone.

How you doing Brandon? He was reading a comic book.

I'm cool, he nodded, paying enough respect to look up from the page to acknowledge this staff his hadn't seen in six weeks. Brandon liked Kevin enough.

Welcome back.

He nodded a second time and returned to his book.

Kevin knocked at Tyrone's door. It was only cracked open. Even so, he could see Tyrone silently weeping in his pillow.

Can I come in?

Tyrone's head nodded.

You mind if I sit?

Again, Tyrone nodded. Kevin was always clear to remind the boys, especially Tyrone, that they were in complete control of their personal space around him, unless they needed to be contained in order to prevent them from hurting themselves.

Kevin sat at the base of the bed. He knew, based upon Tyrone's previous experiences taking beatings from his father, that he needed to approach slowly.

You OK big man? Kevin asked sympathetically.

No…Tyrone continued to weep.

What happened?

Tyrone pulled the pillow away from his face to reveal his cheeks smeared with tear streaks.

Mang, we was just playin' ball, and everyone started ganging up on me, so I threw it back at 'em, and then I went off, and now I'm on house restriction and I'm not gonna get to go to the dance with Rhona next week…

Did Joe say you're in that much trouble?

Naw, but I know he and Agnes and Rita gonna hate 'cause it's my third time going off.

Kevin put his arm on Tyrone's shoulder. Surprisingly, he didn't flinch. He knew Kevin well enough to know he wasn't a perp.

I'm sorry T.

Man that shit wuddn't even my fault, he whimpered again at the thought.

Kevin reflected hard for a moment to choose the right words to comfort him. He settled on the truth, probably the best in this situation.

Well T, you know the best thing you can do for yourself is to run your program right.

Tyrone fought back more tears, confronted with his own failings at impulse control. But it ain't fair Kevin, 'cause kids be hella provokin' me knowin' I can't get out and take no walk or get outta they space when I'm agitated. 'Cause if I get another AWOL the cops'll take me back to the hospital.

Kevin considered his dilemma thoughtfully. From Tyrone's perspective, this seemed totally valid. He wondered what he would do in his client's situation if he couldn't go take a long walk unaccompanied whenever he got steamed about something.

Well there has to be some other way, Kevin finally offered. Can't you take space in your room next time you get heated?

Tyrone only shook his head. Naw, 'cause it be hella claustrophobic up in here, that's why I be kickin' shit all the time when I'm mad...

Kevin had little more to consider. We'll let's see if we can talk to Rita about you taking space down on the circle if you need to gather yourself next time, sound alright?

Tyrone nodded. Yeah, if staff ever trust me walkin' off again.

You know running your program right is the best way to build that trust back up, right T?

Tyrone didn't want to take full responsibility for what an answer to that would demand.

I mean, even if Joe and Agnes do keep you from goin' to that dance, getting violent again is the last thing you want to be doing for yourself, right?

Tyrone whined once again, Shiiiiit...

Alright then dawg, you gonna be cool tonight? Kevin asked with true sympathy in his voice.

Tyrone looked back to him, gave a quick nod and knocked fists with Kevin.

Good, Kevin breathed, satisfied. And tomorrow, I'll talk to Rita.

Tyrone, much calmer now, buried his face in the pillow once again. Taking his cue to give Tyrone his space to process this, Kevin left the room, cracking the door just as he found it.

Kevin returned to the living room space to find the Xbox off and all four of the boys engaged in animated conversation.

Yo mang, Tupac got capped by Biggie's peeps, everybody know that.

Hell naw, cus they wuz friends for hella long.

They be makin' hella dollas together off they beef-

Shit they shoulda put 'em in da ring, I bet Pac would a fucked Biggie right up.

Naw blut, Biggie be hella fat, all he gotta do is sit on the dude...

Hell naw, cause once Tupac start swingin' on that fool he be losin' his fist in one a dem rolls. Then' Biggie grab him and the shit's over!

Biggie wadn't as big as Tiny. And ain't nobody box a dude like that 'less he pull some kind a weapon.

Shit, Tupac hella cut, you see that six pack? 'Cause he wus boxin' hella dudes in jail.

Biggie ain't never been to the penn.

Naw, he wuz just cappin' fools from the block when he was slingin' dat rock.

Just like he done to 'Pac.

Naw mang, the government took both those dudes out, for realz.... Ain't nobody lettin' no niggas get too rich.

Shit, Puffy be stackin' mo' bills than all 'dose dudes put together. And he ain't even dead.

That's because Puffy be hella white, vacationin' up in da Hamptons and shit.

Naw blut.

For realz...

But seriously yo, those motherfuckin' crime scenes wuz airtight. How else you gon' shoot some famous dude in the middle 'a Las Vegas after a boxin' match wit' hundreds 'a people on the street and no one saw nuthin'? Only the gov'ment can pull off that kinda black ops shit.

FBI, CIA, sumpin'.

Whoeva. And da coroner's report said dem slugs in his chest wus military issue. I seen hella dudes dropped in da hood with that kind 'a shit. You remember, Kendrick?

Yup.

They probably hit Pac from on top 'a some building. From one 'a dem casinos on da strip.

Hell naw.

Shoot, I wouldn't put it past those motherfuckers for realz! Ain't nobody in the government give a fuck 'bout two dead niggas no matter how rich they is...

That's why they didn't solve the crime.

OK guys, watch the language now. Kevin usually interjected only when the boys swore at each other, not in normal conversation. But now they were taking it a little too far.

Clearly agitated from events earlier in the day, Rydell focused in on Kevin in order to slowly escalate the other boys to turn on him. He calculated that with enough pressure applied to

Kevin as solo staff in Cottage 2 this evening, he could wrestle his handle on the situation away before too long.

So Rydell initiated his full-fledged assault campaign. Mang, why you gotta hate all the time, Kevin?

Duane agreed. Josh let us be swearin' all the time.

Kendrick left the room to use the bathroom. Rory remained silent.

Rydell continued on with Kevin. Nobody like you dude. Go away. Go back down the hall. Just get outta our faces.

Eric's hands became animated. Yo, his hands be hella chalky after gettin' with Tyrone!

Eric, stop it, Kevin commanded, already sensing what Rydell was trying to do.

Uugh, Nate looked over. Bitch can suck a dick!

Nate! Inappropriate language. You're going to lose your citizenship points if you keep it up.

Yo, stop ear hustlin' man!

Yeah, this an A and B conversation so C your way out of it.

OK, well, it's chore time anyway.

We already done those.

Yeah, chores got done early tonight, so SNAP!

BOYAHHH!

OOOH brown regal, damn it's illegal.

Check.

Bitch can suck a dick.

Nate! Go to your room.

Mang I ain't going in there. Shoot.

Rydell smiled at all the commotion he'd caused.

Kevin now walked assertively over to Rydell. He towered over the couch where Rydell sat, figuring if he could take down the ringleader, he could effectively calm the other boys.   Rydell looked up at him with a blank stare, clearly relishing the challenge Kevin set with his eyes. They both knew Julio was no longer around to diffuse the situation about to arise between the two of them.

Mang, you best get away from me fo' I kick yo' shins in...

You touch me and you go right to jail Dell. And you know it.

Mang you best step off, 'cause I got witnesses.

Eric was clearly distraught at the lack of safety permeating his environment. Signs of an active episode of Tourrettes Syndrome started leaking out of him as he nervously flicked his hands.

Chalky hands, ha ha ha, chalky hands!

Kevin rolled his eyes. Eric, stop it already.

OK, Eric obliged, muttering incorrigibly to himself.

Rory attempted to bargain Rydell down. C'mon man, just cool it already.

Nobody asked your smelly ass nuthin', Rory, Rydell retorted icily. He turned back to face Kevin. Why you leaning over me punk?

Kevin bent down to get right into his face, aiming to intimidate by violating his personal space, with his arm extended, pointing his finger down the hall. Get in your room. You've lost all your citizenship points for the evening.

Mang, I don't give a fuck about that-

Then there go your language points too!

Mang, fuck you!

But instead of pummeling him with his legs, Rydell slinked away from Kevin, afraid he would snap. Because Kevin did, sort of. As Rydell slithered down the hall towards his room, Kevin started to follow him.

That's a verbal abuse Rydell. You're back to Level 1 for all of next week-

Mang, fuck you...Get away from me before I do something.

Yeah, and what you gonna do? Kevin taunted him now, trying to save whatever face he'd lost by letting Rydell check him back on the couch. Touch me and you become a 602. Is that what you want?

Mang, I told you, motherfucker. Stop following me.

I'm going to make sure you go right to your room.

Mang, you can't do shit to me!

Rydell paced into his room and grabbed his jacket. Kevin was steamed by his insolence now, so he followed Rydell inside, going so far as to block the doorway, a clear violation of Excelsior House policy if a client did not need to be physically contained.

Yo mang, get the fuck outta my room!

You are on room restriction for the night, Kevin proclaimed.

Like I said, fuck you, you don't tell me what to do, you hot breath, raggedy shoe-ass bitch. Nobody like you because you don't know when to stop. Rydell approached Kevin, apparently to get him to step aside, but Kevin would not back down. So Rydell hollered out to the other residents.

Yo, this is child abuse! Kevin be forcing hisself on me! Tyrone and Brandon peeked their heads out of their rooms while Nate and Duane watched from the front room.

Dude, just stay in your room already, shit! Tyrone, having heard their actual exchange, called out to Rydell.

Hell naw! Rydell yelled toward his door, through Kevin.

You need to run your program, Dell, Kevin reiterated, more calmly now.

Don't listen to a damn thing he say! Nate called out to encourage Rydell's defiance. Bitch can suck a dick!

Nate! Enough. You get into your room now too!

Eric escalated his own taunting of Kevin. Chalky-ass hands, uhh Kevin bootybusting Rydell!

Alright, the entire cottage is on shutdown!

Duane balked. Aw, hell naw. I ain't even done nothing!

Duane, get in your room please. He did, but not without protest.

Mang, this is some bullshit!

Hatin'-ass staff!

Encouraged that several of the boys had taken his direction, Kevin called out again to Nate and Eric standing at the end of the hallway. You two, in your rooms!

Naw, fuck that!

Nate, watch your language.

Bitch can suck a dick.

He turned back to Rydell.

Excuse me, Rydell insisted, gesturing for Kevin to step aside.

When Kevin did not move, Rydell repeated himself more sarcastically.

Excuse you.

Where do you think you're going? Kevin snapped.

I'm outta here.

You aren't goin' anywhere. He put out his hand to the wall to stop Rydell.

Yo, get yo nasty hands away from me, everyone can see I ain't being violent.

You're not leaving this house! Kevin paced, knowing he had no real control over him.

Mang, fuck you! Rydell yelled right into his face. You gonna push me, bitch? Then do it for realz, otherwise you best get out of my way!

Clearly shocked into reason, Kevin backed off, in a fresh attempt to de-escalate the situation.

Fine, you wanna not run your program, fine, you know the consequences. If you're going to go, then go. He pointed toward the hallway.

Rydell calmly walked past him and strutted triumphantly down the hall to the other end of the house. That's why nobody like you dude, you can't handle shit on your own.

Rydell slammed the door to Cottage 2.

You know you gotta go after him, Duane informed him with mild concern.

No he don't, Tyrone responded flatly from his room.

Kevin tried explaining himself to the boys. If he wants out, that's his right. He's AWOL now. So the police will pick him up when they find him.

Naw mang, that ain't cool, he's just doin' it so you go after him...

Everyone else, in their rooms now!

With their shit-disturbing ringleader now off the premises, Nate and Eric headed sulking to their rooms. Only Kendrick and Rory were allowed to remain in the front room.

Mang, you said the whole cottage wus on shut down! Brandon complained to Kevin, as his brother interrupted his privacy by joining him in their double room.

Yeah, that ain't fair!

Staff be hella playin' favorites.

Alright fine, Brandon, you are right. Everyone to their rooms. Rory and Kendrick, that means you too.

But we didn't do anything.

Holey-ass shoes...

Staff be BUGGIN'.

Mang, that's why nobody like you, Brandon rattled off to Kevin, understanding well now how to manipulate him, based upon Rydell's efficient demonstration this evening.

Go to bed y'all, Lights out.

Mang...

Kevin a bitch tonight.

He always a bitch.

Quiet down or you're going to lose your language points for tonight.

Mang, fuck all that.

Fuck off.

Fuck this!

Just 'cause Julio ain't here to cool us down.

Dude can't handle himself...

Staff be hella haters.

That's why nobody like you dude...

As the voices trickled off, Kevin called the police. When they arrived at the front door at Cottage 2, the boys had already settled down. So Kevin dutifully filed a missing persons report on Rydell, then informed Joe by phone of the situation.

You need me to come down there?

I think they're done for the most part.

OK. But we gon' have it out in the mornin'.

Right.

And don't be fallin' asleep tonight, 'specially in case the cops bring 'Dell home.

I know Joe.

Ayite then.

Bye.

Rydell hiked the twelve blocks across I-280 to Holly Park and lay his body down on the third bench from the jungle gym, the one with the phat view of Hunters Point and East Oakland beyond. He could have trodded the quick eight up Excelsior Avenue to spend the night in McLaren Park but naw, fuck all that. Cops would be keepin' they eyes out there fo' him fo' sho', lookin' to swoop him once that hater Kevin grew the balls to call them. And besides, who knew what crazy fucks roamed around there after hours. Besides, po-po wouldn't have no reason to shine they spotters up in this playground anyhow. They probably was thinkin' he'd gone downtown. Dumbass pigs. And this way the sun would wake his ass up to a nice view, fo' he grabbed a donut down on Mission street and made his way back up the hill to Excelsior House just after shift change, 'cause he didn't want to see no more of that hater-ass bitch Kevin tomorrow. But it wuz cool, 'cause whatever came of his AWOL tonight, Rydell knew he could handle it. 'Cause any punk staff thinkin' he can play 'Dell over some authority bullshit ain't never got nuthin' over on him. And that's all that matters when you'z livin' the institution life. So tomorrow, he'd be back to deal with the AWOL, take it one day at a time for a while and handle his business, come what may till shit blew over and everybody be back to normal. Like he always had, like he always would. Besides, Rita'd be sure to have his back all da way, she even said so straight up...She promised she'd fight for him 'till the bitter end, so ain't no way some motherfuckin' weak-ass staff be causin' Joe to dump her favorite client over some cut and run bullshit for one night. And even 'dough the park table was cold as a morgue slab tonight, it sho' beat falling asleep on one 'a dem Muni owl buses. Shyite. Too high profile in 'dere anyways if po-po came checkin' fo' him in a serious fashion. But not here. Not tonight. For now this'd work. Because it was his spot. Always wuz, always would be.

***

Lucy Gutierrez came home to find Keyshawn hard asleep on the couch. She heard Tre crying in his crib in the other room. Moving swiftly into their bedroom, she picked him up to pat his back.

There you go 'gain, young soldier. You're all good now. Mamma's home.

She walked back out into the living room where Key was snoring all gravelly-like. She lightly tapped his feet.

Yo Key.

Damn. What woman?

Your son was in the bedroom cryin'.

He fine up in his cradle.

I told you he could suffocate if he rolls over. You checked on him lately?

Yo he ain't chokin' if he cryin'.

That's not the point, K. You said you'd watch him while I went to the market.

Just like I done.

How long you been asleep?

Key put a pillow over his face to block himself both from the sunlight spilling through the front curtain and from her nagging.

What if I hadn't come back 'till later? Your son'd still be sittin' there cryin' all night for his daddy.

Well good thing you's home now ain't it? He ain't done nuthin' to hisself.

She put up her hand with a sign to dismiss him. Of course, Keyshawn did not see this.

Shoot woman, you knows betta than t' wake me from my nap. I gots to work tonight.

Yeah, your father always workin', she muttered under her breath to Tre while patting his back. Ain't got no time for his son or his momma neitha.

Tre remained calm throughout this exchange as Lucinda, finally exasperated with Keyshawn, carried their son back into the bedroom and shut the door.

***

Clara Rodriguez arrived at Altegard Public Housing Complex in the Western Addition just before five o'clock, her last home visit of the day. Officer Michael Moreno was scheduled to meet her in the parking lot by 4:45 PM. She hoped tonight she wouldn't have to pull Boyce Turner from his mother, Tayisha Briggs, because Tayisha had been so good about making all of her drug rehabilitation and vocational training meetings these past several months, in accordance with her probation stipulations for keeping her son. But recently Tayisha had skipped out on several of her appointments. So Clara was naturally concerned for Boyce, who Clara had earlier advocated be placed at home with her during

Tayisha's recovery. It didn't make sense at the time for Clara to remove Tayisha's son from her life while she was doing everything right, keeping herself on the straight and narrow. Of course Tayisha's PO, Jorge Andrade, had other inclinations; he was ready to pull her back into county at first instance of parole violation, but it was more Clara's job (and she was determined) to make the case that her son still benefitted from the stable home his mother, now drug free, had been working to provide him. Of course, should mom be re-incarcerated, Boyce would enter into foster care like his brother. So Jorge offered to work with Clara and the judge on this. As Boyce's CPS worker, Clara just had to verify through this unannounced home visit that Boyce was still thriving under his mom's care and that Tayisha was clean despite her repeated absences from work. But if the opposite was true, then there would be hell to pay on all sides. Jorge would immediately yank Tayisha back into county for probation violation, while Clara would have to place Boyce in a new group home. And how all of this might affect his older brother Marcus - Clara didn't even want to begin with that. Marcus still couldn't stand the site of Clara after she pulled him from Tayisha and his brother the first time their mother went into police custody for drugs. It was Clara who ultimately advocated for prison time for mom in order to help Tayisha clean up her act. Though she did it for Marcus's own sake, she never expected Marcus to ever see it that way. Because Marcus was the man of the house, and with his own terms for placement at Excelsior House, Clara knew of his subversions of the mandatory monitored home visits imposed by Juvenile Court to keep him at safe distance from his mother. And yes, Clara know Marcus made his own unannounced trips to see the family, mostly to keep an eye on his brother and to set Tayisha straight whenever she needed it. Because in many ways he was the only man his mother ever knew to depend upon. But because of this unique codependent nature of their relationship, and for his own emotional safety, Marcus' judge mandated no unsupervised contact with the family. Yet Clara knew Marcus would have none of that. He had a brother to raise and a mom to keep on the right track. So she kept her knowledge of his periodic bus rides north to herself.

And so today would create a shit storm if Tayisha was high and Boyce was home. That's why Moreno offered to come and assist her with the extraction. Things would surely turn ugly with the neighbors if she had to pull Boyce and have Tayisha put back into custody for abuse or neglect.

Officer Moreno rolled up at 5:07 PM. Yo Tia, sorry I'm late. Moreno planted a kiss on Clara's cheek. She'd watched him grow up as a child in the Outer Mission neighborhood they both called home.

I know you only make it on time for fútbol.

Naw Tia, see, I had to wrap up my paperwork so I could get right over to school.

Michael Moreno was taking night classes at San Francisco State University to earn his Masters degree in Counseling. Clara had encouraged him to apply to graduate school after he completed the police academy. Miguel was always a good egg. He wanted to build the necessary skills for better understanding the psychology of the people he worked with through outreach as an officer on the streets.

We can do this another night, Clara offered.

Naw it's cool, Tia. I can be late if this stretches out.

Clara patted his shoulder and the two ascended the steps up to Tayisha's unit. Halfway up an elderly junkie shooting up in the stairwell waved at them menacingly. Everyone in the complex understood the intent of her breach into their domain.

You want a taste of the monster? You best leave those kids alone.

He half-threateningly poked a dirty syringe in the direction of Clara's leg as she passed.

Moreno did not miss a beat. He immediately forced himself between Clara and the junkie, kicking him in the chest hard while grabbing the wrist of the hand holding the needle. The junkie dropped the syringe quickly, wincing in pain.

Yo mayne, I wasn't gonna do nuthin'!

Yo holmes, that's attempted murder, Moreno declared, knowing the situation was diffused.

He quickly handcuffed the junkie, grabbing the syringe and returning to his vehicle to dispose of it properly in a sterile waste bin in the trunk of his patrol car. He then moved the apprehended man into the backseat without reading him his rights.

Yo porkchop, you need to leave us people alone!

Shut up, Moreno scoffed and shut the door. He opted not to call in an additional patrol car to monitor the scene while he accompanied Clara upstairs.

When he returned to Clara sitting in the stairwell, she was pale from the encounter.

Do you think he was serious about that?

Don't matter, Moreno dismissed.

Thank you, Niño. She put her hand on his shoulder again.

Now let's go do what you gotta do, Moreno replied.

By now, word of mouth that Moreno had roughed up the local dope fiend had passed between many residents of the complex. They attempted to shout the duo down.

You goin' to jail for dat, po-po!

Police brutality!

Smile fo' da camera, yo!

What your badge number?

Can't no one leave a brother be.

Dem Mexicans here to steal our babies again.

Run Tayisha Run!

Moreno and Clara ignored the hollering as they approached the unit. Clara knocked twice. Boyce answered, immediately recognizing his social worker and letting her in. He eyed Officer Moreno suspiciously.

Clara bent down to give Boyce a hug. He returned her gesture.

Have you come to take me away again? Boyce asked immediately.

No, Clara half lied. She genuinely hoped it will not come to that. But first she had to see Tayisha to know for herself. Is your momma home?

She at the store getting groceries.

Clara inspected the house, opening the refrigerator door. Empty.

She checked the rest of the house. Though it was not clean, there were no immediate signs of neglect, beyond the fact that Tayisha was not home.

Clara knew that with the scene played out in the stairwell only moments before, Tayisha would make a ghost of herself if she did in fact have something to hide. And if Tayisha didn't show up because she knew Clara was sittin' here waiting for her, Clara would be forced to report Boyce as abandoned and would have to pull him tonight. So Clara made a quick calculation. Stick around or leave now and give Tayisha the chance to come back home high if she needed to, only to buy her enough time to get her stuff straightened out once and for all, knowing Clara would be back. This was the only way Clara reasoned to give Tayisha one last shot at keeping her son.

So Clara would return another time. She squatted down to address Boyce, setting her hand gently upon his shoulder.

Will you tell your mother I came by to see her?

With the police?

Clara sighed. Yes Boyce, please let her know that, too. Tell her we need to talk, OK?

Is momma in trouble, Clara?

Not yet, Clara smiled. Not if she calls me when she gets home. But when you see her, please to tell her to call, will you do that?

The boy's expression betrayed a hint of worry.

You believe me Boyce, don't you? She looked kindly into his eyes.

With this gesture, Boyce nodded genuinely. Because Clara had never lied to him before.

OK dear, then I will see you later. Clara hugged him.

See you, Clara. Boyce waved back to her before shutting the door behind them.

Moreno appeared dejected from the entire encounter. You know you're gonna have to pull him sooner or later.

Let's hope it's later.

You always had faith in people who no one else would, Tia.

People can change Niño.

Yeah, but not as often as you think.

Look at you. Was I wrong then?

Moreno couldn't answer her.

I wasn't, she replied, smiling to him confidently.

He returned her gesture gratefully.

You call me when you want to come back, OK?

OK, I will. See you, Niño.

Ciao, Tia.

He kissed his neighborhood auntie and returned to his unmarked patrol car with the dope fiend still sitting in the backseat.

Clara waved to him as he waited protectively for her to get into her car and drive off in the opposite direction.

Officer Moreno turned the block and dumped the dope fiend at the nearest corner with a warning to avoid a police report, giving his mentor Clara Rodriguez and her clients cover to make her "initial" unannounced home visit again when they returned in several days. He then mouthed a silent prayer for the safety of Boyce and Tayisha as he made his way to campus for night class, while Clara returned home from this emotional day to a warm bubble bath and a bottle of her favorite pinot grigio.

***

Joe Rodgers convened group with the boys of Cottage 2 immediately after school. Rita and Jamey, his two on-site therapists, were on hand to moderate.

Yo, what up, Joe?

Y'all know why we here.

Hell yeah, 'cause Rydell be AWOL.

He ain't never comin' back.

Good.

Kevin be hatin' on him and that fool walked right out.

Shit, Rydell was about to pop him good.

Staff be all up in his face.

Damn, hella haters up in here.

Kevin got hisself a PHD.

Y'all gonna fire him already?

Nobody like that dude.

Boys, Rita interjected, we need to get to the bottom of what happened last night.

The clients grew silent.

Oh, I'll tell you what happened, Brandon offered. Kevin was bein' hella strict and Rydell was talkin' shit and Kevin didn't like it so he got all up in Rydell's face and dude wus about to chin check him, so Rydell goin' back to his room to cool off 'cause he got hella steamed but then Kevin can't leave a brother be so he walked back into the dude's room, invadin' his personal space.

Did Kevin ever threaten Rydell? Rita asked solemnly.

Hell yeah, I heard the whole thing, Brandon asserted without question.

No he didn't, Rory interjected soberly.

You didn't see shit, Rory, 'cause you wuz in the other room.

Yeah, well, I know he ain't done that.

Why you all up on Kevin's side anyways? Shit, Brandon retorted spitefully.

Tyrone intervened. Don't even lie, Rory, you wus in the kitchen. But I was in my room on restriction and I heard the whole thing, just like Brandon.

Rita again asked, but now to Tyrone. Did you ever hear Kevin threaten Rydell?

Naw, but that dude don't know when to let us kids cool off. He wus all up in our faces tryin' to get us to bow down to his shit. And it was hella annoying. But naw, he ain't threatened D.

And 'Dell be hella checkin' on him. But he didn't do nuthin'.

So how did this all start? Jamey prodded.

Tyrone reflected silently for a minute, then spoke truthfully. Kevin was killin' everyone's fun, turnin' off the Xbox sayin' they needed to do some homework so 'Dell came at him. And Kevin be gettin' hella steamed at 'Dell in general, so he threw a Verbal on him, and 'Dell told him to fuck off and Kevin sent him to his room, but he wouldn't go, so Kevin started hovering over him near the couch, gettin' all up in his face and 'Dell be like, 'Get away from me dude!' But Kevin kept hangin' over the him 'till 'Dell walked away, calling him a faggot and throwin' up a fuck you with his fist. That's when Kevin followed him down the hall...

So you all feel Kevin was physically inappropriate with 'Dell? Joe clarified.

He just hella annoying.

Yeah, that dude bugs.

It's cause he ain't got no pull with us so he's got to use his body to be all intimidatin'...

But did he touch any of you? Joe inquired bluntly.

The boys reacted viscerally. Uugh, naw. Hell naw.

Chalky ass hands!

Eric, Jamey reprimanded, shaking his head. Eric quickly retreated back into his Tourettes shell.

Rita then shifted the tone of the conversation. I want to ask all of you a serious question now.

The boys quieted down in respect for their matriarch.

Do you all feel safe with Kevin as your staff?

Hell naw, that dude can't control shit! Brandon immediately proclaimed.

But he don't mess wit' you if you don't talk shit first, Tyrone defended.

Nate now spoke up. But you gots to admit, that dude do get hella pissed when you flip shit on him or check him.

True dat, true dat, Tyrone agreed.

Duane? Kendrick?

He cool I guess.

Shoot.

OK, Jamey was satisfied.

Rita shifted the interrogation to its next order of business. So we want to ask you all then, how do you feel about Rydell continuing to live here?

The look on each of their faces make it painfully clear to the therapists and staff alike that the boys didn't want to sell him out. But it was also equally clear none of them liked him much either.

Remember, this is a safe, confidential environment, Jamey reminded. What is said in group stays right here in this circle.

Marcus was the first to respond. In all honesty, that kid's a little bitch.

Like you ain't, Tyrone mocked to defend Rydell. He just jacked up on his meds all the time.

Bitch can suck a dick, Nate stated bluntly.

Nate! Language!

He always gonna be an asshole, Julio offered.

He cool, Tyrone responded, though it was obvious he was too scared of Rydell to badmouth him outright.

He talks hella shit, but then again who don't, Eric replied honestly.

Duane?

I'm straight. But it was clear Duane held no love for him either.

Brandon chided them all. Man, y'all a bunch 'a snitchin'-ass bitches up in here.

Brandon? How do you really feel about Rydell continuing to live here? Jamey prodded him.

Why, you want me to talk head so you got a reason to get ridda him? Hell naw. He already AWOL. So he goin' straight to the halls when he come back anyways.

Marcus corrected him. Naw blut, 'cause Rydell a 300. 'Till you's 602 springin' placement ain't no crime.

He's right, Jamey agreed. But that doesn't mean he needs to stay here if he is disrupting the stability of the home.

What Joe, you ready to toss him to the street just like that? Brandon's tone was layered with disgust.

Ain't no decisions been made yet B, Joe confirmed to him.

Shit is fucked up, man.

He ain't even on probation...

First you want us to snitch out D, now you wanna kick him to da curb? Naw, I see what y'all doing, and I ain't sayin' nuthin', Brandon huffed proudly. 'Specially to none 'a you suckas.

Yo, take a step back, young soldja, Julio admonished him quickly. Staff just figurin' out they mess is all. The dude don't make life easy 'round here, and y'all knows it.

Can't you just give him more Dexedrine like you do on weekends to shut him up? Eric asked the therapists bluntly. Staff won't be having no more problems then.

We'll explore Rydell's treatment options with him when he comes home. You all know each of you have a say in your dosage and regiment, Rita assured them. Rydell is no different.

A few of the boys scoffed out loud at the blatant baselessness of this previous comment. Dissatisfied with his own prescriptions, Tyrone quickly changed the subject.

Yo Joe, ain't yo' pig friends put out an APB on that fool yet?

You know half the city looking fo' his ass 'cause shit, Joe be in hella tight with the cops, Duane snickered. Shoot, that fool'd be stupid stayin' out too long.

He ain't never comin' back, Nate declared.

How you know, nigga?

Brandon-

Shoot.

Hell naw, not as long as Kevin workin'.

Y'all watch, he'll be home right quick, Duane proclaimed confidently.

How you so sho', homie? Julio chuckled.

Duane snickered devilishly. 'Cause every time Lucy come 'round, that damn fool be shakin' in the knees, thas' whassup...

Fo' realz'.

Shoot, I'd like to see D show up at her place, all kickin' it wit' Special K and his boys. Shoot, homeboy got no flex, dude be runnin' back home quick as a mothafucka wit' his tail 'tween his legs, all like c'mon Joe, take me back pleeze. That dude sprung, no doubt for realz.

Joe, Rita, Jamey, and the boys all laughed in agreement at Duane's remarkably salient observation. Because for better or worse, they all knew Duane was right; with Lucy still in the equation, it was only a matter of time before Rydell returned home.

***

Later that afternoon, Lucy Gutierrez brought Tre to Cottage 1 of Excelsior House to meet with Joe and to visit her girlfriends.

What's up mamacita! Sylvia shouted immediately upon their arrival.

What up homegirl!

Lucy and Sylvia exchanged a genuine embrace.

Hey.

Damn, Tre gettin' hella big. What 'chu feedin' him, steroids? Sylvia patted him down. You missed your Aunt Sylvia, oh yes you did! She immediately kissed the boy on the cheek and he responded with the biggest smile any of them had seen in a long while. The girls all lit up.

Ohhh, now he gonna be a ladykiller when he older, Agnes admired, pinching his cheek.

He already is! Sylvia played with him as she, Brenda and Agnes gawked over Lucinda's magnificent baby. But we be schoolin' him on how to treat his ladies right!

Meanwhile, Rhona kept her distance. She quietly prodded Sarah, who stood with her across the room.

Damn, homegirl must need something, she always come 'round when she do.

Sarah could only nod her head affirmimgly. Hey if she gets hers, why not?

'Cause that girl always leechin' off 'a Joe. It was clear from Rhona's caustic tone that she harbored some strong resentment for Lucy's relationship with their Executive Director. She knows he's sprung on her, so she always workin' it.

What's not to like? She seems nice, Sarah deviously suggested with an innocent tone, hoping to rile Rhona, who was obviously obsessed with Joe's not-so-subtle affections toward Lucy.

Girl seems to have her shit straight more than any of us, Sarah taunted further.

But instead, Rhona contorted her face into a confounded knot at the suggestion. Ah hell naw! That bitch even mo' twisted than yo' sorry ass.

Sarah huffed her off with only a smile.

Meanwhile, Carly and Agnes said their hellos.

Hey Lucy, you and the baby lookin' good.

Is Joe around?

He's across the street with the boys in group.

Mind if I wait with y'all?

Girl, you know you always welcome with us, Agnes replied, somewhat suspiciously.

See what I'm telling you? Rhona whispered again to Sarah.

She just workin' it like you wish you could, Sarah retorted vindictively.

Aw hell naw bitch, now you's trippin'! Rhona declared defiantly. But she immediately backed off Sarah, because this girl had her card read and was playing her to the tee. I ain't got nothin' doin' wit' no fuckin' hood rat baby momma bitch.

Yeah obviously. Sarah waited for Rhonas quick display of frustration as Joe walked into the room.

Whoa, whose this fine lady comin' 'round here? Joe beamed.

Hey Joe...Lucy closed her eyes and smiled as he kissed her affectionately on the cheek.

My dawg! He turned to Sylvia and took Tre's tiny hand into his own to shake it. How it doin', little man?

Doctor said he's hittin' all his necessary benchmarks for his first year.

Damn, he already had his one year checkup? Joe's sense of pride for Lucy's accomplishments with Tre showed through his broadened smile. Time sure movin' quick.

How are the guys? She inquired.

Fine, Joe admitted happily. But your secret admirer went skippin' out again last night.

What he do this time?

Joe blew the question off with a wave of his hand. Just his typical nonsense, mixin' it up with Kevin.

His mouth still too big for the head he carryin'?

You know our boy betta then anyone.

Yeah, well when I see him I'm 'a set him straight, Lucy insisted.

Good, 'cause he don't take much talkin' to by us, Joe laughed with Agnes and Carly who nodded in agreement.

Lucy slowly shifted her tone. Hey, can we talk?

Joe immediately knew what was up.

Fo' sho', Joe put his hand out, pointing to the girl's cottage staff office, and the two walked in. He shut the door behind them.

Once they were out of sight, Rhona could not help herself from blurting out loud what all of the other girls and staff in the room were thinking.

There go our money for Six Flags...

Inside the staff office, Joe pulled out a chair for Lucy to sit across the table from him.

So how you really doin' girl?

Not good Joe, Lucy admitted flatly to her surrogate brother/father figure. Key's still in da game.

You knew this was gon' happen when he got out.

I know, but I thought now with Tre, when he saw his son, things was gonna change. But he still out earnin', says he reclaimin' what he says is his. And he out every night, she looked down at the floor, showing her displeasure with her man.

Like I always been sayin' to you girl, wit' that dude, once a thug always a thug.

But he's betta than that Joe, I know it, she rationalized to him. You don't see that side 'a him I do. When we alone with Tre, he becomes this whole other person. He just that sweet little boy nobody be understanding. Nobody but me.

Luce, I'm tellin' you, you cross him and he'll turn you out on a dime. Like he done to hisself a long time ago. You gots to get yo'self free, get out and get on wit' yo' life. You owe it to yo' boy. You owe it to yo'self...Shyite, you owe it to all a' us who care fo' you, Joe trailed off silently.

Lucy could see his true love for her pouring through that last statement. But just as strong was the denial that allowed her to remain with Keyshawn, so was her choice at some level to ignore Joe.

But we in love, she continued on with an unabashed, internal fury. I know he'll change. I just gotta give him some time to come around.

Girl, you ain't never gonna change another man's heart, Joe insisted plainly. He's got to do that for himself. If there's one thing you ever let me teach you, let it be that.

But I know he loves me. And we have a son. I got to believe that's enough.

Fo' now, maybe, Joe hinted.

Forever, Lucy stated drearily, as if not able to convince even herself, at the deepest levels of her own heart, that she would ever truly believe this to be true.

Though it crushed him to admit it to himself, Joe was convinced he could not speak any more reason into her mind at this time. He could only wait for Keyshawn to fuck her up real bad, and when he did, because that time would sure as shit be comin' 'round, then Joe knew he would be there for her until she picked herself back up.

So how are you on money?

Section 8's payin'the rent and I got my food stamps covering groceries, but I can't lie Joe, money be hella tight right now.

He nodded, satisfied to hear her basics were taken care of. How's the job hunt doin' you?

That damn temp agency be takin' they sweet-ass time hollerin' back, no joke. And I know I promised not to take no drug money off 'a Key for our baby's needs, so since he still busy gettin' his flow legal, and I ain't got no job yet, here we is talkin' again.

Joe and Lucy both understood Key had no intention of ever finding legitimate work. But that was the heart of their unspoken arrangement: as long as Joe didn't demand that Lucy leave her baby's father outright, Lucy agreed not to cut Joe out of her life and to not accept any of Key's dirty money for raising her son. So long as Joe was willing to subsidize her until she got up on her own two feet and found her way to self-sufficiency before Key wound up dead, messed up beyond recognition or back in the pen.

So how much you need?

Lucy felt terrible asking him again.

Just for diapers and wipes Joe, I promise I'll be gettin' my callback soon.

Joe waved her off, wanting to spare her the guilt of having to beg him outright.

Naw girl, you know I always got your back, no explanations needed.

He unlocked the cash box stored in the bottom desk drawer and pulled out two hundred-dollar bills.

Go on girl, you take this.

He stuffed the bills into her hand and closed her fingers around them, nodding intently. She stood up and hugged him. It was a tender embrace. The father in him, temporarily winning out over the scorned and wistful lover within, received her appreciation now not as payment for his help, but as a proud provider helping his grown daughter in her genuine moment of need.

As Lucy left Excelsior House and walked with Tre in her arms down the front steps of the cottage, Rydell nonchalantly strolled up the block. He spotted Joe doting on her and Tre, and immediately quickened his pace until he caught Lucy's glare. Joe tossed him a predictable stare filled with reproach, but he was clearly relieved that Rydell had turned up safely.

What up Luce!

She just shook her head at him. What's this I hear 'bout 'chu runnin' off again? Boy, don't you know how lucky you got it here?

You know I'm just teachin' staff a lesson, Rydell fronted happily. Like I always done.

Well 'f you ever wanna grow up a man, you gots to handle yo' business wit' some respect for those who be caring for you, right?

Rydell would have surely slammed any other chick getting up in his grill like this. But all he could do with Lucy was bask in her attentions and hope to up his credentials with her.

Aw girl, you know how we do up in here. I'm doin' it movin', know what I'm sayin'? He fronted. 'Cause that's manstyle.

You got yo'self a job yet? She asked briskly. 'Cause THAT'S manstyle.

Yo girl, my rap career about to flip straight up, hear what I'm sayin'? He fronted hard for her attentions. You need to bring yo'self and little Tre down to Café DuNord and here me spit my master flow at the open mic, 'stead 'a hangin' with dat dopeslinger boyfriend 'a yours. 'Cause I been killin' it for realz.

Dawg, get your delusional ass back in the house fo' I give you somethin' real to spit, Joe demanded.

Hey, good to see you too, Joe! Rydell mocked Joe's sincere distress over his absence. Mang, how are you, D? I was worried sick all night, was afraid we wus gon' find you under a bus or clipped by a shottie up on Alemany, dude I'm so glad you's alive…

Joe could only rolls his eyes. Get 'cho ass in the house, boy!

Lucy laughed at Rydell's utter ridiculousness. Well, if your raps any bit as good as yo' bullshit, maybe you's on yo' way.

Girl, come to my show and see fo' yo'self, Rydell beamed at her suggestion. 'Cause I'm a get you wetter than all dem fools you's tryin' to know combined.

You know what really gets me wet D? Lucy offered saucily.

Aw, I gots to know this! He didn't miss a beat.

A youngsta who can run his program right and maintain wit' staff 'till he old enough to support his own self.

Rydell feigned a look of sincere contemplation over this suggestion, complete with a hand held over his chest.

Then 'f that's my way into yo' heart girl, consider it done. For reals.

Cool. So you gon' do your thing D? Lucy smiled.

Straight up, I'm 'a run it right and tight fo' you, Luce, Rydell nodded.

She finally sent him packing across the street with a hug.

But before leaving, Rydell shook Tre's hand. See you little man. I'm 'a be yo' daddy one day, you'll see. Fo' sho'. Feel me, Joe? He turned sarcastically to Joe for a handslap. My nigga…

Joe just stared him down, leaving him hanging.

Ayite then, I see how it is, Rydell retreated from the stoop where they all stood, saving face in front of Lucy. But once across the street at a safe distance from Joe, he couldn't help but turn and call out to her, cupping his hands to his lips.

I'm 'a tell you right now, Luce, I'm 'a win you 'f it's the last thing I do! You take that one to the bank! For realz.

She simply laughed and waved him off. But it was a pledge Rydell would never forget as long as he lived.

***

Kendrick and Duane readied themselves in the bathroom of Cottage 2 for the big dance at Thurgood Marshall High School that evening. Kendrick clipped his nose hairs precisely while Duane splashed cologne across his lower neck and jaw.

Dang Kendrick, she ain't gonna be lickin' yo' nostrils, mang, Duane proclaimed, rubbing the fragrance into his skin with his wrists. But I'm 'a get' some off 'a Brenda tonight, just you watch, fo' shore.

Kendrick grabbed the last of the cologne his brother put down on the sink. Man, Duane, why you gotta go using my stuff all the time? Damn! Kendrick pouted, futilely shaking the empty bottle with his free hand.

You best recognize, Duane declared.

Get a job and buy your own, shoot.

I don't wanna smell like no French fries, like your stanky ass. He gave a light push to his little brother.

Watch it fool, Kendrick growled peevishly, continuing to clip his nostril hairs. Why you gotta waste it all, Duane, shoot. Brenda ain't gonna do nothin' wit' 'chu!

Mang, I'm a tear dat pussy up for realz, know what I'm sayin'?

Kendrick scoffed, moving the clippers to the inside of his ears. Noticing Kendrick's fastidious attention to detail with his own facial hair, Duane asked his brother all of a sudden, Yo, who you sprung on so bad Kendrick? Must be some tight hoochie wit' all that deep sea divin' you doin' and shit.

Never mind, Kendrick dismissed him abruptly.

C'mon Kendrick, tell your brutha whassup. Whose ass you tryin' to tap?

Man, you don't never know when to quit…

I bet you checkin fo' that girl from Social Studies, huh. That hella smart one. Whus her name? Duanda or sumpin'…

Shoot hell naw, that girl be stanky, smells like Crisco whenever she walk by.

Duane cracked up. Huh huh. That's 'cause she livin' in da projects!

Hell naw, she just nasty.

Duane was now in stitches over his brother's derision. Shoot, you know you'd still hit that if she let you.

Yeah, probably.

Both the boys were busting up now.

Meanwhile, in the bathroom of Cottage 2 across the street, Sylvia and Rhona were busy bickering over whether or not to share their cosmetics.

Ayite, which one 'a y'all skanks grabbed my weave? Rhona griped, rifling through her purse.

Ain't nobody want yo' nappy-ass hair 'stensions, Sylvia confirmed, applying eyeliner as she checked her work in the long mirror.

Shoot, now one 'a my nails is busted. Rhona held up her right hand. You got any more Clairol?

Hell naw, Sylvia replied, teasing her hair. She then proceeded to spray her work with a ton of Aqua Net.

Rhona waved off the cloud. Girl, you destroyin' the ozone with that shit. You a walkin' fire hazard.

Yo, flame on, B…

Damn blut, do that shit outside fo' I suffocate', shoot. Rhona backed away from the mirror, covering her mouth. How my highlights?

They straight.

You got any mo' 'a dat eyeliner?

Right here, Sylvia begrudgingly handed her housemate the vial.

Cool…

Sylvia proceeded to glitter her chest.

Easy on the gold, homegirl, shoot, them niggas be thinkin' you's Tinkerbell.

Sylvia ignored her and called down the hall. Bern, you want me to do your curls?

Shure.

Brenda walked in wearing a sparkling silver dress.

OOOH MY GAWD! Rhona exclaimed, holding her arms out to greet her girl.

Oh hell yeah, Sylvia cheered. Girl, you fixin' to get worked tonight!

Duane gon' get hella sweet on you. Rhona turned her friend around, checking Brenda's tight figure up and down in the dress. Blow his world wide open workin' dat ass. For realz.

Brenda smiled. You think so?

Syl? Rhona asked for her input. Sylvia didn't miss a beat to affirm her friend.

You wanna have his babies, huh? She teased.

Brenda blushed as Rhona continued on. Shoot, first he gon' have to fight off all dem hood rats swoopin' you tonight. 'Cause hella dudes be checkin' fo' you fo' realz, ooh…

Hell yeah, Sylvia pumped Brenda up. The three girls cracked up. Then, Sylvia went back for more eyeliner. This time, the bottle was empty. She balked, handing the vial to Rhona. Blut, now I know you's on yo' way to da store to replace that.

Rhona gave her the look of death. You must be smoking crack girl 'cause that shit cloudin' your mind.

Aw hell no. OOOOH!

A short time later, the Excelsior group headed to the dance piled into the boys' cottage Silver Astrovan. Tyrone, Duane, Kendrick, Rhona, Sylvia, and Brenda shared the mid and backseats while Carly drove and Agnes rode gun.

Once they were on the road, Rhona hollered out to Tyrone, Blut, I thought you wuz on restriction!

Hell naw, Carly's lettin' me go.

Sylvia questioned this. Don't restrictions mean nuthin' no more?

Tyrone took no time to respond. If they did then yo' big booty would be doin' some time, 'cause that shit's criminal.

Fuck you, T.

Only in yo' wet dreams girl.

Agnes could only shake her head. Carly blurted out from the driver's seat.

Tyrone, language! We can turn right back around and go home-

Sorry Carly!

He ain't sorry, Sylvia bristled.

Naw, but you is, Tyrone smirked in retort.

You best shut that big mouth fo' I slap you silly, boy.

Tyrone did.

At the dance, Duane, Tyrone, Kendrick, Brenda, Rhona and Sylvia busted a move to Keak Da Sneak's 'That Go.'

That's how we do it in Da Bay!

Tyrone worked desperately to impress Rhona with his dancing. She checked him.

Yo' cross weave need work fool!

Yo, turn 'em out T, Duane hollered.

Tyrone demonstrated his flow.

Throw it out der!

Tyrone first busted a simple B-boy maneuver, before dropping a three quarter turn on his hands, followed up by a perfectly landed twist arch. He came out of it vibrating his body.

That hoodshake be sick, dawg! Duane yelled over the music.

Rhona was finally starting to pay attention as Sylvia interrupted them. Aw, check out little Duane with his two step!

Ayite, ayite, he cool, Rhona agreed.

Brenda could only laugh nervously.

Chew 'em up' blut, Tyrone encouraged Duane.

Duane immediately laid down some sloppy popping followed by a quick lock.

Now hit it and quit!

Duane did.

Mang, that shit's dope, dawg, Tyrone slapped Duane on the back.

Meanwhile, Sylvia, Brenda and Rhona did some hoodshakin' of their own.

Aw, now you 'hoes goin' suburban commando and shit.

I'm about to…

Rhona stepped up to Tyrone. So what else you got, little boy?

Tyrone smiled, taking the challenge. He backed up off 'a her and got into position.

Aw hell naw, that fool ain't landin' no Brookfield! Sylvia waved him off dismissively.

But Tyrone killed it. Barely. Even Rhona was impressed.

Yo T, what it do? Rhona hollered out, smiling.

You feelin' me yet? He called out back to her.

You doin' it movin', I give you dat, she nodded approvingly.

Hells yeah.

Reppin' Excelsior.

Later, the D-J shifted to a slow dance jam, 112's Only You.

Locked in each other's arms, Brenda with Duane, and Rhona with Tyrone swayed softly to the music. After a time, Rhona spotted Duane's hands all over Brenda's ass.

Damn, your boy gettin' his grip on, Rhona, bemused, said to Tyrone.

Aw, hells yeah. I taught him true. Taking a cue from Duane, Tyrone slid his own hand down Rhona's skirt and tried to grab her in the same way.

Boy, if you even think 'bout it I'm 'a put yo' ass in da hospital.

Mang, how come you never wanna get with me? Tyrone asked, suddenly flustered.

We dancing, ain't we, fool?

Naw I'm serious. You be doin' all them dudes up on the block, but you never show me no kind 'a love. How come you don't want to get with me?

Rhona found herself unsuspectingly caught without anything to say. Instead of locking him with her eyes as she normally would to stare him down, she just pulled him closer and whispered into his ear, so she did not have to face his innocent gaze with the shameful truth of her words.

Everything I do, it come with consequences.

Tyrone didn't know what to make of this.

What 'chu mean? He pulled her forward to meet her eyes, genuinely confused.

For just a moment, she was about to let him kiss her, the child in her finally freed, withdrawn from its shell. But instead of taking the leap, the moment quickly passed over them, and Rhona found herself totally exposed in this boy's arms. She quickly curled her face and threw it back at him, her defenses fully up and running again, finally.

Fool, it mean what it do, shoot, and if you can't understand what I'm saying then that's on you. She pulled out of his embrace and walked to the other side of the dance floor, shielding him the entire time from a view of her fighting back tears.

Tyrone turned away from her, ashamed for putting himself out there.

As Rhona walked to the girls' bathroom to clean herself up, Taniqua stepped to her.

Aww, who let the ree-ree's out tonight?

Rhona's sadness immediately shifted to a more safe emotion, unbridled rage.

Bitch, I'm 'a slash you like I shoulda done last week.
Fuck you skeeza!

Without warning, Rhona instinctively grabbed Taniqua by the ears and dug her fingers so deeply into the girl's cheeks that she broke off several nails in her complexion. Taniqua winced in pain as blood poured from the fresh gashes now leaching from her face, giving Rhona the opening she needed to knee Taniqua in the gut, dropping her to the floor. Receiving repeated kicks to the face and stomach, all the fallen girl could do was cry out in terror as Rhona delivered her onslaught of verbal and physical lashings to the astonishment of the onlookers, too mesmerized by the ensuing carnage to stop her. Finally, Rhona grew tired of pummeling the visibly unconscious girl, allowing Sylvia and Brenda enough time to pull her away from the scene.

Now who's the ree-ree, bitch! Rhona shouted to the mass of pulp lying on the floor.

Soon, half of the school and several administrators scrambled into the gym hallway to clean up the fallout from the fight that began only moments before.

Following several more minutes of shouting, Rhone was eventually escorted to the school office where the police arrested her for aggravated assault. She spent the next few nights in the San Francisco County Juvenile Hall until Joe could decide what could be done to bring her back to Excelsior House. But given Rhone's prior violent behavior and recent proclivity for prostitution as confirmed by the Chlamydia detected in her urinary tract during a routine pap smear performed during intake, her Youth Court judge had no choice but to deem Excelsior an unsuitable living environment for accommodating her special needs any longer. For her assault, Rhona was sentenced to six months in Juvenile Hall followed by placement in a Level 14 psychiatric facility across the bay in Alameda County upon her release. She would never return to Excelsior House.

***

Sylvia and Rydell showed up to Café DuNord on open mic slam poetry night. When her name was finally called, Sylvia got up on stage to a round of applause and requested a beat from the DJ.

Cool.

She beat her head back and forth back a few times to cop the rhythm of the rolling backbeat.

OK OK uh uh, here's what I'm sayin', uh, uh-

Yo check it, feel me out...

The crowd repeated. Uh. Uh.

...Uh, uh OK...(out with abominable flow)

...All I'm sayin' is you betta get yo' game tight and yo' money right f' you want to get yo'self some 'a dis!

She grabbed her crotch and the crowd roared.

Ugh! You go girl!

Tell it true, sista!

You fine!

Gimmie yo' number!

...I want a nigga who be handling his shit, not one 'a dem hustla types rollin' down the block wit' his Nextel AND Skylark...Fool, you can't find time to holla back? Who else be callin' you need to talk to so bad?

Oh no you didn't!

...Shit actin' so busy can't find time to complement a bitch, much less comb that nappy-ass hair or handle that stank breath...Yo dawg, ever hear 'a mouthwash?

Uh huh that's right!

...I'm just tired 'a these no-job-havin', frontin'-ass niggas who think they all that when you can't even make rent or get a pussy wet...

Oh, damn!

And you know you ain't the shit, that's just yo' breath be puttin' me in my fit!

Uugh! Na girl, say it ain't so!

...Ha HA. But ladies, we got the last word don't cha know? Check my flow, 'cause we da mothafuckin' bomb to all these hard-up haters of da world.

True dat!

We got the pussy, so we got the power. Say it ladies! Say it proud!

The crow hollered back.

...Wit' the coochie we bringin' baybies in da world, droppin' babyboys to they knees, makin' grown men cry...

Holla!

So scraps of the world, y'all can playa hate, but don't never underestimate! The power of the goddess be turning it out, flipping the script. 'Cause there ain't no stoppin' us from gettin' ours' 'fore you get yours some 'a dis.

Sylvia grabbed her crotch again. Amen!…Thank y'all!

Sylvia took a bow to the roaring raucous crowd of the women she left invigorated. Most of the men cheered her on for being so dirty.

Rydell gave her a confounded look as she stepped off stage. She could only laugh at the sight of his face.

Damn girl, you wus roastin' fools tonight!

Hell yeah, boy, these peeps know when the truth is spoken.

But why you gotta hate so bad on tha brothaman? We ain't all bad.

Naw, but y'all some flip-ass bitches.

Rydell shook his head defiantly, There somethin' ain't right with you, girl…

It took you this long to figure it out? She laughed as the announcer called Rydell to the stage.

And now from the Excelsior, a local cat, Prince.

The crowd clapped politely. Rydell waved to everyone.

Yo peoples. I'm gonna drop it to you real. Ain't no sugarcoatin' this. Naw. No music for this one.

The DJ silenced his turntable. The crowd stirred to silence. Rydell paused, waiting for the quiet. Once the beat inside his own head became known, Rydell busted into a freestyle, syncopated cadence.

Yo check it, I ain't your normal day to day playa, I ain't gonna drop no front 'bout gettin' pussy or fightin' ova some stupid gangsta shit, just gonna tell it true. I live in a group home, my momma was fifteen when she had me, died in a car accident at sixteen, cracked out behind the wheel, glass carving out her chest like a Halloween pumpkin, no they could not resuscitate… But that don't mean shit to me 'cause I never knew her…Never knew no family, much less a grandma who didn't want me until she died too…

That's when I swooped my first group home. Life in the system ain't nothing polite, yo. It ain't no prison, but it sho' ain't paradise neitha...

Staff be buggin', everyone a hater, you gots to stay sharp wit' fools steppin' to you at every turn, keep 'em in check 'cause they ain't findin' you wit' nuthin' but to get high or get by. Everyone be crazy, staff thinkin' they can help you but they can't do shit, so instead they fill me with meds to control me, shit's straight jacked yo', when little boys and girls all makin' they mark you gotta push back, words cut deeper than fists or blades yo, verbiage straight take a dude out quicka than a blow to the head, that's why I'm a lyrical terrorist, and no one likes me 'cause I tell it true, slay them all to keep it that way, hold my true feelings close and my intentions closer, 'cause I know the game bets than anyone, shit I been playin' you since I wus out da cradle, straight lay a fool out 'fore they even see it comin', splittin' staff, turnin' out tricks, playin' all da haters 'gainst each other, straight laying waste bringin' da chaos, all to gets what I want, stayin' out da loop and in da pocket, pushin' everybody to they limits, 'cause when it comes to it, all people come and go, everyone do they thing that way, and when the apocalypse comes I decide how and when it goes down, therapists try to help but they don't know shit, 'cause all they books and head talk don't say shit 'bout how to survive in my world, the real world, shit where everyone be livin' crazy around you, psycho ward like a livin' hell, dudes blowin' each other out fo' some headlove or just cuz they can, too many violations send you through a juvie stint or on to the next placement, shit I've been to 36 homes so far and all they consequences together ain't amount to a goddamn thing, not when you's the hardest dude around, 'cept when a guardian or staff tries to do you, but then you fuck them up right quick, 'cause ain't no one 'bout to take me out, I straight tear their shit up then run away, I can smell a predator a mile comin', so I tell my staff and therapists how it gon' be and it always do, and 'f they can't get it done they way I want then I just bounce to the next hater placement, make their world a living hell for awhile 'till I get what's comin' mine, ain't no one tellin' me how to live 'cause I make the rules, I live everywhere and everything at once, tried and true, and to get mine, but still I gots no control over the big things, like how and where I'm gon' live or die, and whether my life will ever change I do not know, all I can tell is shit, ain't nothin' never gonna happen 'less you get it done for yo'self, and I'm too smart for probation so the system can't grab me, ain't no caseworkers or probates pullin' me on no 602 'till I turn eighteen, then what I'll do in the world I don't know, maybe get a job or somethin', but until everyone realizes I take orders only from me myself and I, they can sweat me o' fire me all they want, shit that's fine, 'cause when I'm aged out da system and society ain't got nothin' more to give me, wit' nobody wantin' me and tax dollas dried up like a dead tree in winter, then I'll be off doin' what I can like I always done, ain't no transition services so probably I'm 'a be homeless, jackin' fools fo' food or for some clothes ova my head, shoot I ain't stupid so you know where this is all goin', pullin' my gat for 'nough cash to survive if I can't find no new system to work, I'll keep doin' it 'till they catch or kill me or lock me back up, where no one gives a fuck about you, but out here everyone tries to understand but nobody understands me, 'cause even now I'm smarta than those that could help me, and I push anyone away who be tryin', 'cause it's all part of the struggle, part 'a the life I didn't choose but chose me, I ain't no criminal but still I'm your worst livin' nightmare, and nobody gots the patience or the strength to break me, so one day I'm gon' have to break myself, though I don't know how that's gonna look like, maybe by death, maybe with a gun or a girl, maybe prison, maybe drugs, or just knowin' there's a God out there who be wantin' nothin' to do wit' me, no matter how hard I try or who I meet, 'cause the world be sweatin' you at every turn, conspirin' to get you slippin' to where you beyond savin', whateva the case may be take it from me, 'cause I know it best, holla dat, when all you's got is all you's ever gons to get, yo'self and that's it. And still that ain't neva be enough…Though you already knows it, and still you can't do nuthin' to change it…

　　…So that's my life. And that's what real. Thank y'all.

　　The room was silent. Sylvia became the first to clap. Everyone quickly rose from their seats to follow her with thunderous applause. Rydell took his bow. Tonight, this night, validation was all he got. But it was something.

***

On her way home from school, Brenda pocketed a package of press-on nails, eyeliner, and skin glitter while paying for a brown wig with blond highlights at Westwood Beauty Supply on Ocean Boulevard. Once home by 4, she waited out the rest of the afternoon and early evening with apprehension before Cottage 1 shut down for the night. All the girls were in bed without incident by 10 o'clock, right on schedule.

Lights out!

Girl you workin' TONIGHT?

Brenda wished she could ignore the loud, whispering voice of her friend from down the hall while she fiddled with the latch to her bedroom window. Never you mind.

But Carly be checkin' on us every half hour wit' Rhona gone, staff 'specting us all to flop out now or sumpthin'.

Naw, she ain't comin' round tonight. Woman got school in the morning.

Well, what am I supposed to say if she do?

Say you wuz asleep. Shit, I don't know.

Be careful B, Sylvia begged her.

Ayite.

Brenda hopped out her bedroom window, traversed the side gate of Cottage 1 and strolled down Persia Street to Mission Blvd, where she hung a right and crossed the 280 overpass bridge, then dropped down across Cesar Chavez to the 24th street BART station. If all went well she'd be in Oakland by 11:30.

She stepped onto the last Fremont train heading out of San Francisco and hopped off at the Fruitvale station. She then trudged the several long blocks up to International Boulevard, then through the 20's and onto the MacArthur corridor she knew so well. Brenda smiled at the Middle Eastern attendant at the Chevron station on 23rd Avenue who always let her use the bathroom to slip into her nighttime attire. Once inside, she fastened on her wig with braid clips and fixed her makeup in the mirror so none of them daddies cruisin' the corridor for some new cherries would recognize her as Brenda from the block. Finally, the lip gloss. Ready for prime time.

She cruised several blocks down MacArthur, sure enough to avoid eye contact with the ever-present pimps. One or two freakshows passed and hollered out to her, but she didn't pay them no mind, 'cause they must be thinkin' she wuz taken if she kept on walkin' straight. Finally, her first trick of the evening pulled up in a black Mercedes.

Yo girl, you need a ride somewhere?

Brenda didn't miss a beat.

Fifty dollars a suck, 100 to fuck, 200 for any nasty shit, and ain't nothin' go down less you wearin' yo' raincoat.

Damn girl, you ain't much fo' pretty talk now ain't cha'?

We gon' do this or what?

How old are you?

Brenda hesitated. She sensed something was off with this dude, his approach was way too whack even for one of them Suburban Johns. She coulda swore she recognized his flip ass from somewhere, but couldn't quite put a fix on his goofy swagga until...Bingo.

Brenda backed up steadily away from the car. You go have yo'self a good night offica.

Naw wait a minute, hold up babyho! The man backed up his car to follow her walking the opposite direction. C'mon now...You just look a little young fo' the hustle's all.

Shit, we's all workin' out here. She looked around at the other girls on the prowl. So you wanna bust a nut or what?

Yeah. Fo' sho'. The homeboy nodded and pulled out a grip of bills. I gots you covered.

Ayite then. Brenda instinctively knew she should walk away from this one, but it'd been several months since she'd tricked last so she got into the car. She directed the man to head back down International to 23rd Avenue. It was clear this dude ain't never been down this way before.

But before they arrived at her spot, instead of following her directions, he abruptly swung the car into an alleyway several blocks before the turn.

What 'chu doin'? Brenda asked, clearly annoyed with the change in plans.

We good here...

I told you to hit 23rd.

He started to unzip himself.

I said we good...

Shit, dem daddy's catch you poppin' you load 'fo' you pay a bitch you get jacked up good.

Brenda looked out of the car windows nervously. Because she knew in this spot, nobody would be comin' to her rescue.

Then we do it quick...

Brenda sensed something was off but still convinced herself she had a handle on the situation. So did what she always done at this point in the transaction. She pulled a rubber out of her purse.

Here go yo' skin.

Oh yeah, about that shit... I ain't slippin' on nuthin' 'fo gettin' in that pussy.

Then I'm out...

Whoa ho, hold on babyho, ain't nobody goin' the FUCK nowhere!

The man grabbed her by the back of the neck and rolled her free hand around her backside, twisting her arm before she could grab at the mace bottle in her purse or open the door. Quickly and forcefully with minimal struggle, he overpowered her, pulling her wrist down with his other hand gripping her neck and dragging it under his leg to compress her arm against the seat.

Desperately, she tried to head butt him but was stuck underneath by the force of his bodyweight. Then, before she could catch her breath, with his grip on her throat he pulled a razor out of his pocket and applied it to the skin of her neck, hard enough for her to almost feel it cutting through...

Now you listen good, 'cause your life be dependin' on this shit. You's about' to take dem lips and suck the fuck outta this cock 'till it nut. Only then'm I decide if I'm ever lettin' you outta dis car, you dig?

Brenda teared up and nodded to signal that she understood. As he shoved her head down into his crotch, and unbuckled himself, she knew from his sheer force that she'd be dead if she resisted.

Good...Now work yo' game little girl.

Homeboy pushed himself forward into her face as she opened her jaw to receive him.

Damn, you know what you's doin' dontcha'...Little girl can suck a dick fo' damn sho'! He laid his head back and opened his jaw, clearly enjoying the sensation of her wet warmth upon him.

Several minutes went by. Brenda bobbed him furiously, increasing the rate and the suction, trying to get him off as quickly as possible to make this all over with. Finally after several agonizing moments he popped his load. Brenda felt the pressure of the blade roosted upon her neck recede momentarily as the full flush of orgasm flooded him, giving her the critical opportunity she needed, probably the last in her short life to be. Without hesitation, she grabbed for the door and pulled the handle with all her might. Sparingly, it opened and she spilled out of the car, allowing her to run with all her might towards the opening of the alleyway.

The flustered man swung for her skirt as she stood but missed her- just barely!

Yo I'm 'a fuck you up fo' real now, bitch!

She trotted in a fury for several blocks without turning her head. The homeboy did not follow her. Finally, out of breath, she turned the corner and headed to an empty bus stop bench, where she sat, bending over to cough out the man's ejaculate before wiping her lips with her sleeve. She could no longer control herself. The sobbing rushed through her quickly.

On the street where she sat, a patrol car slowed down as it passed. She buried her head deeper into her hands so the officers could not make her age from the vehicle. They did not stop, instead turning their sirens on to respond to a call, rushing across the next intersection and down and adjacent block.

Brenda held her expressionless face cupped in her palms for several minutes before composing herself. But when she lifted her head, her worst nightmare was suddenly realized. She locked eyes with the first person she saw standing in front of her. Not the dude from the alley, but worse. A daddy who had been standing there, probably for some time, just waiting for her to raise her head to lock eyes with him. She tried to pull her eyes away and break his gaze but by now it was already too late. He had already seen her vulnerability, her full abandon to him. In this moment they both knew she was his.

He walked over to her and without asking, put his hand under her chin. He then lifted her head up softly, almost fatherly, slowly forcing another round of prolonged eye contact, assuming his ownership of her. Turning her face slowly back and forth to survey the features of his new catch, he rubbed her cheek with his burly thumb, smiling. Four teeth were missing from his insidious smile.

Babygirl, you ain't much to look' at, that much fo' sho', is all he said. But you's thick. He then smiled, feeding off of the last shred of her exposed inner innocence. He pulled back a pinch of her baby fat firmly from her cheeks to break her down. But that be a good thing in dis game. You's virginal?

The confines of his grasp forced Brenda to answer truthfully. Naw…

The pimp smiled. Well from tonight on out you is.

And they both knew right then and there she was fucked.

***

Lisa Gatwyn prepared her students, Tyrone, Brenda, and Rydell for class Monday morning following the dance Friday night.

Good morning everyone.

Mornin'.

Hey.

I'd like to begin by discussing what happened this weekend.

The kids all moaned. Especially Tyrone.

Mang, y'all be killin' it. Let dead dawgs lie…

Lisa sympathized with Tyrone, as she was well aware of his affections for Rhona.

You doing OK, Tyrone?

Mang, staff be talkin' our ears off already. Can't y'all just let it go?

Lisa genuinely tried to validate her students feelings. I understand your frustration, Tyrone. But because we are a close community here, I think it's relevant to our class that we acknowledge when one of us is missing.

This shit's gettin' old, Tyrone blurted, clearly not wanting to discuss the matter any further.

Obviously Tyrone is frustrated, Lisa acknowledged, turning now to Rydell, whose new medications were burning up his mind enough to force him to rest his head on his desk. Do you have anything you'd like to add?

Naw. 'Cept why you lettin' Tyrone cuss? You must really think we need a talkin' to.

Lisa twitched as he spoke, noticeably peeved by Rydell's astute observation of her relaxing classroom profanity rules. Still, she addressed his speculation outright in order to maintain the integrity of honest communication within the group.

Whatever feelings you all are having around this incident are fine. I guess what I'm trying to do is to encourage you to express them.

Nobody said anything to this.

Well then, can I ask, are any of YOU at all upset by what Rhona did?

No reaction from Brenda, who just sat with her forced smile across her plump face.

Brenda, I don't think I've ever seen you wear a turtleneck before, Lisa realized.

She just tryin' to hide them love bites Duane be givin' her at the dance, Tyrone blurted.

Brenda smiled.

Well Brenda, I think it looks nice on you, Lisa offered.

Brenda's smile appeared genuine now.

Tyrone, I understand you and Brenda were witness to the events which led to Taniqua being hospitalized.

Yeah. But it ain't no thing.

Apparently it was to Rhona and Taniqua, Lisa flatly reminded them.

Taniqua OK? Tyrone asked compassionately, allowing himself to wonder aloud.

Lisa smiled, a bit relieved by his eagerness to talk. Yes, Tyrone, she had several stitches and a shot of antibiotics but she is doing well.

Yeah, 'cept for Rhona carvin' her face out like a pumpkin. Rydell's comment drew a chuckle from Brenda and Tyrone. That bitch ain't never gonna look right no mo'.

She already be sportin' some crooked ass teeth, Rydell continued. So all Rhona did wus finish the job. Brenda and Tyrone nodded in agreement, almost proud with the damage their friend inflicted on her.

That's not funny at all, Lisa admonished him.

But that 'ho had it comin'!

No doubt.

Rydell, that's inappropriate.

I know…But it's the truth, he returned with a groan, pushing his head back down on the desk.

Yeah, Lisa played along, so then how do you all figure that makes what happened OK?

Tyrone jumped in with a raised hand to explain the callousness of his peers. Lisa nodded for him to speak.

Rhona ain't do nuthin' but try to ignore that skeeza all year but Taniqua couldn't let shit be. So she got herself cut.

So you think Taniqua deserved to be a victim of Rhona's violence? Lisa looked at him with a mixture of scorn and confusion.

Hells yeah. Shit, she always makin' Rhona look like a bitch when she tried walkin' away so finally Rhona had to do it, that's just how it work...

But by dealin' with the situation that way Rhona chose to, isn't she the one who now has to pay the price?

Brenda and Tyrone both became saddened by Lisa's analysis, imagining their friend in jail for many years.

Y'all may see it that way, but Rhona had no choice, Tyrone confidently informed Lisa.

And why do you say that? Lisa challenged. Why don't you enlighten me?

OK, Tyrone spit back. I'm 'a drop it to you straight. None 'a y'all done shit for Rhona all year long while Taniqua wus comin' at her. Staff didn't listen to no one, and the teachers all be lookin' the other way whenever her crew stepped to us, callin' us ree-ree's and talkin' they shit while y'all's preachin' to turn the otha cheek. Taniqua been spittin' her mess fo' months and y'all didn't say nuthin', y'all just let it go, let it work itself out. Well, what you see is what you get. Now turn the otha cheek!

Brenda nodded. Holla dat!

Rydell moaned in approval.

Lisa tried using Tyrone's tension to diffuse the situation. OK Tyrone, I hear what you're saying. It's clear that the school staff could have done more to diffuse the situation earlier.

But naw Lisa, 'cause there ain't nothin' y'all coulda done really. Shit went down the way it had to, Tyrone explained. 'Cause Taniqua'd keep steppin' to her 'till she handled her own business, so Rhona had to turn that bitch out. But Taniqua weak, so she couldn't go out without narc'n out some fools like the snitch bitch she is, straight up.

Tyrone was clearly steamed by his own conclusion. That's just how it be.

Do you all really believe that? Lisa asked sincerely.

None of them answered.

Everyone knows it's da truth...

So Tyrone, Lisa countered, then by your logic, can you see any end to this? Any other ways you might cope with conflict when someone is bothering you, to prevent it from becoming this endless destructive cycle of violence you've so elegantly described?

Naw, he admitted flatly. 'Cause when Rhona beat her down, now her girls gotta step up. And when they do they's gonna get fucked up, too-

Until everyone ends up in jail, or dead? Lisa finished his train of thought.

Tyrone thought for a minute, then nodded. If that's how it goes down, then yeah.

And that's OK with you?

Ain't what's OK, just what is.

Then that's it huh? All of this time and energy we're spending together to change our thinking, our patterns of behavior, our reactions to conflict, all of it's just a big waste of time, in your opinion?

Tyrone looked around to his classmates who nodded him on fatalistically. You said it, not me.

Well, I want to hear you say it.

Then yeah...

Lisa sighed.

What? Tyrone was surprised by her reaction.

Well you want to know what I think? Lisa offered.

Tyrone considered for a minute. Not really…

Lisa ignored his insolence. I think that's lazy thinking. I think you all know what's right, y'all just too scared to take it head on now 'cause it takes work, and courage, to think differently, to change your reactions to people, to change your ways, in order to make the world a different place. But that desire has to start from within, Lisa tapped her own chest. Each of us has a choice to make on the inside first. You have to ask yourselves, Do I want to live this way? Or do I wanna take a different path, a new direction my own life, and give people a chance? How do I get my own self correct, knowing what's right and by acting on it regardless of what anybody else thinks? How are you going to live your life by example until you become that example for others? Because when you got it right yourself, by rejecting the bogus idea that you don't have a choice in how your own life turns out, then you get to decide what kind of person you wanna be, you get to choose how to live in this world for real, as a powerful human being, not because the world made you that way but because you make your world that way. You all have the power to overcome anything that holds you back. If you just keep alive that courage inside you to defeat this dead-end mentality that goes against everything you want to create for yourselves…So don't ever forget that.

The group was silent. Finally, Brenda raised her hand.

Can we do art therapy now Ms. Gatwyn?

Lisa surveyed the crowd, hoping for any sign, any reaction to suggest they had internalized her message. Best to give them some time to process, she reasoned. To open up the right lobes of their brain. To internalize, churn, discover.

I think that's an excellent idea, Brenda, Lisa proclaimed. Go ahead and get out your materials.

And the kids of Excelsior's Special Day Program proceeded to do just that: make their art.

***

Deirdre prepared dinner for the boys at Girls Cottage 1. The staff watched from the kitchen as the boys unloaded from the van the groceries they had just purchased during an off-hill after school field trip to Costco. Julio stocked the pantry as Carly dealt out afternoon meds.

She tried to hand 'Dell a small Dixie cup that she had filled earlier with the boys' prescriptions from the pharmaceutical dispensary. He turned her away with his hands.

Are you refusing your meds?

He did not answer.

You know what's gonna happen if you do.

Mang, I don't give a fuck.

OK.

Carly walked away, indifferent. She moved on to Kendrick, then to Tyrone, and finally to Rory, who all compliantly swallowed their doses.

Deirdre, Carly called out to her for Rydell to hear. Rydell has decided to refuse his meds.

OK, I'll call Joe.

You sure you wanna take another trip to the hospital, 'Dell? Deirdre asked one more time, standing outside of the office for Rydell to see her dialing the staff office phone.

Mang…Yo, gimme my cup, Carly.

Deirdre hung up the receiver as Carly handed him the Dixie cup. He put it to his mouth, swallowed, and placed the empty cup back on the tray defiantly.

Carly tilted her head forward. Now lemme see.

He stuck out his tongue at her. AHHHHH! See, I ain't cheekin' 'em.

Thank you, Carly bowed sarcastically as Duane and Kendrick grew antsy. Yo Carly, when can we play ball?

You guys finished your homework yet?

Yeah, I done mine at lunchtime, Kendrick replied.

Hell yeah, me too, Carly, Duane echoed.

Then let me sign it.

Kendrick proudly grabbed his assignment from his bag. But Duane yanked his paper away just as Carly was about to read it.

Naw, I'm just playin'.

Well, what you should be doing is finishing your schoolwork, Deirdre preached from the hall.

Mang, why we always work befo' havin' any fun up in here? Staff always be playa hatin'.

Why don't you follow your brother's example and finish it at school? Deirdre suggested reasonably. Then you would have plenty of time for basketball at home.

Mang, I ain't got time for that at school, 'cause I be too busy gettin' my freak on with those Visitacion 'hos, know what I'm sayin'?

Tyrone and Rory both cracked up at his comment.

Shoot, Kendrick chided his brother's ridiculous posturing. The only freaks you be gettin' on is Brenda and all her tricks who up in her backwash.

DAAAAamn, fool be clowning! Tyrone cracked.

Rydell would have surely interjected his snide opinion at this point but the near-comatose state induced by his new meds silenced him.

Deirdre and Carly both frowned upon seeing him curled up in a ball on the couch.

Kendrick still pressed for a game. T, you wanna ball?

Yeah, I'll show you whussup, he agreed.

Tyrone, finish your work first! Deirdre instructed.

I BEEN done with that. You can even call and ask Ms. Gatwyn! He yelled over his shoulder as he exited the cottage, bouncing the ball all the way to the driveway court.

No dribbling in the house!

Sorry, Carly! He shot back just as the door shut.

The staff watched Kendrick and Tyrone through the front window, playing their one-on-one outside as Julio came out of his room, holding his gym bag. He stopped at the pantry and grabbed his staple Fruit Punch Capri Sun and Nature Valley Granola bar.

Mang, now we's stocked!

Yeah, you should have seen us at Costco, Deirdre laughed. We looked like a bulimic's shelter buying out half the store.

Julio chuckled. We all a bunch 'a mooches, no doubt. Hey Carly, you pick up my CD?

Carly put her hand over her face, flushed with genuine embarrassment. Shoot, I knew I forgot something.

Julio shook his head. Mang, I ain't never gonna hear the end of it 'f I don't hook up my boys wit' some phat tunes tonight.

Sorry, Carly apologized again.

Julio gestured with three fingers extended out toward her. It's ayite, ain't no thing. Just hook me up the next time.

I promise, Carly insisted.

He rectified the situation by grabbing whatever CD was docked in the Excelsior House boom-box.

Tell Duane I'm 'a borrow this.

Tell him yourself, Deirdre motioned to Duane, who was finishing up the last of his schoolwork on the kitchen table.

Mang Julio, why you always be jackin' my stuff?

Don't worry D, I'm 'a hit you back…

Damn, Duane shook his head in disbelief. Mang, some greedy-ass kids up in here.

I see y'all later, Julio hollered out to his staff. Got my meeting, them I'm 'a catch up wit' my PO 'fore I get back.

You home for dinner?

Naw, we's grabbin' burritos.

Then have a good one, Deirdre called out as he flew out the door.

On his way across the driveway, Julio grabbed the ball from Tyrone and landed a hook shot before rustling Kendrick's head with his free hand.

The staff watched him head down the street.

What a good kid, Carly declared. He's doing so right by himself these days. And he's gon' be fine when he gets older.

Shoot, he already is, Deirdre joked.

The girls both laughed in agreement.

You hear his old lady left him?

Yeah, but don't look like it's fazed him none.

No, Deirdre agreed. But I'm sure it's gotta burn. According to his urine tests, his PO says he's still clean. You gotta give the boy props for that.

Who would've thought?

Yeah…

The women turned to check on Rydell again, who was now swaying back and forth like a zombie on the couch, not fully asleep, but not really awake either.

And then there's this one. Deirdre shook her head, perturbed.

You think he's ever gonna find his way?

Not with what Rita and Joe got him on. I mean look at this shit. Deirdre held up his med sheets. All slobbering himself in some kind 'a coma half the day. He may be an asshole, but this shit ain't right.

They know staff can't handle him without it.

Yeah, well they just doubled his dose of Dexedrine. I mean, what's next, saturate his little brain with Klonopin and put him in the hospital for good? He isn't even a fully developed person yet, Deirdre fumed at the thought.

Apparently it's calming him down in the evenings, according to Josh and Maurice.

But at what price? Deirdre was insistent now. I mean look at him. He's a pathetic shell of himself. We've been studying the long-term effects of various psychotropic drugs in my Cognitive Behavior Therapy class for the last three weeks. Turns out, Dexedrine destroys brain cells as fast as the most neurodegenerative of medications out there. His brain's still forming critical connections that are supposed to last him the rest of his life. But by keeping him settled down for Maurice and Josh in the evenings, they're potentially screwing up his long term processing function, which could ruin him forever. That's the price we're paying for keeping him cool, but ain't no one here's gonna have to deal with his psychotic breaks when he gets older in the future, so nobody gives a shit now.

Yeah, I completely hear what you're saying.

Just 'cause a bunch of lazy-ass staff can't handle his mouth runnin' all day, the therapists destroy his head so everyone can get through their day easier...It's not like you or I've ever had any real problems with him.

Yeah, but Rita loves that kid like her son. She's not gonna give him anything to mess him up long term. And if she sees what she's doing is hurting him, she'll change it up like she always does.

Deirdre shook her head defiantly. But that's it, don't you see? 'Cause nobody's sure what the side effects of all these meds have on a young developing brain. You know, the book they base their diagnosis on, the DSM IV, it's so socially constructed by this core group of clinical psychologists who base their diagnoses on arbitrary case studies where nobody really knows what the fuck they're looking at, so they just throw together some symptoms after they watch a bunch of kids exhibit the same behaviors for awhile. Then they put it into the book. And THEN, when they see some kid with the same behaviors someone else saw in another kid, they put into the book and diagnose them all as having the same condition. Then they throw all this medication at them that they think will mitigate the symptoms listed in that book without having any sense of what's really bothering the unique, individual kid they're treating. And no one really knows how these meds are gonna effect the person down the road. 'Cause their either too new or 'experimental treatments.' What I'm sayin' is there are always missing pieces to the story.

Carly frowned. But the meds usually do help them stop from acting out.

But is that worth it? At the expense of burying all their traumas in a flood of pharmaceutical haze where the root psychological problems are never fixed because their brain chemistry is so constantly garbled by the chemicals they've taken just so we can manage them day to day? That's unfortunately the way our current treatment paradigm works, using meds to complement their 'behavior dialectic therapy.' Either find a match in the DSM or diagnose our kids as 'borderlines' so we keep financial resources available to keep combining new med treatments with behavioral interventions while we watch and wait and hope for the best. By calling them 'borderlines,' that allows our therapists to medically justify lumping a whole variety of traumatic medications on our kids, who act out because of their supposed 'behavioral disorders', until they find something that sticks. And of course, if they are truly undiagnosable, then we just call them NOS, or Not Otherwise Specific, or 'Wastebaskets' and for these we've got no treatment or no cure. So God forbid one of these kids has one of the 9 personality disorders that we do know about and that there are no meds to treat. Of course then we couldn't keep throwing any more chemicals at them to chill them the fuck out, so let's just not diagnose them and keep labelling them 'borderlines' and instead medicate the shit out of their behavior any way we can…It's all so arbitrary, Carly, when you really look into how it works out on the front lines. Like right here. It's all bullshit.

Well, it sounds like it's all they have to go on, so they're doing their best, I guess. Carly surmised.

If they wanted to do their best, they'd do real diagnosis and apply their behavioral dialectic therapy without meds to help kids work through their issues without frying their brains with every pharmaceutical on the shelf. Deirdre was very insistent on this point. You know how much money pharmaceutical companies make each year in this country just off of treating children with supposed 'psychiatric conditions'? Billions! Every year! It drives an industry. That's why it continues.

Carly snorted. I don't know about all of that. But I do know our therapists seem to care about the kids in their charge. They're trying to do the right thing. I mean, Rita and Jamey are always so careful when they change up meds, and they always do it with the best intentions.

Yeah, maybe, but is that supposed to make it more reassuring? Is that supposed to make me sleep better at night, knowing that with half a million kids in placement in the US, and so many are on some kind 'a cocktail combinations once they receive a diagnosis for a mental disorder, because kids in placement are more likely to get diagnosed with psychiatric conditions as a cause for their acting out, if you compare them with kids who aren't in foster care, who have families more willing to deal with their shit, they don't have to take meds, they just get sent to their room or grounded, but because all our kids have these extra traumas, and the fact that staff turns over so fast and that most of our clients have no consistent parenting in their lives, the best we can do to help them manage their 'behavioral' issues is to give them a pill and fry their brains? Deirdre surmised. NOT!

Meanwhile, Rydell woke from his stupor.

Yo Deirdre, Rydell yelled out.

Yeah honey?

You livin' with the devil ain't you?

Deirdre rolled her eyes at his lethargic delivery. Why do you say that?

With all that makeup you be wearin', you look like you 'bout ready to sacrifice some babies or somethin'. Go drink they blood and shit…

Go back to sleep, D.

Go on now, go back home…Tell Satan I say hi. He spouted in his haze as he faded back into oblivion.

***

Ron Thompson stood in his office overlooking the gym at the Excelsior Boys and Girls Club, watching his star player Marcus Turner shoot from the three point line. The kid had sunk seven straight so far. He knew Marcus's story all too well. One in a million here at the club. Unlike the others, Marcus had a shot at greatness now that he was off the streets.

Marcus channeled perfection from the free throw line. He set it up, tossed the ball from his hands, visualizing the swish. It came seamlessly. He thought of Boyce and his mom, of better days when they all lived together with Grandma, how one day he would make that happen again when he turned 18 and ditched school after getting signed by the NBA, preferably the Lakers. Unlike most of these other ghetto scraps from the hood, like Pee Jay and Juke, those dudes could ball no doubt, but Marcus had discipline, so he wus the cat to beat come All City in a few months. Marcus couldn't help dreamin' 'bout all them college scouts comin' to scope out new talent, for new blood, and how he'd secure his scholarship by showin' dem skids how a real baller do it movin', makin' his play at the State Championships, it was only a matta of time 'fore all them shady agents came a knockin'. 'Fore they rolled out his All Star contract and dropped his fat signing bonus into his lap, shit ain't no joke, and he'd be laughin' all the while 'cause he'd been knowin' for years this day would come. Shit, 'cause it was always Marcus' dream to provide for his family, make life right for his moms and his little bro. And once an NBA star, Marcus'd flip his resources to pull Boyce and his mom outta them dilapidated ass Altegard projects quickstyle, free 'em from the grips a that bitch caseworker Clara Rodriguez who be foreva draggin' him out from unda his family any chance she spotted. Marcus knew with every free throw and every last shot he was one step closer to makin' his dreams true for his mamma and little brother, being the real man none 'a them ever had. He planned on raisin' up Boyce right for realz once he wus stackin' serious paper, too legit no doubt, livin' together under the roof of the dream house 'a Marcus's creation, a fat million dolla life where Momma would never have to lift a finger workin' and could go back to school to get her Nursing degree like she'd always wanted once she was off of drug probation for good. Marcus would pull out all the stops to get her into one of them rich-people treatment centers, all Betty Ford and shit, get Momma enrolled in a real 12 step, none 'a this court-mandate three month bullshit that tore her away from her kids every time she slipped, settin' her up to falta wit' they unannounced home visits and piss tests that ain't done nobody no good. But under his watch and with his megadollars soon flowin', Boyce'd be set up in a real school out da hood where he could have hisself a real girlfriend too, not one a them ghetto skeezas from da block where he could focus on gettin' his academics right and go to college. All on account of Marcus. The provida. If only he kept makin' these shots, come on now, 'though his wrist be hurtin' like a motherfucker every time he threw one-

Ron Thompson walked out onto the court, interrupting Marcus' daydream. He knew something about dreams himself, and admired Marcus' sense of determination. But with that lower arm inflamed the way it was, it was best to lay off awhile.

Ron grabbed the ball as it fell from the net and passed back to Marcus.

How's that wrist healin'?

It's doin' what it do.

Might wanna lay off a bit.

Ain't no thang, Marcus' concentration was not swayed.

As Marcus' mentor for three years, following Marcus's court-appointed placement into Excelsior House, Ron had done his best to nurture Marcus' dreams. He wanted more than anything to see this kid succeed, not just because of his life story, but so he knew that one 'a his could make good enough, it was possible for any of them to make it, with a little luck and a lot of heart.

Listen, Ron began, catching the ball as the last shot dropped from the net. I got a call back from that basketball camp in Atlanta. They said they might have a place for you this summer if you can raise the funds.

Marcus held his hands out for Ron to pass the ball. After a beat, Ron did. Marcus took another shot, eyes never leaving the rim. How much they want?

Three grand?

Marcus tossed his mentor his Are you fucking kidding me? glance as he retrieved the ball. Damn. Ain't nobody I know with that kind 'a skrill 'cept a few slingers.

Ron laughed truthfully. No doubt. But I think I've got a way around the signup fee.

Yeah? What's up? Marcus looked up, genuinely interested now. Ron tossed him back the ball.

Magic Johnson's Young Leaders Fellowship is offering scholarships for disadvantaged youth looking to make something of their futures. I went on his website. If you're looking to go to college, you can write an essay, maybe make the case for having him sponsor you.

Marcus shook his head while batting an eye, then made another free throw. Ron dutifully passed him back the ball.

You still thinking about school?

Yeah. Marcus made his next shot.

That's good, Ron agreed.

But I ain't bankin' on no Magic Johnson to get me there. That's what the scouts are for.

You don't want to put all your eggs in one basket, Ron countered. Every little bit helps.

Marcus shook his head indifferently. We both know I ain't got but one shot wit' dat, and its right here.

Another swoosh.

Ron betrayed a dejected look from Marcus' ingratitude. Marcus noticed this and corrected himself, knowin' regardless of who was more realistic, Ron always had his back, come whatever may.

Yo, so when you wanna show me that scholarship form?

Ron smiled. It's printed up in my office. Check out the site when you have a minute.

Yeah, I'll be there. Marcus took another shot. Another swoosh. And another satisfied smile from Ron. Somehow, some way, he knew this boy had a real chance.

***

Lucy Gutierrez walked past her dream wedding dress in the window at Mi Encanta on Mission Street before crossing Cesar Chavez Avenue to check her job application status at the Centro De Empleo. Her case manager Lucretia Weintraub was brief.

Did the law firm call back?

I'm sorry Lucinda, your typing skills weren't fast enough to match their needs.

Lucy's heart dropped before Lucretia could finish. She had a lot banking on that interview.

So's anyone else hiring?

Not for the moment. So should we go ahead and reactivate your status in our temp bank?

What you sayin'? I wasn't active before?

In order to satisfy our clients, we only draw from those of you with no permanent jobs pending.

Lucy knew bouncing back into the temp bank was a dead end.

Shoure…

OK. Then we'll let you know if we need you for anything.

All right, thank you.

Say hi to yo' little one.

Lucy forced a courtesy smile. Always a 'let you know' but never a 'yes' or even a 'maybe'. Well this just meant you don't have what it takes, you're too stupid or too uneducated for any real office work, so get back in line with the rest of the single moms trying to learn Word or Excel, maybe you can find a housekeeping job or sumpthin' with the rest 'a them Latina maids from the block and they sistas.

But Lucy didn't allow herself to stay fazed for too long. 'Cause with Key back in the mix, she needed to be on her own two feet for Tre more than ever, and she needed to pay Joe back legit. So she'd pick her head back up and see what was out there tomorrow.

Lucy passed the jornaleros waiting for work along the Cesar Chavez strip as she walked home, across South Van Ness and Folsom, before turning left down Harrison back to her baby and to Keyshawn. As she passed the many migrant men standing there downtrodden, as alone as she was with no hope for any steady future employment, she could only think, damn, those dudes' families must be hurtin' too…At least I ain't the only one.

***

     Across town about an hour before, Deshelby Rollins jettisoned past Tim's Market on Grove Street with a fury, hustlin' for his life, with two thugs on his back. Keyshawn's crew had just spotted him copping a deal in Alamo Square, Keyshawn's turf no doubt, so he made his break for it. But Key's people was trailin' fast. He didn't have time to look over his shoulder to see if they'd pulled out they clips yet. Best to assume they had or if not, then they was about to. But If he kept 'em runnin' long 'nough, it'd be all good. Deshelby was the fastest scrap on the block, so he knew he could smoke any 'a these flip-ass slingas skimmin' here and there off 'a Keyshawn's bags. The only reason they hadn't capped him yet wus cus dey wus too busy makin' they play for the Lower Addition fo' him to be worth they time up in Alamo. But now wit' Knockout Posse fallin' back after a few 'a they peoples got sidewalked, all 'a Western Addition was Key's territory now, and them independent contractas like Deshelby now knew they wus on notice. All 'cept for Deshelby himself, who still for fuck knows whatever reason thought he didn't count. But Deshelby didn't plan on their shakedown creepin' up to Alamo this mornin', 'cause ever since Key be takin' ova, his boys only been flexin' on dem crews down on Grove and Turk. But no more. Now they wus expandin' operations, lockin' down the square as well as every drop north to Geary, 'fectively putting nonaffiliates like Deshelby outta business for good. So when Deshelby took it upon himself to say fuck dem hoodrats and keep a lock on his corner, Key's boys made it they business to turn him out right quick. And if he didn't make it past Buchanan now and over that Altegard gate, those dudes wus about to have they way fo' sho'.

     So Deshelby ran like a motherfucker, cruising down Grove several blocks with Keyshawn's boys Antonio and Bizmark in tow 'till he made it to the entrance to Altegard. For his life, he turned hard into the gate and jumped the fence with all his force, but stuck himself trying to slip his otherwise dopefiend-skinny ass between the guardbar and over the metal door. That was all the opportunity Key's thugs needed to run out the clock and finish they job.

Whassup nigga! Deshelby yelled as the two assassins caught their breath, aiming their Glock Nines right at D's stuck body. He called out more for the neighbors, knowin' a couple must 'a been hidin' behind them glass windows or on they floors, listenin' to the murder that wus about to go down. 'Cause maybe if somebody grew balls 'nough to show they face or call da po-po, maybe none 'a this shit would play out like it was about to. But naw, fuck all dat, who was Deshelby even tryin' to kid-

Yo blood, Eddy Rock crew don't run Grove no mo'!

Mang, fuck da 27's! (Keyshawn's Crew)

The first two shots impacted Deshelby's body hard enough to push his body through the divide between the upper gate and the door and off the backside. He was a corpse long before he hit the pavement below with a deadened thud. Casually observing the fallout from their kill, Antonio and Bizmark didn't even trip. They just stood there, winded and hunched over, wheezing from all the runnin' they'd done. Once they caught their breath, they walked casually back to Tim's Market for a soda. One of the neighbors heard the two boys muttering as they passed below the window.

Motherfucker could turn it up though, gotta give 'im dat.

No doubt.

***

Lucy Gutierrez walked up the steps to her dilapidated Victorian apartment and turned the key in the door latch. Home at last.

Baby, I'm back.

Keyshawn was on the phone receiving the news of Deshelby's untimely demise from Antonio and Bizmark. Yo I gots to go, Cinda here. Holla.

He hung up. Lucinda came in to find him gently playin' with their baby boy. She gave him a snuggle. Hi baby! Momma's home.

She planted her lips first on her son's forehead, then turned to kiss Key. He didn't look at her, focusing instead on Tre. She found his coolness odd.

How was your day, baby?

Coo', he mumbled. Just takin' out the garbage, playin' wit' our little soldja here.

Lucy was afraid to ask. She watched intently as Tre fumbled with the plastic black GI Joe doll Key had bought for his son at the dollar store last week.

See dis dawg? This is you. Keyshawn beamed as he played with Tre's hands. But you ain't runnin' off gettin' yo'self killed or shot up for no damn military like so many 'a our peoples. Naw…'Cause you's gon' be hood certified, straight up. He shook Tre's arms. Tre gave him a cherubic smile. Fools'll be shakin' in they draws when you runnin' the block like yo' daddy, steppin' to any motherfucker who be slippin'. Hells yeah. 'Cause you's gon' be hardest of the hard, notorious just like your pop, the family way. You's a livin' legacy now, gon' set my exploits to shame, little man, takin' this village for all it got, you'll see.

He shook the GI Joe doll to entertain his son. And when all those flip-ass motherfuckas from round da way comin' back to the hood from whatever war they been in, thinkin' they's hard, shootin' whoeva they done, all dressed up in dem cammo rags fightin' fo' some govn'ment don't give a fuck 'bout they peoples no how, you straight ain't gon' give a fuck, know what I'm sayin'? Cuz you gon' be runnin' they shit too. You'll be the meanest, smartest hustla' 'round, and all them fools 'a have to bow down, pay their respects, 'cause they all know you be the one handlin' the real business, come on now…

You talkin' your mess to him again? He just a baby.

Ain't never too young to indoctrinate, ain't that right, Tre? He bobbed Tre up and down on his knee.

Tre smiled as his father returned his affections. Yeah…My nigga. But Key's affection quietly turned to a scowl as he looked up now to focus on Lucy, who was boiling some water in the kitchen to make spaghetti.

Yo, girl.

Yeah baby?

Where you come by the money for all dem groceries?

Lucy shuddered at the question's implication, and did not turn around in order to avoid betraying any expression. Instead she hoped to hide her discomfort by preparing the meal as if nothing was wrong.

You ain't on no food stamps now, Key growled.

Naw baby, that hundie you handed me a few nights back took care 'a things, she returned lightly.

Key got up from the couch, carefully setting Tre down on the sofa. The hairs on her back instantly rose. She could feel the menace in his approach but did not dare turn around to face him.

That's funny, 'cause I don't recall handin' you no hundie.

She tried desperately to deflect. You was busy on the Playstation wit' yo' boys. Maybe you done forgot is all. It ain't no thang, baby...

Key snarled under his breath. Naw baby, it can't be, 'cause I keep track 'a all my money real tight, you know that.

He rubbed up right against her. She could sense his uncurling rage and desperately prayed the next words out of her mouth didn't bring his simmer to a boil.

Where'd you get that grip Lucy? He growled in her ear.

She immediately closed her eyes and prayed to herself silently. From you, bab-

You's lyin'!

He grabbed her wrists and slammed her fingers against the stove. He almost broke every bone in her hand.

Ahh! Stop Key-

Tre heard his mother shriek and began to cry.

Key was automatic. You best tell me where you got that money, girl.

He twisted her arm around now, unleashing the tears welling in her eyes.

Key baby, please!

Tell me NOW!

Ayite, OK, it was Joe-

At the mention of his name, Key's blank face turned from an expression of measured calm to unbridled, furrowing rage. He slapped Lucy hard against the cheek, dropping her to the ground with a full swing as he released her swollen hand from the stove. She almost knocked the pot of boiling water onto him on her way down.

Key just gazed at her.

I told you never to take money from that fool, you got that? 'Cause I'm the provider 'a this family!

Baby, please, I'm sorry, Lucy pleaded. I didn't get my job! I was hopin' to make you proud and didn't know how to tell you so I asked Joe for a solid to hold us over. Key, baby, please - I know I screwed up; I know I messed up bad, baby, I'll never–

You never take nuthin' from nobody but me! 'Cause I'm your man, you my princess, and that's the way things gonna stay from now on.

Tre shrieked in the background, prompting Key to extend his arm outward toward his son and comfort him in this moment of uncertainty.

Ain't no play, little man, mom and daddy just talkin' is all.

He then turned back to Lucy and pulled her up from the floor by her sprained hand, wrapping it in his clenched fist. She winced but found herself too afraid to cry out in pain.

Luce, you'z my woman, and there ain't no way that ever gonna go wrong, understand?

She nodded.

I just want us to be the family we never had. That neither 'a us done, you feel me?

He squinted hard at her with clear intent to do further harm if she did not comply. So she slowly relaxed the full of her body within his commanding hold.

Yeah baby, she rationalized hard. I know you doin' it all for us.

Good. He grew confident again, slowly releasing her brittle fingers from his grasp. So listen up now. Tomorrow you's gonna give all that money back and tell him you's done seein' him no mo', you feel me? 'Cause you's my people now, and I'm 'a take care of you.

His eyes flashed maniacally, searching her expression for any hint of resistance. She knew if she didn't tell him true, the beating would resume.

Yeah, baby…

Then you's gonna come home and cook dinna like you always do when you's waitin' fo' me to get back. And then we gonna get back to bein' the family we is. How's that sound, baby?

She shuddered inside. That sounds nice, Key…

Real good, baby, he responded flatly. 'Cause you my everythin', girl, you know that? And I ain't lettin' nothin' get the way 'a that no mo', you feel me? You's mine, you and Tre, and we got something real goin' now, hear me? So I don't want you over there hangin' round them bitches who callin' you they peoples, then talkin' they mess tryin' to spin ill thoughts 'round yo' head to keep us separated, none 'a that shit, you feel me? Check it all at da door. 'Cause you's straight breakin' 'em off permanent now, 'riddin yoself 'a all they bad influences on what we's creatin' here.

Lucy nodded. Yeah baby, I got it…

Yeah? He shook her, though gently.

Yeah. She was truly broken now.

Good. Then go on now, calm our son down while I'm 'a finish dinner. Then we'z gonna eat like none 'a this mess been comin' on.

Lucy promptly did as she was told. She walked over to Tre, lifting him up and leaning him against her shoulder to pat his back with her painful hand as he continued to cry. It's OK Boobie, it's OK; momma and daddy's just wrestling is all.

After several minutes of this, Key called out to her from the kitchen where he put the finishing touches on their dinner preparations. But this time, he fronted as if nothing prior had transpired. So my princess want mushrooms and cheese on her steam noodles?

Sauce is fine enough baby.

Ayite, but I'm tellin' you, shits da bomb with the Parmesan…

Lucy sobbed silently to herself, burying her face in her son's side. By not leaving the house right then and there with him, in this moment she'd become the very woman she hoped she'd never be.

***

Julio met up with his crew at HOMEY'S (Homeboys Overnight in the Mission Empowering Youth) just after eight o'clock. Little Eduardo threw his favorite Tupac Shakur album into the stereo while Tootz and Edgar from Julio's former 24th Street Norteño set joined Nestor Flores, their group mentor, in prayer.

Paco 415 and Carlos ran with their rival 16th Avenue Sureños on account of little more than geography, but were on this rare occasion kickin' with their old skool patnas from childhood in this neutral setting.

Julio, you want to speak the convocation this evening? Nestor directed the others to grab hands as they joined in group prayer.

What up y'all.

What up.

Word.

And now for the blessing: Lord we come here tonight in the spirit of your love and in celebration of your vision that we are all your children and no matter what race or color or creed or set we affiliate with in this world you love us equally as brothers and we embrace our homies convened on this evening in the hopes that our communities and our families and our peoples can come together in the vision and the spirit of your love. God bless and AMEN.

Amen.

That was tight, Julio.

Damn right.

Yo, blut, turn up the music already!

Ayite…

You bring the disk?

You know I hook you up. Julio pulled Duane's Tupac CD from his bag.

Little Eduardo checked the label and nodded approvingly, dropping it in the stereo and quickly cueing to his favorite song, "I Wonder If Heaven Got a Ghetto."

Yo blut, play the whole thing, shit.

Yo mang, your song be comin' on hella soon.

Stop skipping shit, blut.

Ayite, just this one, Little Eduardo pleaded.

So whas up y'all? Nestor mediated.

Paco 415 shifted the lid of his SF Giants hat and jumped right in. Yo Eduardo, where'd you get that shiner? Playin' soccer wit' my boys up on 20th?

Eduardo shook his head. This shit's gettin' out control, blut. Words out yo' homie Miguel bringin' in some Mara fools from Bakersfield to take out Hector's crew.

Paco and Carlos both spit. Shit blut, 16th Street's goin' to war over what you bustas done to our boy Rodrigo, for realz.

Edgar fronted. Then we gon' flip the rest of you scraps fo' what y'all done to Eduardo.

Y'all best let shit lie, you feel me? Bygones be bygones, know what I'm sayin'? 'Cause even 'dough we all here kickin' it like a bunch a God lovin' motherfuckers, on da block, Miguel be addin' y'all names to his hitlist, for realz.

What 'chu spittin' now?

Shit blut, everyone knows y'all pulled the trigger on our boy, no doubt.

Yo, we ain't had nothin' to do with dropping that scrap, straight up-

Y'all's some lyin' ass bustas, Paco 415 insisted. He knew his childhood friends better than that.

You best get yo' stories correct, and stay out da mix 'fore you get checked, feel that? Tootz warned.

Don't even try to front, Carlos admonished them, 'Cause several of our patnas up on 20th made your punk asses on the scene.

Yo mang, I ain't even tryin' to hear all that, Tootz dismissed outright. Them 20th street suckas didn't see shit, 'cause that wusn't us. You feel me, blut?

We know you all wus involved. Julio too.

Naw, 'cause they's some lyin' ass suckas, Julio demanded. I ain't even in da life no more. Shit, them gang injunctions and my old lady 'nough to run me off fo' good, but I been comin' round to set my niña right, and thas all, mang. I been jumped out months, just ask these motherfuckers right here.

Paco and Carlos looked to Tootz and Hector for validation. They were still so pissed at Julio for not helping them hunt down Rodrigo they contemplated selling him out, but out of respect for their past together, instead confirmed his alibi. Homeboy's talkin' true. Shit, we turned his ass out real good several months back, blut said he wanted out da life, so shoot, we gave his ass what he asked fo', know what I'm sayin'? The fond memories of kicking Julio's ass remained fresh in his voice.

Well, y'all best wake the fuck up blut, Carlos scoffed. 'Cause when you wasted Rodrigo and Ramon front 'a the whole world to see, you set shit in motion.

For realz.

That bitch Rodrigo got what was comin' to him anyhow, Edgar tried to rationalize.

And now you 'bout to get yours, Paco declared.

Paco and Carlos were surprised by their adamant denials. All kinds of people saw them do it, so retribution was inevitable. Yo mang, whatever you say, it don' even matta now, 'cause every busta runnin' wit' you crew a target now, them Bakersfield scraps straight make all y'all pay for droppin' our homies, you feel me? La Eme ain't makin' no distinctions, for realz.

Yo mang, true dat, those valley vatos don't mess around, shoot.

They out fo' some busta blood now, blut.

Shit, them Bakersfield soldjas Miguel called in are Cardena's boys, you feel me? So you best stay the fuck out da 20's and keep yo' heads down 'cause guilty or not, y'all some hunted-ass cholos now, you feel me?

Yo blut, long as you ain't lookin' down the barrel 'a my glock, then we's cool.

Shoot, Paco empathized. We ain't got no pull with Miguel now that he bringin' in them Mara elders to take out your set.

Fo' sho', so watch your backs yo', Carlos added.

Aw hell naw.

Fo' realz.

Shoot, you scraps got some dumb ass love for a busta 'round here tonight.

Yo blut, I'm tellin' you, y'all best leave Slum Francisco while you still can, 'cause them valley vatos be putting in work round the clock on y'all 'till they blast every last busta off 24th Street, you feel me? They comin' at 'chu hard now, blut, for realz straight up, fuck everything now, 'cause all 'a 16th Street's lookin' to funk with you, Paco finished.

Mang, they can bring it hard as they want, 24th Street Ene straight don't give a fuck, 'cause our Nuestra people be comin' up from Fresno to drop all y'all, you feel me? Tootz retorted. Get yo' body bags and yo' t-shirts ready, 'cause we doin' it right, Ene straight represent!

All part 'a da struggle, Edgar agreed.

But underneath all their posturing, Edgar and Tootz considered their old friend's warnings solidly.

Shit blut, Tootz offered. We but appreciate y'all stickin' yo' necks out to come holla at us.

Yeah blut; straight up, mang. It's all good with 'chall far as I'm concerned. Edgar nodded.

But Paco grew defensive. You can talk all the shit you want, but if Miguel catches on that we got wit' chall, he be lining us up right next to you dead busters on da curb.

Dude got wood for a snitch yo', Carlos confirmed.

Naw mang we feel you, Edgar promised to not narc them out. We ain't gonna say shit.

Holla that.

The boys reaffirmed their childhood bond, which thankfully at some level still transcended whatever set politics they had bought into with their respective crews.

Paco then turned to address Julio. Look blut, far as I'm concerned, it's all good you out da life, but you best tell yo' babymoms to get your niña out da hood 'fore shits shit starts poppin' off, cause this summer gonna be open season on all you bustas, you feel me?

Yeah mang, we gotta flop yo' ass too if we catch you 'round the way, you feel me? Carlos agreed, not wanting to see his childhood friend shot dead. Your niña don't need no dead-ass papi, holmes, know what I'm sayin'?

Yeah, Julio conceded. Then we out, blut.

So consider you motherfuckin' selves warned then, ayite?

Peace.

The boys all tapped fists, knowing they had to split sides after this evening. But they tried to make the most of their last night together.

Yo, Little Eduardo, mang, flip that CD back on, shit!

Blut, I'm sick as fuck 'a yo' song already!

***

Brandon and Nate eagerly awaited their parents' arrival at Excelsior House while Josh Crenshaw, Carly and Deirdre worked the afternoon shift with Jamey Sherwood, the family's therapist.

Jamey was the first to greet the parents as they entered the cottage. They seem nice enough, Carly remarked to Deirdre.

Deirdre frowned after feigning a smile as the parents stood there waiting for their sons. Together, the two of them can't pass a drug test to save their own lives, much less get their boys back. That's why they have their monitored visits on site, she informed Carly.

They do look like a couple 'a malfunctions, that's for sure, Josh agreed with uncharacteristic subtlety by whispering under his breath.

Just then Nate and Brandon emerged from their rooms. Hey boys, their father hugged them lovingly. How you doing, son?

I'm straight.

Nate.

Hey pop.

Their mother followed.

Is that tuna casserole momma? Brandon asked eagerly.

Made just right for my babies. With the crust how you like it.

Nate smiled. Each boy got the same hug from her. But because it was in front of the staff and several other clients, including Rydell and Eric, the boys became visibly embarrassed.

Mr. and Ms. Sampson, we can go into the next room, Jamey suggested, extending his arm to point down the hall.

I thought we was gonna cook here, Nate reconsidered.

We are darling, his momma smiled. Just like at home.

Yeah, just like home, their father beamed with a paper bag raised in his hand. Got the fixin' for the grits and collard greens right here.

Brandon relaxed his expressionless façade with a smile. You gonna finally show me how you do it? 'Cause I need to be eatin' somethin' other than this prison food they servin' up here.

Come on now, his momma smirked at her son, It can't be that bad now. Y'all makin' a fuss over nuthin'.

Nate and Brandon both rolled their eyes. Brandon dropped his head and rolled his eyes around to call his mom out.

Shit tastes like dog food half the time here, Momma.

His parents blushed. Come on now Brand, his dad smiled nervously, chastened by the deeper implications of his son's comment. I'm sure it ain't puppy chow.

Nate wasted no time backing up his brother on this point. Oh, yes it is. It felt good to guilt his folks for leaving him and his brother out here with the wolves.

Well we gonna have a nice meal tonight baby, ain't that right? His mom tried to recover.

Sho' is baby, her husband agreed.

Y'all gonna let us have some? Eric piped up from the living room couch.

Josh quickly intervened to squelch the interruption. Naw Eric, 'cause you're about to get your two butts out on the circle while we let your two housemates homevisit.

Mang, does this feel like home to y'all? Rydell asked Brandon and Nate, if only to dampen their mood.

Shut your trap, D 'fore I double your dose! Josh bellowed.

Mang, shoot. Rydell dismissed them, pissed that everyone besides him had themselves some kinfolk.

Josh just shook off Rydell's comments to the boys' parents. Don't pay him no mind. He's just a little asshole…

Each parent responded with an autonomic jerk of their bodies, shocked by Josh's blunt assessment in front of the very client he was speaking of. But both of their boys quickly reassured them with a nod to confirm full agreement with Josh.

Jamey, in charge of the visit, tried to remain poised with a smile throughout the interaction. He motioned diplomatically for the family to move on into the kitchen.

Yo, Dell, Eric, asses up and out now! Josh commanded.

Eric obliged while Dell dragged himself slowly out of the house.

Yo Brandon, you best save me some greens, he called out without turning around. Peace out!

Josh, Carly and Deirdre followed the boys out the door to allow the family and their behavioral therapist their privacy.

***

Maurice showed up at Excelsior House later that afternoon with a bag of movies and snacks for the boys in Cottage 2. Kevin was scheduled to cover the overnight shift, but both staff would be supervising the boys this evening. It was a rare occasion that everyone was home. Maurice relieved Josh just after dinner as the boys finished up their chores.

See ya, maggots! Josh snickered.

Later Josh, Duane called out.

Oh excuse me, maggots and Duane.

Mang, Duane pouted.

Brandon finished wiping the dishes down. He was complimenting you, crackhead.

Nate was still agitated by the brevity of their home visit earlier in the day. Bitch can suck a dick, he muttered under his breath.

Kevin called out. Nate, language!

I don't care man, shit.

Nate's true indifference to staff's wishes caused Eric to laugh. Damn.

Eric, Kevin advised, Don't get in the middle of things.

AHH HAA OK. He returned to sponging down the tables.

Brandon, on the other hand, lit up when he saw Maurice come in. Did you bring Halo 3?

Got it right here, dawg.

Awesome, he and Duane approached Maurice first.

Dude, y'all better finish up your chores.

Mang, Tyrone complained, I thought we was gon' to watch Transformers.

Maurice smiled. Brought that too.

That bitch on there is hot, Nate cracked.

Language, Nate, please.

Eric countered. Mang, we got us some hatin' ass staff up in here.

Eric, what's gotten into you tonight?

I don't know.

Kevin took a moment to check the boys' current behavior level rankings as scribbled on the dry erase board in the staff room.

Looks like Rory, Duane, Kendrick, Brandon and Nate are all at Level 3, so you guys can watch the movie.

Tyrone protested. Mang I'm off 'a restriction too!

Says on the board you're still on Level 2.

Shoot, that's 'cause Carly forgot to change it after her overnight. That was supposed to end yesterday.

Kevin looked to him at first suspiciously, then sympathetically. There was from time to time some confusion between staff on updates if one of them forgot to change the board after working a 16-hour combined evening-overnight shift, which usually happened at the end of each staff's work week.

I'll double check the log book then, Kevin agreed.

You do that, Billy, Rydell snickered from the couch.

Dell, you know you're still at Level 1, Kevin immediately countered.

Dell eyefucked him. Yeah, that's 'cause some PHD's up in here don't know when to stop pushin' a nigga to the brink.

Brandon and Eric laughed. Nate went one step further to verbalize Rydell's frustration. Bitch can suck a dick!

Now Maurice jumped in. Nate, cool it dude.

It was unclear to Kevin if Nate's comment was directed toward him, so he let it go.

Maurice followed Kevin into the staff room, commanding to the other boys. Y'all finish up those chores and we'll throw in the movie.

Once inside, Maurice put a reassuring hand on Kevin's shoulder. You cool?

Yeah, Kevin replied. Dell's mouth I expect. But what's up with Nate and Eric tonight?

Maurice sighed. I talked to Joe and he said Brandon and Nate's onsite visit didn't go so well today. The boys thought they might get to go home on their next one, but based on what Jamey saw he ruled it out for now. So they may be a little out the fray tonight. I say we let them all watch the movie, just cuz.

Kevin considered this for a moment. I'm cool with that.

Cool, Maurice replied as they both returned to the front room.

Kevin made the announcement. Maurice and I talked it over and were gonna let y'all watch the movie.

Aw listen to Billy over here, Brandon cracked. Y'all.

Several of the boys laughed. Kevin did not flinch.

That is if you all can handle it, Kevin stared intently at both Dell and Brandon.

Dell took immediate opportunity to stir the pot. What you lookin' at me for hater, I ain't even said nuthin'...

Eric cracked up as Kevin gave him a close stare. You think you can handle yourself too, Eric?

Eric was clearly aggravated for being singled out, but agreed. Yeah I'm cool.

Fine.

Maurice, put in the movie!

Yo Maurice, your girl as fine as Megan Fox? Rory asked.

The boys all waited intently for his response.

Shoot, she hotter, Maurice boasted.

Aw, hell naw she ain't!

You right dawg, I'm just playin', Maurice admitted laughingly.

I bet she a mutt, Nate shot out.

Your woman a hoodrat Maurice? Brandon continued.

Maurice looked the inquiring boys over with wizened eyes as Dell pounced. Damn Maurice, you wouldn't know what to do with a hoodrat if one sat in yo' lap, shoot. I bet she ugly. Nasty face like Sylvia and fat-ass like Brenda.

Naw dude, that's wrong, Rory chimed in, shaking his head.

Y'all little boys don't know nuthin' about women, Maurice declared. My God...

Then edumicate us, Maurice. What kinda pussy you pullin' wit' your chubby ass? Dell mocked. Shoot, fool probably eat her before he fuck her anyway.

All the other boys cracked up at this last comment. Maurice playfully engaged them. Yeah D, maybe, but at least I can get women in my bed. He pointed directly to Rydell as he motioned to the other boys to gather around, as if he was a grio sharing a deep secret. I been watching homeboy here try an'run his game on Lucy for, what's it been now D, something like two years, dawg? Maurice chuckled. And what 'chu got to show from all that effort? Pat on the head? Kiss on the cheek? Maurice feigned a tear. Shoot, I heard she tellin' her girls you too short for her, is that right dawg? Damn, now ain't THAT about a bitch. And when you try to kiss her, your breath be hotter than her baby's diaper after he done dumped his draws, Wheew whee, Maurice waved his hand in front of his face. Ain't that right D?

DAAAMMMMMNNN. Tyrone and Brandon, Nate and Rory, Duane and Kendrick and Eric all broke up in stitches over Maurice's dis.

Damn, Lucy thinks Dell smell like dukie! Eric hollered out.

Shut up, fucknuts, Rydell hissed. Least I ain't never stuck my willy in my sister.

Eric got real quiet. But clearly, Maurice struck a nerve bringing up Lucy.

Mang, you know I'm just playin' with you, dawg, he offered his hand out to Dell for a fist tap. But Rydell refused, pouting instead.

Mess with the bull, get the horns, Rory surmised.

Yeah, Brandon added, 'Specially when it's a fat bull.

The other boys continued to ridicule Maurice's weight as he looked over to Kevin, who was busy at the table with Kendrick. Sometimes you gotta let 'em win one, he shrugged.

Kevin laughed. But Dell was still quiet. So Maurice grabbed him in a headlock to carpet burn his nappy scalp instead.

Mang, why you gotta get all sensitive and shit?

Damn Maurice, ayite, stop! Rydell rubbed his head in defeat. Shoot.

Now y'all watch the movie, Maurice declared and hit play.

Later, as the clients of Cottage 2 finished up their evening routines before bed, Rory and Tyrone shuffled into their room.

Damn Rory, Tyrone waved his hand in front of his face. Put some socks on, shoot, the war's over. Where your spray at?

I can't help it T.

Tyrone was among the more sympathetic of the boys to his roommate's hygiene problem. But lately the foul scent emanating from across the room was trying even his patience.

Then put yo' damn feet under the blanket or sumpthin', shoot.

Duane entered their room and after taking a whiff, pulled the neck of the t-shirt he was wearing up to cover his face like a bandit. Rory, yo' stank makin' my eyes water!

Tyrone didn't laugh, wanting to avoid a diatribe from staff last minute before bed. So he just buried his head halfway under his blanket to avoid the smell permeating the room as Rory finished dressing for bed.

Yo Rory, you got that new 50 Cent CD? Duane asked, changing the subject.

Yeah.

Can I borrow it?

Just don't scratch it, it's my brother-in-law's.

Rory reached into his dresser and pulled the disk from its upper drawer. He handed it to Duane.

Cool, Duane dropped, turning to the hallway with a nod of thanks. He returned to his room with Eric who was now fidgeting with his hands. A pencil sat at the base of his bed with a spiral notebook opened to a page with half-finished picture carved out of its berth.

Next door, Nate got changed for bed while his roommate Kendrick read from a debate book with a clip-on light.

In the last room, Brandon and Rydell sat awake talking to, of all people, Kevin. He broke from their chat momentarily to call out to the other boys. Lights out in ten, alright?

Brandon asked Kevin to hold up a minute. Yo Kevin, can we ask you a personal question?

Kevin turned back around thoughtfully, surprised by the request from either of these boys. Seeing an opening to possibly bond with them, which he desperately wanted to do, he agreed. Sure Brandon, he replied. What's up?

Do you masturbate?

Rydell sat in stoned silence waiting for Kevin's reaction. But Brandon was not smirking. He was dead serious in asking this. Kevin understood this moment to be one of those few instances in a child's life where gaining real knowledge required candid illumination from an older brother or other male mentor figure. And for whatever reason, on this night Brandon and Rydell had chosen Kevin for that role. Kevin contemplated momentarily considering the best way to answer, but could see in the boys' eyes that for their sake, he had to do so honestly. So he went for it.

I'm not going to get into my own habits Brandon, but what I will tell you is that healthy adults do it once and awhile.

The boys seem confounded by this response. Brandon pressed it, as if dismissing his stock answer in search of something more meaningful. Yeah, but do YOU masturbate?

Like I said, healthy adults do it once and awhile. That's all I'm gonna say. If you want to put me in that category, then so be it. But I'll tell you that's the truth of it. It's not something to be afraid of.

Brandon just nodded, seemingly comforted by the affirmation he required, and so received it without further drama. Cool.

Rydell said nothing, but from the mildly bewildered look forming in his eyes, he too appeared for the moment not to harbor any need to belittle Kevin, but rather to offer an almost appreciative nod for the honesty of Kevin's response. At least for tonight.

All right then.

Maurice hollered out from down the hall.

All right y'all, lights out! Go to sleep!

The boys quickly complied, each out cold by 10:15. And for the remainder of the evening, all was quiet in Cottage 2.

***

Kendrick brushed the dust off his book in history class. The Homecoming dance for Balboa High School was next week. He peered over his desk to see the object of his affections, Ranisha Jenkins. She was the most beautiful woman he'd ever seen. Confident after clipping his nostril hairs and eyebrows earlier this morning, and giving his scalp a quick buzz with Tyrone's electric razor to sharpen his cut along the forehead Kobe style, he approached her just as class ended. Ranisha's friend Shaniqua Robinson stood with her near the front of the class.

Ranisha gave Kendrick an unsure once-over as he came upon them. Though she was primped and pretty, Ranisha was a real intellect. Not like those Excelsior House skeezers or scandalous-type bitches he'd known from the block or in his numerous placements. No, for Kendrick, Ranisha was a prize to be had, the real deal.

Hey Ranisha.

Hi Kendrick.

He thought he saw her blush.

So, you going out for the debate team?

Sure am. You have to if you want to get into a good college.

Yeah, true dat. I was thinking of trying out myself.

Ranisha smiled at his boldness. Really, Kendrick? I didn't know you were into debate?

I argue with my brother all the time, so I think I got some good practice goin' in...

Shaniqua rolled her eyes. Boy, you gots to bring more than THAT to get up with my girl here. She's smarter than any 'a them fools at this school or any other. She'll tear you up for realz.

Ranisha laughed off her friend's protectiveness. I'm not like that.

There you go again, downplayin' yo' skills. My girl here is fierce like Sasha Fierce. Shaniqua turned to dis Kendrick. So what 'chu think you got to match that, shoot?

I don't like to brag about all that, Kendrick joked to take her off the defensive, returning his attentions instead to Ranisha. But I'm still thinkin' to make the team. One of us does well, we all do better, right?

Ranisha smiled again. That's exactly the kind 'a mindset you have to have to be successful.

Kendrick used his professional voice. And just think, maybe if we beat some 'a those other schools, them colleges scouts will notice our girl here and sign her right up.

This intimation made both Shaniqua and Ranisha giggle.

What, she your girl now? Shaniqua chided his overtness.

A brother can only wish, Kendrick replied confidently.

Well he bold, I give him that, Shaniqua shook her head, giving him another once-over.

Ranisha fixed him with a cool look. You really think you have what it takes to make the team?

Kendrick smiled. We'll see, I guess.

Ranisha hesitated, tilting her head upward, maintaining eye contact. She then returned his grin. Yeah, we'll see.

A silent pause as the two scoped each other out. Shaniqua could not maintain any subtlety as the tension surrounding their flirtations escalated. I think homeboy checkin' for you, Nisha.

Kendrick didn't deny it, but instead steered the direction of the conversation elsewhere, slightly.

So how many hours a week do debate preps take?

Ranisha worked her face into a contortion as she counted in her head. I'd say about five to ten. We meet three times a week after school before competitions.

How long that go?

Why, you got something more important going on? Ranisha inquired almost defensively.

Or someONE, uh huh, aw now I see how he do, Shaniqua called him out, once again rolling her eyes.

Naw, it ain't like that at all, Kendrick insisted.

Isn't like that, Ranisha corrected him brazenly.

Yeah, isn't I mean, my bad. He accepted her correction without resentment. This also impressed her.

So what's the problem then? Ranisha now challenged.

Its just that I got work right after school.

Dude got hisself a job, that's a good sign, Nisha. But Ranisha looked puzzled.

Where you workin'?

I been at McDonalds. He sensed her hesitancy to believe him and so was happy to respond. It puts some flow in my pocket.

Shaniqua was the one who appeared impressed now. Shoot, homeboy got a job, sounds good 'a reason as any to me.

But Ranisha assumed an arrogant, dismissive expression which made Kendrick want to get with her all the more.

Well if you are serious about your future, you'll set work aside to put your academics first.

Kendrick came back at her playfully, without a shred of regret. That's easy to say for someone whose given everything you need.

Ranisha grew defensive at his suggestion. I earn every penny I have, thank you very much.

Yeah. How?

By being a good student.

Kendrick laughed out loud in spite of himself. Oh, OK.

I'm serious, Ranisha reinforced.

I know, that's why it's so funny...

My parents understand the need for school and appreciate that my earning good grades is my primary job. Surely your folks must feel the same way.

Kendrick could not help but laugh out loud at the naiveté of her statement. But it was precisely that which made her so endearing to him, that they were nothing alike. Here she was, this sweet, innocent, bright, happy girl that no punk like him was ever supposed to get with.

Shoot Nisha, my mom's is in the penn and my pops, well I ain't never met 'im. But if I do, I'll be sure to holla at both a them, suggest what 'chu sayin'. I'm sure they'll see the light.

Ranisha and Shaniqua turned to each other uneasily, genuinely embarrassed by their smug combination of ignorance and insolence.

I'm sorry Kendrick, I didn't know about your situation, Ranisha apologized. I shouldn't have jumped to any conclusions about you.

Shoot, ain't no thing, he shrugged. Is what it is, right?

Another awkward silence lingered as it was clear the girls now wished to end their conversation with him quickly.

But Kendrick jumped at the opportunity to flip it on them. So y'all goin' to the homecoming dance with anyone yet?

Ranisha blushed again. Shaniqua got a date.

How come ain't no one hollin' at 'chu yet? Damn, girl as fine as you, that's criminal.

Ranisha playfully held out. Actually, I'm putting that night aside to study instead.

She just too good for anyone who already asked is all, Shaniqua assured on behalf of her friend.

Ranisha looked to her friend with disdain, No I ain't.

Yeah you is...Shoot, don't even lie.

Kendrick jumped at the chance without knowing how or from where the courage came. Well if you ain't busy that night-

Shaniqua huffed, Fool, you already know what she be doin'. She pointed to her girl.

Yeah, I mean, fo' sho', but Ranisha, if you ain't gonna be studyin' ALL night, then maybe we could meet up.

Ranisha smiled, smitten by his offer. But she could not find the words to respond, so once again, Kendrick compensated by filling the empty void.

It don't need to be all that, just a couple of hours.

Shaniqua elbowed her silent friend. Girl, say something.

Ranisha finally firmed up. All right. Well, we'll see.

See what? You ain't got nuthin' doin' that night, Shaniqua rolled her eyes at her friend's solicitude.

Kendrick appeared embarrassed that Ranisha did not seem to want to go with him.

Let's wait until after debate tryouts, she finally smiled to him. If you make the team, I'll consider it.

What, you think I ain't up to the challenge?

We'll see, won't we?

Ayite then.

Shaniqua huffed again. Girl, you crazy.

I'm a make that team for you, then we be goin'?

I said I'll see, Ranisha insisted.

That's cool, but I ain't about to let you down. You can take that to the bank, Kendrick beamed. Ranisha laughed off all of his posturing.

I'm 'a get at you girl, for realz, you watch. I'll be crackin' on them dudes like you never believe.

Oh really…

Hell yeah, just you wait.

I will.

Cool, then I'm 'a holla at y'all later.

Bye, Shaniqua and Ranisha looked to each other and giggled as Kendrick exited the room.

Girl, he crazy.

You's both sprung far as I'm concerned.

On his way home, Kendrick was ecstatic. Duane and Tyrone were never going to believe him.

***

Sarah Hillsbrook ran the knife along her upper arm. Tiny, precise cuts, then the release: slow, warm, satisfying, inviting. She closed her eyes. Felt the endorphins rushing through her blood; a sweet, satiating symphony crackling through her arms. She needed a fix bad. Screetch would surely be missing her by this point, and with Brenda so easily concealin' the bruises from her pimp's claimin' her ass the night before, it was clear staff didn't monitor her roommate's comings and goings for shit, so it shouldn't be too difficult to slip out tonight. She packed the razor tightly back underneath the sole of her shoe and washed away the tiny droplets of blood she'd squeezed from her miniscule cuts down into the sink, patching herself up nicely with a paper towel nabbed from the kitchen and a couple of pieces of scotch tape from Agnes's office. She wrapped the sleeve of her thermal over her throbbing wrist to cover her tracks; those cuts'd be enough to quench her Rodgers until this evening. But she sure as shit better find Screetch when she finally got out, and hope to God he was holding when she caught up to him.

Outside on the circle, Eric was busy boring a hole into the driveway fence with a sharp pencil. No weapons for crazies, Sarah thought to herself as she slowly ventured up to him. Looking down the street, she spotted a tall black man sitting in his Chevy El Dorado Scraper straight scoping out Sylvia and Brenda as they walked in rotation around the circle under Agnes' watchful eye. Agnes didn't notice the man in the car but Eric did. His eyes brightened and his face lit up as Sarah sat down beside him.

Hey stranger.

Whassup.

This seat taken?

Just waiting for you.

I see your being productive.

Yeah. Just one of my moods.

So you like to destroy shit?

I call it creative destruction.

She laughed as he poked the pencil relentlessly into the wood. The lead was long since snapped out of its shaft.

Oh, is that what this is, she replied snidely.

He looked down to her arm. It was bleeding slightly through her thermal sleeve.

You carving some fences of your own?

Oh shit. She tried rubbing the small traces of blood out with her saliva. You don't miss much do you? She replied keenly, sucking her wrist.

Never have. Least that what my folks always told me. Always was the curious baby, they said. He continued carving at the fence.

She drew herself forward. Where they at now?

They're all hippied out, living down in Venice. Pop sells weed, mom just smokes it. They said I could come back to live with them anytime I want, I just have to say the word.

So why don't you?

Dad was busted for drugs one too many times, so they made me a ward of the state. But when I turn Sixteen, sure as shit I'm gonna get up outta this place. I'll emancipate early if that hater Jamey gives me my medical clearance.

How long 'till then?

Let's see, three months, twelve days, seven hours.

She made a face, signaling that she didn't want to bother with the mental math.

January 21.

So you're a Capricorn on the cusp of Aquarius, Sarah much more quickly deduced. That must be what makes you so interesting.

What, you believe in that shit? He reconsidered her tattoos and their previous conversations. Wait, shit, of course you do. Dumb question.

She laughed.

So what does all that mean?

Capricorn makes you grounded, observant, and a shrewd yet social spirit, where your Aquarian side makes you a dreamer.

Pretty much sums me up except for the stable part.

You seem to know what you want well enough.

He looked to her coyly. That's pretty much true.

She smiled back, then broke his gaze.

Well I hope you get back to Venice, Eric. Sounds like a nice dream.

Oh, it's gonna happen. What would make it a dream is if you came with me.

She laughed out loud. Now I see the Aquarian side coming out.

Naw I'm serious, I never say anything I don't mean. He forced his gaze upon her now, taking her hand into his own.

Sarah looked back at him intently. I believe you.

Good, he nodded. 'Cause I won't ever leave you.

She broke his stare again. Okay, Romeo, she chuckled. See that?

She pointed to the dark man keeping his eye on Brenda from the car down the street.

Yeah, he's been checking them out all afternoon.

All blatant like and staff don't even notice.

They probably know him.

Brenda's been sneaking out with the dude last three nights. Girl came crawling through her window with bruises up and down her neck at 4 in the morning, I saw her in the bathroom tryin' to cover 'em all up, but I knew what was up.

Eric checked out her turtleneck. Yeah, it's a little warm for that shit.

Dude's straight pimpin' the hell outta her. And still she takes off with homeboy just about every night Deirdre works. Carly checks our shit regular but Deirdre, that lady's asleep by 11:15 every night.

It's because she's in grad school.

Sarah fixed her gaze upon Eric hard so that he was unable to look away. He locked in a prolonged stare with her. The two sat for several moments reading each other. Neither blinked. Finally, once she was satisfied she'd seen whatever it was she needed from him, Sarah moved away, almost guiltily, a bit further than before.

Point is, I don't wanna go crushin' your romantic fantasies, but I'm outta here tonight.

In light of the intimacy they'd just shared, Eric was taken aback.

I've gotta cop quick. Shit's knockin' real bad cooped up in here.

Is that why you're cutting again?

It ain't passin' the grade no more…

So where you going? He asked, trying to mask his sadness that she was leaving him.

I know a few dudes in the Haight who can hook up what I need.

You know if you bounce they'll send you right to the hospital.

Knowing my parents, I'll be sent somewhere across country for good. That's why this is goodbye Eric. She paused, looking up to him. She couldn't ignore the despondence in his eyes. Indeed this was her very intention, to break him off cold and final right here and now, once and for all. 'Cause she didn't need his infatuation following her around town when she had other business to tend to. You ain't gonna snitch me out, are you?

Eric wanted to cry but his meds kept him from forming any tears.

Naw, I ain't. But you don't have to go. We can run to Venice tonight, you and I, and no haters up in here have to know anything about it. Just you and me, gone. We can get you fixed up and then poof! Vamoose sonofabitch. He blew into his fist and opened his palm.

Sarah laughed. Man, there goes that Aquarius in you again. Eric, I ain't gonna last through the night if I don't cop fast.

Then we'll go to the Haight on our way out.

Dude, you only got three months left. Bolting early won't make a case for your emancipation.

Kids go 300 up in here all the time and they don't do shit about it.

That's 'cause these chumps are all stuck here. You get locked up and you'll go nowhere. I'm telling you stick it out, then you'll be free. LA will be yours.

I want it to be ours.

You don't even know me, she scoffed.

I know enough.

She just shook her head.

Say you'll come back and I won't rat you out.

This rattled Sarah fast. She knew she had to cut this dude off straight now. Bitch you better not say shit-

Then tell me you'll come back.

He grabbed her arm hard enough to cause a bruise as she tried to wrestle him free. Her plan totally backfired. She winced.

Agnes heard her yelp out from across the street. Eric you let go 'a her right now!

Hands off her, malfunction! Josh yelled from across the lot as he hustled over to them.

Eric released her, and she pulled her hand out of his. You're a fucking loon. You know that? Sarah declared, then quietly added, and you best not say shit!

Josh caught up with them. Don't you know better than to talk to this psychopath? It was not immediately clear whom he was addressing.

Josh, I've got some very important information I have to share with you, Eric began.

She stared at him with utter disdain. For the moment, he held all the power.

What is it, bitch? He scolded Eric. Sarah continued with her look of death, sure he would rat her out.

I was just trying to give her this…

He pulled a note from his pocket.

Josh grabbed it and contemplated tossing it to the ground, but seeing Eric's grief made him change his mind.

Well then you should do it like a gentleman, like this. Josh handed the note to her properly, and she snatched it from him quickly.

It was the poem I was working on until I got stuck.

Sarah realized this is why Eric had been carving into the fence. It was written with the same pencil type.

Josh surprisingly encouraged her to read it aloud. Go on. This dude may act like a freakshow but he's got talent with the words.

An unusually sincere endorsement, one of the first times she'd ever seen anything resembling empathy from Cottage 2's most bellicose staff.

I'll read it later. She stuffed the note hastily into her sweater pocket before walking back across the street. See you around, Eric.

Eric drooped his frame on the fence. Soon, I hope.

Josh was oblivious to the context of their previous exchange and so huffed in mild disgust. That the best you can come up with?

Shit, with you cockblocking up in here, what am I supposed to say? Eric scoffed.

Hey, never can tell with you predators, Josh returned forcefully.

Dude, why you always gotta bring that up?

You tell her you diddled your sister yet? He said loudly, just out of earshot from Sarah.

Man, that shit was a LONG TIME AGO.

Hey, that's cool, Josh put his hands up, genuinely lamenting that he had to throw salt his favorite client's game with Sarah. I ain't here to judge, but you still gotta keep your space from the girls.

Eric was still so pissed at the idea of losing Sarah forever that he directed his rage to his staff.

Fuck you, Josh!

No thanks brother, I don't like boys. He backed off, walking away with his palms raised in mock surrender. But for the ladies, that note was a good start.

Eric huffed at the taunt and threw a rock into the shrubs beside Cottage 2.

***

Lights out in Girls Cottage 1. Sarah waited for Sylvia to fall asleep, then quietly slid open the window. It was a foggy night in San Francisco, and the chill swept through the room. But Sarah did not feel the cold. Quietly, she lifted her leg over the ledge and pressed her foot down on the foliage below. Sylvia stirred in her bed from the cold.

Where you off to? She inquired in a groggy haze.

I'm out. You finally got the room to yourself.

Damn girl, Sylvia sat up, making sure to maintain her voice at a whisper. What 'bout 'chour probation? They gonna throw your ass back in the halls straight up when they catch you.

That's why they ain't gonna find me. I ain't comin' back.

Well damn, Sylvia processed it all. Shit ain't gon' be the same without you 'round.

Take care 'a yourself Syl, huh.

Shoot whitegirl, you know I be doin' it movin'. You keep your head on straight, ayite?

I holla at 'chu.

Then see ya' when I see ya'.

Peace.

She gave a nod then rested her head back down into the pillow to fall asleep. And close that slider, shit's hella cold up in here.

Sarah did. She then walked quietly to the side gate of Cottage 1. Careful not to wake Deirdre, she unlatched the handle silently and slipped out into the Excelsior night, making her way down to Mission Street, catching the MUNI Owl Bus to 14th Street, then out to Fillmore Street where she walked the mile and a half up Haight Street to Buena Vista Park, where she found Skreetch underneath his favorite tree, the one with the carving professing their undying love.

Yo Skeet it's me.

He looked to her with vacant, placidly watered eyes. Never thought you was comin' back.

Well, here I am.

He hugged her, shaking off his last bender.

Don't ever leave me again, okay?

I won't, baby.

You know I can't make it without you, right?

That's why I'm back. Ain't nothing to worry about no more.

I'll always love you the best. Just what his Barbie's all wanted to hear.

You holding?

Yeah.

It's been a long time baby...She drawled, craving to be juiced again.

Then let's get you fixed up.

He pulled his rusty spoon and needle from his pocket, unwrapped the sticky clog, spit his chud into the mix, fired it up, drew the syrup into the syringe and pumped his baby's shit back up something right.

She lay back with her eyes rolled into her head as he unzipped his pants and took back what was rightfully his.

She didn't feel a thing anymore. Just as she wanted.
You know I'll always love you best.
I know baby…
Oblivion.

***

Agnes and Kevin worked the Saturday dayshift following Sarah's disappearance from Cottage 1. The tension on the living units was high. The boys were especially agitated by the stir-up. Joe Rodgers was busy on the phone with his contacts in the SF Police Department's Juvenile Missing Persons Division, while Sarah's father called the City Attorney and several members of Excelsior House's Board of Directors to lobby for immediate closure of the program while his lawyer prepared the necessary filings to sue the city for criminal negligence in case things didn't work out his way. Meanwhile, Joe was at a loss for words to explain to his board how his longtime staff member Deirdre fell asleep during her overnight shift, neglecting to monitor their client at highest risk for suicide. John Hillsbrook as well as Sarah's therapist, Rita Wilson, were actively calling for Deirdre's termination while half of the city's on-patrol officers combed the streets for Sarah. But all the while, the burden of accountability ultimately fell on Joe. He was so livid at Deirdre yet sympathetic to her at the same time, understanding that their probate clients went 300 on just about every occasion possible, regardless of how many times overnight staff checked the rooms. Still, with Sarah's IEP explicitly documenting her need for constant supervision, Deirdre's position of negligence could not be readily defended to either his supporters or detractors who needed real convincing now to allow his program to continue. Damn it, Joe realized, he should have just demanded that Sarah be sent directly to General Hospital at the time of her admission, where she ultimately belonged. If only he hadn't needed the extra funding. A risky play to increase the profile and reputation of his program now all gone to hell, and Joe was having to clean up the mess he always saw comin' at some level. He knew they'd be lucky to keep Excelsior House operating following an episode like this. Joe squirmed again in his chair. He wished he knew what to do. One thing was for certain. An emergency staff meeting for the afternoon had to be called.

Agnes and Kevin monitored the clients outside while Joe worked the phones. Between Brandon and Nate's anticlimactic parental visit yesterday and Sarah's disappearance, a perfect storm was brewing for a difficult day on the circle. Nate paced warily in the front yard while Eric sat in the house drawing his next set of morbid torture devices for a future album or book cover. Julio meanwhile lay in his bed pondering his niña, whom he hadn't seen in forever. Kendrick, Rory, Duane and Marcus shot hoops while Brandon and Rydell kept a steady pace on the circle behind Tyrone, who was busy choppin' it up with Brenda and Sylvia ahead of them.

Agnes, Lead Supervisor for the living units that day, called her line staff into the Cottage 2 office, leaving Kevin alone to monitor the clients outside.

You okay with watching the crew solo?

Sure Agnes, I'll be fine, Kevin declared.

Be sure to keep an eye on Brandon. I know it don't seem like it, but he's the ringleader runnin' the show today.

He seems really mellowed out. And I had a good interaction with him last night.

He'll smile right at you while he stabbin' you in the back. Remember, he ain't happy wit' havin' to stay.

Okay Agnes, I got it.

Rory walked into the room unannounced.

Hey Agnes, can we use the other basketball?

Now Rory, how many times I told you not to interrupt staff outside of an emergency when we talking business?

Sorry Big Momma, he lamented, retreating to the edge of the portal, standing just outside.

Now that's better, dear, Agnes laughed under her breath, shaking her head mildly. So what'd y'all do to yours?

It went flat, I don't know how.

She scolded him squarely. Of course not. You boys ain't never taking care of the things you have, so eventually your gon' learn when you break them, there are consequences.

Agnes left to grab the last basketball in the staff office, which miraculously was still inflated. She quickly returned and handed it to him. Here you go. But be careful. Once this one goes, there ain't gonna be no more basketball, 'cause y'all know money ain't growin' on trees 'round here.

I know, Rory agreed dejectedly. It is clear he was not the cause of the last ball winding up deflated.

Now go on and take better care 'a your stuff.

We will Big Momma.

Rory ran back past Kevin, who was busy keeping tabs on the heated one-on-one exchanges brewing between Kendrick and Marcus in the driveway. Kendrick, of course, was no match for Marcus' imposing figure on the court. After several shots, it was clear Marcus owned him.

Man, damn, bunch 'a cheatin'-ass bitches up in here! Kendrick chaffed.

Kevin had to call him out for this.

Kendrick, language.

Mang, forget 'chu!

Kevin was surprised by Kendrick's overt insolence.

Kendrick! Take five please.

Man, screw you! Marcus and Duane both cheatin' and you call me out 'cause you think I'm the only one who'll listen to you!

Of course Kendrick was right, but Kevin had to appear unfazed by the comment, at least on the surface. Kendrick, you know you gotta run your program like everyone else.

Mang, fuck your program, damn! He sputtered into the house. Kevin tried to blow it off.

Duane and Marcus, play fair.

Marcus shook his head. We wasn't doin' nothing to him. He's just pissed 'cause he too short to rebound.

Duane agreed. Yeah Kevin, we ain't done nothin'.

Well maybe try to go easier on him next time.

Ayite.

Cool.

The boys continued to play without any further disruptions while Tyrone was busy pressing Brenda and Sylvia for any news on their girl. So y'all talked to Rhona yet?

Nah, Sylvia replied honestly.

Shit, she ain't even call you?

Fuck, if that bitch wanna chop it up with me, Sylvia snorted.

Brenda chimed in. Man, I heard Deirdre say she still up in Juvie waitin' fo' her trial. Says that skeezer Taniqua's parents gon' sue Joe 'cause they daughter be lookin' like a Jack O'Lantern wit' all dem scars.

Sylvia laughed. Yeah, Rhona straight carved that bitch out permanent.

Fo' sho', Brenda agreed.

Well if she call, tell her to holla at me, ayite? Tyrone insisted.

Shoot T, you best let yo' baby crush fizzle right quick, Sylvia advised. 'Cause homegirl ain't never comin' back. She 17 so she gon' be tried as an adult, bitch be off to Chowchilla chillin' wit' Rory's mom 'fore you know it...I ain't even lying.

For realz, she gone for good, Brenda agreed solemnly.

Tyrone's brave stance withered in response to their words. Just then, Brandon and Rydell called out from behind them.

Yo, y'all STILL hangin' out with fatboy? Rydell was only overtly mean to Tyrone when trying to impress the girls, which was basically every other day. When y'all gonna show us some love?

Dell punctuated his comments by gripping his package. Brenda flipped them off.

Come on now Bern, we all know you's back to suckin' dicks.

Brenda turned to face him angrily. You couldn't afford this booty if you tried, broke-ass mothafucker!

Rydell continued harassing her for the pure sport of it, pulling out several cash bills. Shoot Brenda, I got my skrill flowin' tight, so let's go, I take you behind the cottage and tear you up somethin' right.

Bitch, I bet you cum like a six year old.

Brandon and Sylvia both hacked with a stuttering chuckle. Damn!

Why don't you bend that fat ass over and I'll show you, Rydell dared her.

Instead of taking the bait, Brenda held her palm straight up to dismiss him without turning around.

Rydell and Brandon stood back. Shoot, dem cottage cheese thighs couldn't make me blow 'f I tried...

You don't know shit about shit, little boy! Sylvia dissed as the girls continued walking away.

Brown regal damn it's illegal! The boys snickered, heading off the circle.

Hearing the entire disturbance, Kevin called out to them, hoping to liven up the basketball game in the driveway.

Yo Brandon, Dell, why don't you come show these guys how to get their hoop game correct?

Brandon curled his lip. Naw we's cool.

Dell laughed. No thanks, Billy.

Kevin remembered Maurice's words of wisdom. Let them win once and awhile. So he called over Tyrone instead.

Yo T, wanna help Duane and Kendrick take on Rory and Marcus?

Naw, I'm straight, Tyrone also refused.

But Sylvia encouraged him on. Why don't you show off some 'a yo' game T? We be kickin' it right here when you come back.

Tyrone shrugged. Okay then, I'm 'a show y'all how a real nigga ball.

Marcus laughed at the sheer audacity of this cocky kid two years his junior. Don't worry T, we'll be gentle.

Long as you don't cry while I flip you on yo' ass, then I'm straight.

The boys proceeded to tear each other out on the court, complete with trash talk.

Tyrone attempted a layup but Marcus blocked him easily.

Homeboy front like Kobe but shoot like Shaq-

I'm 'a Ron Artest your ass if you don't pass the damn ball!

Kevin look, foul, shoot! Marcus complained as Tyrone blocked him with an accidental arm chop to the neck. You ain't calling nuthin'!

Duane balked. Yo Turner, this ain't the Boys and Girls Club.

Kendrick laughed. Yeah, we streetballin' now.

Marcus threw one of his characteristic temper tantrums. Y'all bunch 'a cheatin'-ass niggas! He walked away. The boys were not surprised by his unreeling on the front lawn. But nobody save Rita understood the true toot of his PTSD releases, which time and time again kept him from beating the hell out of the rest of the Excelsior House clients whenever he grew frustrated by them.

From the circle now, Brandon and Rydell continued running their game with Sylvia and Brenda, walking as a foursome.

Oh damn, Marcus be crying again? Sylvia called out.

Brenda shook her head. Shoot, that boy fine but the dude sho' can't get hisself under control.

Brandon was the only one sympathetic to Marcus, having some inkling of the pain he was releasing with his outbursts. But Rydell of course mistook Brandon's silence as tacit approval for him to continue riding Marcus in order to impress the girls.

Yo crybaby, so how you gonna win All City wit' tears in your eyes?

Duane and Tyrone laughed, but Kendrick and Rory held back, the latter waving his hand at the mocking boys. That's messed up y'all...

Kendrick seemed annoyed that the game had stopped again on account of some flip ass drama. Damn, can't anyone 'round here just let a nigga be?

Kevin stood up. Kendrick, watch your language!

This time, Kendrick laid into Kevin. Man damn, he tantrumed, chucking the ball across the street. You call me out when Marcus and Dell sayin' shit ten times worse? Forget 'chu!

Check, Rydell cracked.

Kevin first focused on squashing Rydell.

Nobody asked you to jump in.

OK chalky hands.

What did you say?

You heard me.

Now Brandon joined in the fray. Damn, I thought whackin' yo' willy's supposed to make you go blind, 'stead you lost yo' hearing.

Several of the boys cracked up at this.

Kevin now understood what Rydell and Brandon were referring to, but he hoped to avoid addressing the subject directly in front of the other clients if at all possible.

Now Eric made his way outside. Ahh hah, chalky hands!

Stay outta this Eric.

Yeah Eric, better watch out, or he gonna grab you like you grabbed your sister.

Ugh, scaly hands, scaly hands!

Brandon and Rydell walked up to stoke the other the boys into bagging hard on Kevin.

When they approached, Kevin put his hand on Brandon's shoulder, appealing to his more amicable side. Brandon, you need to run your program, too.

Instead, Brandon used this touch to further provoke the other boys into disarray. Ughh, dude, don't touch me! He immediately backed away from Kevin. Y'all better watch out, 'cause this dude's a tosser!

UUGHH! Even Kendrick and Rory joined in.

Brandon just smiled at all the chaos his revelation brought out of them.

Scaly hands!

Eric!

Don't nobody like you, Billy...

Brown regal damn it's illegal!

Kevin grew pissed. All right, everyone inside, I'm calling a group circle.

The boys protested, knowing full well Joe and Agnes were running damage control on the phones inside. Rory just shook his head as Tyrone ran across the street to retrieve the ball.

Kevin took this opportunity. T, in the house, now!

But-

The girls ain't even packin' up yet-

Ladies, you need to go inside too.

But Kevin, shit.

Just go please.

The girls grudgingly complied.

Thanks T, Sylvia and Brenda chided him from across the street as they headed inside Cottage 1.

Once inside Cottage 2, Kevin attempted to run group, but with the relentless onslaught of hostile verbiage spewing from the boys, Joe was forced to step out from his office in order to make his dominant presence known. His aggressive posture looming in the doorway made it perfectly clear he wasn't having any of their business this afternoon.

Y'all picked the wrong day to screw with staff. I'm shutting this cottage down now! Everyone in their rooms for the rest of the day.

The boys' protest erupted to resemble anything but going gently into that good night as each client, one by one, sullenly made his way down the hallway.

Joe, fuck that!

Naw, hell naw!

This is some bullshit!

Kevin tried touching me!

Chalky hands!

Bitch can suck a dick.

Y'all a bunch a biznitches up in here!

Haters, mang!

Brown regal damn it's illegal.

I want my therapist.

I don't feel safe here!

Rory, you stanky-ass feet motherfucker…

Duane, where my CD at?

What the fuck y'all doing back here?!

Kevin a buster.

Get him away from me!

Joe, this is some bullshit!

Fuck all y'all!

I'm 'a go AWOL and you can't do shit to me.

OOHH don't look at me dude…

I wanna call my PO I don't feel safe here anymore!

Now Rita gonna make sure you fired, you PHD!

Pedophile!

I'm 'a kill myself if that tosser come back here one more time...

Eric, stop touching yourself!

Dude, nobody like you!

Fuck you!

Get in your room, Marcus.

But I didn't do nothing!

When the cottage shuts down, everyone stays in.

Watch out before Kevin go booty-busting you too!

I ain't sleeping with him in the cottage!

Fuck that diddler!

He just can't handle himself.

Don't nobody fall asleep...

We should all run, then the city have to fire Joe's ass too, fo' sho'!

Screw all these haters. They can't stop us all.

Boys, y'all need to take your meds now...

Fuck that Agnes, I'm rejecting mine!

Me too Agnes...

OK, but you know what happens if you do.

I'll take mine as long as you keep Kevin outta here.

Boys, y'all best run your program.

Fuck you!

Boy, you best get your ass in your room now, 'cause I ain't playin' with 'chu no mo'.

Joe, you's a bitch too.

Oh yeah, well I'm 'a knock you out 'f you don't get back in your room, that's for damn sure-

This is some bullshit, Joe...

***

One by one, the Excelsior line staff arrived for Joe's meeting at Cottage 2. Carly watched the girls across the street while the rest of the staff convened at the kitchen table. Down the hall, the boys settled into their cottage shutdown. Jamey conferred with Brandon and Eric as Rita returned to her seat after calming down Rydell. The boys still yelled a few periodic slurs about Kevin so the rest of the team could hear their protests throughout the meeting.

Josh turned to address him. You must have done something to really piss them off.

Joe was all business. Okay y'all, a couple of things. Obviously you all know Sarah AWOL'ed. We got the city cops on an APB for her.

If she stays off of her meds too long, Rita warned, she's at high risk for attempting suicide. We've got to get her back.

Rita and Joe couldn't avoid looking to Deirdre as they described the immediacy of the situation.

Deirdre frowned. Look, I know I fucked up, but we all knew she was a Level 14 and never should have been here in the first place.

Joe grew livid at the thought of this client's AWOL unraveling all they had worked so hard for. Well, what's done is done, so all we got left to do is wait till they find her. As for the future of this place, I don't know.

They can't take it away from you on account of one 602, Deirdre pleaded with this jury of her peers.

Agnes shook her head. They can do whatever they damn well please.

We all knew the risks going in.

Deirdre withdrew her arguments, knowing Agnes spoke the truth.

Well, we just gonna have to wait it out is all.

Jamey interjected. On another pleasant note, Rydell says that he no longer feels safe with Kevin working the overnight shifts. When I asked why, Brandon said you tried touching him after talking to them about masturbation.

Maurice rolled his eyes. Those boys are both shit disturbers, you know that.

Well whatever you did Kevin, you got a real rise out of them, Jamey suggested.

Kevin copped to the situation. Look, last night, Brandon and Dell asked me if I masturbate. And I told them that healthy adults do it once and a while.

Agnes immediately gasped. Ohh wee.

Joe just stared at Kevin as if he was out of his mind. Maurice could only laugh.

Upon hearing this, Jamey seemed a bit surprised, but no longer concerned.

But Kevin still had to defend himself with the other staff. Look, I knew they were asking me an honest question about something they didn't understand and were worried about. They've got no one else in their life to talk about it with, and they certainly aren't going to bring it up with female staff. So I knew I was the only one in a position to say something helpful to them. They were reaching out, and I felt I had a responsibility to be as honest as possible, to treat them as young adults and to give them the information they needed to make a healthy decision for themselves. That was it.

Joe shook his head again in disbelief. Damn...

Agnes shook her head as well. There are some things you just don't talk about with these kids.

Rita, however, came to Kevin's defense. No, I don't think that's right. I think what you did was healthy for them, helping them to understand that it's not something to be ashamed of.

Kevin nodded. Exactly. I mean, who else were they going to hear that from?

But Agnes was not convinced. Rita, you know I love you, but I just can't get my head around this one.

It was obvious that the staff were in disagreement.

Kevin continued. And as for the touch, I put my hand on Brandon's shoulder to ask him to mellow out when some of the other boys were going off, and instead he used our conversation to escalate Eric and Rydell to make it harder for me to bring them inside, 'cause he didn't want to come in for group right then.

Maurice agreed. That sounds like Brandon all right.

Little manipulator, Josh scowled.

Agnes certainly agreed with Kevin on this much. That boy is always trying to split staff. Told you he was the ringleader.

Kevin nodded. I probably shouldn't have done that, but I never went into any of their rooms other than to poke my head in the door during rounds when they were asleep.

Josh laughed. Sounds like they're all pounding their puds after all.

Joe took a deep breath and released an audible sigh of relief. Those boys are just pissed 'cause they ain't going home.

Jamey agreed. Mom and dad didn't pass their drug tests again. Obviously they are disappointed. Especially Brandon.

Agnes sympathized. Ain't those folks ever gonna get it together for they kids?

Jamey grimaced, wishing he had that answer. You'll probably see Nate acting out directly, whereas Brandon will keep pushing the other boys, either Dell or Eric to aggravate the staff. That's his M.O.

Maurice offered his preferred approach. Seems to work best with Nate just to let him be when he gets into his moods.

I agree, Josh nodded. Just let him sputter out his crap long enough, he calms down.

As for Brandon, Jamey continued, he's going to keep manipulating staff to get his revenge. So we gotta come to an agreement as to what were going to do when the boys bring up Kevin and his masturbation comments.

Tell them it's inappropriate language and slap 'em with a verbal, Agnes stated flatly.

I say we just take points every time they make a comment. That will keep it to a minimum, Deirdre reasoned.

But it's Brandon that's instigating them, Kevin observed.

Well we can't punish the boy direct unless we hear it from him, Agnes countered. And he's too smart to say anything out straight.

But you'll see him nudgin' the other boys to bring it up.

Then we confront it in group.

I'll continue to talk with him in our sessions, Jamey assured them.

Rita was more forceful in her prescription for modifying the boys' behavior. We still all have to agree on consequences regardless of whether or not we like them. Because letting it slide will only split the staff and make Kevin's life hell around here. We've got to be consistent.

The staff all agreed on this point.

Deirdre was the first to suggest the solution. Points it is then, with a room restriction if they make any masturbation gestures or link it to Kevin?

Sure.

Okay.

Maurice patted Kevin on the back. Dude, you straight opened up a can 'a worms on this one dawg, he laughed, with the intent of busting on, as well as consoling, Kevin.

Sorry guys, I didn't realize this would blow up in my face.

Maurice retorted with a stroking motion of his hand in the air. That's just 'cause you ain't doing it right dawg…

Josh and Joe immediately cracked up at Maurice's lewd suggestion. Deirdre and Agnes winced, and the therapists remained blank, though Jamey was clearly repressing a smile.

I guess I set myself up for that one, Kevin laughed.

All right y'all, Joe chuckled, intent to refocus the group. We gotta buck up 'round here, specially on the overnights. So here's how its gotta be. Kevin will continue with his shifts as usual, but absolutely no snoozing for anyone no more.

The staff all nodded.

That includes you too Maurice, Joe finished.

Man why you gotta get up in my grill? Maurice feigned aggravation with Joe's insistence. But of course they both knew that's how it had to be from now on.

Joe then turned the meeting to Agnes. So how our girls doin'?

Agnes reported dutifully. Sylvia seems consistent, but Brenda's been a LOT more agitated since Rhona left.

For sure, Carly agreed.

How so? Joe inquired.

She just more aggressive, acting out on the boys.

What does Ms. Gatwyn have to say?

Says Brenda's been withdrawn in class, and Tyrone's sad as hell.

'Cause his girlfriend gone, Joe finished her thought.

And his mother's coming to visit. We're still planning it, but it won't be for another month or so. I'll keep you posted.

Please do, so we can save up for some new furniture.

He knows whatever he breaks, he pays for. He's been doing better on that.

Yeah, instead of kicking shit, he just takes a walk.

As for Rory, he seems stable but withdrawn on his Ritalin. I'm planning on dropping his dose to try to get him to come out of his shell, Jamey interjected.

And when does that go into effect? A med-sensitive Deirdre asked irritably.

We're gonna start him up next week.

Eric hasn't been as stable lately either, Kevin observed.

Josh stepped in. He's been all pouty since his vampire girlfriend took off, ain't writing no more poems or doing his drawings or nothing. Just sits there fumbling with his hands, muttering to himself.

Jamey took note. Were having our one-on-one session tomorrow, so I'll bring it up.

Boys have been talking shit about him and his sister, trying to throw some salt in his game with Sarah, Josh observed further. But all that crap seems to have settled down temporarily since she left. But I'll keep an eye on him.

Jamey nodded, jotting a note to himself on his legal pad. Thanks, Josh.

Anything else y'all?

The staff couldn't think of anything.

So Rita finished. One more thing, Rory's brother-in-law is coming for a visit this weekend.

Agnes was very concerned about the prospect. Shouldn't we wait to take him off his meds 'till after that?

Maurice agreed. You know that dude can be the biggest handful if he ain't juiced up.

Rita considered their concerns for a moment. I think it's time we reduced his dose, but let me know if you see any behavior to make me think otherwise.

A few of the staff huffed.

We still haven't addressed the elephant in the room, Deirdre suggested finally.

Oh, and by the way, I ain't gonna fire you, though I probably should, Joe returned sarcastically.

Deirdre took his comment in stride. You know who I'm talking about. One day Rydell is a complete prick, then the next morning he's a medicated blob on the couch. What's the long term plan for him? She directed her comments squarely to Rita.

Rydell is trying, Rita defended. You should see him in therapy. He's making great strides…

Maybe with you, but nobody else can handle him, Kevin surmised.

Maurice and Agnes agreed. Place would be a lot calmer without his bullshit.

He's just a little asshole, Josh dismissed.

I just want him off all that Dexedrine, Deirdre replied. The dosage he's taking is destroying his brain.

Joe visibly stiffened, concerned that his line staff couldn't agree with Rita on what to do about this.

Kevin continued to lobby most forcefully. We'd all be much better off if he were gone.

Silence. Agnes nodded her head in agreement, along with Josh and Maurice. Deirdre and Rita seemed the only holdouts.

He's got no one else.

And therein lay the rub. Each staff member knew Rydell was Rita's baby and that she would do anything and everything to keep him at Excelsior House. So Joe made his decision in the hope of finally unifying the staff around this issue. Well he's Rita's patient and so she makes the final call.

Rita jumped at the opportunity. I'll talk to him to address all of your concerns, Rita agreed. Tell him he really needs to start behaving better if he wants to get along here. I'll hold him to that. And if he can do that, I'll reevaluate his med regimen.

The staff had no choice but to accept her decision.

All right then, Joe concluded the meeting. Y'all keep doing good...

***

Judge Donna Rogers convened Family Court on Tuesday afternoon.

Good morning.

Good morning, Your Honor.

Regarding the third and final reunification hearing for Sylvia Sanchez, Case number 4210365, the judge addressed Sylvia's social worker, Ms. Clara Rodriguez. Is everyone present?

Yes, Your Honor.

Mr. and Mrs. Sanchez, hello to the both of you.

Hello, Your Honor.

Judge Rogers gave a warm nod to Sylvia's Court Appointed Special Advocate, Rosaria Higalda, muralist and founder of Almas Apasionadas.

Mrs. Higalda.

Your Honor.

Finally, she turned to the client whose fate she would be considering today.

How are you doing today, Sylvia?

Sylvia forced a smile. Fine, Your Honor, thanks. And you?

Judge Rogers straightened in her chair with an unexpected smile. Just fine Sylvia, thank you for asking. She then turned to the court reporter.

Please note for the record that all guardians and special advocates are present for these proceedings.

The court reporter nodded. Noted.

Judge Rogers addressed the group. So let's review, over this past year this court's goal has been to reunify you, Sylvia, with your birth parents, Jose and Maribel Sanchez. At our last hearing we set up a reunification plan for your family. Ms. Rodriguez, will you report on status of all parties in meeting their stipulated requirements?

Clara Rodriguez stood, facing the bench. Yes, Your Honor. Sylvia is currently enrolled in Thurgood Marshall's Special Day Program where she works under the observation of Lisa Gatwyn to treat her residual PTSD. She continues her extracurricular art activities with Rosaria Higalda at Almas Apasionadas and is currently undergoing anger management counseling with her therapist Jamey Sherwood at Excelsior House, where she has resided for the past twelve months. Mr. Sherwood and Ms. Gatwyn could not attend this meeting today but both have indicated in their reports to the court, as well as in reiterating in person to me, that Sylvia has excelled in all areas of treatment and is a model client at Excelsior House as well as a committed student in her academic program.

Noted by the court.

Sounds like you've been living very responsibly these past twelve months, Sylvia. I want you to know the court recognizes your efforts and I commend you on your commitment to this process.

Thank you, ma'am...I mean, Your Honor.

Clara continued. As for Sylvia's parents, both Mr. and Ms. Sanchez have exhibited considerable difficulty in complying with their obligations under the court's reunification plan for their family. Based on several unscheduled home visits made over the past three months, it is my determination that Ms. Sanchez's alcohol use continues to dominate her daily routine. Similarly, Mr. Sanchez has failed to attend the minimum number of court mandated domestic violence counseling sessions as stipulated under the terms for reunification, according to his group's facilitator, Damien Horowitz.

Judge Rogers frowned, visibly dissatisfied with this news. I see. Noted by the court.

Clara continued. Given that reunification has been our goal, Mr. Sanchez has been repeatedly warned that failure to complete his program would jeopardize his daughters' chances for returning to the home.

Do you understand the implications of your failure to complete the program, Mr. Sanchez? Judge Rogers asked sternly.

Sylvia's father nodded, ashamed. I do, Your Honor.

Than do you have a reason you'd like to give the court for why you were not able to attend these classes?

Yes, Your Honor. I've been working several landscaping and kitchen remodeling jobs and could not meet on a consistent basis. Both my sponsor and facilitator will tell you the same.

I see, Judge Rogers replied. But then if your schedule created problems for attendance, did you ever follow up with your facilitator to make up your missed sessions?

He told me if I wasn't committed to the schedule, then I'd have to find another program.

And you never did?

No, Your Honor...

You do realize this could cost your family reunification. Did that thought ever cross your mind Mr. Sanchez?

Yes, Your Honor, Mr. Sanchez sighed.

Judge Rogers stared hard at him. He looked visibly broken. Noted, she finally acknowledged. Ms. Rodriguez, please continue.

Clara did. It is my belief after multiple interviews with the family over the past twelve months, that Mr. Sanchez is no longer assaulting Ms. Sanchez and poses no threat to his daughter, based on the progress he made in counseling prior to his employment-related truancy from recent meetings, according to his facilitator, Mr. Horowitz.

Judge Rogers nodded to Clara before looking directly at Mr. Sanchez.

Mr. Sanchez, are you beating Ms. Sanchez anymore?

No, Your Honor.

Judge Rogers believed him. She then turned to his wife, sitting beside him.

Ms. Sanchez, is this the truth?

Sylvia's mom nodded without hesitation. Si, Your Honor.

Are you still drinking Ms. Sanchez?

She thought of lying but choose not to cross the judge at this time.

Yes, ma'am...

Every day, Ms. Sanchez?

Again, Sylvia's mother nodded. Yes, ma'am.

Sylvia just looked down into her lap and shook her head. This was not going well.

OK, Judge Rogers affirmed. Ms. Rodriguez, please continue.

As far as Sylvia's safety is concerned, however, as her social worker, I am particularly concerned by the fact that several family members and acquaintances continue to occupy the Sanchez home as their primary residence. Given her father's absence for purposes of work, her mother's self-admitted substance abuse, and repeated use of their living space by transient older male guests, there is a high probability that she will be returning the very same circumstances that led to her removal in the first place if reunification is granted. Furthermore, given her history of sexual assault by her uncle, whose current whereabouts are unknown, the termination of her pregnancy, and her family's steadfast denial to address and accept the events that led to loss of custody, their current failure to meet the terms for reunification remains a serious concern. Though the family has made some modest progress, and though they certainly appear to love Sylvia and want her returned to their guardianship, given her marked improvement this past year working through her rape in therapy with Mr. Sherwood and her few episodes of acting out in placement, her treatment team believes the risks involved in returning her to conditions conducive to further sexual assaults remain. From what I have gathered in repeated interviews with the family, I must agree with their assessment and so therefore have no choice but to deny recommendation for reunification. As an alternative, it is my preference that Sylvia remain a ward of the court and retain her placement at Excelsior House until emancipation on her eighteenth birthday.

Sylvia's parents were visibly livid at the suggestion. Her mother silently mouthed 'Culo' to Clara.

Is this your complete assessment, Ms. Rodriguez?

It is, Your Honor.

Judge Rogers nodded. Very well. Ms. Higalda, do you have anything to add on this matter?

Yes, Your Honor. Rosaria stood to address the judge. As Sylvia's CASA, I can say that she is in a great place in her life. She is an amazing muralist and has a warrior spirit, among the strongest of her ancestors. Her art is informed by her struggle, as is all of ours, but I know in her heart reunification has been a real dream for as long as I've known her...So though I respect the recommendations of her social worker, I'd hate to see her lose being a part of her parents' lives, 'cause it's much of what drives this girl. Her family is the source of much of her pain but also a source of real love, and so I cannot advocate for anything but to allow them to continue to exist within the tapestry of each other's lives.

Rosaria sat back down, confident with her response.

Thank you Ms. Higalda. I thank you for your sage advice and for your proactive commitment to Sylvia's treatment and well-being. The court acknowledges and appreciates your input here.

Judge Rogers finally turned to Sylvia.

Sylvia, I'd like to hear what you'd like to see happen here today. Having watched you grow into the responsible, thoughtful young woman you've become over this past year, I understand that you carry immense love for your parents, but I want to hear what YOU believe is best for you. You're sixteen years old now, and soon you will be an adult. So your recommendations for yourself carry a great weight with me, and in what this court will decide for you today.

Sylvia felt the gravity of the responsibility Judge Rogers now placed upon her. She knew she was ready to decide her own future. But she was still unsure how to bear the reaction of her parents when delivering the decision she'd made months ago. So she stood and directed her response specifically to the judge.

Well, you know, Your Honor, I want to be at home, there is no doubt 'bout that, but I also know my mami and papi ain't about to change they ways neither. I could sit up here all day and spit all kinds of mess to you 'bout how good I take care 'a myself and all, but fact of the matter is things going solid the way they is. I don't wanna jeopardize seein' them, 'cause they my world, you know what I'm sayin', and I can't blame dem for being the people they is, stuff just happens the way it do. But I know I ain't ready to seek no special 'mancipation, and sure as heck don't want no other placements. Excelsior ain't so bad far as they go, so I ain't lookin' to get moved or fo' some other family to take me in, know what I'm sayin'? So I'm straight with keepin' things the way they is, if that works for you and the court.

Judge Rogers smiled. Yes dear, I think it does. That was a very thoughtful and mature assessment of your situation, Sylvia. And I think everyone in this room should be proud of you and recognize the amazing young woman that you have become. It's obvious you seek to balance your love for your parents with what is healthy for you. And I think that demonstrates the very adult manner in which you are choosing to handle yourself, and your life.

Shoot, Your Honor, it's all I know how to do.

Judge Rogers smiled again. Well I'm glad to hear that, Sylvia, because that approach will continue to serve you well throughout your adulthood, as it has today.

The judge then stiffened to formally address the group.

Based on the obvious wishes of Sylvia, and for the well being of this family, it is the court's decision at this time to terminate pursuit of reunification, making Sylvia a permanent ward of the court with monitored visitation rights for the family, where she will continue in her placement at Excelsior House until her eighteenth birthday. I hope you are satisfied with this ruling, Sylvia.

I am, Your Honor.

Is there anything anyone else would like to say?

No one spoke.

Then this completes our third and final reunification hearing for Case number 4210365. Court is adjourned.

Sylvia's mom bowed her head and cried in her husband's arms as Sylvia hugged her parents. With a thoughtful nod to the judge, Clara and Rosaria left the courtroom and waited outside for Sylvia to finish with her family before returning her to Excelsior House.

***

Lucy Gutierrez opened the door to Joe's office. His eyes lit up as she walked in with Tre's head resting on her shoulder.

I can't take your money, she proclaimed, dropping the hundred-dollar grip firmly on his desk.

Joe immediately sensed the tension in his favorite former client.

What's going on wit' 'chu girl? He asked, afraid he already knew the answer.

She chided him coolly. It ain't like that Joe.

I thought you was in a bind.

Yeah, and I got it straightened out now so it's all good.

Girl, don't go running your game on me now. I know you too good for that. He got up from his desk and approached her. Is something goin' down between you and Key over this?

His fingers brushed her cheek gently. She shook them off abruptly. Joe held his palms up, despondent. She'd never resisted his affections before.

It ain't like that...

Then how is it? How you suddenly straight when only yesterday you was more desperate than I ever seen you?

She looked her protector and benefactor square in the eyes and then broke his gaze before responding. We got an understanding now, is all.

Yeah, he glanced down and saw the bruises lining her neck. And I suppose these butterfly kisses got something to do with that.

He raised his hand to touch her but, embarrassed, she brushed him away. Forcefully now.

I can't see you no more.

Joe looked down at her with a mixture of rage, pity, and sadness painted across his expression.

So that's how it's gonna go down now, huh?

Key been talkin''bout-

I don't give a damn what that fool says.

Lucy looked up to him with sympathetic eyes. He my baby's daddy, Joe. What do you expect?

How 'bout some respect? Shyite. Suddenly my opinion don't matter none?

You know it ain't like that...

Hold on now. Didn't I raise you with 'nough sense to step off when somebody go disrespectin' you? C'mon girl. You know that fool don't give a shit about you, 'cept for what you can give to him.

He loves Tre. You should see them together.

Yeah? Then if he loves his boy so much, how's he go beatin' on his moms then? Ayite then, Uh huh. That's right. You know I'm tellin' it true girl. 'And you know that motherfucker ain't about to stop knockin' on you now he started. Uh uh, 'cause now that door's open, and all you can do is get out, 'fore he do worse on you and Tre. You got to check yourself for real now Luce, do it for your boy, and step the fuck off. 'Cause there ain't no way this story gonna end right for you. Not no more. Not with that fool. Uh uh. Cause he's taken it to the next level. And I know you. You think you's in it for the long haul, and that it's all good, that he gonna change and whatnot, but next time shit goes down, and it will, you can believe that, I promise you you ain't gettin' away wit' just a chokehold, that's for damn sure.

What would you want me to do Joe?! Lucy yelled. Leave him when he wants to be my baby's father? Key done stepped up, and so he's my world now. When you gon' finally bend yo' mind around that?

Her attack tone rattled Joe, but he countered quickly. This is your life I'm talkin' about Luce. Yours and Tre's. Shit, how you gon' let your boy grow up with no momma? Come on now. What's little man gon' do when you's dead or laid up in some hospital beat up so bad you don't know which way to Tuesday? Shit, you want Tre raisin' hisself like you done in a place like this? I know that motherfucker Key don't love you in no way 'nough to make that worth it to you. You know I'm keepin' it real now.

Key's the only father he got, Joe! And he loves me, he do, even though I know you don't see it. He tryin' to change. I know it 'cause I see it in him. And the only way he's ever gon' get there is if I don't give up on him. Like everyone else in his life done.

Girl, you talkin' crazy now. You just see him the way you want to, 'cause the alternative is too scary to dink out.

Yeah, and how'd you see I should do? Take Tre out on the streets? Or come back here to live with you? Is that what you really want?

He still couldn't bring himself to admit the truth, that he was deeply in love with Lucy.

So what then, you gonna keep on takin' you chances wit' Keyshawn instead, and go riskin' yo' life and little man's?

Naw, that ain't fair Joe…Her eyes started to well up with tears. He sensed a moment of possibility with her now.

It don't gotta be this way Luce, Joe pressed. Feel me? He looked at her in a way now that, for the first time in their relationship, revealed his true feelings for her.

So what 'chu sayin' then? For a minute, she really saw in his face what his compromised heart truly wanted to express to her. But a nagging sense of disappointment and rage from waiting all those years for him to step up, combined with her sense of utter terror over what she knew Key would bring down on the both of them if she ever flipped his way, was too much to bear. So Lucy stayed her course instead, and turned the knife back on Joe.

What, so now all'a sudden you gonna play knight in shining armor, come swoop down and take care 'a us? Shit. You done had your chance for that…many times. But naw, you stood tall, behind your morality and your holier-than-thou big brother front ever since I done 'mancipated. Well this ain't no front, Joe. Yeah, you always been there helpin' out with immediate needs and whatnot when Key was away, and I appreciate all that, I do, but it was Key who stepped up and loved me the way I needed…as a woman. So I'm his now. And I gots to have his back. He's trying hard to change. And he gonna do even better. I just gots to give him the chance to do us right. He workin' hard to get hisself correct now, so he deserves that much from me.

Joe slumped his shoulders, defeated. That boy ain't never gon' love nobody right Luce.

Then it's on me to help him change. 'Cause ain't no one else 'bout to.

She finally pulled away.

By the way, Key don't want me comin' round y'all no mo'.

Is that what you want, girl? Joe insisted that she commit one way or the other. Is that how you really want to play this?

Looking down for a brief moment, Lucinda finally met his glance once again. He my man, Joe. And if it's what he wants, that's how it's got to be.

She turned and left his office, closing the door behind her. Joe stood defeated, absorbing the knowledge, the reality, that had not only faced him for so long, but had finally overcome him: that his entire relationship with Lucy had become an utter and undeniable failure.

***

Yo B, you hungry?

I guess, his little brother nodded, almost ashamed to be a burden.

Marcus Turner was late for the Sunday pickup game with his boys. He'd stopped by his mom's house on the way over to the Western Addition courts to pick up his little brother Boyce. With that crazy white girl from Cottage 1 on the run, he hoped to steal some quick time alone with his family. Joe and the rest of the Excelsior staff were so distracted he could no doubt cop to a few hours away at the Boys and Girls Club without anyone checkin' his alibi. But his momma was nowhere to be found. Bad sign. Must be another bender, Marcus thought. Sure 'nough Clara'd be comin' 'round to check on their situation real soon. The place was trashed. And that lady been knowin' what time it was for more than a quick minute. So he quickly straightened the place out while he whipped up a cold mac and cheese sandwich for Boyce, with a slice of bread and the few extra noodles caked in Velveeta he found stuck to the belly of a pot on the stove from god knows when.

Where momma at?

Boyce shrugged. She out.

Of course he knew his brother wouldn't have another answer.

She cookin' for you? He asked Boyce with a glint of hope.

Naw, that's Damone's from last night.

One of momma's boyfriends. Or fix of the week.

Last night? Marcus griped. This Damone up in here regular like?

Naw, Boyce buried his head in his chest nervously, as if ashamed for ratting out his mother. Only sometimes.

He out too?

Boyce nodded.

Marcus was sure now that his momma was coppin' herself a fix, and that this dude Damone was her new score. So there it was then, for himself, and for Boyce, any hope of continuing to stay with their momma lost, in only a matter of time.

Ayite, here it do, Marcus wrapped the sloppy cheese mix in a paper towel, handing it to Boyce who proceeded to lop it up like a hot dog. I'm a roll you by Taco Bell on da way over.

Marcus and Boyce showed up to Jefferson Square Playground just as members of Knockout Posse were calling out their teams. His boys from Eddy Rock strolled onto the basketball courts with calculated swagger, fronting confidently in this territory designated neutral among the crews.

Yo Turner!

Boyce, check it. Eddy Rock and KOP together in the crosshairs…Damn.

Mang, y'all look like some United Nations motherfuckers signin' a peace treaty up in here.

Naw, we just choppin' it up, Turner.

The rival sets talked the requisite smack and then some before the game.

Shit, what 'chu doin' walkin'? I thought I shot yo punk ass last month.

Obviously you missed, bitch.

You gots to get 'cho eyes checked motherfucka!

Punk-ass crackhead so thin bullets be flyin' right thru the dude and shit.

That's 'cause you aim your clip like a bitch.

Normally, D-Ride, Pee, and Jay would be turnin' each other out hard on the asphalt, but today, on Sunday, Day of the Lord, everyone was comin' together for a not-so-friendly game of streetball.

The rival gangs tagged each other out in a ridiculous display of camaraderie. Nine years together in public school could revert even the hardest of street thugs back to old childhood friends on common turf when the score was basketball.

Yo, where Deshelby at?

He comin' round 'fore too long...

Naw, Keyshawn's boys caught up to that dude last Thursday, blut. Shoot, motherfucker got got hoppin' the gate to Altegard.

He died right on his auntie's porch.

Hell yeah, you know it. His little bro found him all bloodstained and shit.

Man, ain't that about a bitch.

Some of the crew sported his picture on their T-shirts.

Damn, is all Turner could muster. RIP Deshelby...

That's some coldblooded shit, D-Ride lamented from the rival crew.

Aw, you just mad 'cause you didn't cap his ass first.

Naw, blut, it ain't like that. I mean sho', Deshelby a bitch like da rest a y'all, but we used to jack fruit rollups from the corner store back in the day, know what I'm sayin'?

Keyshawn's niggas got no regards. They clearin' out everybody.

Fo' realz.

Scandalous-type Individuals.

They claimin' the entire block yo, wastin' any fool get in their way.

Yo, but KOP 'bout to flop they asses hard when we see 'em, for realz, know what I'm sayin', cuz Deshelby didn't die in vain, mang.

We keepin' ours close, blut.

Yo, I ain't seen none 'a you fools stepped to Keyshawn yet.

Mang, Eddy Rock holdin' it down solid, yo.

Y'all best put in some work on that dude for what he done to yo' boy.

Drop his ass for realz, 'cause if I see him, he takin' a dirt nap.

Y'all know floppin' them niggas ain't no joke, yo, Dudes is grimy. Knock you off yo' two toes.

We straight put some slugs in them thugs, no doubt.

Takes the hood to save the hood, know what I'm sayin'?

Yo, keep yo' game tight mang...

For realz, blut.

Y'all get a homepass down Eddy next time we see Keyshawn chasin' you through our cornas.

Mang, fuck y'all!

Marcus stared down D-Ride. He called out to Boyce.

This dude still messin' wit' 'chu?

E already squashed that beef, Turner.

D-Ride was defensive. Mang, I ain't touched yo' little bro...

Why you pokin' yo' big ass nose round somewhere it don't belong?

E smiled to Marcus to let him know his own crew had already checked D-Ride.

Best not.

Damn, ain't you 'bout a bitch, D-Ride hissed to Marcus.

Then let's play already, nigga!

For the rest of the afternoon, Eddy Rock and KOP ran a normal pickup game of ghettoball. Marcus dazzled his old neighborhood patnas with his changeup shots and crossfake layups. He even incurred a few minor scuffles. At one point, D-Ride dropped him hard on the blacktop, but he didn't even trip.

You gonna call me out Crybaby?

Naw, we's straight.

Damn right we is.

Dude playin' with da big boys now, D-Ride clasped hands with a member of his rival crew.

Marcus rolled himself back up from the blacktop without flinching. The game continued on with only a few more minor scuffles. Until again on another changeup, Marcus flipped around

D-Ride to take an easy layup. While the other boys stood in admiration of his fake, D-Ride wasn't about to let this dude get the best of him, so he put out his arm to clothesline Marcus to the ground.

Marcus winced in pain as his body came down hard on his wrist. The boys all heard a crack.

Yo mang, that ain't no joke!

Shyitte!

C'mon shake it out Crybaby!

Damn you's broken!

His friends from Eddy Rock sprung to his defense.

Naw mang, it's just a sprain, Marcus waved them off. But he knew from the surging pain running up his arm that he was in serious trouble.

Dang, yo...

What's yo' beef, D?

He just jealous 'cause Marcus be schoolin' him all day.

Ain't no niggas gettin' schooled out here 'cept y'all, D-Ride retorted.

Livid at his arrogance, E pushed D-Ride. Mang, have some respect. Dude be riskin' his scholarship to play wit' yo' ghetto ass.

D-Ride tapped his hands to his own chest in defiance. Mang, do I look like I give a fuck?

Cuzzo ain't gettin' no scholarships now.

We do it out here for realz dawg.

The boys stepped to each other hard, ready to throw down.

Why you gotta jam up my boy? E pushed D-Ride to the ground in retaliation.

Because they were all playin' ball, none of the boys on the court were strapped. Yet.

You just bent over that bullshit last week when he dropped yo' ass...

Eddy Rock be doin' dirt up here!

As the rival crews squabbled, RT casually walked towards his gym bag to pull out his clip.

Meanwhile, Marcus cooled their heads out. Naw mang, y'all drama ain't necessary. D just holdin' it down, yo.

D-Ride dogged Marcus. You can't see me bitch...

Naw its cool D, but we gots to go.

Mang, fuck you!

We ain't in no kind 'a mood for y'all noise, yo.

Yo back off, D-Ride. Dequan from KOP now stepped in to block his boy off. He nodded to Marcus. You all right Crybaby?

Yo, I'm straight.

Then tap out, dawg.

Marcus and D-Ride knuckled their fists together and gave a quick eyefuck to one another. Beef squashed.

That's whassup, y'all.

Mang, I'm out.

Whassup Turner, you grow a pussy all a sudden?

Naw mang, just got to get. Gettin' late. Marcus left his old childhood friends behind him. Let's go, B.

Boyce ran over to follow his brother off court.

On the way out, Marcus tagged out with a few of his homies from Eddy Rock and KOP.

Y'all soldja's stay strong, you feel me?

You keep yo' head up, Marcus.

Do it movin', cuz.

Like I been.

Keep it crackin', yo!

He took his brother Boyce by the hand and led him away from the game. As they walked back to their momma' apartment, for the first time he could remember, Marcus was truly grateful for Joe, Judge Donna Rogers, and Excelsior House. Even Clara. By the way times were changing in his old hood, he knew he wouldn't be seeing more than a couple of those fools again.

When Marcus returned with Boyce, he found Clara Rodriguez and Officer Michael Moreno standing solemnly in his mother's living room. He knew immediately what was about to go down from the way his mother slouched on the couch, dejected. Their cat and mouse game with CPS was up.

What 'chu doin' here? Marcus nastily hissed at Clara, walking past her into the kitchen.

Baby, Marcus's mother moaned aloud to Boyce. Clara's gon' be takin' you away for awhile.

Marcus tried to look his mother in the eye but she would not respond. So what, after everything I did for us, you gonna let it go down like this? I mean, damn, momma…

His mom could only stare through the front window, cigarette in hand. She barely answered him. I can't do no better that I been doin' Marcus.

That's some bullshit. I mean what the fuck? I can understand you givin' me up, but B? What we supposed to do now? He just a boy. Where he gonna go?

We gonna try to get him assigned to Excelsior House with you Marcus, Clara interjected.

You don't fucking talk to me, you hear me!

Hey take it easy! Moreno interrupted the boy.

Marcus checked himself, but refused to subdue his rage toward his CPS worker. Don't you ever run yo' mouth at me ever again! He pointed at Clara fiercely. 'Cause I got nuthin' more to say to you.

Clara did not try to justify her actions.

Settle down, Marcus, Officer Moreno reprimanded him. We're taking your brother to a safe place now.

Oh yeah, I know y'all idea a safe, like half the homes I been in, shiyite. He shook his head with hostility. How could you, momma?

Marcus started tearing up when his mom refused to meet his eye, instead taking empty drags from her cigarette, sitting there with arms folded, staring out the window. She was too high to cry, though she desperately wanted more than anything to give in the gravity of this moment, to express her true feelings of shame and sorrow to her son for what she had done to them. But all of that now remained buried within her disjointed haze.

I failed you baby, she mouthed to the window, still unable to face him. I KNOW that. But I can't change...

Clara put her arm around Boyce. Come on, dear, let's go get your things. Let mommy and Marcus talk. She escorted Boyce from the room. Moreno remained.

Marcus wanted to destroy his mother right then and there, but instead he found himself almost automatically crawling up onto the couch and placing his head into her lap, clinging to her. She was still too wasted to respond, but she did let him hold her. Just staring out the window, cigarette in hand, smoke trailing through blinds towards the reflecting sun with every drag in her hazy stupor, knowing that she had once and for all destroyed her family.

Marcus just cried and cried on the couch beside her, clinging to her, sobbing. Why momma? Why? Why? He repeated between pants to catch his breath before the tears resumed. Why?

Moreno couldn't force himself away from watching this tragic but necessary moment. As Marcus lost himself in emotion while his mother coldly faced the opposite direction, with her blank eyes into an endless, vapid stare, Moreno could only think about the numerous textbook cases he wrote about in his graduate school essays and papers, analyzing broken families in crisis and individuals of all personality types and dispositions, wondering if there was any rhyme or reason or hope left in any of this madness, or if some people were just too far gone. And where did people like Marcus and his mom find the resilience to keep fighting, against all odds, the endless battle that was their lives? Moreno couldn't make any more sense of this moment than Marcus or his momma or even Clara could. He could only sit back as the silent observer and watch all the love and efforts and intentions of these three blood relatives finally derail into the wreckage of what would most likely be their last time together as a family. To bear witness to such softness and brutality and tenderness all at once was too much for Moreno to bear. Almost. But for some reason, he could not keep himself from it. Indeed, to see such resilience in Boyce, in Marcus, even in the boys' mother as they all faced the harsh realities of their separation, confronting such indefatigable loss with their combination of dignity and rage, their fortitude fascinated him, indeed seduced him; though Moreno could only steward them through this miserable moment to its forgone conclusion, working to minimize any fallout for the participants until long after they went their separate ways. He recovered only when Clara touched the back of Marcus's shoulder. She clutched Boyce's hand in her own.

Marcus dear, it's time to go home now.

Marcus had no tears left for his mother now. The boy took measured leave of the house and walked down the apartment complex stairs with his brother and caseworker in tow. Boyce's belongings dragged behind the younger boy in a black plastic trash bag that he gripped with his free hand.

Moreno followed them out of the apartment, without further incident from the mother or any of the building's residents. Many of the neighbors stood silently as the troupe passed through the complex, then down the stairwell to Clara's Buick. No one spoke a word. They all understood what a loss this CPS intervention represented for Marcus, given his efforts over the past two years - the countless trips across town, the excuses, the cover stories, the subversion – all done in order to keep his mother and brother together, his efforts now come to naught. And now that he faced the reality that his brother, like himself, would no longer know the home he always wanted for him, there was nothing more to do about it. Other broken families among the neighbors mourned the loss of the Turner family, witnesses along with Clara and Moreno. Any family's separation was a shared one within this community where everyone had to find a way, as this family did, despite this loss, to continue on.

***

Rory clipped into his Oshkosh denim overalls in preparation for meeting up with his sister and brother-in-law. Jamey hadn't approved a home visit yet, but his sister was looking into adopting her baby brother while they waited for their mother to get out of prison, or until Rory turned eighteen three years from now, whichever came first. He got along well enough with his sister, thought she could be a real biznitch at times. Her husband Kyle was cool enough, though. He was all into cars, fancy Corvettes and Chevy Novas and Camaros. He had Rory's favorite car, a souped-up '68 Camaro with a 454 chopper block, 48" wheels, the whole nine. He loved taking Rory for rides in that. They'd hit the quarter mile in Modesto where his sister had a place. Neighboring Riverbank and Oakdale were competing for the title of Crystal Capital of California, and Kyle had his own lab in a trailer out behind their house where he did all the cooking and mixing, with recipes tried and true courtesy of Rory's old man, the Meth Chef. Pops caught himself a solid up in Folsom for blowing their old house up, nailed for possession with intent to distribute. Thankfully the arresting officers who busted him and Rory's momma never caught wind of the fact that Kyle was helping the old man out on the side; no harm, no foul. Needless to say, Rory didn't mention nothin' of his brother-in-law's involvement in the family business during intake or to Jamey Sherwood during their numerous therapy sessions together. In many ways Jamey was the best friend Rory had up in Excelsior House, but a dude had to keep his family's secrets at all costs. That was just the code.

Rory was looking forward to hooking up with his big sis and brother-in-law today. They'd made the two and a half hour drive from the valley up to Frisco early this morning so they could maximize their visit with him. Kyle called from his cell phone sayin' they would be running a few minutes late.

No problem, Rory informed Jamey. I'll just get my game on.

Rory's meds were fucking with him recently since Jamey switched him off Ritalin. The new Klonopin made his head heavy and caused him to break a sweat just before his vision got blurry. This always happened about 45 minutes after taking his morning dose, without fail. Jamey suggested his brain would need about a week to adjust. They were already on day four, but Rory still didn't feel up to his daily whirl and twirl.

You still dizzy? Jamey inquired from the front porch, watching his client consistently miss his basketball shots this morning.

Yeah, I'm 'a sit out a few.

Jamey gave a look of concern. He was trying to keep Rory's malaise at bay, and Rory did appreciate that. It was all good. His head just ached like a bitch. But he'd experienced no major mood swings yet this week, which was the point of the changeup. Always a tradeoff, it seemed.

Kyle and Cherri rolled in within ten minutes of Rory cooling his head on the porch.

Hey little bro, Cherri walked up and gave her brother a big hug as she'd done all those years they'd lived together. Rory immediately felt back at home. She kissed him square on the cheek.

Man, Cherri, you gonna get all these fools up on my case kissin' me like that.

Ain't no little boys gonna stop me from showing my bro some love.

What up Roryman? Kyle put out his hand out for a slap. His white muscle shirt and Levi shorts exposed parts of a large American Eagle tattoo inscribed across his frame underneath. And his muscles were bulging.

Man Kyle, you's yoked! Rory admired out loud.

Been working out.

Good. Another sign Kyle was off the meth.

Hey Jamey, Cherri waved to Rory's therapist.

Hi Cherri, Jamey put his hand up from the porch in acknowledgement. Kyle.

Whassup, Kyle half-assed. He turned immediately back to Rory. You want to shoot some hoops?

Sure, Rory replied. I'm 'a run circles round yo' bisack.

Ah, you think you is, Kyle laughed. Boy, you're gettin' bold.

That's 'cause I been practicin'. Rory showed him his characteristic layup. Not bad, little bro. Guess I'm 'a have to pull out all the stops now.

For the next half hour, Kyle and Rory went one-on-one style, with Kyle obviously alternating between blocking the kid's shots and letting him score.

Mang, play for reals, Kyle, 'fore I go to town on you! Rory taunted him.

I ain't holdin' back on you, dawg, Kyle obviously lied. More back and forth.

At the end of the day, Cherri, Kyle and Rory hugged out their goodbyes.

Yo Roryman, you know we're gonna talk to Jamey and the Judge 'bout having you come live with us for good this time. No more of this 'ward of the court' nonsense.

Yeah bro, Kyle boasted, we got to get you outta living with all these niggers.

This last comment made Rory sick, hearing it come from someone like Kyle whom he admired so much. Rory immediately thought of his best friend Tyrone and how he would feel knowing where Rory came from. He hated his brother-in-law's racism. But when it came to his family, that just always came with the territory. So instead of fight it, Rory did as he always done, he simply didn't respond to Kyle's baiting.

Cherri could sense Rory's discomfort on the spot. That sound cool with you?

Shore it do, Cherri, Kyle finished for him. Man gotta stick with his own blood, you know.

Even with all that white pride bullshit they'd grown up with, Rory and Cherri still knew what Kyle was really talking about. Rory wavered because he wanted to stay as far away from his brother-in-law's drug operation as he could. As much as he loved catching the wind in his face on those quarter-mile runs whenever Kyle took him out in the Camaro, or the idea of freedom living with his sister in the valley, being able to come and go as he pleased, along with the prospects of attending a new school with new girls, Rory could never forget how meth destroyed his family. How it rotted out his pop's mind, all the beatings he and his sister and his mom caught whenever pop was high, his father's weeks at a time away, then his mother's own drug use, her stealing for her fixes all those years she was tweaked out, then her arrest, and now Rory's own time away from that way of life. He wasn't keen on running back to any of that, his sister knew, but they were both sure he'd never narc them out to Jamey.

Well then, you stay strong brother. Kyle tapped his fist with Rory's. We're gonna be in touch 'bout getting you back with us, you hear?

Rory nodded with a feigned a smile. He was pretty sure their words were just another hollow gesture, a shallow half-attempt to squash their guilt for not filing any custody papers for him sooner.

Right on. Peace.

Kyle revved up the engine to his Camaro for Rory and the rest of the boys at Excelsior House to hear, screeching out the tires as he and his sister turned the corner. Jamey could only shake his head.

We'll work on reunification if that's what you want Rory.

Cool, is all Rory replied.

***

Sylvia Sanchez arranged her spray cans alongside those of the other Almas Apasionadas artists in preparation for the mural they would be spraying today on Harrison Street, commissioned by the City of San Francisco, Free Palestine Now! and the Jewish Community Center. Her mentor, Rosaria Higalda observed Sylvia's selection of colors approvingly.

Sylvia was in charge of the Falcon of War flying over a group of soldiers marching through the fields of her native El Salvador. Other artists would be painting the palms of their fallen ancestors extending from the clouds, the hand of god releasing a white dove alongside the spirits of the dead peering through from heaven, soldiers from both sides and the peasants they murdered alike, all holding hands in an embrace of peace and tolerance in the afterlife, where all mortals good and evil, rich and poor, FZLN and Nationalistas joined in solidarity now as equals to support the struggles of their descendants in the world below. The Gaza Strip and West Bank interventions intertwined with the State of Israel and Palestinian Flags depicted alongside the Salvadoran War mural. All the teams were set to paint their sections this afternoon, and more than a few members of the community had lined up along the sidewalk to watch the artists tag up this wall adjacent to the corner taqueria. A few local news crews and members of the community were scattered throughout on this big day for the residents of the Outer Mission.

Sylvia was nervous about her design. She meticulously cut each of her cardboard print boards to fit their appropriate dimensions. Rosaria reassured her efforts with a smile. Let the spirits of your ancestors guide you, hija.

Sylvia nodded, ready to roll. She stood upon the ladder, and began spraying primer through each of the boards in series. First the body outline of the bird, then the wings emerging and finally the head, the beak, and lastly the trim to denote the feathers. She shook the last board to slough the paint off, shooting off several finishing spurts to elongate the feathered wings, blurring the contour to give the viewer the impression of hurried flight. Rosaria Higalda was impressed.

You've channeled the collective intentions of a hundred thousand souls dead from the war, hija. Well done.

Sylvia stood back and observed the face of the wall, proud of her work. The talons of the falcon could use some touch up, but that would come soon enough.

Hay mami, you doin' it right wit' them paints.

Sylvia immediately recognized this hot boy she'd seen comin' around Excelsior House a few times.

Whattup, she nodded to Julio, hard.

Where you learn to paint like that anyways? He asked with unfazed admiration.

She nodded over at him. I been taggin' since I wus out da womb, yo. You mighta seen my script 'round da block.

I might 'a. Who's you?

Chita.

Damn, yeah, I've seen you. So whaz your real name Chita?

She hesitated only because she could. Sylvia.

Julio scanned her up and down with obvious interest. Yeah. That 'bout fits you right.

You're in Cottage 2, right? She shot back.

Yeah. Why, you watchin' me 'round da way?

Sylvia laughed off his swagga. I seen you scopin' on my patnas from the driveway a couple 'a times.

Shit girl, 'f I wuz scopin' anyone it wuz you.

Sylvia huffed. Yeah? Then how come you ain't introduced yo'self yet?

Aw, my bad, he blushed. I'm Julio.

Sylvia.

Ayite.

What 'chu in for?

Doin' dirt.

Yeah, that much can be told just lookin' at 'chu.

Fo' sho', Julio cracked. But, naw, blut, I'm just finishing off my probation. Joe lettin' me stay at Excelsior for a quick minute to keep myself outta trouble now that I got booted from the block, for realz.

You ain't one 'a them fools slapped with' them gang injunctions?

Damn straight.

Sylvia nodded, Ain't that a bitch.

Shit, you know what it do. Judge said I'm a Menace to Society. But fools can't even go nowhere to see they peoples no' mo'. Shoot, you c'take the thug out da hood but you can't take da hood out the thug, know what I'm sayin'? For realz, Julio tsked. DA Herrera, he a bitch straight up.

Sylvia cracked a smile. So what 'chu doin' round the way then?

I come to visit my baby moms, blut.

You's a father?

Yeah, Julio smiled. My little niña, she my world, you feel me?

That's cool, she said dismissively.

What, you don't believe me?

Naw…

Damn Chita, you checkin' me already? I just met you. Shit.

She bellowed again, swiveling her head flirtatiously. Well apparently SOMEBODY's got too.

Julio enjoyed her banter. Mang, I wish my baby moms' had yo' kinda spunk.

Shit, by the looks 'a you, she already got plenty to deal wit'. fo' sho'.

Mang, I ain't about all that, Julio reaffirmed to himself. But Sylvia didn't expect any self-deprecation from him.

Seriously blut, you don't know me, you feel me?

I'm 'a bet that's a good thang.

Aw hell naw, he retorted. You's cold. He smiled again, for real this time.

Gots to be messin' wit' yo' kind.

Aw, what 'chu mean my kind?

I mean all you wannabe gangstas and shit.

You don't know me-

I don't wanna know you, fool.

Mang, but I'm different, blut. You ain't never seen the likes 'a me befo'.

Shoot, I been dismissin' scraps like you since I was off da nipple... She put her hand up. Check! She then waved her hand to blow him off.

Julio ignored her insolence. Aw, don't even front. You know you like me.

Shoot, chump, you's delusional.

You ain't told me what 'chu up at Excelsior fo' yet.

Like I'm gonna.

You Salvadoran?

Sylvia looked at him hard but admired his persistence. Mami crossed the river with me when I was 2. Papi's been here since '94.

So how'd you end up in placement? Julio asked, genuinely interested.

Mang, why you want up in my business so damn bad?

Just tryin' to conversate with you, shoot, know what I'm sayin'?

No I don't, she dissed him again. But she didn't turn away. So you Eme?

Naw, I's Mexican...

First generation? She finally asked.

For realz...Jalisco, blut. He threw up a J with is right thumb and index finger.

Then you's Norteño.

I was. 'Fore I jumped out...

Sylvia dropped him a look of disbelief.

For reals.

Then how you all up in da hood with no cops 'restin' yo' ass?

Aw, now you see about all that, 'cause we got an understanding, blut.

You's so full a shit, Julio.

Naw, check it girl, for realz. They look da other way whenever I come visit my niña, long as I stay out da mix.

Tha's cool, I guess.

For realz, mang. 'Cause I been in some shit in my day, blut, no doubt. I know all the 5-0's up in these parts. But since I'm out da life, I been keepin' it straight... Got the cuts to prove it, for realz.

He held his arm up to reveal a long scar carved across its length.

My homies did that with a bottle to make sure I never forgot where I come from.

Shoot, sounds like you got off easy, she proclaimed with a twist of her hand. Ain't y'all supposed to be kickin' it wit' yo' sets fo' life?

Shoot, I'm a papi now, for realz. My homies know my niña my priority now.

Sylvia nodded. That's cool...So then why they gotta cut you?

Motherfuckin' hood code, blood in blood out, straight up.

Her blank stare indicated to Julio that she was unimpressed with his front. So he changed the subject, pointing out her falcon on the mural. So what's this bird all about? He asked, genuinely interested.

To her surprise, Sylvia actually found herself eager to share the symbolism of her work with him.

It represents the spirits of the Salvadoran military and rebel army, all the soldiers fightin' and dyin' in the civil war. Shows how our peoples, dove and falcon, suffered at the hands of war and the atrocities of man, but how in death we all share the skies of the afterlife in peace. Just like the peace that came to my country.

Damn Chita, Julio nodded solemnly. That's deep.

You know it...She stood taller with his affirmation of pride. Came up with that concept myself.

So you always the creative type?

Just like you always been a buster...

Hell naw, I told you I ain't bangin' no more yo. Get to know me, y' see I ain't even lyin'.

Well I ain't gonna lie neither, you seem like every otha busta from the block I ever known.

How many you known? He asked, genuinely interested.

She played it off. 'Nough to know once a gangsta, always a gangsta.

Hell naw, 'cause I done changed, blut. Mosta the perpatratin' I done came from all them drugs I was funkin' wit' once upon a, you feel me? But when I found Jesus Christ, he was my salvation out da life, know what I'm sayin'? He my redeemer now, my savior...

Aw naw, Sylvia admonished, You ain't one 'a those!

One 'a what?

Mother of Guadalupe worshipping cholos. You sound just like mi mami, all father this and the Holy Mother that. That shit ain't done nuthin' for her 'cept give her 'nother reason to tell everybody else what they gotta do. Naw mang, far as I'm concerned, y'all can have your Jesus Cristo while I'm 'a stand right over here. She backed away from him.

Naw girl, you got it all wrong. I mean check it out, the Lord helped me change my life around 360 yo, for reals, you feel me? I'd be dead by now 'f he wasn't speakin' to me in my ear whenever I feel like doin' wrong...

You hearin' voices now? Like the rest 'a them psycho boys up in yo' cottage, mang? Shoot, you best talk to yo' therapist 'cause you need to change up your meds or sumpthin', blut.

Naw Chita, cuz Jesus don't talk with words, he doin' it with actions.

Sylvia was perplexed. Boy, the deck you's playin' wit' be missin' the face cards.

Naw I'm serious, you feel me? 'Cause I read my bible every night, and every time I start slippin', the Lord's guidance keeps me on the straight and narrow, no shit. I know it sounds loco, but it's the truth.

Julio gripped the metal cross hanging around his neck. The power of the love of Jesus Christ keeps me on the path to forgiveness, you feel me? And the power a my niña keeps me goin'. Tha's whus real.

Julio paused to gauge her reaction. Judging by her clear frown, she was still visibly unconvinced. And I ain't slipped once since I been clean, blut, that's how powerful he is, you feel me?

Hey, Sylvia countered with a shrug, whatever floats your boat, mang.

Julio stepped back towards her. Surprising herself, she let him.

So when you gonna let me take you out, girl? He scanned her up and down.

Aw, hell naw, she checked. I don't even know you.

Then get to, shoot, he countered.

Yeah, and what yo' baby momma gon' say 'bout all that'?

Julio reeled back slightly, shaking his head. She and I ain't got no future, you feel me? For realz. That's the truth of it, yo. She thinks I'm in too deep to ever change.

Sounds like she doin' right by her little girl den, Sylvia observed dryly. Gettin' real wit' yo' ass.

Naw, blut, Julio rejected her intimation flatly, 'Cause she wrong 'bout me. She never really known what I'm about, the real me, you feel me?

He seemed so intently serious, Sylvia had to give him a second look.

Yeah, and what's that?

What's what?

This real you you's talkin' bout?

Julio smirked. Shoot, you gon' have to chill with' me to find out, for realz. Know what I'm sayin'?

Yeah, well we see 'bout that.

Julio locked eyes with her and smiled. It excited her, much more that she wanted to admit either to herself or to him.

He sensed this. To keep her from getting uncomfortable, he playfully checked his wrist where he had no watch. Well, hey girl, I gots to get, check in wit' my PO downtown befo' 2, you feel me?

Sylvia chuckled. That's cool Foolio.

Ah, hell naw, he cracked. But I'll see you 'round da way, fo' sho'.

You might.

Julio smiled again. She showed just enough interest.

I'm 'a catch up with you on da circle then, he beamed. 'Till it do keep it real Chita, you feel me?

Coo'.

See you then.

Whatever, she playfully brushed him off.

I'm serious, for realz I'm 'a holla at 'chu real soon.

Ayite then...

He kept backing up into the crowd but clearly he didn't want to leave. So she had to finally shoo him away.

Go on then. Get yo' grimy ass out 'fo I call ICE to come swoop you for good!

Julio hollered and pointed. Ah, hell naw, I'm 'a check you 'gain for realz, you can take that to the bank.

Go on, she finally waved him off more defiantly now, against her own will.

Most definitely.

***

Bauhaus! You're out today. Let's move it!

Andrew perused his cellmate at San Francisco Juvenile Hall with a final once over. Smell you later.

The other boy couldn't be bothered to move his head from the pillow where it was buried in order to say goodbye.

See ya, wouldn't want to be ya.

***

Officer Michael Moreno and Tommy O'Shea transitioned out at shift change near the front desk of SFPD's Mission Station.

Officers Jonson, Hernandez and Stalward approached O'Shea, putting their hands up on the officers' shoulders.

Just the men we wanted to see. Pizza at Pasquale's and beers at the Shamrock. You in?

O'Shea gave an eager smile. Nothing beats puttin' a few back with my fellow Micks.

What about you, Moreno?

Naw, I'm 'a have to catch up with you fools another time.

Oh, and where you gotta be?

His old lady must be calling, Jonson cracked.

Naw, Moreno's a single man again, Hernandez gave his fellow officer a sympathetic pat on the shoulder. He just wants to go home and stroke it to Dancing With the Stars.

Dude, that Cheryl is the finest one.

You would know all of them, Jonson.

Moreno cracked up and shook off their taunts.

Let the man do what he's gotta do.

My Latin liver can't keep up with all you peasant potato-eating motherfuckers anyway, Moreno reasoned.

Least we ain't getting no heart attacks off 'a no cheese papusas and bean tacos.

Moreno feigned offense. Man I'll still run all your asses off the track.

Name the time and place my friend, Jonson invited.

But you gotta come out with us, Rodriguez pined. Nikki's working the bar tonight.

She likes you…It ain't no secret.

Word is she loves herself some brown meat.

Yeah and if you wash a few dishes, she might do yours.

Leave my partner alone. O'Shea insisted. He's got to go hit the books.

Moreno confirmed with a nod. Got a midterm tonight.

Oh man Mike, I ain't never pegged you as the scholarly type.

Just promise me you won't forget us little people when you make it big, Professor.

What's your test on?

Social Construction of Human Relations.

Construction of what-the-fuck? The officers laughed. Man, what kind of ivory tower bullshit are they filling your head up with?

You'd be surprised, Moreno mocked.

O'Shea defended his partner. You chumps laugh all you want, but our man's been dropping' some mean psychology on our bangers lately. Homeboy got their brains so twisted up they even tipped us off to those Mara Salvatrucha street soldiers who dropped into town from Bakersfield this week.

Seriously?

Moreno shrugged off his partners praise. Just bringing some new tools to the game's all.

So when you gonna edjumacate us?

What those kids need is for some strong relative to deliver an ass whuppin' each and every time they mess up, not some shoulder to cry on.

Actually, therapy can kick your ass harder than any knock on the block.

Man, get your silly ass to class already.

Don't you dobby bastards have some beers to drink?

You ain't never bustin' my head up with that pop psychology crap, Jonson insisted.

Naw Jonson, 'cause your skull's way too thick for that...

Well if they ever teach you 'bout dealin' with some real life situations up in your classes, like how to get a neighbor to narc out the thugs terrorizing their block or how to hold a banger in witness protection long enough to keep him from gettin' splayed across the pavement for being the snitch he is, or what makes a dope fiend keep lovin' her fix more than her baby, promise to share.

Will do.

Then get your ass to school already bookworm, those tests aren't gonna take themselves.

Moreno chuckled and gave them a wave. Say hi to Nikki for me.

I'll tell her you're busy reading the Kama Sutra, so next time you come out you can show her some new moves, courtesy of all that higher learning! Jonson yelled out, making an upward thrusting motion with his hands.

You guys take HIM with you and she won't be talkin' to any of us anymore.

The officers laughed it out and headed out for their night of revelry.

***

Cardena, Nacho, and Smiley made the trip up from Bakersfield to Frisco quickly enough. Their Upper Mission Sureño homies needed some serious muscle now to deliver their retaliation on the 24th Street Norteños who murdered Rodrigo Suarez, the younger brother of La Eme's leader in Chino, Antonio Suarez, and Cardena's homie for life. Word had just come down the pike from Pelican Bay that none of the three elders of Nuestra Familia had authorized the killing of their arch enemy Suarez' little brother, runnin' with the San Francisco Mara Salvatrucha for his elder kin while he was away dinkin' a dime for double murder one. But still, homeboy got got. And La Eme had a code. Brother for brother. Blood in and blood out. The fathers made it clear. No soldja left behind. Like the military. 'Cause each of their sets was linked city to city, across all of California, from Crescent City to San Diego, and ain't no bustas be breakin' the chain. And Suarez never let his people down. Shit, back in the yard in Chino years ago, Cardena woulda never saw that La Familia bitchpunk runnin' up on him if Suarez hadn't flopped his ass first, for realz STRAIGHT UP, and Suarez went to town on that fool, straight busted his head up so bad he caved the vato's face in and shit, no doubt. Suarez dinked a dime for saving Cardena back then, took ten solid, no questions asked. That scrap even got his ass shanked with a dipstick in the scuffle, two twists through the back into the liver and dude was dust, straight septic, prison docs couldn't do shit about it. No way, but dude's homeboy assassin straight never batted an eye. So Cardena owed him his life. And so when Cardena came up for his solid but got a reprieve for good behavior after Operation Black Widow ran all they peoples out the jails, he'd promised to look after Suarez' kin on the outside. 'Cause if Chino taught him one thing it was this: who his homies was. And now Suarez' little brother was gunned down in cold blood, and his old crew wuz deep in some major scuffle with dem bitch-ass Norteño bustas frontin' as Nuestra from the Lower Mission, damn Frisco been lit up past couple 'a weeks in some tit-for-tat bullshit. And now they wus turnin' up the heat on 16th Street, they wuz soon 'bout to feel the full reach de La Eme. Cardena would keep his Sureños holdin' they rags high up and down the block 'till Mara Salvatrucha straight owned every inch of Norteño Mission territory, droppin' bustas like deuces down the corridors for good. Fillin' they funeral homes with blue rags 'till they ain't none more standing. 'Cause if Pelican Bay Nuestras thinkin' they still got flex up in Frisco, it ain't mean shit now that Bakersfield on tha job, takin' ova da block straight up…

Miguel, leader of the 16th Street Sureños who represented for Suarez long as he was in lockup in Chino, and his youngbloods Paco 415, Benny, and Javier, hooked up with Cardena, Nacho, and Smiley at the fence near John O'Connell High School on Bryant. Cardena finished his lengua taco from the truck and the boys exchanged signs, Thirteen bitch, with hands crossed.

La Eme.

Throw 'em up.

Mad hugs exchanged between Miguel and Cardena.

Paco, Benny and Javier nodded in respect for the valley
Emes.

Wha''chu been up to…

Doin' dirt.

Cardena smiled. Hell yeah, clasping hands. As always, no
doubt.

What it do, Cardena?

This is Nacho and Big Smiley.

Eme...

Each member threw up their three fingers against their chests.

Meet my little up-and-comer homies.

The leaders from Bakersfield nodded to Paco, Benny and Javier.

Thirteen, blut...

What it do.

Miguel spoke for them. Yo homie, you know we got all kinds 'a mad respect for y'all makin' the trip up like this, know what I'm sayin'?

Bakersfield represent.

The leader shrugged. Ain't no thang, young thug.

Ain't missin' no chance to blast a busta.

Cardena noticed Paco staring at him and met his gaze. He walked up to this eager youngblood and put his hand on Paco's shoulder. Paco nodded. Here's to our fallen homie, blut.

Paco extended three fingers to his heart. The others bowed their heads in tribute.

RIP...

Damn straight.

Respect.

Well now we gonna make it right, you feel me?

Hell yeah, blut.

Y'all holdin' it down tight, light 'em up, let 'em know Eme be rollin' through for they payback?

Shore 'nuff.

No doubt.

Keep shit locked down, homie. Just waitin' on y'all now to put in some real work.

Well, we here...So where them cholos at?

Corridors be crawlin' wit' Ene tonight, mang.

So why we still choppin' it up, yo?

Yeah, let's go blast on these bustas.

Do or die...

That's what I'm sayin', mang.

Some mothafuckin' cholos be dyin' tonight.

Nacho and Smiley approved of these up-and-comers in their 16th Street Frisco set. These Sureños were more than ready to drop a few knocks.

So Cardena and his local affiliates walked South down Treat Street, crossing 23rd thick into Norteño territory on a sleeping mission. Rolling six deep, these scraps they straight didn't give a fuck, out for blood. About halfway down the street, they caught wind of their first victim, Edgar, who felt the hair on his back climb into his shirt well before he saw the Sureños who were about to end his life. He knew the score immediately at the sight of them. So did Tootz, who was down the block but not strapped, so whatever went down with his homie, he could only sit by helplessly and watch, with no way to flex on these fools. He yelled out to Edgar to get into his house but by the time Edgar stood up it was too late, Cardena's crew was well upon him.

Whassup Paco? Edgar fronted to his childhood friend among the group, Y'all know Ene ain't got no love for you scraps up in here.

Paco could not meet his old friend's eyes in the company of the Bakersfield muscle. Cardena noticed Paco's hesitancy and approached instead.

Is this him, homie?

Paco only nodded.

Edgar stepped to Cardena, I tell you whus up...

Cardena calmly shifted his physically overbearing frame into the young Norteño's space, forcing Edgar to bend backward in an awkward display of submission. It was clear to everyone that this vato owned him in every way.

Cardena only smiled back. Ene ain't in Frisco no more, holmes.

Edgar tried to hold his hard face but his body clearly shook from the exchange. Nacho and Smiley laughed at the spectacle.

Eme can suck a dick like the bitches you is! Edgar spit on the ground near Cardena's feet instead, trying to save whatever face he had left. If he could just stay alive long enough for Tootz to round up his patnas. But in his heart he knew he was done for.

Cardena hissed coldly through his several missing teeth. Go with God, youngblood.

Edgar froze, taking several panting, shallow breaths as Cardena menacingly stepped back from him and drew out his clip from under his shirt, taking his time to wipe the gun and lock the barrel into position. Edgar panted harder, clearly distressed, unable to stop his body from shaking. Cardena waited a few moments longer than necessary to allow the younguns in his set to watch Edgar slowly lose control of his posture, to harden them up. But Paco, Javier, and Benny closed their eyes instead, ready to mourn their old friend out of the view of the misdeeds this older Bakersfield leader was about to perpetrate on their old rival. They were clearly inexperienced in the ways of killing. But Cardena delighted in the opportunity to grow this next crop of Frisco gangstas to represent La Eme correct in their hood. Several neighbors watched the scene expressionlessly, while others shuffled behind their windows to avoid becoming witnesses.

Cardena turned around and mused at the hesitancy on the faces of the young Sureños in his tow, perhaps remembering his own initiation into the business of killing for his crew long ago. He put the gun squarely in Paco's hand.

Chulo's heart's still beatin', holmes…

Clearly an indication that Cardena wanted Paco to assume ownership of the kill, to blast his childhood friend dead in the chest and finish the deed. As the one chosen by Cardena, Paco had no choice. His face hardened for Benny and Javier to see. Cardena smiled again. He knew this youngun had what it took to step up. Javier and Benny could only stare at him blankly, thankful neither of them had been given the brutal task. The Bakersfield La Eme crew was motionless, having watched this ritual repeat itself a hundred times. Now Paco was among those to be initiated, one of those now on his way.

Looking directly at his friend, Paco mercilessly raised the clip, pointed, and fired several shots into Edgar's chest near his heart, blasting him point blank execution style in the street for all to see, killing him instantly. Tootz heard the two shots rings out from a block and a half away as he ran down 24th, trying to bury his tears in his hands.

After a brief moment, Cardena grabbed the clip back from Paco, stowing it methodically back under his pants along his waist. Paco stood before the crew expressionless, though clearly transformed by the experience, riding the full wave of emotion from fear to thrill, befuddlement to panic, then finally to complete self-abandonment. Regardless of where he settled, he knew his life was forever different now.

Ain't no thing, homie...

Cardena patted Paco's back, knowing full well this little Sureño had never killed before.

Now Frisco crew ain't got no love for Ene neither.

The street was silent. Not a neighbor stirring or seen. The Sureño crew had sent their retaliation. With the street as their witness, the rest was only a matter of time.

***

Eric walked most of the distance from Excelsior House to the Upper Haight where he knew Sarah would be. He did not quite know what to expect if or when he found her, he only knew that he had to.

He combed Yerba Buena Park, paying particular attention to the skater punks and homeless youth that lined the outer grass rim on Haight Street. No sign of Sarah. He perused the shops around Ashbury and Carl, popped into Amoeba Records just to be sure, checked out a couple of Tool imports in the bargain bin for good measure. Fuck Amoeba, he thought to himself, anybody so privileged to listen to the likes of Maynard James Keenan better sure as shit be paying full price before it washes all away, see you haters down in Arizona Bay…

Eric quickly regained his focus. His Klonopin made any thoughts that sputtered through his cranium grow fuzzy, but he knew his mission. Pull Sarah outta her daze and get her back downtown and on the Greyhound with him to L.A. where they would live happily ever after on Venice Beach near his parents. He only had to find her first.

He crossed Stanyan and descended into the tunnel connecting Hippie Alley to the rest of the park. It was on the other side of the portal, in a patch of leaves near a wire mesh fence protecting the exit from the street above, that he saw her lying in the bushes behind a small tree. Stewing in her own sweat, moaning. Foaming at the mouth. He went to her immediately.

Who did this to you?

Eric…

Sarah was fading in and out of coherence. He slapped her face gently, mindful of the cuts along her cheek and bruises across her temples.

What'd you take?

She could only mumble through the stench of her cottonmouth.

He tried taking her pulse, but fumbled. He would not have known what to do anyway, but because he didn't feel any throbbing in her neck, he got really SCARED.

Eric knew he couldn't take her to the bus station now. Given her likely overdose, he had to get her to a hospital NOW. She could kill him for that later.

On automatic pilot, Eric dragged her up out of the foliage, carrying her in his arms though the tunnel, panting the entire way. He was too exhausted to haul her up the full two blocks left to St. Mary's Hospital alone, so he tried flagging a taxi down, but instead a Five-O passing down Stanyan immediately noticed what was up and pulled around to him. The officer called the paramedics and they picked up Sarah. After allowing Eric the courtesy of riding with her in the ambulance to the hospital, the officer called in his information. No AWOL had yet been registered. So Eric placed a call to Excelsior House and Deirdre answered the phone. Upon speaking with her, the officer agreed to transport him back to his placement, no questions asked. Nice work, Deirdre.

Due to her considerable experience taking the boys off-hill, Deirdre volunteered the next day to drive Eric back to St. Mary's to visit Sarah, who had undergone a stomach pumping the previous evening and was recovering in the ICU. He put his hand on hers the minute he arrived. When she awoke, Sarah looked at him through vacant eyes.

Doctors said I'd have been gone in less than an hour if you hadn't found me. You should've let me die.

How can you say that? I love you.

I don't deserve it.

Well, I can't help it. I want us to go to Venice.

I can't. I'm being transferred to a psych hospital, she said flatly.

Not with Charlotte!

No. Out of state. My father wants me to disappear from California for good before I kill myself or ruin what's left of his political career.

Do you know where yet?

Colorado, I think.

Well you can escape that. I'll come get you again.

Eric, she paused, insistently. You saved my life. But I don't love you.

Eric processed this for a minute.

Yeah, I know. But I know I can make you if you just COME WITH ME...All of our dreams will come true. He hit the palm of his left hand with the back of his right to punctuate the point.

Sarah was not startled by this, but closed her eyes in order to be as forceful with him as now needed. No, they won't. Because I never will.

How can you be so sure? He bargained desperately.

Sarah shook her head. I just am.

He didn't have any way to respond to this.

Go to Venice alone, Eric. There's nothing left here for you with me.

Sarah kept her eyes closed so she would not have to face his agony. Deirdre meanwhile, was completely enraptured in the teen drama. But she too had no way to comfort him.

Goodbye, is all Sarah said, without opening her eyes.

Vanquished, Eric started to blink out in an apparent Turrets episode. Deirdre saw the fluttering of his eyelids and immediately distracted him in order to stifle its onset.

C'mon Eric, we have to go. She paused for a moment to let his thoughts settle within. I'll buy you a Big Mac.

Eric threw her hands off of his shoulder, but came to blankly. Surrendering to the finality of the situation, he followed Deirdre out of the hospital room without further incident. He would never see Sarah Hillsbrook again.

***

Carly and Deirdre prepared to take the boys on an off-hill to the Oakland A's baseball game one Saturday morning. Joe walked in with the tickets as Josh Crenshaw finished up his shift on the overnight.

Joe alerted the boys. Ayite, I got some extras last minute. So who all wants to go?

Brandon raised his hand. I been on Level Three for a month.

Me too, Nate announced.

But Deirdre rebutted him. No Nate, you're on Level One.

How come?

For all that swearing.

That was only for a week.

She checked the board in the cottage office.

Nate followed her inside. See, it's right there.

He's right, his name's been changed to Level Two.

Joe shuffled the tickets in his hands, counting them tauntingly in front of the clients. Boy, get your butt back out da staff office!

Nate quickly ran out.

OK, so we got enough for Levels Two and Three only.

Eric was disqualified because he had violated his house probation by AWOLing to go track down Sarah. Tyrone and Rydell were still on Level One for swearing at staff the previous week, so they couldn't go. But Rory, Kendrick and Duane were all eligible. Kendrick started packing his things, but Josh stopped him cold.

Kendrick you know you can't cross no bridges.

Rydell agreed. Damn right, you's a 602 like the diddler here. Rydell pointed over to Eric to taunt him.

Kendrick resisted the comparison. Man damn. I ain't no chalky hands, shoot!

Carly sounded off from the floor. Rydell, Kendrick, language!

But unfortunately, as Rydell had ungracefully reminded them all, San Francisco County's jurisdiction did not extend across the Bay Bridge into Oakland, so it was in fact true that any resident at Excelsior House who was also on probation with the county could not go to the game.

But Joe was known to bend this rule from time to time if his clients demonstrated good behavior. Kendrick, How long you been on Level 3?

Kendrick pouted. I don't know, shoot...

Carly chimed in for him. Something like four months.

Joe looked hard at the little man. You been doin' right since you been here. I think we can make an exception here. Just don't tell no one, right Kendrick?

Kendrick jumped out of his seat to join the boys leaving for the game. For shore!

Deirdre looked over to Joe with hard eyes. This made Joe melt. She knew he couldn't stand punishing his boys on a technicality, especially when they were good, knowing full well Carly and Deirdre could easily handle any issues that might spring up bringing the boys into Gen-Pop. Besides, any opportunity to socialize their clients into society was healthy for them, as well as part of the Excelsior program's mission, so Joe had little problem with making such a call along the broader margins of their treatment plans whenever possible.

Josh hollered out to Kendrick as the boys prepared to leave. Don't you go grabbin' no more kids shoes at the game now.

Duane laughed. Aw, he clowned you Kendrick!

Who gave your punk ass permission to talk, Duane? Josh started to noogie the naps off of Duane's scabied scalp as the kid ran around the front room in feigned hysterics. Naw, mang, Josh stop! HELP!

Joe, Carly and Deirdre cracked up watching Josh play-wrestle Duane into a half nelson and rug burning his scalp with his knuckles. He then released Duane, who kept laughing during the exchange, despite the clear pain he exhibited with a wince across his scrunching face while rubbing his hands across his head to squelch the burning.

But of course, Duane fronted as if he had won the melee. That's what I thought, baldy.

Joe crushed any opportunity for sympathy. All you knuckleheads goin', in the van now!

The boys took the cue from Joe and ran out to Excelsior's silver Astro van parked in the driveway. Carly took the driver's seat while Deirdre rode shotgun. See you guys in a few hours. The boys pulled away, chipper as all hell.

A quick win for all involved.

Mid-afternoon, Kevin showed up for work at Cottage 2. Tyrone, Brandon, and Rydell walked the circle as he approached. As Kevin waved to the boys, they at first ignored him, then quickly on Brandon's prompting, all turned around in unison and crossed their arms to form a series of Figure X's, proceeding to bounce them up and down from their crotches. It was a direct rip off from wrestler Triple H's taunting maneuver to flip off his own opponents, without raising the conventional middle finger or directing a clenched fist to the sky.

Rydell yelled out to Kevin. Brown Regal, damn it's illegal.

Kevin blew them off, focusing instead on Eric, who sat on the front lawn drawing solemnly in his sketchpad. All of the boys were awaiting the arrival of Excelsior House's new client from Juvenile Hall, Andrew Bauhaus. Joe thought it would be best to move Andrew in while some of the boys were at the A's game, in order to minimize any potential disruption during intake.

Soon enough, Andrew arrived with his bag. The boys on the circle at this point were chatting up Sylvia about Sarah's recent ejection from Excelsior House, when they all finally saw their new arrival walk into Cottage 2.

Aw, hell naw. 'Nother white boy movin' in? Damn.

We's outnumbered now.

Andrew was tall and shifty in his gait. He ignored the boys' gazes fixed upon him, displaying a mixture of suspicion and intimidation as he walked into the house. Once inside, Andrew staked out the empty bed and drawer set in Tyrone's room. Rory had already moved his things down the hall into Kendrick's room in anticipation of the new client's arrival. Brandon and Rydell would still be bunking together, while Nate and Eric kept their digs as well. However, none of the other boys had been informed of the changes.

So Joe showed Andrew his room while Tyrone, Brandon, and Rydell, ripe with curiosity, followed them to the house to scope out the scene.

Joe introduced the boys. Hey y'all, this is Andrew. Give him the Excelsior welcome.

You don't even want none 'a that, Tyrone joked. Hot dogs and chili farts.

But Brandon and Rydell chose to size him up instead, with several hardened nods.

Whas up, Brandon sneered.

It was immediately clear there was no love shared between the boys.

Yo man, this is Tyrone, Joe pointed to him. He's gonna be your new roommate.

Sup, Andrew offered his fist.

Sup, Tyrone fronted, tapping it with his knuckles.

I'm a let you two get acquainted. C'mon y'all. Joe shooed away Brandon and Rydell, who immediately retreated to their room to eavesdrop on the back and forth sure to follow.

Tyrone made the first attempt at conversation. So where you coming from, mang?

Andrew remained blank in his stare, but didn't reveal if this was out of toughness, nervousness, stupidity, or pride. Probably a combination of all, Tyrone guessed to himself.

Andrew finally answered. Was up in Hillcrest doin' a stint for aggravated assault. Bashed in this jig's skull for lookin' at me wrong.

Yo mang, what did you say? Tyrone shook his head, dumbfounded. He still thought Andrew's demeanor was just a front 'cause he was scared in his new surroundings. Tyrone had seen all kinds of fools in his time gettin' transferred up in here from the halls. You's 602 then?

Yup, Andrew finally replied.

Then you best not be messin' up in here, know what I'm sayin', 'cause Joe be throwing probates back to the courts quick as a motherfucker when they be doin' dirt.

Listen dawg, Andrew interrupted. I'll tell you straight up. I ain't used to bunkin' with no niggers.

Tyrone was stricken. This dude was as racist as they come.

And I bet you don't want to be shackin' up wit' no crackers neither.

Aw, hell naw, Tyrone could only shake his head.

So I suggest we both just keep to each other's side 'a da room, you feel me? I wuz bunkin' wit' one 'a y'all up in da pen, and we both made it work, but I ain't about to get all friendly with you now, you feel me?

After sharing his room with Rory for six months, Tyrone didn't quite know what to say.

Dude, you ain't gon' last ten minutes up in this place coppin' that front.

Yo this ain't no front bitch! Andrew immediately broadened his shoulders. I'm 'a flex on whoever thinks he can step to me, you feel me, 'cause I keep it real dawg, white pride motherfucker!

He hovered menacingly over Tyrone, who quickly backed off, startled. It was clear that Andrew was more than a little nuts.

That's what I'm sayin', Andrew flailed, sitting back down on his bed after having established his dominance. Tyrone's was mildly panicked but didn't quite know how to process it.

I'm here to do my time and get the hell out this place, straight up straight out, Andrew lamented. I don't even know why my PO put me up in here with y'all in the first place. You'd think the motherfucker know better and shit. He hucked his socks angrily from his duffel bag into his drawer.

Yo, whatever works for you, dawg, cool. Tyrone retorted passively.

Andrew did not acknowledge his new roommate again. Instead, he closed his drawer and lay back on his bed with hands folded behind his head to rest. Andrew's muscle shirt revealed not much meat on his bones. Tyrone figured he could take him if he had to. But still, Joe had to be hearin' how Tyrone wasn't about to kick it with this dude no more.

The boys in the Astro van arrived home stoked from the game. Joe immediately called them all into group and they assembled in the front room of Cottage 2 with Kevin, Deirdre, and Carly sitting in the circle. Andrew was comforted now by the sight of a few white staff in the mix. They would have his back, he reasoned, if shit with the other clients went the way it always seemed to with him.

Agnes and Jamey made their way across the street from Cottage 2 to say their hellos as well.

I want y'all to offer up a warm welcome to Andrew, He's gonna be stayin' in Tyrone's room, Joe announced.

The boys were encouraged to introduce themselves by saying their names around the circle.

So Andrew, Jamey began. We don't want you to feel on the spot since you're new, but we like to convene group several times a week, and whenever a major event affects our cottage community. Group helps us express our feelings about what is going on with us and to voice any concerns or work out any issues we might have with others in our community here before they escalate. But generally this is an opportunity we take to encourage clients to check in with their peers and to plan for the week. Group is intended to be a safe environment to express yourself; nothing you say here is used against you as a consequence. It's the one time of the week you are encouraged to express whatever is going on for you in a non-judgmental, supportive capacity. Does that sound okay to you?

Sure, Andrew replied, only slightly comforted.

Meanwhile, Brandon, having overheard Tyrone's earlier conversation with his new roommate, whispered into Rydell's ear.

So Andrew, Welcome to Excelsior House. Do you have any questions for us? Jamey offered.

Naw I'm straight. This was clearly a front to everyone in the circle.

After an awkward silence, Rydell raised his hand for Jamey's approval to speak, a gesture usually uncharacteristic of him. Jamey appreciated his willingness to break the group's deadlock so nodded to him. Go ahead Rydell.

So where you from whiteboy?

Deirdre, Joe, and Agnes stared daggers at him.

Keep a lid on it boy, Joe insisted.

You're losing points for being inappropriate, Deirdre stated.

Man, you can't take points from kids expressing theyselves in group, Nate correctly pointed out.

Mang, all I did was ask a question, Rydell feigned annoyance. Just trying to help our new homie feel the love.

Nate, Brandon, and Eric snickered at the comment.

Andrew sneered at them. In another setting, he might have let the jab go unaddressed, but here, he was put over the edge by the fact that Eric was complicit in their taunts.

So Andrew lashed back out. Why you laughin' with these jigaboos, fool?

The cottage was taken aback by his unabashed bluntness. All except for Tyrone, who already expected this kind of outburst from the cottage's newest client. Game on.

Agnes was the first to respond. Did you just say what I think I heard?

The staff were obviously not impervious to offense. Though Deirdre and Carly felt it unwise to engage Andrew's clear attempts to goad or split staff, they certainly did not dare try and temper Agnes' inevitable admonishment that was bound to follow, because staff made a point of never second guessing each other in front of the other clients.

Andrew immediately sensed the tension he created in Agnes and so felt more than obliged to engage her. Yeah, you heard me right coon lady.

Deirdre immediately risked escalating the exchange by rebuking him in Agnes' defense. Andrew. STOP IT!

But Andrew refused to back down. What, you gonna back her too fat girl? Just 'cause you too big fo' a white dude to wanna fuck you don't mean you go against your own kind.

Deirdre's blood rose to a boil as her cheeks flushed a dark crimson under her furrowed brow. Joe rested his right hand on her shoulder.

Boy, you best keep your mouth in check, 'fore you get yourself knocked out.

Yeah nigger, and whose gonna do that, you? What kind of home you runnin' here anyway?

Joe stood up immediately and got right in Andrew's face, hot as hell. Don't think I won't knock your butt from here to Tuesday!

Shit, go ahead and touch me, I dare you, Andrew taunted, reveling in the power his words now held over those in authority of his new surroundings. My PO will have this place shut down so fast you'll be sittin around eatin' watermelon and fried chicken all day like the no-job-havin' porch monkey you is, stupid jig motherfucker!

Although his taunts resonated as pure nonsense, Joe was still about to kill this kid before Jamey pre-empted him with an extended hand to Joe's midframe, stunting his advance.

Agnes diffused Joe's representative rage by just shaking her head at Andrew. OOOHHH. Uh uh. You ain't gonna last long at all around here with that kind 'a attitude, I'm a tell you that right now.

Jamey intervened. Andrew, it's obvious you have some issues with race.

Mang, I ain't got no issues 'cept havin' to bow down to a bunch 'a jigs every beck and call. Shit, Andrew pouted. You said I was free to express my views in group. Well here they are, so deal with 'em.

Jamey clarified. That is only if you are trying to be constructive.

What, you one of them now too? Man, my PO's a straight busta sendin' me here, I never seen so much white trash in one room at the same time. He looked to Deirdre and Carly. These niggers done rotted y'all's brains. Where's yo' pride? Buncha bitches up in here is all I see.

Rory was the client who finally stepped to him, thrusting his chest into Andrew who stood firm as well. You the bitch, bitch.

Andrew flexed on him. Man, sit your hillbilly ass down. You ain't gon' do shit when I bury you.

Let's go, right now then, shit. Show me what you got-

You disgrace your race-

Let's go biznich, I'll take you out!

Rory raised his arms and pushed Andrew farther than any of them expected. From the force, Andrew fell squarely onto the couch below.

Joe and Jamey immediately snapped into action, forming a barrier between Rory and Andrew. Joe blocked Andrew squarely in his seat as he tried to stand back up.

You get your hands off 'a me nigger, that's assault!

Rydell smirked with pleasure. Staff can contain your ass all they want, bitch.

Now I'm 'a press charges and you're goin' to jail, too, hillbilly boy.

Sit your ass down, Rory growled, waving his hand as he returned to his chair.

I don't feel safe here Jamey, Andrew pouted. I want to call my PO.

OOOH, Agnes retorted.

Joe would have none of it. Shut your ass up, boy.

Surprisingly, this time, Andrew did.

But of course, from across the room, Rydell wouldn't let it lie. Fuck you, cracker!

Fuck you, grouphome! Andrew hissed back at him.

To diffuse the confrontation one client at a time, Jamey first turned to Rory and pointed him down the hall.

Rory, to your room. Rory was clearly worked up, but out of respect for his therapist, he followed the order. Man, this is some biznitch, he protested, kicking his way along the wall down the hall before slamming his door shut.

Meanwhile, the group was still on considerable edge from Andrew's outbursts.

Sensing this, Andrew kept spewing his vitriol. I'm walkin' my ass up outta here first chance I get straight back to the pen. Fuck y'all. Just call my PO and tell him what's up. I'm out.

Agnes calmly demurred. If that's what you want Andrew, then fine, let's go call him.

Five minutes and I'm outta this place for good, just you watch.

Jamey clarified the situation to staff. Unless he's a threat to himself or the others, we have to hold him tonight. Otherwise we're instructed to send him to the hospital for psychiatric observation. A wry smile of morbid satisfaction crossed Andrew's face upon uttering this fact.

The boys immediately relished at the thought.

Hell yeah!

Send him to Charlotte!

You gon' get booty busted by dem gay ass kids at General!

Andrew appeared genuinely nervous for the first time by the group's sudden excitement at the prospect of him ending up in the hospital tonight instead of returning to the halls.

So you gonna be a threat tonight Andrew? Agnes smiled triumphantly. Please tell me you is.

Not to you, nigger, I wouldn't touch you with a ten foot pole!

Ah, hell naw! Now it was Nate who stepped up in a rage to defend Agnes.

Nobody be talking to Big Momma like that without getting they ass beat!

Sit down baby, Agnes asked of him soothingly. Big Momma can take care of herself just fine.

Deirdre reassumed command over herself. Andrew, it's time for you to go to bed.

No way Whale Tail, I ain't even listenin' to you.

Joe could no longer contain himself, rushing to Deirdre's defense. Boy, you best show staff some respect and get your ass down the hall before I drag you down there myself.

The underlying rage in Joe's tone suggested to Andrew that he harbored deeper affections for this woman that could be conveniently exploited. What, she your girlfriend or sumpthin' jigaboo? Andrew mocked incessantly. Damn, y'all blackmen LOVE you some big bootied white bitches, don't you?

Go to bed Andrew, Deirdre commanded indifferently, finally in command over her emotions. She pointed methodically along with Joe toward the hallway. Go.

Yeah, okay, Andrew finally relented, knowing that going to the mental hospital was his only other option following his present course. Then I'm 'a see you later fat girl. He continued to taunt Deirdre. Mmm. Damn shame you dis nigga's pussy. 'Cause I'd tear that ass up something real.

Andrew licked his lips. Joe was seriously about to lunge at this cracker before the soft hand of Agnes placed itself firmly on his chest to stop him. Let it go Joe, Deirdre got this, Agnes assured him quietly.

Of course, Andrew continued slinging his racist epithets at the group as he backed down the hallway to his room.

Yo' y'all know what they call a damn shame in the South?

He didn't bother to wait and answered his own question. What's that? A bus half full of jigs driving off a cliff!

And why IS THAT a damn shame? He continued taunting by answering his own question. 'Cause the bus is only HALF full....AHHHH!

The staff and clients were genuinely at a loss for what to make of this kid.

That piece of crap is outta here tomorrow, Joe finally announced to the group once he was out of their sight. His assurances comforted everyone, including Tyrone, who had to take a moment to set the record straight in front of the others. Told you so Joe, damn.

***

Julio Hernandez caught up with Andrew Bauhaus the following morning after Deirdre distributed meds to the boys. She finished out her overnight shift without incident and quickly left. The boys gathered in the front yard earlier than usual on this casual Sunday morning. It was agreed by everyone to collectively ignore Andrew until another one of his outbursts got him kicked out for good, save of course for the occasional eye fuck, which the boys delivered whenever they passed him in the hallway or out on the circle. Andrew, for the most part, lay low from the evening before; In light of his initial acting out during intake, his interim therapist Jamey decided it was in the best interests of all the residents to stabilize Andrew's transition to group home living with a combination of one-on-one therapy sessions and an incremental increase in his drug regimen. So Jamey upped his Dexedrine dose from 500 mgs to 1000, to be administered once in the morning and once in the evening.

Outside, Andrew sat alone, leaning on the front yard fence watching Tyrone, Rydell, Nate and Brandon pace endless circles with Sylvia along the cul-de-sac while Maurice and Eric played cards inside. Kendrick was in the bathroom, grooming himself for a busy day working the drive thru window at McDonald's on Ocean Boulevard, while Rory and Marcus shot hoops in the driveway. Duane was the only client left sleeping in his room, dreaming of his parents and his six other brothers and sisters all gone, longing for a time when they were still all together as a family, so many years ago.

Walking backing home from his morning NA meeting, it was Julio who, noticing Andrew in distraught isolation, took pity on him. He rolled up on him before entering the house.

'Sup man...

Andrew's initial reaction was to be startled, but Julio's body language implied he was not stepping to check him, so Andrew returned his greeting with a nod.

Julio spotted a menagerie of fresh bruises lining Andrew's face and arms.

See you met the welcome wagon.

Andrew just shrugged, defeated. Ain't no thing. Been though tons worse in the halls.

So you's a 602 too? Julio inquired. Thought I was 'the only one left up in here.

Staff always let us beat on each other like that?

Only if they like you. Naw, blut, Julio laughed, That shit was on account 'a Deirdre sleepin' on her overnights. Sounds like you had it comin' though, blut, for realz. Julio gave Andrew the once over no bullshit nod, hard. This kid's complexion was black and blue across the board, blemished from the previous night's hazing where Nate, Brandon, and Rydell caught him in his sleep, held him down under his bed sheets and took turns on him with pillow sacks stuffed with books. After their reprisal beating, Andrew was allowed to crash on the couch to await his return to the halls the next day. But you can bet he didn't cop another wink that night, ready to deliver payback to any punk motherfucker who dared step to him again.

As a result, Julio could see the deep circles of sleep deprivation welling around Andrew's eyes, imposed by the demands of last night's sentinel duty.

Yo, I usually don't chop it up with spicks but you seem cool enough.

Yo blut, you think I'm all about kickin' it wit' yo' cracker ass? Shoot, then you is nuts.

Andrew could only laugh, equal parts proud and embarrassed, because he had to agree.

Naw, mang, Julio countered. This is 'bout maintainin', handlin' yo'self correct around here. Yo blut, you feel me? Doin' yo'self right doin' right by others, know what I'm sayin'? Holdin'

it down wit' yo' head up high, blut. I do it movin', you feel me?
Ain't no other way to go.

Andrew knew he couldn't cop a front and talk shit or be a
dick to Julio, 'cause this dude already had his number, that much
was for sure. But still, for some reason he could not figure out why
Julio was being cool to him, so Andrew reasoned to take the high
road, if only to see where it led. Yeah, I hear you man.

'Cause this motherfucker they call life ain't no picnic out
here, you feel me, blut? Dude could use a homie or two.

Andrew nodded in agreement. True dat.

But I'm 'a tell you right now, this shit ain't 'bout how
many fools you step to, how you' get 'chours, make your way or
get paid, or yo' payback, know what I'm sayin'? Nuh uh, this
shit's about change, mang. I'm talkin' rehabilitation, you feel me?
'Cause we's straight institutionalized. Fools all tryin' to step over
one anotha', doin' what they do 'cause that's all dey ever done,
know what I'm sayin'? Ain't nothin' but missed motherfuckin'
opportunities up in here 'f you keep coppin' to that racist front,
mang, you feel me? 'Cause up in here we all niggas and spicks and
crackas, you feel me? Shyite, so it's up to us to decide how we
gonna get ours, you feel me? Straight up…I tell you right now I
ain't no angel, for realz, I done some shit would make the hardest a
motherfuckers crack, no doubt straight up, and I'm 'a never live
long enough to live it all down, you feel me? But forgive and
forget, tha's how I see it now, mang.

Start over. I'm trying blut, shit's all part 'a tha struggle, you
feel me, know what I'm sayin' is, that's 'bout all a motherfucker
can do for hisself, you feel me? I'm tellin' you blut. Shit, I don't
know you, but I know where you at, and I'm 'a tell you right now,
you got two choices blut, stop livin' all dat Aryan pride bullshit,
check that shit right at tha door, for realz, and maybe you got a
second chance 'a make somethin' more 'a yo' life then what you
been doin'. 'Cause da only loser from all 'a that shit gonna end up
bein' you 'f you don't, know what I'm sayin'?

Andrew nodded in agreement, taking Julio's warning to
heart, which both of them could see.

Man, you's like a preacher or sumpthin'?

Julio laughed. Naw mang, just gettin' my NA on blut.

So what's your story?

I was a gangbangin', punk-ass motherfucker 24th Street
Eme, know what I'm sayin'? Hittin' licks, boostin' stolos, straight
actin' a fool 'till I got locked up for shootin' some scraps up in
they house while they wuz havin' a party. I killed some KIDZ blut.
No joke. And all kinds 'a fools wus makin' me on that shit.

Andrew did not know what to say. Damn dude that's deep.
He finally acknowledged, solemnly.

No shit blut, for realz. Julio agreed with a grave, square-
jawed nod. Shit, and if only I could take it all back, I'd do it in a
heartbeat. But that ain't the way da game's played, mang. So you
just gotta find a way to live with that shit.

Julio trailed off. Andrew was touched that he would share
such an intimate vulnerability with him. But he could not bear the
growing silence between them. He felt compelled to fill the void,
to say something, anything-

Man, if only my patnas up in the pen could see me now,
choppin' it up wit' 'chu like this, Andrew laughed at the irony of
his blossoming friendship with Julio. We's been at war with you
wetbacks for something like foreva.

Tha's whus weird homie, 'cause I ain't never seen no
brotherhood motherfuckers before I been in lock up, know what
I'm sayin'? Y'all ain't in the hood. But shit, hell yeah blut, I
straight knocked one 'a yo' punk asses right out the gate when he
flexed on me first day in, flopped his ass right 'n front 'a his set,
blut, no shit.

Andrew laughed at the audacity, genuinely respecting the
brashness of his act as Julio chuckled with nostalgic pride. Shit,
they gave me another six months right 'dere on da spot, straight up.
But I tell you, none a them Aryan fools stepped to me after that,
they straight checked me off from the get go. Cause 24th Street
crew wus' representin' back in the day, know what I'm
sayin'…But games changed yo'.

No doubt.

And I got my babygirl to do right by now, you feel me?
Shit, ain't but one way in one way out otherwise. Fatherhood be
alterin' yo' perspective on shit, blut.

Andrew nodded to his new friend. Straight up.

Yeah, and these cats in here understand it too. That's why they's helpin' us. You do right by staff, then they do right by you. Respect is the name of the game, yo.

Andrew paused, somewhat ashamed. So you think I ruined my chances of that last night?

Naw blut, just be cool and that's that. Bygones be bygones. You be surprised the kinda mess some 'a these little boys be pullin'. But they always bring it back. Forgive and forget, blut. You'll see. Know what I'm sayin'?

The boys pacing the circle came upon Julio and Andrew again. But this time, with some hope of redemption, Andrew tried not to immediately retreat into his mad dog front. Of course, Brandon and Rydell, investing no trust in this seemingly newfound vulnerability, provoked him hard.

What up, Julio?

Whatup, D.

You playin' yo' peacemaker bullshit again?

Don't listen to this dude Billy, Rydell cracked to Andrew. He think he got the voice of Jesus whisperin' in his ear.

Nice face, dawg, Brandon prodded. You fall down sleepwalkin' or sumpthin'?

The passing boys snickered again.

Andrew turned bright red, but the new meds Jamey prescribed this morning helped take the fire out of his heart so quickly he couldn't muster the energy for anything but to control himself. So he said nothing.

But letting these boys check him was a bad idea. Smelling hesitation, Rydell, Brandon and Nate wasted no time, although surprisingly to Julio, they didn't come back on him nearly as hard as they normally would have. This was the most generous offer of a second chance anyone at Excelsior could ever expect to receive.

My god.

Nate mockingly did his best white man's voice. Well guys, you know I'm really sorry for all of that doohickey malarkey I was spitting last night...

Aw, hell naw, Tyrone cracked up.

Check!

Nate kept up his routine. It was really silly for me to be so confrontational with all you niggers.

Andrew could not help himself but to counter their taunts. You can't see me!

The boys appeared dumbfounded with joy at the neutered rise they were able to pull from him.

Nate laughed. Oh, what I meant to say was, I'll catch up with you negros later!

The boys cracked up amongst themselves again and went along their merry way.

Aw, hell naw…

Julio just rolled his eyes.

Catch you later, Billy.

They'll come around, Julio assured Andrew.

More progress.

Later in Cottage 2, Julio and Andrew kicked it on the couch in the front room watching Kendrick and Duane, who sat on the floor playing Speed Racer on their Xbox 360. Meanwhile, outside of the door to the cottage staff office, Marcus argued with Maurice as he answered the phone.

I don't want to talk to her Maurice!

Dude, you know she's gonna keep calling until you get on the phone.

You tell her if she wanna talk, she can come up here.

Alright, but then if she does, you know you've got to see her.

See if that bitch makes the trip, Marcus hissed, his voice layered with spite. I'm 'a bet you five dollars she ain't got the balls to show here face 'round me.

Kendrick overheard Marcus' declaration and laughed out loud. Shoot Marcus, your caseworker got balls!? No wonder you's so scared 'a her!

Marcus was offended. I ain't scared 'a her, Little Kendrick. I just don't want to see the bitch is all.

Why, 'cause she gonna show you her nuts?

Naw, 'cause she took my little brother away, Marcus pouted.

Duane laughed so hard at Kendrick's comment he knocked into him, messing up their game.

Mang, damn! Duane you cheat! Kendrick threw his controller down in protest.

Duane tried unconvincingly to defend himself. I ain't no cheat, Kendrick! Come on now…

Maurice hollered out from inside the staff office. Don't be tossing my controllers, Kendrick!

That ain't all he be tossing, Maurice, Duane retorted for his brother.

Marcus and Julio laughed out loud. Andrew, sitting across the room from the other boys, was not sure yet if he was allowed to.

Kendrick huffed, Man…

Or I'll toss your head so you can see how it feels!

Yeah Maurice, I bet you'd like that, Rydell interjected.

Maurice just ignored him, calling back to Marcus. Dude, your caseworker's on her way over.

Marcus was clearly perturbed by the news of Clara accepting his challenge. So Kendrick and Julio comforted him.

She just doin' her job.

And ain't you still on probation?

Yeah, Marcus admitted.

Julio offered him some perspective. Then you's lucky she ain't reported your ass to yo' PO. My caseworkers' a buster. If he caught me takin' any field trips like you done, he'd have my ass thrown back in the halls so quick-

Marcus had no patience for Julio's platitudes. Shit, if I don't call my PO every day, she tellin' the cops to get at me just to be sure I ain't doin' dirt.

At least you ain't takin' no piss tests to make sure you keepin' on the straight and narrow, Julio contended. Mang, I had some bunk ass caseworkers, but I've had me some good ones too. Shit, when I sprung outta CYA, my PO wanted to toss me back in after just one day for disobeying Deirdre. Shit, she was writing up my incident report and everything, but when Deirdre found out my PO had it in for me she backed off. Still, I was about to get pulled for good. Luckily, my old PO Larry vouched for me, he wrote me up a good report to contradict my PO's assertions in court so the judge and Public Pretender would forgive it. Damn juvenile courts, motherfuckin' left hand don't know what the right's doin' half the

time. But shit, if Deirdre hadn't bent the rules I still woulda been shipped outta here. I owe that lady big. But once you in it, the system's a bitch homie. You just got to deal and be glad you got someone in yo' corner at DFS.

Your caseworker still a bitch for separating your family dawg, Duane agreed.

Thas whussup, Marcus emphatically agreed. I still don't even know where my littlest brother at, Marcus emphasized.

It was here that Duane and Kendrick felt compelled to chime in. Shoot, three 'a our brothers are up in some other group home in L.A. And our little sister got adopted by a foster family who done moved to Georgia. Her new family don't even let her call us no more, and her old caseworker can't do a damn thing about it. Shit, now she adopted, they get to decide whether or not we keep in touch. And they don't want her around us, so now Duane and I are the only ones together 'cause we's the oldest, Kendrick surmised.

Duane completed his brother's account. Shoot, if you wasn't on probation and Joe didn't make space, they woulda split us up too.

Speak for yourself, Kendrick chided. Ain't nobody woulda adopted your crackbaby ass, shoot.

Aw, hell naw, Duane asserted with little more to come back with.

But Kendrick was adamant on this point. We ain't seen our family in a quick minute. And ain't no group home paying for no family reunions.

Joe said we could go down there if we wanted, Duane corrected him.

Yeah mang, and with what money? Kendrick dismissed flatly. I'm the only one of us workin' fool.

Shoot, I work.

Oh yeah. Givin' handjobs to crackheads don't count.

Aw, hell naw.

This time, Andrew laughed outloud. But the boys did not chide him.

Damn, you's cold Kendrick, Julio interjected with a chuckle.

But Kendrick returned to finish his serious point to Marcus. You ain't never gonna see your peoples again once they get adopted, for realz. And CPS ain't about to make no special arrangements for your brother to live with you if he too young.

Duane agreed with this. Mang, we been in twelve homes already and most of them never had the space for more than two 'a us.

That's why everyone else got moved away.

Yeah man, that's cold.

No doubt.

Straight up.

Shoot, and even if you get placed together, Kendrick continued, If people ain't gettin' along, they move your asses anyway.

Duane took over from here. Damn straight. When Kendrick got beat on by an uncle of one of our foster families, I straight smacked that fool with a stick to his head. You remember that Kendrick?

Kendrick laughed nostalgically at the recollection. Yup.

Then they flopped my ass in the halls so quick and put you in another home.

Shit, those fools wuz beatin' on all the kids up in there too, Kendrick recalled without emotion, and my caseworker couldn't do nuthin' about it, 'cause there wusn't any space for all dem kids. But that time I held my own.

Duane finished his thought. So when I got out, I straight skipped outta there and went back to the neighborhood to kick it with Tiny's crew. Shoot, now I been AWOL from so many group homes, my PO straight put me on house arrest up in here, forget a home pass, he be settin' all kinda restrictions and stuff. Yo, mang, now I gots to call his ass each time I go and come back, even for school, blut, ain't nothin' cool wit' that. Got myself a curfew and everything. Shoot, they got my ass on lockdown, but its better den kickin' it in the halls with all 'a you and Billy's peeps. Duane pointed to Andrew. That's what I'm sayin'…hell naw, after a while you just get tired of going to jail. For realz.

Julio agreed with Duane. No doubt.

The boys all sat and reflected on their own individual experiences for a minute in silence. Then Andrew put himself out there to Duane and Kendrick in a moment of reconciliation.

Yo man, so how long it been since y'all seen your kin?

Shoot mang, must been fo', five years, sumpin' like that.

Kendrick corrected his brother. Naw Duane, it's only been like two.

Hell naw Kendrick, 'cause I was up in Crestview a year ago, and then we was in them two homes before that.

Yeah, for like six months.

The truth was probably somewhere in the middle, because neither of the brothers could remember just how many homes they'd passed through. But what mattered most in this moment was that Andrew actually seemed to give a shit about them beyond looking to tear anybody down.

That sucks dawg, Andrew sympathized.

Hell yeah, Duane agreed.

The boys returned to their game without further thought. Julio and Andrew meanwhile calmly continued to kick it, watching the brothers race circles around each other on the game's Monaco track, while Marcus fidgeted with his hands discreetly, waiting for his visitor to arrive. Clara would be here for him soon.

***

Clara Rodriguez arrived at Excelsior House in her beat up beige Ford Taurus with mixed news for Marcus Turner. As she locked her car and her eyes wandered to the stoop of Girls Cottage 1 across the street, Sylvia Sanchez gave her an awkward wave from the front porch. Clara knew she wasn't too popular with some of her Excelsior House clients right now, but nonetheless it was her job to do what was best for them, regardless of how any of them might see her role in their lives in the short term. There would be time, she hoped, in later days or months or years, for them to understand that, as their primary protective services caseworker, she was fighting for them. But for now she had to get down to brass tacks with probably the most noble yet stubborn of her clients. She met him in the staff office of Boys Cottage 2 for their onsite meeting in private.

How are you doing Marcus? She empathetically greeted him with arms extended. Marcus, of course, refused to hug her.

An awkward pause. He would not look at her, instead staring defiantly up at the ceiling.

So what, you not even talking to me now?

He shrugged. Got nothing to say to you…

OK then. She put her things down and took a seat in the staff chair, leaving him the couch next to the bulletin wall.

Well here's the situation as it stands. Your mother has been admitted for treatment into the Salvation Army Women's Shelter in Oakland, because there was no space immediately available for her here in San Francisco. According to her case manager, she's doing as well as anyone does in her first week of treatment. I spoke with her yesterday and she wanted me to relay a message. She wants you to know how much she loves you. And misses you.

Marcus waved her off. Where my brother at? He still would not look her in the eye.

Boyce is currently on a waitlist for permanent placement. He's staying at a short-term transitional care home here in the city, run by a trustworthy Asian family in the Outer Richmond. I've worked with them a lot over the years, and I think you'd like them.

So when I get to talk to him?

Clara paused, uneasy. As it currently stands, because you were at the scene when DFS arrived with the police, we're going to have to wait for a judge to decide that.

Marcus clenched his jaw.

We've scheduled a hearing for next week.

He shook his head. Man, why all you people gotta hate on us so bad? You know we's just gettin' by like any 'a y'all would do.

Clara acknowledged his frustration. Marcus, given that you violated the terms of your placement with numerous unmonitored visits with your mother and brother together, DFS has no choice but to wait for Juvenile Court to decide how any future contact with you and Boyce will be established, to prevent any further endangerment to your brother's safety moving forward.

Marcus wanted to lash out at Clara, but was overcome with emotion.

Naw naw, 'cause YOU IS DFS. You could change all 'a this if you wanted.

Clara understood his frustration, but had to be firm. Marcus, with your previous history of home visits, I have no other options but to follow protocol here.

You know I ain't done nuthin' but do right by the both 'a them. He teared up slightly.

Clara tried meeting him with her usual unflappable stare, cultivated over years in the field, but her soft eyes betrayed her deeper sympathy for him. Because in this case, in his case, she too believed he was wronged.

I know Marcus, I know. She insisted. And the judge will understand this too when we meet with her. We're gonna make things as right as we can. We just have to wait for the court to hear your situation out, okay?

So you got my back then?

Yeah, she nodded. Of course I do. You know I do.

He started to cry. She stood up and walked over to the couch, sat down beside him and held him, gently stroking his back with her free arm.

I know, dear…I know.

He nodded his head onto her shoulder and allowed his tears to flow free. As she patted him on the back, she could not stop a few drops from welling in her own eyes.

We're gonna do everything we can to keep you and your brother together, okay?

He simply nodded in appreciation with his face still buried in her shoulder.

A few minutes later, after Marcus gathered himself, Clara dialed the number of her friend in the Outer Richmond and handed him the phone. Boyce was on the other end.

So how you doin' little man?

I'm ayite.

Those fools know how to make a mean grilled cheese or what?

Not like yours, Marcus.

Then what 'chu been eatin'?

Noodles and wontons and stuff I never heard of.

Just don't let them feed you no dogs.

A momentary silence across the phone implied his brother's panic at the thought. UGH. Are they really gonna make me eat a dog?

Do you see them havin' any pets?

Boyce sounded sheepishly scared. No…

Then that's what I'm sayin'…Naw B, I'm just playin' with 'chu. Hear me out now. Marcus tried to recover by playing it straight. You be good 'till I come see you, ayite? Keep it real, and mind yourself so I can come get you.

When you comin', Marcus?

Soon B, just as soon as I can, like I always done. You heard from momma?

Naw.

Well, I heard she okay. She loves you, you know, that's what she told me.

You talked to her? Boyce more than wanted to believe he had.

Naw little man. But she relayed her message to me.

How?

Clara told me.

Marcus?

Yeah, B?

Are we gonna still be a family?

Hell yeah we is, B. I'm 'a tell you straight up, we gon' be just fine. Just fine. Just gots to get through dis rough patch now, you feel me?

No answer.

Remember what I always told you?

Yeah, keep your head up, stand tall, stand strong, ain't no fools gonna get you down.

You believe me then don't 'chu?

I guess.

Well you be good, and I'm 'a hook you up with a pair of them LeBron Nikes like I been promising. Sound cool?

When you comin' to get me, Marcus?

Soon B. Just as soon as I can.

I gots to get off the phone now, Mrs. Chu making me come for dinner.

Then you be good. Like Tupac say, stay strong, keep yo' head up, I'm 'a see you soon.

See you, Marcus.

Love you, B.

Love you too. Bye.

Peace.

Marcus hung up the phone. For the first time with his little brother, he was not sure if he'd ever be able to make good on his promise.

***

Sylvia and Brenda walked up Ocean Boulevard overpass from the Excelsior, crossing I-280 into Ingleside where they spotted Johnhay Deguzman's fresh PANOY-1 tag sprayed across the freeway exit sign below. They made a quick pass by City College, walked up to the drive thru window at the McDonald's across the street, where they grabbed a few free cheeseburgers from Kendrick before doubling back to Westwood Beauty Salon. Sylvia checked her cell phone a few times and shot off several rapid texts.

Fools be hella blowing me up...

As she looked up from her phone, Brenda saw several tiny bruises percolating across Sylvia's neck.

You got yo'self some hater marks, girl.

That's 'cause Edwin be hella feelin' me lately.

You givin' it up to that scrap?

Hell naw, Sylvia fronted. Dude be dirty.

But you's still sprung…

Hells naw. His breath so hot it smell like gutter.

UHH.

So den why you still checkin' for him? Brenda couldn't help but ask.

Dude thinks he a grinder. Always rolling up in one 'a his uncle's stolos, tryin' to impress me buyin' me shit. Like this Nextel.

So you's pimpin' yo'self out den?

Hell naw. Dude thinks he hard, always coppin' to some kinda dirt. But he just anotha' flip-ass cholo when it come down to it. That's why he likes me. 'Cause I'm always checkin' his ass, fo' reals.

Dude sounds grimy, Brenda said doubtfully. And ain't no fool gonna keep you just 'cause you his friend. You just another trick he ain't funked with yet.

Sylvia slapped her fist into the palm of her other hand. Fool try to step to me anything shady like and I bring the wrath on his freaky ass.

Fo' sho', Brenda laughed. So what we doin' here den?

I need to check somethin'.

The girls scoured several aisles until they came to find the weaves, on display behind the glass counter up front.

Yo Bern, how you think I'd look in cornrows?

All gangsta wifey and shit.

Yeah you's right, Sylvia agreed. That shit's flip.

Yo, dude? She asked the elderly Chinese man behind the counter, pointing up to a specific package hanging behind him. How much for those weaves?

It depends, he explained. Extensions run anywhere from 40 to 150.

Damn. Sylvia checked her cash. She was only holding 25 bucks.

I'll front you the rest if you need me to, Brenda offered, digging into her purse.

Naw, Sylvia looked over them again. Those nappy ass strands be looking like they made outta horse pubes anyhow. I don't need none 'a them slippin' out on me and stuff.

Brenda was surprised by Sylvia's momentary need to change up her look, realizing something must be going on with her. What 'chu allvasuddin lookin' to do yourself up fo'?

Sylvia dodged the question by checking out the chest sprinkle tubes instead. But Brenda knew Sylvia better than that. She never wore anything but the same ton of eyeliner the rest of them Latina ladies from her block did when they was lookin' to pull a scrap of they own.

You some kinda shady tryin' to be all Mariah Carey now.

Sylvia tried to cop her front. But Brenda wasn't having it.

C'mon Butterfly, who got you so sprung?

Sylvia winked to her friend bashfully, acknowledging her suspicions.

You know the dude...

Spit it then already, I ain't got all day.

Sylvia remained coy.

Not 'Dell.

Sylvia twisted her face I genuine disgust. Ugh, hell naw. Nasty. He grimy.

Who den? Brenda persisted.

Sylvia took a deep breath. It be Julio.

Brenda smiled. Damn girl, I knew it.

Sylvia continued to deny it. No you didn't!

Hell yeah! I seen you all sweet on that fool every time he be out walkin' the circle. And he checkin' fo' you hard. Just didn't say nuthin' befo'.

Sylvia blushed. Well, there it is den.

Brenda smiled hesitantly. Girl, you know he crazy? You best square yo' shoulders diggin' it out with him. 'Cause he be all livin' by the Lord now.

I know girl, Sylvia admitted. But he fine.

Yeah, Brenda agreed. I give you dat. Hella protective too. Like when that shit went down with 'Dell and Kevin. He ain't afraid 'a keepin' the peace with his patnas, all respectable like.

Just make sure he don't play you.

It ain't like that.

People gonna do what they do.

But he ain't no sucka. Sylvia couldn't believe she found herself defending him to her friend. Been through it and he still got a good heart.

Dude be livin' the fast life fo' sho', Brenda agreed. But 'f you ain't livin' large, you ain't livin'.

He different though, Sylvia admitted, smitten. He's all sweet and shit. And real daddy like to his baby girl.

He got a baby mama too? Brenda reeled. OOOHH Syl, no you didn't! You don't need to be a part 'a none 'a that mess. Believe me, Brenda was insistent now. 'Fore you know it's all good, some flip-ass skeeza come runnin' up on you outta nowhere spittin' all kinds 'a drama and then shit gonna jump off! She shook her head for emphasis. Uh uh.

I can handle myself, yo.

Yeah, and I'm 'a believe dat, for sho'. But you don't need to go messin' wit' some dude whose hoes be steppin' to you all jealousy trippin' all 'cause her man be playin' her.

Maybe I do.

Brenda paused for a minute. What 'chu talkin' about?

I could be a momma to his baby just as good as anybody.

Oh, HELL NO! Brenda stepped back. You ain't up wit' no bun in the oven?

Naw, Sylvia brushed her off. I'm just sayin', if it did happen with Julio, I could handle myself.

Hold up girl, don't you go gettin' all twisted on some dude, talkin' 'bout havin' his kids and shit, 'fore you know how he got his bidness handled. You hear me? Brenda huffed at her friend. Naw girl, 'cause right now you all gas and no brakes. Take a step back, check yo'self fo' realz, 'cause too many bitches be up on these fools thinkin' they in love while they man out jackin' it up wit' his breezies, bumpin' and grindin', cupcakin' wit' that dude while you gettin' all wifey respectable with his kids and he just playin' you, feel me? Fools give a little and get a lot, they just all ballin'.

Sylvia understood what her friend was saying.

Yeah girl, I got 'chu. But I known plenty 'a scraps in my day. Julio different.

That's what they all want you to be thinkin'. But you don't know nuthin' 'till you know fo' sho', Brenda counseled.

True dat, Sylvia admitted.

Brenda lightened up on her for a minute, allowing her friend to enjoy her moment of happiness.

Oohh girl, you's sweet on him, most def. So he best treat you right, know what I'm sayin'? But you gots to demand it fo' yo'self first, hear me?

What, like you been doin'? Sylvia mocked, referring to Brenda's night expeditions with her pimp in Oakland.

Brenda rose to the defensive. You ain't got no business in none 'a that, you hear?

Sylvia countered, having wanted to say something to her on the subject for a while. You know he ain't treatin' you right.

Brenda shut off the conversation immediately. Girl, you don't know nuthin' and you ain't gonna. So don't even try to go pryin'. I'm gettin' it done like I needs to. Like I always done. Handlin' my own business. You might stand to learn sumpthin' 'f you shut yo' mouth and listen to what I'm saying', you feel me? Ain't no other way that shit works.

Sylvia looked at her for a minute. You know that dude don't got no real love fo' you Bern. He just made you his.

Brenda knew Sylvia was telling it true, but from her own experience there wasn't no girl on the streets made it without their own daddy's doin' to them what Lumpy had already inflicted on her. But Brenda was not yet ready to admit her situation to anyone. Not to Sylvia, not to Agnes or Deirdre, not to Rita, not even to herself. Not no one!

So Brenda refused to respond. You handle yo' business and I'm 'a handle mine, thas it thas all mang.

Sylvia knew she'd crossed the line, taken it too far. But it had to be said.

I'm sorry Bern, I shouldn't 'a…

S'all good, Brenda offered. You just speakin' what 'chu know.

We cool then? Sylvia hoped out loud.

Brenda returned a confirmation. 'Course we is, bitch.

Sylvia smiled, putting her arm up to give Brenda a hug.

Brenda put hers around her friend's shoulder. Well c'mon then, let's get you hooked up right.

Brenda grabbed several French braids and singles from the shelf, matched them quickly to Sylvia's two-tone complexion, and splayed them out along the counter, pulling a grip of bills from her pocket and resting a twenty on top of the goods.

Dude gonna come crawlin' fo' his ghetto princess when we's done with you.

Sylvia laughed out loud. Girl, you's whacked.

The two friends returned to Excelsior House to do their do's.

***

Lucy Gutierrez walked with purpose down Mission Street to 24th. She hit every beauty shop up and down the block, desperate for a job. I can do curls, I can do weaves, mannies, peddies, you name it. But nobody would hire her. She'd been doing up herself and her girls for God knows how long. But none of that meant anything to the proprietors, the old Mexican chulas or fresh off the boat Vietnamese madams with their heaps of trainees from beauty school. To them, Lucy was just another teenage mom with no experience and every reason to fail even when she wanted to, needed to, succeed more than anyone. Now desperate, she hit the last shop she could find, Maria's on 22nd. It was her final lead in the neighborhood.

Can I speak to the manager?

I'm the owner, the thick woman in her 50's responded.

You need any help up in here?

You lookin' to work?

Yeah, Lucy responded.

Do you have any experience?

I been hookin' up my girls since I can remember.

The woman looked into her eyes deeper. You certified to cut hair?

Naw. But I know what I know. I do my own.

The woman smiled. It looks nice.

Thank you. I can do nails, sand bunions, anything you ask, you just name it.

The woman paused. Lo siento senorita, I can't hire you without a degree from a certified beautician school. There are plenty of girls like you lookin' for work. But the city has rules.

Please, Lucy asked one more time. I've got a boy. I been tryin' for an office thing but nobodys lookin' to hire right now. I need a job. Anything. I promise I'll do good.

The old woman wished she could act on her empathy. I'm sorry, but I can't hire anyone unless they are certified.

Lucy sensed the compassion in her tone, and spoke to her in Spanish to drive home her point. Yo trabajo poner la mesa, qual es conpenasa que puerda no es la problema para mi...por favor senora, mi moy estoy despararte, por favor.

No puedo, ella; lo siento.

Please senora, por favor, she begged at this point.

No puedo, senorita, I will lose my business license if the employment officals find out I hire you, lo siento…

Lucy, knowing there was nothing more she could do to convince this woman, slumped her shoulders as she retreated out the main door. Si. Gracias, mami.

The woman gave her a sympathetic smile goodbye. Si, esta bien. Ciao.

Lucy took her time walking back to her house on Harrison Street. She did not know how she would face Keyshawn with another defeat. None of the local dental offices would hire her without computer skills, and the Centro De Emplejo had not called with any leads for over two weeks now. She knew Key had been rooting for her to get a job and would surely be upset for her when she got home. But mostly, what she needed now was the love of her family. Her and Key would make it work together for Tre, she assured herself. She only needed more time. And Key would keep paying the bills until she could do right by both of them and earn her part.

She arrived home and the place stank of mota. She would have to address that with Key at some point, because the smoke was no good for Tre's developing lungs. And it could even cause brain damage!

She found Key sprawled out half-sleeping on the couch.

Hi papi, she greeted him timidly.

Ai mami? Key whispered in a half stoned daze. What it do?

I couldn't find nothin' today.

You try all the way up Mission?

Yeah, she conceded. Every place was tapped.

I'm tellin' you girl, the Fillmo' got it goin' on if you's lookin' to work. Shit, my baby up on all them other hoodrats tryin' to make some stanks look pretty out there, no doubt. But they got a chore ahead of them, know what I'm sayin'?

Lucy laughed at Keyshawn's compliment, hugging him from behind the couch. All our sistas are beautiful Key.

You seen some 'a them hoes up tha block? Key grumbled to himself, then turned his head to look to her. Now you just bein' nice girl.

Hey, we ladies got to stick together.

True dat, Key agreed. True dat.

So how our baby been doin'?

He fine. Little man gettin' his rest in the otha room.

Just like his daddy, she kissed his cheek softly.

Key smiled again. He lookin' mo' like his pops every day.

I'm 'a go check on our boy.

You do that, Key nodded approvingly.

Lucy got up and moved down the hall to Tre's bedroom.

She opened the door. Tre was lying on his side. Lucy grew concerned. She'd told Keyshawn a hundred times to check on Tre regular like as to not let their baby roll on his side in the crib for the first couple of months.

Lucy shifted over to the crib to find her baby's tiny blanket wrapped around his neck in a twirl. Tre's face was dark blue.

Lucy screamed.

With time standing still, she grabbed her baby in a panic, untwirled the knot from his tiny neck and blew air frantically into his tiny mouth while pumping the child's stomach like just she remembered being taught to do in CPR class six months earlier. Tre did not respond. She repeated the action several times with increasing desperation. Nothing. Once again, she could not stop herself from shrieking. *Please God please God oh my God if you just let me fix this if you just let him live I promise I swear I will never do another bad thing again I will live my whole life only to protect him and I'll do anything if you just let him live please just let him live give him one more chance give me this one chance-*

Miraculously, after several more pumps to his chest, Tre coughed. A miracle. The boy's face slowly returned to its original color.

Frantic, Lucy grasped him tightly in her arms, holding him deep to her chest to guarantee that his breathing continued. She felt as if she would never let go of him again. Ever.

Ohmygodthankyouthankyou thank you-

At this moment, Key walked in to the room to find her crying profusely.

My God woman, why you makin' all that noise? He stood between her and the door.

Instinctively, she lunged at him, pushing him repeatedly in the chest, clutching Tre tightly in her arms as she marched toward the front of the house.

Were you even watching him!? Do you even care about my baby?!

Yo mang, stop yo' drama already and give me our son.

No, I'm never letting you touch him again!

Yo woman, you best give me my son-

Don't touch him!

She started to open the door but he pushed her into it, slamming it back shut. He leaned the full weight of his body hard against hers, pressing her and Tre against the closed door.

Oh no, you ain't even thinkin' 'bout leaving this house.

Get away from us! Just stay away! She shrieked into his face to move him back.

Bitch, you ain't never takin' my boy from me!

In what felt like an out-of-body, orchestrated dream dance, Keyshawn began punching Lucy repeatedly in the face, from each direction and every angle, while she left her body to watch him destroy her from above. Yet despite each pulverizing hit, she did not release Tre from her grasp. Instead, clinging to life, she took each one of his forceful blows with increased furor and determination, gripping her son tightly to shield him from his father. Finally, after several minutes of beating, Keyshawn appeared winded. This was just the moment she needed to save her son. Keyshawn backed up momentarily to gather himself before continuing his onslaught, and in doing so gave her the critical opportunity she needed to pull the door open. She twisted around the edge of its frame, squeezing herself through the tiny slit with Tre clenched tightly in her arms. Key came after her now with renewed fury. Out on the porch, he belted her in the head from behind, but she dared not turn around for fear of losing her grip on Tre. Escape was so close now…

But the sheer force of Keyshawn's blow pushed her to the edge of the stoop, where a second kick to her right shin followed by a backslap across her neck throttled her down the small flight of stairs onto the sidewalk below. She twisted her body as it fell to prevent Tre's fragile body from hitting the pavement and landed on her back instead. It cracked. She wondered if she would ever move again. Several passersby stood closely mutely watching the scene unfold before them, too frozen with fear to intervene. Lucy knew she was on her own. If she could only make it to her feet, she'd have a fighting chance.

With renewed vigor, she rolled her bloodied body across the sidewalk to stand up, prying herself and her son up from the pavement with her free hand. She could hear Tre's cries from a distance now, in her mind, a muffled frenzy overtaken only by the thundering of Keyshawn's voice as he stood atop the stoop unleashing his virulent commands at her, through her, yet futilely in his apparent reluctance to run down and beat her outright in full view of so many witnesses. She knew she would finally be free of him, if she could only gather her remaining strength and walk away.

Sensing this, he waved his hand at her dismissively. Fine then, you want out, then get your stank ass up outta here. Go on! You'll be comin' back tomorrow cryin' for me to take you in, you watch. But I ain't havin' none 'a that shit. 'Cause if you leave now, don't even think 'a showin' your face round here 'gain. I'll kill you myself.

Everyone on the scene knew his threats were hollow, because they could all see that Lucy was never coming back. So Keyshawn pointed his arm down the street with increased ferocity. You want out, then get the fuck out! Go on. Get!

Lucy was in serious pain but did not waver for a second. Instead, without a word, she stood herself up firmly, straightened out her damaged back, and dragged herself and Tre up the street to the corner of 18th street, out of Keyshawn's life forever. She then turned west out of his sight and kept walking. Away from everything. Except for herself, except for her son.

Several hours passed. She slowly made her way across the city to the Overnight Woman's Shelter on Polk and McAllister. She knew the way, as she had planned this escape months before, without any real willingness to act until now. The shelter was already full for the evening. Observing the cuts and bruises now clearly presenting themselves on Tre, the shelter's intake coordinator offered medical treatment or to call an ambulance to take her to SF General. She would never give those bastards any reason to have CPS take her son on suspicion of child abuse or reckless endangerment. The intake coordinator was sympathetic and instead offered to call another women's shelter. Lucy thanked her and the coordinator placed the call. There was a room free. The coordinator gave Lucy a cab voucher and directed the cab to an anonymous address.

Suzy Manfield, the overnight staff at the Rose Center, met the cab on a corner near the shelter in the Lower Western Addition. Lucy knew this area well, as it was part of Keyshawn's drug territory, and his crew would surely be on the prowl for this evening's customers. She had to be extra careful and keep out of sight. But for this evening alone, the house would prove a safe sanctuary.

Once inside, Suzy was kind and deliberate. She first helped dress Lucy's wounds while convincing her to seek medical treatment for herself and Tre, assuring them that as victims of domestic violence seeking refuge from their batterer at the shelter, they would not be reported to CPS for child neglect or endangerment as they received hospital care.

So Lucy agreed to go to the Emergency Room at SF General, the county hospital where she could access services without health insurance. Suzy arranged to have her assistant oversee the shelter while she escorted their new client there, to help Lucy navigate the process. At General, the doctor took several x-rays and informed Lucy that she'd suffered a spinal fracture, broken nose, detached meniscus and several bruised ribs from her fall. The fracture would eventually require minor surgery. To Lucy's surprise and immense relief, Tre's bruises did not indicate serious injury, he had suffered no broken bones or harm from having his air cut off. He would be okay.

CPS was in fact called the next day at the request of Lucy's attending physician. Clara Rodriguez arrived at the hospital within the hour to take down Lucy's information, determining that under the care of the Rose Center, Lucy's willingness to seek shelter demonstrated her sound judgment as Tre's guardian, and no further threat was posed to her or Tre's safety. Clara, however, tried in vain to convince Lucy to undergo a joint interview with officers Michael Moreno and Tommy O'Shea (who were already at the hospital on an unrelated call) that could be later used to press charges against her batterer. Lucy politely refused, knowing Keyshawn's reach through San Francisco exceeded the ability of any police or CPS to protect her and her son from retaliation if an arrest was made. So the officers took down her information instead, promising to keep an informal eye on her ex-boyfriend's activities for the time being. Lucy appreciated their gesture but disclosed nothing more to them that could be used as testimony against Keyshawn in a court of law.

Later that morning, Lucy was discharged from General. She returned to the Rose Center and stayed for several days at their Richmond District living unit, away from the neighborhood where Keyshawn's people were on just about every corner. At the shelter, she bonded with several other women, all of them facing circumstances similar to her own. She found it in equal parts comforting and saddening to know that all of these beautiful, broken women were just like her, all hiding from their batterers, fearful for their lives, facing an uncertain future just as she was. Yet at the same time, these women were an inspiration to her, reminding her of the power and dignity and resilience of the human spirit to overcome just about any circumstance, against any odds. They too were all alone. But, as Lucy learned during their group therapy meetings together, they were all among the lucky ones to have survived their abuse. Considering that one out of every three women experiences some form of domestic violence during some point in their lives, and that an average victim returns to her batterer six times before leaving for good, where uncounted others died at the hands of their abuser before escaping his or her reach, these women were among the lucky ones. If she could only maintain her strength and courage in the face of an uncertain future alone and keep from returning to Keyshawn the way these women tried to keep from those who had hurt them. Knowing the entire time that every seven seconds, a woman somewhere was being battered by her significant other. Remembering in fact, that among the survivors, she and the rest of these women were truly not alone.

Lucy insisted to the women in her group that she would never under any circumstances return to her life with Keyshawn. They all cried and hugged her, assuring her that she was brave and a true inspiration to them all. Feeling uplifted by their support, she returned to her bedroom with Tre to play with him with the toys provided by the shelter. During one of their games, she killed a roach scurrying across the carpet.

Several days later, Suzy accompanied Lucy to court as her advocate to seek a restraining order against Keyshawn. The judge approved it quickly and outright. For the first time since she could remember, Lucy felt safer, empowered. The Rose staff accompanied her to Target to pick up diapers and new clothes for Tre. Since their stay at the shelter began, he had already grown a size larger.

All the while, Keyshawn was nowhere to be seen. Over time, Lucy's sense of security and empowerment only grew. The staff at Rose Center suggested that she pursue her plan of entering into vocational school to become a certified beautician. They helped her find programs in San Francisco and assisted her with the application process and fees, downloading the required forms from the internet. All and all, she was extremely grateful for the Rose Center's generosity, but deep down, she knew this life was only a temporary solution to her situation. In her heart of hearts she was sure that unless she left San Francisco for good, the one city that had been her home her entire life and the only place she had ever known, eventually she would be found. Ultimately, there was only one place where she could go without being judged, where she'd be fully understood and accepted, and all the protections her unique situation now required would be unconditionally provided.

So, several weeks after her intake at the Rose Center, Lucy packed her and Tre's things and took a cab back home. To the only place she ever really knew to call that. Or had ever felt truly safe. Or had belonged.

A tall, dark man answered the door. He took one look at her face and needed no further explanation. Any guilt, shame, or fear that she might have felt in this moment of return, all at once it disappeared before his watchful, approving eyes. She was finally home again.

The man embraced her firmly, lovingly, rubbing the head of her son in the palm of his gentle hand. She buried her face in his shoulder and began to cry.

Come on now, the voice assured. You home now girl.

Lucy, for the first time in years, was overcome with relief. Thank you Joe.

***

Lisa Gatwyn paced her classroom, watching for signs of breakthroughs during art therapy. She was avidly rooting for her special education students here at Thurgood Marshall High School this morning. Tyrone, Brenda, and Rydell, each members of the school's Excelsior House Special Day Program, were the first subjects in her targeted pilot study. Each had lives steeped in turmoil, childhoods so plagued by physical and psychological violence that Lisa felt a personal responsibility to succeed with each of them. Notwithstanding, there was always the possibility that, if her work with them proved a success, she and her mentor Dr. Metcalf could make a solid case to the San Francisco Board of Education to expand their cutting-edge program citywide over the next few years, reaching hundreds of children at similar risk for suffering PTSD who lived in the city's most violent neighborhoods in crisis. Such an opportunity would provide them not just the foundation for implementing their new treatment model at the the state level, but even one day bringing their work national and revolutionizing education across the country! The possibilities were endless. Yet regardless of any future goals, it was Brenda's, Tyrone's, and Rydell's ability to live healthy, productive lives *now* that Lisa fought for in this moment, that was her highest priority. Because the stakes for *them* could not be higher. So today, like every other, these kids had her full attention.

The students began with a brief meditation session. Lisa then encouraged them to recall and to draw their fondest childhood memories. She checked their work as they labored, searching for any association to key events in her three subjects' case histories. With a brief explaination, each child understood the intention behind the exercise.

Now, we are trying to trigger any memories you might have buried within your subconscious, in order to begin working through them consciously. Remember, you are under no pressure to come up with anything. Just draw whatever feels right to you.

They trusted her. And this was essential to achieving any meaningful awakening or breakthrough in this process.

Brenda sketched herself first. In her picture, she sat in front of her mother's old curio cabinet mirror making herself beautiful with mascara when she was five years old. Rydell recreated a picture of himself and his grandmother visiting the Oakland Zoo. A tiger and elephant were present, along with a chimpanzee hucking its droppings through its cage at a small child who was too young to duck away from its impending collision. That shit was hella funny, Rydell recalled deviously.

Tyrone found himself drawing both of his parents. In his picture, Lisa noticed a marked difference from the others he had made in previous sessions. In this representation, his parents were wearing each other's clothes.

Your drawing is very interesting, Lisa observed, encouraging him to develop it.

Can you tell which one's which? Tyrone asked her, relishing in his ability to create ambiguity.

Not really, Lisa laughed. Isn't that the point?

Ain't really no point at all, I guess.

Other than to be provocative?

It ain't no mystery, Rydell injected himself into their conversation because his desk was right beside them. Tyrone's momma butch 'cause she a lesbo. He recited this narrative so frankly, and without a tinge of his characteristic venom, that Lisa believed this was a common discussion point between the boys in each other's company.

Tyrone only gave him a dry look. Least I got a momma.

Rydell was not fazed. Naw blut, what you got is a daddy.

Yeah, and she could kick yo' ass, Brenda proclaimed in Tyrone's defense.

Not if you sat on her first, Rydell shot back.

All right 'Dell, let's keep it positive.

Mang, Gatwyn, why you always callin' me out?

'Cause you always a busta, Brenda checked him bluntly.

Naw girl, you the busta, Rydell turned on her. Bustin' nuts here, there, everywhere up and down da block...

All right D, that's enough, Lisa admonished.

Hey Brenda, here go five dollars, why don't you come busta nut over here?

Brenda ignored Rydell's reference to her nocturnal activities and returned to her drawing.

So when you gonna read my rhyme, Gatwyn?

I will after our activity, Lisa assured Rydell.

He just high maintenance, Brenda said out loud, clearly stating what was on everyone else's mind.

Mang, screw you. Rydell grew sullen and returned to his work.

Lisa returned her attention to the Tyrone's drawing. Did this really happen T?

Naw, Tyrone smiled. My daddy never dressed like that. He'd kick any dude's ass who he thought was a faggot.

Lisa pondered his observation for a minute. Because she understood that the visual expressions created during cognitive therapy sessions could take on many forms. Here, the trick was to get the subject to express their work in their own words, prompting the conscious mind to retrieve what the subconscious already knew. Wherever it might be buried.

Did you ever see him do that? Lisa finally asked directly.

Letting his mind wander at the prompting of her question, Tyrone remembered his father when he came home one night from his guard shift at San Quentin. He was arguing with Tyrone's mom about separating. Why did she wait for him to be all tired out from work to tell him she was gay and was leaving their son with him, so he could be raised a man while she went out to discover who she was and what she needed outta life? Tyrone would never understand that. But he remembered how his dad would never let no one think his own son was a faggot. So it was Tyrone who caught his father's beatings those months after his mother was gone, and Tyrone remembered *those* very clearly. Ain't gonna let you come up soft, his father always said between hits whenever Tyrone acted in a way he considered weak or pleaded for him to stop. My boy ain't gonna be no faggot like his mom! So his father beat him whenever he cried, whenever he lost a fight. Whenever he came home late. Whenever he slipped on anything. His father kept him hard when Tyrone showed any sign of gentleness. But they both knew Tyrone couldn't help himself. He was just too much like his mother, so his father toughened him up with the beatings. And T being T, he never fought back. He took every punch, internalized every blow, hoping his father would eventually see how solid he could be. So he'd know his son was no sucka. One day his father came to the conclusion that he couldn't do nothing more by hittin' on him alone. So they robbed a gas station together. Tyrone pointed his gun at the store owner while his father cleaned out the register. He made Tyrone put the barrel in the owner's mouth. You's a man now T, his father proclaimed afterward, as they sat in the car counting the money they'd swiped together. Ain't no one can think nothing different 'bout 'chu from now on. Tyrone distinctly remembered his father in that moment putting his hand triumphantly on his shoulder. I'm proud of you, son, he declared, satisfied with their work. And that made Tyrone feel good.

The cops made their car soon enough and rolled up on them still sitting in that parking lot, right under the streetlight. But none of that seemed to phase his father now. 'Cause he'd already finished the job with his only son. You got what it takes to raise yourself right, his father said quietly before the police took him away, and Tyrone knew for better or worse that was that. He never went to his father's arraignment, nor to the trial, never visited his pops up in Folsom where he was surely still having things his way despite being one a the knocks who'd crossed the line from the other side. Tyrone had tried forgetting about him, worked hard to shut his father's memory out of his life for good, 'cause for better or worse, he knew his daddy had been nothing good for him, and had nothing left to offer him. Tyrone himself was all he had now. And that was just the way things were going to be. So no sense going back on it.

Naw, Tyrone finally replied to Lisa, closing out her line of questioning. Just know he could is all.

***

The staff of Excelsior House arranged a co-ed dinner to reintroduce Lucy back into the group. In Cottage 2, the boys made their preparations for the girls' arrival. Rydell put on his favorite 'do rag, adjusting it perfectly, skewed just left of parallel from his brow to maintain his best I-don't-give-a-fuck front while Tyrone and Kendrick took turns combing their hair in the mirror. The boys all thought Lucy was so damn fine they all had to look their best for her.

What you doin' yourself up for, y'all know she's mine, Rydell challenged.

Yo dawg, she gonna get with whoeva she want to.

Mang, y'all's some whack-ass niggas 'cause I'm about to lock that girl in right quick, watch and see.

Whatever, D, Tyrone retorted.

Kendrick agreed, dismissing Rydell's claim on Lucy. Shoot, that fool been checkin' fo' her for like forevez.

Meanwhile, Eric, Nate, and Brandon played checkers at the kitchen table as Andrew watched their game from the couch. In the kitchen, Julio cooked his famous mole, with Rory as assistant.

Roryman, you gonna make some lucky lady very happy when you learn to cook like me, Julio blustered.

Man, she gonna cream herself fo' sure, Rory agreed.

Damn little boy, why you always gotta take it there? When you get a little older, you gonna see this for what it is. Romance.

Hell naw Juli, 'cause I ain't never gettin' that old, Rory replied.

Julio laughed. Yo dude, chop up these peppers fo' me.

Alright, Rory happily agreed, pulling out the cutting board and going to work on them with the cottage's blunted cooking knife.

Across the street in Cottage 1, Lucy and Brenda did themselves up, fixing Sylvia's hair for the occasion of seeing Julio again.

How do I look?

Girl you fly, Lucy assured. That boy don't know who he messin' with. Mmm mmn. When he sees you…Ooh wee, she shook her hear head. It's gon' be on.

Brenda rolled several strands of Sylvia's hair in her fingers, trying to tease up a back curl with some spray.

Now don't go wreckin' it, Lucy admonished Brenda for altering her hard spent beauty work.

I'm just touchin' it up a bit. Brenda finished another one of Sylvia's curls, satisfied. There you go.

Sylvia looked to them for final validation as the girls admired their work through the bathroom mirror. Lucy, I'm glad you's back. Sylvia hugged her so hard Lucy almost fell from the chair where she sat.

Lucinda was the big sister Sylvia never had. And Sylvia had missed her furiously ever since Lucy got pregnant two years back and had to leave Excelsior House to live in a transitional home for teen mothers.

Me too, girl, Lucy replied, hugging her back. And now look at you. All grown up and done up right, like the goddess you is.

For realz.

Brenda shook out the empty container of Sequins into her hand, chiding them with feigned disgust. Yo, where all my glitter at?

Sylvia's chest sparkled with the last of the bottle's shiny contents. The three girls cracked up.

Everyone was excited for the meal, as displayed by the shameless swagga the boys layed on to front for Lucy once the girls arrived at the cottage.

At six, Agnes walked them across the street. Though several of the boys leapt off the couch when they first heard the knocking, it was Rydell who made it to the door.

Of course Agnes was having none of his phony charm offensive, throwing salt in his game immediately as the girls filed in. D, sit your happy ass down so we can get ourselves somethin' to eat already!

Josh, Maurice, Joe, Agnes, and Deirdre had eagerly waited for the boys and girls to share a meal together like this. It made everyone feel like a real family for the first time in a long while. The mess with Andrew had for the most part blown over, Eric seemed relatively stable after losing Sarah, and everyone was glad to see Lucy back in the fold. In short, the flavor was good. Even Rydell was in the best of moods, strictly on account 'a Lucy bein' back.

Girl you know I been missin' you, he began smoothly.

I'm just glad you got yo'self and Tre away from that buster.

Yeah, mang, that dude is whack.

Lucy agreed in not so many words. It's good to be back, y'all.

Hells yeah, Rydell chimed in. Lucy, check this out.

Rydell stood up from the long kitchen table to throw down a few lines from his latest rap. To the beat of Ludacris' 'Get Back': To my girl who be comin' back 'round, whose once all flip and whack 'till 'Dell threw out the Mack attack, here we is all now chillin' and scrillin' soon cribbin' you'll see, 'cause when I make you mine cupcakin' we'll be...

The group universally moaned, while Sylvia bagged hardest of all. Mang, Dell that's some whack-ass shit!

Yeah, dude, give it up already, Nate shook his head.

You a STI, Sylvia balked. Scandalous-type individual!

Yo, he a STD too, Duane cracked himself up. But nobody else was laughing.

Do you even know what that is, Duane? Brenda shot her boy a cold look.

Shoot, Duane lamented.

Sylvia shook her head. Hella shameless little boys, damn...

Naw, cause y'all can't even hate on a playa who be runnin' his game tight as mine! Rydell threw back to them.

At this point, the group didn't even try to reason with him.

Julio simply frowned, turning to face Sylvia instead, who was busy ignoring Rydell's lack of swagger. He noticed her makeup and quickly changed the subject.

Ay mami! Julio whistled aloud.

Ay papi! She retorted.

Girl, who died and made you so fine? Julio was clearly worked up. Shoot. MMN MMN. He scanned her body up and down, pursing his lips in approval of how delicious Sylvia was looking tonight. The staff and the clients all quickly tuned in to the sparks flying between them. Trouble, they thought to themselves, and each for different reasons.

Brenda and Lucy just smiled at the sight of Julio who was clearly aroused by the sight of their girl looking fly.

How come ain't no dude done swooped you yet?

'Cause I always be doin' it movin'. For reals.

Hell yeah, Lucy agreed. My girl ain't nothing polite.

Julio shaking his head while keeping his stare locked on Sylvia. No she ain't.

Sylvia returned his affections with an observation of her own. So you the chef tonight?

Why, you ready to dig into my mole, mamacita?

Only if it's good, she played along.

Got my special family recipe all up in this, he bragged. It's all about how long you soak the carne. I been marinatin' fo' at least two days. So you's about to get sprung. Hear that!

Meanwhile, Brandon fixed his eyes on the girls' getups and changed the subject. Mmn, damn. Y'all hoochies been up to sumpthin' scandalous.

The boys all laughed at Brandon's verbalization of what they were thinking. But the girls scorned Tyrone when he popped off, So when y'all gonna bust yo' moves?

We handlin' it right after dinner, you can believe dat! That is, if y'all's lucky, Sylvia teased.

Awww, hell naw! Nate, Duane, Kendrick, Brandon, and Rory all went wild at the very thought of these girls dancing it up in their cottage soon. Do it now-

Hold yo' loads shorties, 'fore you go disappointin' these skeezas you checkin' fo'!

Duane couldn't wait to see Brenda shake that big booty 'a hers. Especially since she'd been giving him the cold shoulder as of late.

Brenda and Sylvia had practiced their hip hop routines for weeks in the backyard of Cottage 1, out of sight from the boys, so they were more than ready to make their debut tonight.

Julio emerged from the kitchen with a hot dish in hand. Yo bustas, dinners served! Last one to the table doin' my dishes!

And as quickly as eight boys could run to a table and sit at the same time, that's exactly what they did.

Everyone wolfed down their dinner promptly in order to watch Brenda and Sylvia drop their moves. Brenda and Sylvia jumped up first, with Lucy soon making her entrance from the side. Agnes and Deirdre played with Tre while the three girls ground it out with each other, prompting the boys to go apeshit, hootin' and hollerin' before joining in directly.

Mang, this shit beats a strip club, yo!

I got my dolla billz right here!

Put your money away little boy, 'cause you ain't getting none 'a this, Sylvia taunted with a slap to her booty in full view.

DAMMMNN!

Rydell cracked that Tyrone, Duane and Rory now had plenty of material in their spank banks for later tonight. Still, the flavor was all good. Soon, Rydell, Tyrone, Marcus and Julio freaked it up with the three girls as the younger, less daring boys stood back to the side, sizing them up jealously from a distance. Of course this all turned inappropriate real quick, so staff had to call off the co-ed dancing.

Predictably, they were met with some resistance. Too many playa' haters up in here! So Agnes had to pull the plug on the supervised party altogether.

C'mon girls, we goin' home! Too many loose hands up in Cottage 2.

Aw hell naw!

Agnes, don't do us like that!

Bunch 'a haters up in this place!

With more audible protesting, the boys grudgingly said their goodbyes. As Sylvia walked by Julio, he grabbed her hand and turned her around to face him.

Yo, so you like my mole?

I had betta.

C'mon now, admit it, you ain't tried none like mine. It was clear he was fishing for anything.

So she coyly obliged him. Ayite, I give you that.

He licked his lips in approval, furrowing his brow as he checked her up and down once more. You got some moves too, girl.

What you see is what you don't get, she shot back.

Damn. So when am I gonna see you again then?

Shoot fool, I live right 'cross the street. Come visit.

He nodded his head. Ayite. I'm 'a do that real soon. I promise you.

She smiled and headed off to the door.

But Julio couldn't let her go. You did like my mole though?

This dude seemed genuinely into her. So instead of cutting him off his nuts with a rude retort, she obliged him, nodding with a coy smile. It was ayite…

His own smile grew large as she passed deliberately out of his sight. Mmm hmm.

Later that night, Sylvia and Brenda heard a scratching at their window. It was Julio.

She rose with full bed head and opened the window.

Fool, what 'chu doin' here?

You said come visit-

I didn't mean at three in da morning, shoot!

C'mon Chita, let's go to the park.

I ain't goin' nowhere with you…

C'mon, it's a full moon. I promise I'll show you a dope time.

How you even get out?

Deirdre be sleepin'. C'mon girl!

Carly gonna be hella pissed if she find me gone.

You know she crashed out too.

Sylvia considered this for a moment. Ayite, shit. I see you out on the curb in five minutes.

Five minutes? Julio scoffed impatiently. Damn what 'chu gotta do?

Girl shit, damn. She batted him away from the window. Five minutes, chump. She shut the window down extra hard, almost taking off his fingers before he whisked them away quickly enough to avoid the impact. He gave her a hard frown through the glass.

Five minutes, he bargained, holding out his palm.

I be there when I get there, shoot. She waved him off again as he rustled out through the bushes under her window and back over the side gate to Cottage 1. She quickly applied her makeup, grabbed her signature 49ers jacket and grey sweatpants, and within minutes was out the door.

But as it turns out, on this evening Deirdre was not asleep.

Several hours prior, at 10:15 PM, Crazy Therapist Charlotte had brought Zeke, the boys' biggest nightmare client, from the hospital to Cottage 2. Charlotte and Deirdre conferred in the staff office while Zeke sat on the couch, listening to the other boys brush their teeth and ready themselves for bed.

I need to have him stay here tonight, Charlotte declared with no further explanation. He's having some problems with another client at the hospital so I have to make new arrangements.

What kind of problems? Deirdre inquired, unsettled by Charlotte's explanation. Deirdre didn't trust Charlotte's unsavory treatment methods for this very reason. Not only did she play favorites with certain kids who were clearly a menace to other clients, but her insistence on conducting her treatments in secrecy from other staff, combined with her Nurse Ratched proclivity for overmedicating her more 'challenging' wards into oblivion, just made Deirdre sick.

It wasn't Zeke's fault, Charlotte passionately defended her client, who after seven years under her therapeutic wing had become like a son to her. He just needs to be separated from the others for now, she assured Deirdre. He's heavily medicated, so he's harmless. And it will only be overnight. Right now, I've got to rush back to the hospital to deal with the other boys.

Deirdre fumed. You know he can't stay here. He's Level 14. And the boys are all afraid of him.

In the background, she and Charlotte could hear them brazenly taunting Zeke from their rooms. Zeke, meanwhile, sat listlessly on the couch, staring through the wall with glassy eyes as his unclenched jaw dangled inanimately from his mouth. Deirdre was afraid to imagine what thoughts now flooded through his chemically soiled brain. Was he somehow staring at his tormentors, silently biding his time, waiting to lash back out at them? Or was there still a trapped little boy somewhere in those vacant, watery eyes, struggling within the confines of his littered mind simply to reemerge? There had to be. Or was he simply an emotionless vegetable now, battered into oblivion by years of Charlotte's wretched medical interventions.

The shouts continued to emanate from the main hallway.
I ain't sleepin' in no cottage with this dick sucker!
Help! He gon' booty bust us Deirdre!
I want to go across the street with Carly…
Don't you be lookin' at me faggot!
Chalky hands!
Y'all best lock yo' doors. He just like Eric, only with boys!
UUGH!

Watch out white boy or he gonna suck you off in yo' sleep.
Fool be thinkin' its Tyrone…

Charlotte looked to Deirdre blankly. They don't sound scared to me.

But Deirdre and Charlotte both knew better. Having a perp in the cottage usually triggered similar anxiety responses in the clients. And Zeke, being the unusually large sized boy that he was with a known range of demonstrable psychosis, could best be managed within the confines to the hospital. The boys were all well aware of this, so any potential outbursts from him would certainly escalate and set off the whole group.

Y'all best be ready to scream if somebody gets booty raped!

That dude's breath smell just like dukey…

That's 'cause he eats dicks too!

UUGHH.

Charlotte grabbed Deirdre's arm and tried to reassure her. You're doing us a solid on this. He's much better now than when he lived here before.

Deirdre just gave her a look of subdued rage, because she could do nothing. Charlotte was the supervising therapist at Excelsior House and so ultimately made any final treatment decisions for their clients, including those under Rita and Jamey's care. Deirdre considered protesting Zeke's temporary residency for her own safety, but upon further consideration of the grief this would have caused Joe, having to get up in the middle of the night to supervise the cottage in her absence, she ultimately stood down. Creating friction between Charlotte and Joe would only complicate matters, and Deirdre knew she could handle this kid for one night. Especially if she hoped to run her own group home someday, she'd have to learn to roll with such challenges like these as they presented themselves.

The boys also knew they would be safe with Deirdre staffing the overnight. Because that woman didn't take shit from anyone around the cottages. And with such a reputation to maintain, it became a point of pride for her to take on the challenge, regardless of what her gut urged.

You've already given him his meds?

Charlotte only nodded. When he goes down, he'll be out until morning.

Deirdre unwittingly allowed herself such assurances. Fine then. But he's sleeping out on the couch.

Several hours passed without incident. The boys slept soundly. Deirdre checked on Zeke a few times, but he too was out cold, snoring on the front couch. So she lay her head down on the staff office sofa and, soothed by Zeke's sedated cacophony from the front room, closed her eyes.

About 20 minutes after Julio embarked on his nocturnal escapade from the cottage, and roughly ten after Sylvia climbed out her window to meet him on the street, just as they headed up the Excelsior Avenue hill towards McLaren Park, Zeke woke up suddenly. Though groggy, he was clear enough in mind not to immediately recognize his surroundings. Invigorated by the new prospect of freedom from the confines of the hospital, he moved silently down the hallway, remembering finally where he found himself. His old placement. Zeke wondered aloud who could possibly be staffing the overnight. He shifted over to the office entryway and peeked inside, where he found Deirdre sound asleep.

He quietly shut the door and pushed the lock into its place.

Seconds later, Deirdre woke to find Zeke hovering over her, his pants dangling around his knees.

She screamed.

He overtook her.

Nobody gonna think I'm a faggot now.

She tried kicking his groin, but could not bring the thrust of her leg up in time before he managed to obscure her mouth with the thick palm of his hand. She bit into his fleshy grasp, but the numbness from his medication only muted the pain. Menacingly, he didn't seem to measure any response to her struggle beneath him. He only grimaced at the difficulty of pulling her denims apart to consummate his deed.

Tyrone was the first to wake at her tapered shriek. Though Deirdre was silenced, he heard a faint rustling from behind the staff office door. He instinctively moved down the hall and discovered Zeke missing from the couch, so he returned to the staff office door, meeting her muffled shifts with a hesitant knock.

Deirdre...Zeke sleepwalkin'.

It was only then where he heard a faint whimper escape from Zeke's muffling hand. He turned the door handle. Locked. He knew he had to raise hell quick. He banged the door hard. Deirdre, Deirdre, you okay? Deirdre!

Rydell, Brandon, Nate, Eric and Andrew were up and into the hallway in an instant. They heard a more aggravated struggle from behind the door.

Dude, Zeke got Deirdre locked in the staffroom!

Call Joe!

Eric, go get Carly!

Naw, mang, we gots to do something now!

Let's break this bitch down!

Go on then!

The boys lunged their bodies into the door one by one with the force of their entire frames, though frustratingly it did not budge. They kicked and pounded as hard as they could but they could not force it open, not even a crack. So instead, they slammed it repeatedly with their open palms, hoping the noise would deter Zeke from whatever despicable deeds he might be imposing from across the other side.

Zeke, you best step off 'a her 'fore we fuck you up!

We gonna kill you 'f you don't open this door!

Open the door, bitch!

Finally, it was Tyrone who made the critical leap in logic to grab the fire extinguisher. He yanked it from the wall and swung it hard into the doorknob.

Hit it again, mang!

Brandon, Nate, and Andrew all pushed at the door while Rydell screamed more taunts to Zeke, insisting that he let them in. With a few more solid hits, Tyrone broke the door handle but still could not push through the barrier. Desperately, they could sense from the silence inside that they were losing precious time. Eric ran across the street to grab Carly and call the cops.

Though their impacts were boring a deep dent into the wood, the door still would not budge. Rydell yelled frantically to Tyrone, who was growing tired from delivering the repeated thrusts. Keep bustin' that shit!

Through the hole left by the broken knob they could see into the room, Tyrone and Rydell spotted Zeke on top of a motionless Deirdre. Realizing she was unconscious, they stepped up their efforts. Together, they grabbed the metal extinguisher and pounded it hard near the door latch until they finally cracked it open.

The boys poured into the room and immediately pulled Zeke up and out of Deirdre. Nate, Brandon, and Rydell pummeled the living shit out of his exposed face and body as they dragged him across the office floor away from her. Meanwhile, Tyrone attended to Deirdre, who did not appear to be breathing. Her lower face had swollen in Zeke's grasp, which had suffocated her. Tyrone began slapping her cheeks in desperation to wake her when Carly finally ran into the room. Instinctively, she pulled Deirdre's pants up from her ankles, refastening them around her waist while the boys continued to inflict damage upon Zeke's upper body across the room.

Once Deirdre was covered up, Carly yelled out to the boys to stop kicking Zeke, but she was too late to prevent Rydell from delivering one final, near fatal blow to his head with the fire extinguisher. This sent Zeke's body flopping into convulsions.

The cops were on the scene within minutes, just before Charlotte arrived with an ambulance to whisk Zeke away to General Hospital, where he was treated for a fractured skull and internal organ damage. The blunt force trauma inflicted by Rydell had left him in a catatonic state. Rydell was taken into custody immediately and transferred to San Francisco's Juvenile Hall to await arraignment on charges of attempted murder. The rest of the boys were eventually calmed down and debriefed as much as possible by a clearly rattled Rita. She guaranteed to Rydell upon his arrest that that she would do everything in her power to procure his release.

Once back across the street, it was Carly who discovered Julio and Sylvia's AWOL. She placed a call to Julio's PO and asked Officers Michael Moreno and Tommy O'Shea to try and locate the missing clients discreetly in order to provide cover for Joe, should they turn up before shift change tomorrow morning. The sympathetic officers agreed to keep an eye out.

Meanwhile, Joe accompanied an unconscious Deirdre by ambulance to St. Luke's hospital, where doctors in the ICU monitored her closely for signs of brain damage caused by lack of oxygen during Zeke's assault. When she awoke several long hours later, she and Joe embraced. Over the next several days, the boys from Excelsior House each came to visit her. She thanked them profusely for coming to her rescue, telling them they were her heroes. She also informed them that though she was eternally grateful for their courage in helping her to survive her ordeal with Zeke, she could not see herself ever being able to return to Excelsior House. The boys, though disappointed to see one of their favorite staff leave, whom many considered their big sister, they clearly understood, having borne witness to her traumas firsthand. Needless to say, upon their return from the hospital, Cottage 2 would never be the same to any of them again.

***

Julio and Sylvia sat atop the jungle gym structure at Holly Park overlooking Hunters Point, the Bayview, and east across the San Francisco Bay to Downtown Oakland, San Lorenzo and Hayward. They kissed passionately there for several long minutes before Sylvia pulled away.

So who am I to you Juli? She asked solemnly. For reals?

To Julio, her question betrayed an underlying insecurity about taking their intimacy to the next level. So he stepped right up to the question. Girl, far as I'm concerned, the day we met I knew we was meant to be, you feel me?

Pshhh yeah right, there you go spittin' your game.

Naw, for realz. The Lord spoke to me when I first seen you...at the mural, he told me he put you on this earth for us to be together. Amen.

She laughed hard at this and pushed him away dismissively.

You's busted, all hearing voices and shit.

Naw Chita, I'm serious. It was clear that he was utterly sincere.

Why you gotta go droppin' that 12 Step gospel shit like we's in Sunday School?

Naw, 'cause I just know. Like everything that came before us. It wus all gettin' me ready for you, and now you're here, my world's got purpose.

She paused hard. Yeah. And what's that?

I can't help how you make me feel, Chita. You's got me sprung, straight up. I'm bein' real wit' 'chu now.

She scoffed, pushing his shoulder. You's silly Julio.

Naw mang, 'cause whenever we togetha', the love of Jesus be pourin' though me like it never done before. That's how I know dis is real. That's from the heart, girl.

Sylvia suddenly grew defensive and backed off. Fool, you know I got nuthin' doin' wit' Jesus. So why you gotta bring the Lord into all this? Damn dude, you's killin' da moment. Got my coochie dried right out wit' 'chu spittin' that shit.

Maybe, Julio paused, knowing he had to tread lightly, but it don't matter. Cause he's speaking to both of us now through me. He's showing you his forgiveness too…By giving us to each other.

Sylvia stared hard at him with a sudden red flush of anger that overtook her face. Because he was fully aware of her abortion and the pain of guilt she felt each and every day from that loss. Naw blut, you don't even get to go there-

Julio implored her with open arms. Jesus doesn't hate you for what you did to your baby. He never has, and he never will. He understands. 'Cause he loves you for life-

Get out my face with all 'a that bullshit, she waved her hand hard to push him away.

Naw girl, Julio pulled himself back. 'Cause I'm bein' real wit' 'chu now. Come on now and listen! 'Cause I KNOW you THE ONE for me, Chita. I KNOW it clear as crystal yo, straight up.

HOW! She yelled forcefully at him, her convictions as sharp as ever. How the fuck do you know anythin' 'bout anythin'?! What makes you so goddamn sure? For realz?!

Julio understood he had to let her into his deepest heart of hearts now if she was ever going to trust him enough to open her own to him. It was now or never. So, determined to make her his, he drew himself back to the ledge and took a breath, putting one foot in front of the other, before letting himself fall completely into her grace.

'Cause you didn't have to mess wit' me when you did, he paused. But you did. Another pause. You saw my shit straight through girl, you accepted me for who I wus, with all the shit I done, everything…So in my heart of hearts I'll always be yours, you feel me? That's for realz.

Sylvia searched desperately for any crack she could discover within his shell to break him. Anywhere to hedge, spilt, divide, back off. But there was none. As usual, she was sure he was being sincere. And that, as usual, was enough for her.

Yeah? Sylvia looked him over again hard.

Julio smiled. You know I couldn't never lie to you, baby girl.

So what…It's just you and me against the world then, huh?

Anything and everything for you. Look at me. He softly touched her cheeks with both hands, raising her gaze slowly to face him.

You my world now, Chita. For everz. Thas whassup.

Sylvia stared penetratingly into his eyes and saw his sincerity. She was acutely aware that the choice she made right in this moment would determine the rest of her entire life. But this choice, her choice, had already been made. She just had to meet it halfway. And when she finally allowed herself to, for the first time in her life, a feeling of utter calm washed over her.

You's fuck nut crazy Juli, you know that?

He responded confidently, with his characteristic wry smile. You know what 'chu see is what 'chu get.

Sylvia exposed a smile of her own. But you's always fo' real.

So you gon' be my girl, Chita, or what? Julio asked again, vulnerable, needing verbal verification for the answer he already had.

Seeing him this way now, offering himself to her so fully and unconditionally, broke her.

Like we been doin'?

Julio did not hesitate. Hells yeah. And like we always gon' do. No doubt.

Sylvia stared hard into his eyes for another moment, if only to relish in the memory of the sight of him like this, in the exact instant they gave themselves to each other, to be cherished throughout their future together, forever. She soon nodded again, deliberately this time. Yeah. Let's do this.

Julio's joy rose right to the surface. Damn Chita, you just made me the happiest busta in da whole damn universe.

You certainly is. One of the luckiest too. She laughed. Come here. Sylvia pulled him close.

They kissed more passionately than ever before, sealing their newfound bond of loving matrimony.

***

Sylvia, Lucy and Brenda braided Tre's hair in the front room of Girl's Cottage 1. When Sylvia bent down, her hair shifted to the side. Brenda noticed several of the lovebites peppered across her neck. You got hella hickeys, blut.

That's 'cause Juli be hella likin' me.

I was just talkin' to that dude dis mornin'.

Whad he say?

I told him how he best treat you right, and he's all like, uh huh, oh yeah, I know all that.

Lucinda motioned to Sylvia. Can you grab me that clip?

Dude's hella sprung on you 'dough.

Hells yeah. That's 'cause I told him I ain't about no drama, 'cause I got NO TIME for that. Too busy cupcakin' with my girls, 'cause we do it live, know what I'm sayin'? Sylvia put her hand out for Lucy to slap. For reals, blood.

He's a good one Syl, Lucinda acknowledged.

Yeah, but dude be hella buggin' lately, talkin' 'bout how we all soul mates and shit.

Oohh damn, Lucinda swooned. He's just feeling you girl, ain't no denyin'.

Shoot, I'd straight lose my wata 'f little Duane stepped to me with all that Romeo and Juliet bullshit, ugh uh.

What chu buggin' for girl? You know when he gettin' all romantical, he's serious.

Brenda was a more difficult sell. Ain't no dude all lovey dovey wit' no females 'less he tryin' to get somethin' off a her somehow. So, you two fuckin' yet?

Sylvia blushed.

Don't you be lyin' to me now girl, hell naw.

Oh yeah you is! Lucy called her out.

First time last night.

Lucy and Brenda swoomed. Ohhhh.

A high five from Lucy. And a curled brow from Brenda.

You used protection?

Hell naw…

What? Brenda flipped. Girl, your turned out coochie be oozin' some nasty VD shit 'f you ain't careful. MMNNN. You don't neva know what homeboy shootin' up into you, hell naw! I tell you one thing, dem dudes best be wearin' they jimmy hats or they ain't never seein' none of this. Brenda grabbed her cooze and pulled upward with a thrust of her pelvis, to punctuate for full effect.

So how was he Syl? Lucy inquired.

Sylvia blushed, remembering last night. He was all gentle like.

Lucy smiled, remembering her experience with similar men. They act all gangsta, but underneath they tender.

Brenda was more skeptical. Yeah, well yo' boy ain't on no honor roll so you best watch out. Who knows WHERE he been stickin' his thang!

Lucy scoffed. Oh Brenda, come on now.

You come on now Lucy, hell naw! 'Cause I seen hella skeezas carryin' some shit you ain't even tryin' to have. Them pussies be blowin' smoke signals!

Sylvia rolled her eyes. Yeah, well Julio ain't no trick.

That's what you think, but you ain't know where that dude been. He best get hisself tested fo' realz, fo' you go messin' wit' him. Shoot, Haight Ashbury be doin' free walk-ins whenever you like.

Sylvia considered Brenda's point a quick minute. Until suddenly without warning, Brenda grabbed her hand and twisted it real hard, forcing Sylvia to cry out.

Damn Brenda, stop!

Say you gon' do it bitch! Tell me you goin' to da clinic right quick! Brenda curled her hand tight enough to wrench the chrome off a trailer hitch. Or I swear I'll pull dees fingas right out yo' hand.

OWWW Fine! I'll go! Shit!

Satisfied, Brenda released her. Sylvia quickly shook off the pain in her wrist. Damn, bitch.

My grandmams used to pull that trick on me. And it be workin' every time!

You's 'a straight hata' Brenda.

Shit, I be savin' yo' life with that arm twista voodoo shit, just you watch.

Hell naw.

Hella blut.

Sylvia again tried to wave out the soreness from her hand as she turned around to find Lucinda playing with a fully weaved Tre. So Luce, when are you gonna press charges on yo' baby daddy?

Lucy looked at her intently. I ain't.

What! Sylvia balked. Aw, hell naw, that dudes dirty, he tried to kill you!

Key don't never need to know where we're at. He probably thinks we outta the city already. And I'm all good to keep it that way.

But you can't run from that fool foreva. Shoot, I bet if I hollered at Julio to go put a cap in his punk ass, dude be dropped in a minute.

Now Syl, Lucy insisted with resignation, we gon' let the past be the past now, feel me? Bygones be bygones.

Past be bygones - hell naw! Sylvia charged. That dude fucked you up for realz, so ain't no way he walkin' free. Fuck all that! If it wuz me, dude's nuts'd be straight swingin' off da MUNI cables on Mission by now. Sylvia puffed her chest in a protective posture towards her friend. If I ever see that dude comin' 'round here myself, I swear I'm 'a stomp him out, straight up!

Shoot I bet 'Dell' beat you to that punch.

Brenda laughed hard. Syl, you talk too much shit to back nuthin' up.

Yeah? Sylvia redirected to Brenda. Well what about you then, Miss Trick? Uh huh. All 'a dem turtlenecks you's sportin' ain't hidin' shit. Shoot, least I don't got no motherfuckin' daddies up in my pussy, sellin' my stank ass up and down da block chokin' me out when the money ain't right-

Brenda stood up in a huff. That shit ain't none 'a yo' concern.

Hey, why you gotta trip? Sylvia feigned surprise at just how far she's pushed Brenda. Thought we was just talkin' head, blut. Why you all bent?

Brenda finally snapped. You best wake up bitch, mind yo' p's and q's fo' you get your ass beat or sumpthin' worse. Cause snitches be gettin' stitches!

Shoot, bitch, I ain't no snitch! Sylvia recoiled. You's a hypocrite.

You the hypocrite little girl. Up in my face talkin' 'bout stuff you don't know nuthin' about. Handle yo' own business first 'fore you get dropped.

Oh yeah, and whose gonna do that, you?

You keep openin' yo mouth like you been doin', spittin' yo' nonsense, and see what happens.

Ohh I'm real scared.

Brenda backed up and left the room pissed. Once she was gone, Sylvia turned with subdued rage to Lucinda.

I swear I'm about THIS close to narcin' her out to Agnes for reals, you feel me?

You gotta let that girl make her own choices, Lucy concluded solemnly.

Hell naw, Sylvia blurted. You seen that dude sittin' down the block waitin' for her three nights a week?

Lucinda nodded. Don't know nuthin' about that.

He probably told her to say that shit when people go askin'.

Eitha' way, It's Brenda's business how she gon' check herself. Girl's gotta figure it out on her own some. It's the only way she gon' work through it.

Sylvia threw her hands up in disgust. What, so you expect me to cop a front and wait around 'till she end up like you? She waved her arm back down. Naw, fuck all that!

Lucy remained serene. Even with the prospect of Brenda being hurt – or worse - by that man parked down the street who watched them all walking the circle, waiting into the night for her to meet him out and to do his bidding. I tell you somethin', if you'd sold me out to Joe back when I was gettin' down wit' Keyshawn, I'd a never spoke to you again. Even if I knew you wus right. Brenda's got to get real wit' what she got to do fo' herself f'ore she ever wanna change. So the best you can do is sit back and be there for her when she comes crashing down.

Or ends up on some fool's t-shirt.

Lucy considered this for a minute and, despite what she might want to believe, had to agree with Sylvia's prediction.

Then let me be the one to snitch her out, Lucy offered. I'll talk to Agnes.

Oh hell naw, Sylvia rejected with disgust. 'Cause if anyone's gon' rat out my girl, it's gon' be me.

Hear me out, Lucy demanded.

Sylvia for her part was ready to listen. Because Lucy had been around the block long enough to understand some things.

All she's gotta know is Agnes' a nosy-ass staff who spotted some shady shit for her own self. And then when homegirl comes checkin' on you to decide how people jumped to they' conclusions, you don't gotta lie.

Sylvia thought it over intently before agreeing to let Lucy be the one pull the trigger. Fine. But then you best do it quick. Cause girl's been springin' out our window every night this week. And before Dierdre gone, shoot, I bet she ain't slept a full wink in twice as long.

I'll holla at Agnes this afternoon den, Lucy agreed.

Sylvia smiled, grateful to Lucy, before returning to a somber frown, contemplating all the drama that was soon to follow.

With that settled, Sylvia sat on the floor and played with Tre while Lucy admired them together. She thought long and hard about Tre's father and the cycle of violence having already plagued this little child at such a young age.

Yo Lucy, how is it all them dudes turn into such motherfuckers when they grown?

They ain't all that way, Lucy insisted calmly, her eyes settling into a sign of affection as her thoughts returned warmly to Joe. Just the ones we been messin' with.

Yeah, Sylvia pondered. Well fuck that. Raise this one right.

You know I'm gonna.

Cool.

***

Julio Hernandez wandered to the stoop of Edgar's house on 20th and Florida in the Mission where Hector and Tootz were sitting with Julio's old crew, the 24th Street Norteños. He was on the perimeter of enemy territory now, as were the rest of them. With 20th being the cutoff, that was entirely the point of this escapade. Both sides were stalemated in their street war, ready to provoke a showdown at a moment's notice. Several of the younger crew members stood by flexing on Julio as he approached.

Big Eduardo and his brother Little Eduardo wrenched on the engine of the older sibling's 1965 Chevy Impala. The rest of the boys held their swagga solid, locking up the corners on each end of the block in case any of them Eme scraps from 16th decided to come blasting on them in broad daylight.

As Julio reached the group, their mood was somber, clearly mourning the loss of Edgar.

A young up-and-comer stood in front of Julio with chest out, refusing to let him pass. Well, look who it is. What it do, Juli?

Come to pay my respects, homie.

Big Eduardo nodded to let him in.

Several more stood hard before Julio, copping their front. As he approached Big Eduardo, the leader of his old Norteño set stood firm.

Throw 'em up.

Big Eduardo extended his arms out first, and Julio did the same. The two men embraced. Ene.

Ene.

Foreva yo.

Where you been, blut? Stayin' out da way wit' yo' baby mama drama?

Gots to, you know. For realz...

Another member of the set was clearly upset with the warm welcome Julio received.

Naw blut, this ain't right yo, you feel me? He a traitor!

Big Eduardo calmed him down and addressed Julio directly. Handle your business, yo.

What it do? Julio looked hard over to Tootz, whose face betrayed a mixture of sorrow and rage. Damn shame homie. Edgar was our brother, feel me. Julio tapped his chest in tribute to their fallen friend. Today we mourn, yo.

Norteños 'till we die.

The group agreed. Several members held up their blue rags.

Tootz hissed, resenting Julio's audacity given that Edgar might still be breathing had Julio ridden with them to take out them scraps who popped him the afternoon before.

Julio put his hand on Tootz' shoulder. You did what you could youngblood. Ain't no shame in your stance.

Man fuck them Eme bitchpunks! Tootz lit up as he spit on the ground. I'm 'a blast every last one 'a them scraps.

Justice, Julio intoned.

Just us, the group agreed.

You feel me?

I feel you, blut, Julio affirmed.

So why you still frontin' den, dawg? Little Eduardo mocked him. Look at chu'. He tried to recruit several others to maddog Julio. He ain't no busta no more.

Thug life, homie, Julio retorted. Love it or leave it, blut.

Then wha''chu doin' here?

I come to broker a truce, E. Takes the hood to save the hood, yo. Julio now directed his comments to the older Eduardo, who nodded.

Paco 415 came holla'in' round the way yo, sayin' Bakersfield Eme straight gunnin' for y'all now. Dem valley eldas prowlin' the hood blut, no joke, 'till all 'a y'all in the dirt.

Tit for tat, bitch! Eduardo fronted. Blast a buster, smoke a scrap!

I say we knock them bitches off they two toes once and for all!

We breaking curfew tonight, blut. In solidarity, several of the Norteños clasped hands.

'Till Eme blood coverin' the streets!

Fo' sho'.

Little Eduardo was done choppin' it up with Julio all nice-like, so he stepped to him hard. We sucka-free up here. So step the fuck off, blut, 'cause you's dead to us now, dawg.

Julio checked the group for any clues as to why Little Eduardo's stance was so fierce.

Little homie just jumped in this morning. Big Eduardo proclaimed, patting his brother's shoulder with pride as Little Eduardo continued to eyefuck Julio. I'm proud of you, blut. He rubbed his brother's shaven scalp affirmingly.

Julio could see the changes already instilled in Little Eduardo. Shit, after getting jumped in by your best homies turnin' you out for 12 minutes straight, Julio knew any motherfucker'd be mad juiced to flex on the next fool for more than a little while.

So Little Eduardo focused his adrenaline-hazed rage on Julio. And you still talkin' to them scraps after what they done to Edgar?! Damn blut, Eduardo turned to his brother, who was the final arbiter in all decisions concerning excommunicated members, let's blast this Sureño-lover right now bro, you feel me? Just say the word, yo.

Chill out little homie, save it for dem bitchass Maras, the elder Eduardo advised.

Little Eduardo turned back to Julio and spit near his feet. You ain't one of us no mo' Juli, so you ain't nuthin'. Shit, blut, you less than nuthin'. You's dead. So you best be on yo' way.

Little Eduardo pulled out his clip and pressed it right to Julio's temple. Just say the word, Wardo, and he the first.

Julio looked to this young'un bent on ending his life with hardened eyes. He was fearless. This ain't no way to live your life blut....

Little Eduardo mashed the gun deeper into Julio's head. But Julio did not flinch, instead staying solid in the face of whatever this little up-and-comer had to dish up. I known you since you was in da cradle, E. This ain't you, blut.

Mang, fuck you, you don't know me! Little Eduardo spit at the ground again resentfully, pausing to check his brother for the signal. C'mon, greenlight this motherfucker bro!

Put him in the dirt E! One of the Norteños hollered out.

Shit, Wardo, do what you got to do, another affirmed.

Hells yeah, a third from the back chimed in.

Julio was saddened by what all of his old homies had become to him. But Big Eduardo had always kept it solid with Julio. So instead, he signaled his little brother to stand down with a wave of his hand and a short shake of his head.

Julio got his homepass, yo.

Infuriated, Little Eduardo took his brother's cue and stepped off of Julio, pissed as hell and still maddogging him, throwing up signs as he returned to his crew. Pinche huele maricone!

Y'all gon' t' flex one-on-one with them Eme's? Julio finally chimed in to the rest of them. Y'all Kings Original, birthed outta pain, but 'chall don't know how to put neighbor back in da hood.

Yo, they blasted Edgar. So they pay. Simple as that.

And y'all took out two 'a theirs before that!

La Ene straight don't give a fuck-

Tit for tat, motherfucker!

Yeah, and who you gonna do next? Julio admonished them passionately and with the considerable ease that came with knowing each of these bustas individually. First Paulo, then who? Paco and Nacho and Joser, then who? We grew up with all dem fools! And now they gots to die on account a some scrap walkin' where he shouldn't up the 22 block back when who the fuck knows? Come on y'all, you gots to see this shit ain't got no end, 'lest you stop it now, I say fuck dem haters, let them valley scraps spin they wheels for a couple 'a weeks, run they hustle down da corridors 'till this shit cools down. Then they gone 'fore you know it.

It's too late blut, shit's already in motion.

That's my point blut! Shit always in motion wit' 'chall.

Five-O ain't gon' do nuthin' 'bout our dead homie Juli, he just a 'nuther RIP'd busta, you know that.

So then where does it end blut? Julio preached to any who would listen. Fuck it, half 'a us already fillin' the boxes at Driscolls. And for what? So some fool can walk 'round da hood frontin' yo' silly ass face on they t-shirt when you the dead mu'fucker you is. What good that gonna do?

Show dem hater-ass bitches we ain't no punks!

Thas right blut, blood in, blood out, nigga!

Yeah, well you ain't no punk 'f you's dead in the dirt, I give you that. Julio chastised. 'Cause then you ain't shit, you feel me?

This last statement clearly aggravated several in the mix.

You said your piece blut, Big Eduardo warned. Now get on yo' way yo.

Julio heeded his former leader's ultimatum that his time was up. Mang, well, I hope at least some 'a y'all motherfuckers be listenin' blut, for realz. 'Cause all this shit you's spinnin' is busted, for realz. Just remember, Jesus loves y'all! No doubt, straight up. That's the gospel. Each and every last one 'a ya'. Even you Little E. Let his grace into your heart, give him a chance to make yo' life whole and he'll turn you around.

We's splittin' motherfuckin' wigs tonight, one of the Norteños rebutted as he left.

Julio retreated with only a slow blink of his eyes. Stay strong, homies.

And if you wusn't no bitch you'd be right dere wit' us, Little Eduardo taunted, echoing the sentiment of several of the others in his crew.

A few of the Norteños patted Little Eduardo on the back. C'mon blut, now let's go earn yo' ghetto stripes.

For realz blut.

Hell yeah.

Jesus got nuthin' but mad love for all y'all!

Bitch you pass me again, you gonna get butched, Little Eduardo called out as Julio finally walked away. 'Cause I don't know you, blut!

Julio waved him off as he stepped off the block and back down the street, turning the corner on his former homies and that old way of life once and for all.

**

Brenda fixed her weave in the passenger seat of her pimp's 1986 Oldsmobile while he surveyed the corner of 82nd Street and International Boulevard in East Oakland. They watched a pair of cops arrest a suspected john across the street.

Knocks runnin' hard lately, Lumpy offered, Actin' like there some kinda pussy convention or sumptin'.

Brenda applied her eyeliner using the mirror on the visor. And people been hella poor.

Fuckin' 'conomy never stopped nobody from tappin' no ass, Lumpy replied, taking a deep drag from his cigarette. But somebody best turn da spigot on right quick, tha's what I'm sayin'.

Brenda sighed with a hint of a snicker. People gon' do what they do, regardless of what you want 'em to.

Lumpy checked her playfulness. Oh, so thas how it's goin' down then.

Brenda cracked a smile at his fatal. Yeah, you know how it do.

And how you do'in it?

I do it movin'. Right wit' my man, Brenda kissed him affectionately.

Lumpy leaned back, satisfied. Shit, thas what I'm sayin'. He scoped for the police again while puffing another drag.

So when these knocks breeze on out you best do your thing girl. Shit ain't jumpin' off on its own. Lumpy pondered their meager earning prospects for the evening. Or maybe we roll out to the 50's. What 'chu think?

Naw, I'm straight here, Brenda assessed confidently.

Then you best watch yo'self baby phat. Undercovers be toolin' for y'all.

Shit, you ain't gotta school me on how to diss no 5-0.

Naw, guess I ain't. Mmm hmm.

There dey go. They both watched the police release the john and roll off the block abruptly, apparently to cover an emergency call. I'm 'a catch up with homeboy and make dat dude's night.

Lumpy frowned. Girl, you's ripe.

Gotta get mine.

MMMN MMNN. Come on now, doll.

Brenda exited the car and approached the john. Yo, so what 'chu lookin' for? She coyly called out. You see sumpthin' you like?

The dude turned around. She recognized him immediately.

Decoy police! Brenda yelled out loud enough for Lumpy to hear her. He started the car. But he was too late. Two black and whites immediately rolled up to block him from driving off. A sting operation. Lumpy surrendered without incident.

Once she was in custody, Officer Gutierrez from the Oakland PD Special Trafficking Unit sat Brenda down on a nearby curb to watch Lumpy Mirandized and put in the back of another squad car.

This your daddy?

Naw, Brenda dismissed obstinately.

Come on, now. We saw you in the car with him before you made your approach. Who is he to you?

He's my boyfriend.

Oh, is that what you're calling him, Gutierrez pressed. Did you know your 'boyfriend' is a known pimp to at least 13 other girls?

Brenda said nothing.

How old are you?

Eighteen.

Yeah. How old are you really?

I'm eighteen.

OK, fine. Well I'll tell you something Brenda, this guy ain't no one worth defending.

Brenda squealed. How you know my name?

SFPD's been scoping for you all night. Gave us a call sayin' they had reason to believe you'd skipped town, might be roaming the corridors 'round here. Told them we'd keep an eye out.

Damn, Brenda shrugged, perturbed. Sylvia be hella opening her big mouth.

The officer interrupted her internal tirade. You're lucky you know. We don't find most girls right away.

Brenda remained silent.

So we know you're thirteen, okay?

Brenda looked hard at him, then turned away.

We're going to cite you as a minor for attempted solicitation of sex in exchange for payment.

Whatever, mang…

The officer remained all business with her. Sounds like you've been through this drill before.

Brenda nodded. A couple times, shit.

Well then, you know this guy you're hangin' with is up to no good.

I ain't about bein' up in nobody's business but my own.

Yeah, all right. Then I'll let you in on a little information. Your "boyfriend" is a known trafficker of minors. Girls your age and younger. One of his tricks just came up dead, OD'd on MacArthur last week. Girl was beaten so bad, shot up with so much of that shit he's feeding you all to keep working, it stopped her heart. You know how old she was?

Brenda shook her head, maintaining her hardened posture. Naw.

Fourteen. That's just one year older than you.

Brenda squinted, trying to keep her eyes from instantly flooding with tears.

That little girl died all alone, right there in that street, and for what? She could be you 'f you keep on doing this, you know that.

That shit ain't happenin' to me.

Yeah, Officer Gutierrez scoffed. 'Course not. Hell, in some ways, you already are her. Just a matter of time. Maybe a year, maybe three or five. But stay out here long enough, you know how this plays out.

Brenda gave him a blank stare like all the other tricks he tried to crack. Gutierrez only shook his head.

So that's how it's gonna be then? He frowned. Okay.

The officer stood up to escort her to the backseat of his unmarked squad car. As he opened the door to usher her inside, Brenda stopped and asked him quietly. Who was she?

What's that, couldn't hear you? Gutierrez stooped down to earshot level with her now, almost mockingly.

The girl. Who was she? Brenda mouthed again, clearly this time.

Her name was Charisse Noble. Went by Rhona with y'all. You know her?

Brenda nodded helplessly, a tear streaming down her face.

Officer Gutierrez saw the emotion she could no longer suppress spilling out of her. Yeah, guess you do then. He gave Brenda a minute to absorb the news. She skipped out of her group home out in Richmond a couple of weeks back, found herself on the streets again, just like you. He sharpened his glare pointedly at her. You wanna end up like her Brenda?

Brenda shook her head, trying to keep the news of her friend's passing from overtaking her in front of the officer and the rest of her peoples roaming the street nearby.

Yeah. He put a hand on her shoulder. Didn't think so.

Officer Gutierrez paused to let her process this. You ready for some help then Brenda? He finally asked. She knew the life she'd led up until this point left her nowhere else to turn. And this might be the last time anyone who could actually help her make good on a different choice ever asked her this question, before it was too late.

So this time, she nodded.

Well, I got someone I think you should talk to then. C'mon.

Officer Gutierrez shepherded her into the backseat of his vehicle and drove her away. Upon passing Lumpy locked in the rear of an adjacent patrol car, she did not even look up to meet his eyes, instead staring forward through the glass divider in front of her to watch the first hints of the morning sun rise over the Oakland Hills.

***

Eric stepped off the Greyhound at the Main Bus Depot in Downtown Los Angeles. He walked the several blocks down Seventh Street through Skid Row to the Metro and caught the 33 bus westbound to Venice. He would be arriving at his parents house soon enough.

Though his homecoming was unexpected, Eric was sure they would be ecstatic to find him all grown up and ready to be a part of their world again, just as he'd always imagined. How he always knew it would be.

As he laid his head against the bus window, settling in for the long trip across central LA to the beach, his thoughts drifted back to Sarah. He wondered at which hospital she was staying in Colorado, how she might be maintaining, fighting those bastards at every step, first by refusing her meds, then throwing her shit all over the common area, or lunging for the door to escape at every opportunity. When Eric was finally settled in with his folks, he pledged to himself to make a few calls and track her down. Then, once the timing was right, he would take a trip back east to claim his bride. Eric always liked traveling when it had a purpose.

Having Sarah missing from the equation in this moment was the only piece of his dream that had not yet come to fruition. Everything else had worked perfectly according to plan. Nobody had expected him to bounce from the cottage once Rydell got shipped off to Juvie and Deirdre disappeared. Staff all thought shit at Excelsior House was stabilized, so Maurice started sleeping again on his overnight shifts and all was good, just long enough for Eric to slip out first down Ocean Boulevard to the BART station at Balboa Park, then on to the train, stopping at Embarcadero station and walking the two blocks down Fremont Street to the Greyhound Terminal to catch his midnight bus to LA. Eric had been planning this trip for months, outlining all the contingencies, making all the necessary preparations, and now with Sarah gone, jumping ship was all but a foregone conclusion. Fuck his PO and that 602 his hater therapist Jamey would try to slap on him when they eventually caught up with him, because Eric knew this time his parents would take him back regardless of any charges they tried to apply to him. None of it would mean anything once he was no longer a ward of the state, as long as he could prove his ability to take care of himself once emancipated. So everything in his life was about to change for the better, he just had to make it to the beach and show his parents that he was ready to come home for good.

The bus landed him without ceremony near the beach on Pacific Avenue. Eric exited and walked the playa north while waiting for his parents to arrive home. He would surprise them just as they were eating dinner. Dad would answer the door, mom would run from the kitchen table and they would embrace: the three of them, right there on the porch, in perfect majestic harmony, a family complete again-

Tea, anybody wanna buy some tea? One of the homeless hippies on the beach not-so-subtly offered him.

That was a good one, Eric chuckled to himself.

I can read your chakras. There is much power in your soul.

Hey man, you got 30 cents?

Ballers south of Muscle Beach, Baptiste selling his children's song albums, the black dude with big muscles and no shirt on roller blades rolling the glass ball along his arms, all of this was Eric's scene. Back on the Venice strip, he was in his element again, finally. Like that brooding first lyric from Pink Floyd's 'Breathe Reprise' on *The Dark Side of the Moon* so elegantly captured: Home, home again...

Eric grabbed a coffee to calm his jittery nerves. Finally, as six o'clock arrived, and not a moment too soon, he marched up Pacific Avenue, across Abbot Kinney and just past the Hare Krishna temple on Rose before spotting his parents' apartment building. He wormed his way up the short flight of stairs to the second floor, carrying nothing but his small backpack with a pair of underwear, socks, two t-shirts and his sketchbook, filled with his most recent drawings. His parents would surely be proud of all the art he'd created while he was away.

Drawing a breath to muster the courage to face them, he finally knocked firmly on the apartment door. He heard a rustle from within. God, he wished Sarah could be here.

The locks to the door snapped out of position. The knob turned, the door opened, and then, standing there plain enough was a woman he did not recognize.

Hi, are Lily and Bill home?

Clearly spaced out, the woman replied. Yeah, come on in.

Eric entered the apartment. Not too shabbily decorated, though the occupants were much more questionable. Several wastoids from the beach lay on the floor chilling. Miles Davis' "Bitches Brew" hummed from a stereo in another room. His father sat at the kitchen table packing a bong, while his mother dutifully washed dishes piled up in the sink.

Neither looked up to greet their new visitor, so Eric called out to his parents. Mom, Dad!

Upon seeing him, both exuded genuine satisfaction. Hey Eric! Come on in and make yourself comfortable!

His mom was the first to step from the counter, walking across the room to hug her son. Look at you. She ran her fingers through his hair. Wow, it's so long!

Her face beamed with joy as Eric smiled with her approval. I've been going for that whole Marilyn Manson look.

It's so, it's so…YOU, she smiled again. I'm so glad to see you.

It's so great to see you too, Mom. And you, Dad.

His father stood up to give him a brisk hug, with a cracked smile chiseled across his face. Glad you're here son, he rubbed Eric's arm a second time. So, how long you down for?

Eric's mind refused to twist itself around the implication of the question. Well that's the thing. I was thinking I could stick around for a while this time.

His mother continued to smile. That would be a nice thing, Eric.

His father drew a long rip from the bong, coughing heartily. It would be great to have you, no doubt.

Oh Lily, is this your boy? One of the women on the floor stood up and walked over to them. He's so cute.

Yeah, my Eric's always been quite the looker, his mother beamed proudly.

Well, when he gets old enough, I hope you won't mind us getting to know each other a little better.

Lily giggled. Oh Clem, stop it! My Eric's going places!

Well he could go wherever he wants with me, the woman continued with another flirty glare shot his way.

You're so bad, his mother chided her houseguest.

Eric chuckled. No really, it's okay Mom. I'm flattered.

Now Clem, I bet he already has a girlfriend. You do, don't you Eric?

Yeah, of course, Eric announced proudly.

How come you didn't bring her along?

Eric feigned his characteristic, guarded smile. She couldn't get the time off work is all, but you'll be meeting her soon enough, I promise. He wanted nothing more than to avoid disappointing them in any way. Mom, I know you'll love her.

I'm sure I will, Lily proclaimed, still stroking her son's hair.

After an awkward silence between them, his father used the break in conversation to rip another hit from the glass bong.

So how long are you planning to stay? His dad toked as he asked again, interested.

Eric took a deep breath. I wanted to see what you guys thought about me finally coming back to live here for good?

I think it's a great idea Eric! Clem proclaimed.

Lily held her flaccid smile. Of course it is, dear. She continued to pet the back of his head affectionately.

Eric's father tapped his son's leg without getting out of the chair. Well, we'd have to see what DCFS says about that.

But see, that's the thing, Eric continued on with pride. Now that I'm sixteen, I can live alone as my own guardian if I have a place to stay.

Oh Eric, I'm not sure we'd have enough room for you *here* though, his mom immediately lamented.

I can share the guest room with whoever...

We need that space for the plants.

You guys already ditched the warehouse?

His father stiffened. Cops busted it a year ago. Didn't know we were silent partners, so we're all good on that front. But your mom and I have been living on what we can grow out of here since then.

It's not much but we get by, Lily held him by the cheek, still smiling profusely. My, have you grown up, Eric.

Then I'm fine with just crashing on the couch.

Lily nodded and looked over at her husband for approval. His father, however, grimaced at the notion. I just don't know if that's such a good idea right now, you know, calling all this new attention to our living arrangement and all.

Eric did not like the direction the conversation was taking, so he pulled out his sharpest counter-argument to gain their approval. But if I'm emancipated, it won't matter. Nobody will be watching us.

His father hedged. Well the thing of it is is, if they know you're living here, we might lose our visitation rights with Petunia.

Lily came tenuously to her son's defense. If DCFS insists on coming back here to check out the house, of course we can just move our stash.

You know they ain't gonna wait for an invitation to just drop in, his father insisted. Especially if he's staying here, you *know* they will stop by.

Eric realized that his molestation of his little sister Petunia years ago had once again caught up with him. Regardless of any work he did during his years of therapy at Excelsior House to correct his tendencies to perpetrate, any progress he made through intensive reflection with Jamey to explore the root causes of his feelings of inadequacy of self, his anger toward his parents for neglecting him and his sister throughout their childhood, his rage centered around their preference for a carefree life in place of loving him, his subsequent acting out upon his sister so many years before in order to assume power over his parents indifference to him, if only to make them suffer for always favoring her and raising them both in a drug-filled home, or his ultimate responsibility for removal of their children from the home by DCFS. If any of his rage was still at the heart of the matter now, the fact remained that his parents visited Petunia often but seemed to have little or no use for coming up to San Francisco to see him, in spite of his many violent episodes acting out against a system indifferent to their lack of attention, or love. While his separation became more defined now, crystallized even as all three stood together in the same room, all of his resentment and longing for unrequited love boiled back up to the surface at once, the flood of memories and emotions in full clarity now due to the sobering absence of the medication he'd thrown away back in San Francisco, with the intent to start his new life absent the pangs of hurt and abandonment that forever continued to bang away within the walls of his fagile mind, if only to be somehow reinvigorated now, amplified by this unforeseen, unfortunate complication of events-

So how is she? Eric asked them finally.

Petunia's doing well. Real well. They've got her in a great foster home in Downey.

Oh...

It's a long drive but her foster parents let us come out and see her every other weekend or so.

Yeah, Eric, his mother nodded. They're really good about that.

His father finalized the debate. Legally they don't have to let us around her at all. You know, after what happened.

But they know how much we love her.

So they let us stop by once in a while.

We get to stay in her life if things keep on going the way they are now.

And you wouldn't want to disrupt any of that, Eric, now that things are finally getting better with her. You understand, don't you son?

Yeah, Dad. Yeah. Eric replied. I understand.

Oh Eric, but we're so glad to see you.

Me too, mom. Me too.

***

Sylvia made her way to her parents' house with Julio for her mother's birthday party. All of her extended family were in attendance. Uncle Pico, her tia Faviola, her primos Javier, Nestor, Angelito, Carmina, and her abuela Gabriela. Papa greeted her at the door.

Niña, he hugged her warmly.

Hola Papi, esta Julio.

Mucho gusto, Señor.

Julio and Sylvia's papi locked eyes. Their handshake was firm.

Welcome Julio.

Donde esta Mama?

Esta en la cocina.

Cocina empanadas?

Si, y estan muy perfecto.

Soy exciting. No me puedo esparar para taste su recipe delicioso?

Vamos a ver ella.

Sylvia and Julio found Sylvia's madre Maribel in the kitchen, finishing her preparations for the meal.

Upon their arrival she exchanged a quick glance with her daughter, then gave Julio a long once over. Her expression was unreadable; it could go either way.

Hola mami, Sylvia gestured with her palms extended toward the olive tanned man standing next to her. Te gusta introducer a mi novio.

She walked over to them with apparent scorn for her daughter greeting her in this way.

Why do you (bring) el a mi casa con no (warning). No ver a tu para dos mezes and now you come like this? Que lastima, you never fail to invent new ways to break mi corazon.

Mami. No mi (I mean no disrespect).

Maribel became very dramatic. She turned to address Julio with her hands on her chest. My heart cries for my daughter to care for her mama again.

Julio saw the somber effect her mother's drama had on Sylvia. So he turned on his customary Latino charm to redirect her energies for the time being.

Mami, in meeting you this pleasure is all mine. Sylvia speaks of you often, and always very favorably.

She looked at him with amused suspicion as he praised her in Español. She also tells me you are the best cook she knows, so please forgive me if I come uninvited, but I had to see you for myself to believe it. Is that mole I smell? Although I am not the world's greatest chef, I have never tasted any that compares to my own. Will you be so gracious as to let me try yours?

Maribel had no other way to respond than to lighten up. She shook her head. If it is mole you want, then you must wait like the others. She then shooed them away with a wave of her hands, but was clearly excited to have her new visitor taste her cuisine.

Come, Maribel grabbed him by the arm, I'll introduce you to mi famila.

Sylvia was aghast as her madre presented Julio one by one to the family. They all accepted him into their circle graciously. Together, her father and primos discussed souping up their rides with him, while her mother called Sylvia back into the kitchen.

He seems nice, her mother acknowledged, with her usual stone-faced stare.

He is, Mami, Sylvia assured her. No other words were spoken on the subject as they plated the dishes and carried them out to the table.

Within a short time, the feast was set. Enchiladas, empanadas, rice, beans, spicy vegetables, and of course, Sylvia's madre's famous mole.

The familia stared at Julio with anticipation as he brought Maribel's signature dish to his lips.

Que deliciosa! Julio praised. My tongue has never tasted such sensations. My deepest respects to you Mami, the flavors of this exceed even my own!

Maribel lit up with delight over his compliment, beaming happily.

Julio followed up with promptly naming her 'Queen of all Mole'. You must share your recipe with me mami!

At this Maribel playfully scoffed. You know a Latina woman never reveals her deepest secrets to any man!

But, she continued on, if you are half the chef mi niña claims you are, you must already know the combination of spices I've used.

Julio reveled in the taste of another bite. Of course Senora, I'm very familiar with the tomatoes, onions, but wait…is this Tobasco?

She winked playfully.

But the exact proportions…you must tell me!

Ms. Sanchez was utterly smitten with Sylvia's new novio. Almost flirtingly, she replied, Of course I never will. But you are welcome to come back anytime to try and figure them out!

The family all laughed together.

I accept your invitation, Julio cavorted. Only next time, I will bring my own to compare!

Maribel adored Julio. Then we will be looking forward to it!

The family clearly enjoyed the banter exchanged between these two, especially admiring Julio's natural ability to disarm their matriarch with such effortless grace. Somewhere into the meal, as Julio and Sylvia's primos continued to chop it up over their cars, Maribel gave her daughter a solemn nod of approval. From the look of mutual respect that was conveyed, the drama between them seemed forgiven, or so it would appear to the casual observer.

But back in the kitchen after dessert, as the two women washed the volume of plates piled in the sink, Maribel's demeanor cast an emotional chill over the room.

It's good to be home, Mami.

Her mother handed a dish to Sylvia to dry without looking at her.

Did you see my mural on Harrison?

How dare you humiliate your Papi and I like this…

Like what? Sylvia implored.

In Espanol: The last time I see you, you tell the world the most intimate secrets of our familia, then you have the audacity to inform the judge you want nothing more to do with us, and now you bring a man here unexpectedly, to the people you have such scorn for?

Mami, I'm making it on my own now, please. Of course I want you and Papi to be a part of my life-

Enough! Does this Julio know the truth about his new mamacita? Does he?

Mami, please don't start-

That she had the audacity to destroy her own niño, to rip an innocent child from her flesh so she could continue living her selfish life!

Sylvia began to tear up. Mami, stop, please…

And does he know his novia is a whore who fucks anything that moves?

Don't-

Including her own Tio!

Stop it! Mami JUST STOP IT! JUST STOP! You know he was the one who raped me. YOU KNOW IT!

Sylvia's screams filled the house. The men at the table could not bring themselves to look at one another as they listened to Sylvia's cracking voice reveal the horrors of her past to anyone who would listen. But back in the kitchen, her mami only shook her head defiantly at the truth Sylvia now threw back upon her.

YOU KNOW THAT IS THE TRUTH. LOOK AT ME. FACE ME, MAMI! YOU KNOW YOU LOOKED THE OTHER WAY WHILE YOUR OWN BROTHER HAD HIS WAY WITH ME, OVER AND OVER AGAIN IN YOUR HOME, UNDER YOUR ROOF WHILE PAPI WAS OUT WORKING. WHILE YOU SAT THERE IN THE OTHER ROOM, PRETENDING NOT TO HEAR! AND WHAT DID YOU DO? YOU DID NOTHING! YOU HEARD HIM TAKE ME, HAVING HIS WAY WITH ME IN THE OTHER ROOM AND YOU DID NOTHING!

IS THAT what you'd have this chulo you bring into mi casa believe? Maribel hissed to her broken daughter. IS IT?! YOU KNOW WHEN YOU FEED A MAN LIKE A DOG, HE'S

GOING TO EXPECT IT OVER AND OVER AGAIN. YOU
TEMPTED HIM TIME AND TIME AGAIN UNTIL HE GAVE
INTO THE URGES YOU TEASED OUT OF HIM!

MAMI please! STOP IT! YOU KNOW YOU ARE
WRONG, YOU KNOW THIS IS ALL WRONG SO JUST STOP
IT! JUST STOP!

Sylvia screamed several more times and slapped into the air
at her before falling to the floor, crying.

Her mother, meanwhile, remained stoic in her denial.
That's it, cry on the floor like the animal you are. Lie there with
the trash! You are nothing to me anymore, you hear me! You are
nothing. You dog! Her mami spit on the floor next to her.

All of the relatives outside on the patio now made their way
into the kitchen to find Sylvia vanquished on the floor with her
mother standing erect over her. Everyone knew what this meant.
Finally, the confrontation they'd all waited so many years for, the
family's dirtiest secrets unveiled in their full raw glory for all to
see. Sylvia pointed out to the others surrounding them, addressing
her mother directly, recounting the consequences of her crimes.

YOU LET THIS HAPPEN TO ME, MAMI, AND YOU
WILL HAVE TO LIVE THE REST OF YOUR LIFE KNOWING
THAT, UNDER THEIR EYES AND GOD'S...

Julio looked upon Maribel now with his own mixture of
empathy and scorn, seeing both she and her husband for the frail,
pathetic people they were, in failing to protect their daughter and
the child she had been. But by confronting them, by saying these
things OUT LOUD, Sylvia had overcome her loss. And she was
truly her own woman now. Seeing this, Julio walked over to his
novia sitting on the floor and held out his hand.

C'mon Chita, let's go. There ain't nothing left for you here
no more.

She wept silently, knowing he was right. After a moment of
reflection, Sylvia stood up. Empowered. Transformed. Julio
wrapped his arm around her. Out of courtesy, he spoke a respectful
farewell to her papi standing at the doorway, who responded with a
kind goodbye but did not dare otherwise intervene in the rift
between these two women. Neither did any of the other relatives
who stood by silently, just watching. So Julio and Sylvia pressed
on. And as they moved together out the front door, Sylvia left the

house of her childhood and the life she had lived with her parents finally behind her.

***

Kevin walked through the front door of San Francisco Juvenile Hall and down the narrow hallway leading into the visitors' room. Sitting alone at one of the round tables was Rydell, in his orange dregs, fumbling with his hands. To Rydell's surprise, the guards motioned Kevin to his table, where he sat down. Rydell continued to fidget with his fingers.

What are you doing here? 'Dell inquired snidely, though his face betrayed a look of clearly being happy to see him.

Thought you might like a visitor, Kevin responded matter-of-factly.

You bring anybody wit'chu?

No, Kevin replied. It's my day off.

Rydell looked at him, perplexed. Of all the fools who'd come up to see me. He shook his head in dismissive disbelief.

So how you holding up in here? Kevin asked with a smile.

It ain't bad, Rydell admitted, relaxing a bit.

Kevin mirrored his body language and also relaxed in kind. I'm glad to hear it. How's the food?

Shitty.

Probably to be expected. But not as bad as Excelsior's?

Rydell offered a cracked smile. Hell naw, nothin' bad as that.

You sleeping OK?

Yeah.

Not getting into any fights?

Naw, just chillin'.

You writing?

Rydell was visibly surprised Kevin would want to know.

Pshh, staff be all up in my shit if I don't take my meds, so naw...

An awkward silence.

I brought you something.

Rydell looked down to Kevin's hands. He was holding a book. He handed it to Rydell, who flipped through it breezily.

Manchild in the Promised Land, Rydell read across its surface.

One of the best autobiographies ever written about a young black man coming of age, Kevin admitted. Kind of like Catcher in the Rye for y'all.

Rydell laughed hard, appreciating Kevin's attempt at brashness.

Y'all, Dell cracked a smile. I like that. So all this shit really happened?

Kevin motioned to the book. The author didn't have any folks either. He grew up in Harlem. Raised himself, like you. Got himself into some crazy shit back in the fifties. But he was an artist too. Like you. This book's about how he found his inner voice. That's why I thought you might enjoy it.

Rydell looked down at the text again, clearly touched that Kevin put so much time into thinking of him.

I'll check it out den, he replied.

Beats staring at the walls all day, Kevin returned snarkily.

That's fo' sho'.

Another awkward silence.

Finally, Kevin got up to leave.

Yo mang, Rydell implored.

Yeah? Kevin nodded, noting the gratitude in Rydell's eyes amid his hardened stare.

Tell them fools Joe and Agnes they best come visit soon 'cause Rita gettin' me outta here right quick. And tell that buster Tyrone he still a pussy. Tell Rory to wash his feet, and Sylvia to get a clue. Tell Julio he best get my shit and tell Lucy I'm 'a come for her just as soon as I'm sprung. Can you remember all dat or should I write it down?

Kevin smiled, satisfied that in spite of everything that had transpired with this kid, he was the same old 'Dell. And he was going to be okay. So Kevin nodded back, I'll give them the message.

Rydell yelled out again as Kevin walked to the door. You betta!

Kevin waved goodbye as Rydell shot him a final nod. Once alone, he picked up the book and curiously turned the cover to the first page.

THE END

About The Author

Lance Lund is a former Residential Counselor for a Level 12 facility serving SED (Severely Emotionally Disturbed) adolescents. This is his first novel.

www.ingramcontent.com/pod-product-compliance
Lightning Source LLC
Chambersburg PA
CBHW020818180626
46814CB00001B/13